Educated at Bristol Grammar School and Reading and London Universities, where he studied History, Clive Ponting was a senior civil servant for fifteen years. He worked in the Ministry of Defence and also directly for the Prime Minister, Margaret Thatcher, and was awarded the OBE in 1980. In 1985 he was tried, and unanimously acquitted, at the Old Bailey under Section 2 of the Official Secrets Act, for passing documents to the Labour MP Tam Dalyell about the sinking of the Belgrano.

Of *The Right to Know*, his previous book, about the Belgrano affair, *The Times* wrote: 'His story is both shocking and fascinating, and provides a compelling case for legislation for freedom of information.'

D1586083

Also by Clive Ponting in Sphere Books:

THE RIGHT TO KNOW

Whitehall

Tragedy and Farce

CLIVE PONTING

SPHERE BOOKS LIMITED

First published in Great Britain by
Hamish Hamilton Ltd 1986
Copyright © 1986 by Clive Ponting
Published by Sphere Books Ltd 1986
27 Wright s Lane, London W8 5TZ
Reprinted 1987

TRADE
MARK

Printed and bound in Great Britain by
Collins, Glasgow

To Sally

Contents

Preface

This book is based on fifteen years' experience in Whitehall. I had joined the Civil Service if not as a naive idealist at least with some expectation that public administration was about the better government of Britain. Long before the Belgrano affair I had become disillusioned with Whitehall. This book attempts to explain why I had become disillusioned and, more important, attempts to tell, for the first time, what really goes on in the "corridors of power".

The book is critical of Whitehall and the way in which British government works. But it should not be taken as critical of the vast majority of civil servants who work long, hard and loyally. They are let down by the tiny group of mandarins at the top of Whitehall and by the system itself.

In the course of writing this book I have incurred many debts of gratitude which I can only briefly mention. To Hilary Rubinstein who encouraged me to write this book, to my editor at Hamish Hamilton, Christopher Sinclair-Stevenson and to my previous editor at Sphere, Rob Shreeve, who also encouraged me to write this book and had to edit my first book. My thanks also go to my typist, Laraine Fox, who somehow managed to read a confused manuscript. But my greatest thanks as before go to my wife Sally who not only read the first draft with a perceptive and critical eye but also gave every form of support during the research and writing for this book.

I am grateful to Hamish Hamilton for permission to quote from the *Crossman Diaries* and Barbara Castle for permission to quote from the *Castle Diaries*.

CHAPTER ONE

The Misgovernment of Britain

Tragedy and Farce

How well is Britain governed? If the amount of effort put into British government were the sole measure Britain would be well governed indeed. Whitehall is a hive of activity. Ministers meet in numerous committees, exchange hundreds of letters and hold countless meetings with officials in their departments. They write thousands of letters to members of parliament, who have passed on the grievances of their constituents, and also direct to the public who have complained, or more rarely, complimented the government about some aspect of their policy. Civil servants are engaged in a constant round of inter-departmental committees, working groups, working parties, committees of enquiry and just plain meetings. They write hundred of minutes to Ministers about matters both great and trivial, exchange tens of thousands of minutes, contribute to voluminous reports. All of this effort produces huge quantities of paperwork.

Both Ministers and civil servants spend much of their lives in trying to put across to Parliament and public what the government is doing. In the House of Commons every day about twelve questions are answered orally by Ministers standing at the despatch box and about 175 others receive written answers. All of this requires a vast amount of work behind the scenes finding out vital information and compiling background briefs so that the Minister can try to understand the complexities of the problem. Ministers and civil servants are writing long papers and appearing before Parliamentary Select Committees investigating the workings of government and the effectiveness of policies. Information on a large scale is made public through White Papers, Green Papers, consultation documents, press releases, press briefings and masses of statistics.

The pace at which all this activity is conducted is, if anything, more alarming than the sheer volume of work. Working in Whitehall is not a nine-to-five job. Nearly all Departments have resident staff, usually young high-flying civil servants, on duty overnight and at weekends. The Whitehall day starts early, often before the overnight cleaners have left. Most Ministers start work about 8 a.m. and the civil servants in their private offices will have been in before them organising the papers. The day itself is a frantic round of activity, going on well into the evening. Most top civil servants rarely leave their offices before 7 p.m., often later, and then take work home for the evening. Ministers work late, often having to stay in the House of Commons till after 10.30 p.m., and then go home to deal with a pile of red boxes crammed with official documents. The public image of Civil Service lengthy tea breaks needs to be replaced by the hurried lunchtime sandwich at the desk.

Is this all generated by constant and selfless devotion to the public service on the part of Ministers and civil servants alike, grappling valiantly with highly complex issues and problems for the greater good of their fellow citizens, as the participants would like us to believe? It is foolish to deny the hard work, but the real question that needs to be asked is, what is produced at the end of this ceaseless and frantic round of activity? The basic question remains. We need to look beneath the surface and not be diverted by the conventional academic analysis of British government or Whitehall's public relations effort. Is Britain governed well; indeed is it even governed competently? Has British government been able to grapple with the complex and difficult problems facing the country on almost every front both externally and internally?

The thesis of this book is that Britain is appallingly badly governed and that the blame for this state of affairs has to be shared by the political class of both major parties and the top mandarins of the Civil Service. Whitehall has failed the country; that is the tragedy for Britain. The farce is the way that Whitehall actually conducts its affairs. This book throws, for the first time, light into the darker recesses of the closed, secretive and amateur village world of Whitehall and on the way in which Britain is really governed. In the process some of the reasons for the current state of Britain will be revealed.

A Nation in Decline

Britain in the late twentieth century is the remains of an Empire in long-term economic and political decline. That is the background against which Whitehall has had to operate in this century; and even by the late 1980s Whitehall has still not adapted to this harsh reality. The facts have long been apparent, but the ability to respond has been missing. Let us look briefly at some of the depressing statistics that chart the process of economic decline.

In the middle of the nineteenth century, Britain was the dominant economic power in the world. It produced 65% of the world's coal, 70% of its steel and 40% of world trade in manufactured goods. In the second half of the century Britain began to lose its dominant position to the newly-industrialised powers of the United States and Germany. Its share of world industrial output fell from 33% to 14% between 1870 and 1913. It was in this period that the British Empire reached its height. It was only later that Britain found that it did not have the resources to defend that Empire which stretched round the globe.

After the First World War Britain's relative economic position worsened considerably. On virtually every available indicator Britain did worse than the rest of Europe; it experienced higher unemployment, lower growth of exports and a low growth in output:

(annual average)	*1920–29*	*1929–38*
	%	%
Growth of output		
Western Europe	3.6	1.2
UK	1.9	1.9
Unemployment		
Western Europe	3.3	7.5
UK	7.5	11.5
Growth of Exports		
Western Europe	9.7	−2.3
UK	7.3	−3.9

Although the performance of the British economy improved after the Second World War Britain was still doing less well than its competitors. The annual growth in output was nearly half that of the rest of Western Europe, export growth and the level of investment were lower and, apart from the 1950s, unemployment was higher:

(annual average)

	1950–60	1960–70
Growth in Output		
Western Europe	4.4	5.2
UK	2.7	2.8
Unemployment		
Western Europe	2.9	1.5
UK	1.2	1.6
Growth in Exports		
Western Europe	7.8	9.0
UK	1.8	4.8
Investment as a % of GDP		
Western Europe	15.4	18.1
UK	11.6	14.2

At the same time the British share in world trade in manufactured goods slumped disastrously:

	1950	1960	1983
UK	25%	16%	8%
Germany	7%	19%	18%
France	10%	9%	9%
Japan	3%	7%	19%

If one looks back over the twentieth century, the result of this persistent economic failure has been immense. In 1970 Britain was only 2¾ times wealthier than in 1913. Despite losing two World Wars Germany was six times wealthier than in 1913. And it is not just in comparison with the German "economic miracle" that Britain has performed so badly. Only Ireland in the whole of Western Europe has had a worse economic performance this century. Formerly one of the wealthiest countries in Europe, Britain has been steadily overtaken by its rivals and is now one of the poorer countries in the European Community.

Recently, the situation has worsened further. Unemployment has risen to well over 3 million (or over 4 million on the pre-Thatcher government definition of what constitutes unemployment). For the first time since the early nineteenth century Britain now imports more manufactured goods than it exports. The economic bonus of North Sea Oil, instead of being used to revitalise the economy, has paid for the social security benefits provided for the vast pool of unemployed following the collapse of British manufacturing industry. There are few, if any, signs of an economic transformation that would improve the prospects for the rest of the century.

Economic failure has been the crucial, but unwelcome, fact that has dominated the life of successive British governments. It has produced the major political problem of reconciling public expectation of continual improvement with the reality that the resources are not available. Persistent failure to solve this problem has produced a deep public pessimism about the political process and the future of Britain.

Institutional Sclerosis

The institutions of government have not risen to the challenge posed by the state of the economy. Throughout the twentieth century it has been subject to "institutional sclerosis". Success in two World Wars, coupled with the pervasive influence of a conservative and complacent establishment, has produced hardened arteries and ensured that British government is still largely carried on by the methods of the late nineteenth century. Although public expenditure now amounts to about £140 billion per year (or 45% of the national wealth) the accounting methods are almost unchanged since the 1860s. Parliamentary procedure, the debates, the committees and its power to control the executive still follow a fundamentally nineteenth-century model. In Whitehall, new Departments have been created, but the relationship between Ministers and the Civil Service is still based almost entirely on the methods evolved in the late nineteenth century when Departments consisted of a handful of staff working directly to the Minister; far removed from the large bureaucratic structures of today.

At the heart of government the Civil Service is still the

creation of the reforms of the 1850s. It is led by the amateur élite created by those reforms and has successfully resisted change ever since. The methods and procedures of government have changed little this century. The only reform of any consequence was the creation of the Cabinet Office in 1916, when for the first time records were kept of what the Cabinet had decided. And it was only after the fiasco of trying to run a war for national survival without such records that even this reform succeeded. There has been only one investigation this century into the way in which British government should be organised to meet the needs of the twentieth century (the Haldane Commission of 1918), and typically its report was ignored.

In its adherence to old and outdated methods and institutions of government that appeared to be successful in the past, Britain is following the pattern of many other nations in economic and political decline. The major historian of the decline of Imperial Spain has brilliantly described Spanish failure, and his analysis applies without alteration to Britain in the late twentieth century.

> Heirs to a society which had over-invested in an empire, and surrounded by the increasingly shabby remnants of a dwindling inheritance, they could not bring themselves at a moment of crisis to surrender their memories and alter the antique pattern of their lives.[1]

Who is to Blame?

As Britain has declined economically and political difficulties have mounted, politicians of both major parties have looked around for suitable scapegoats. The targets chosen have varied according to the political colour of the accusers. Trade unions, big business, the educational system, international currency speculators, or the lack of an "enterprise" culture, all have been blamed in their turn. But one group has been accused by both political parties – the Civil Service. It is seen as conservative, amateur, incompetent, dedicated to the status quo and to obstructing the reforming desires of any radical government. Many of these criticisms are justified as we shall see later in the book.

The case against the Civil Service has been put most eloquently by Tony Benn.

> They [civil servants] are always trying to steer incoming governments back to the policy of the outgoing government, minus the mistakes that the civil service thought the outgoing government made.[2]

For once Margaret Thatcher would completely agree with Tony Benn.

Some support for this view can be found in Sir Anthony Part's comments made in 1980.

> The Civil Service always hopes that it's influencing Ministers towards the common ground ... it is the civil service trying to have a sense of what can succeed for Britain, and trying to exercise its influence on Ministers to try and see that they do capture the common ground with their ideas, from whatever origin they start.[3]

No wonder there were major rows when Sir Anthony Part was Tony Benn's Permanent Secretary at the Department of Industry from 1974 to 1975. Even a more moderate politician, Shirley Williams, would accept much of his picture:

> The trouble with the civil service is that it's essentially a negative machine, that it exists to try and stop things happening; and, as a negative machine, it's in the Rolls-Royce class.[4]

What is the evidence for the Civil Service conspiracy theory? Do they try to bring all Ministers round to the same policy? One well-known phenomenon is the way in which politicians say one thing in opposition and do the contrary once they are in power and susceptible to the malign influence of the Civil Service. Let us look at three recent examples: official secrecy, the Evans/Christie murders, and compensation on the nationalisation of the shipbuilding industry.

Case 1: Official Secrecy

In 1971 after the unsuccessful prosecution of the *Sunday Telegraph* and Jonathan Aitken under Section 2 of the Official

Secrets Act for publishing details about UK assistance to the federal government in the Nigerian civil war, the Conservative government set up an enquiry into this section of the Act. The enquiry was chaired by the doyen of the establishment, Lord Franks, who reported in 1972 that the section was a "mess" and should be repealed and replaced by a much more tightly-drawn provision that was logical and coherent. Such a change was certainly opposed by senior civil servants since it would tend to open up the world of government and reduce their influence. Nothing happened and the Conservative government left office in 1974. Labour came in with a commitment to repeal section 2. After four years of inaction the Conservative opposition decided it was time to make some political capital out of the situation.

In June 1978 Leon Brittan, later to become Home Secretary, described section 2 as "barely consistent with any proper concept of the rule of law" and went on to say:

> In other words, that Section of the Act is simply indefensible yet it is still there. Why is that? It is still here, in spite of the Government's assurances, because they have not had the courage to fight and overcome the strenuous rearguard action mounted in the more obscurantist concerns of Whitehall. This is the real explanation.[5]

Sir Michael Havers, later Attorney General, made an even clearer statement of intent:

> We think, as we always have thought, that the Franks Committee was in general right. We accept that Section 2 of the Act is outdated and far too widely drawn.[6]

Once in office in 1979, their views changed. A bill was indeed introduced to repeal Section 2 but more restrictive provisions were to replace it. Even so Lord Hailsham, the Lord Chancellor, was adamant that the notorious section must go:

> Are we to leave on the Statute Book a Section which is really manifestly intolerable because it is unjust and anachronistic; and if tolerable at all, is tolerable only because it is unenforceable and unenforced and therefore brings the law into disrepute?[7]

When that Bill failed, the government refused to legislate as Lord Franks had recommended and as they themselves thought so essential when in opposition. Instead the "unjust and anachronistic" section 2 which brought "the law into disrepute" was, under Sir Michael Havers, used more frequently than ever before in a string of prosecutions of increasing controversy. The Conservatives' policy in opposition had been reversed with a vengeance.

Case 2: The 10 Rillington Place Murders

In 1950 the mentally-deficient Timothy Evans was hanged for the murder of his baby daughter. Later his landlord, Ian Christie, was hanged for a series of murders at his house, 10 Rillington Place. There was much concern about the Evans case but two official enquries refused to clear his name. Following a book by Ludovic Kennedy exposing the scandal there was a debate in the House of Commons in June 1961. Sir Franks Soskice, the opposition spokesman, called the case a "nightmare" and demanded a new enquiry and a free pardon for Timothy Evans:

> My appeal to the Home Secretary is most earnest. I believe that if ever there was a debt due to justice and the reputation both of our own judicial system and to the public conscience, that debt is one the Home Secretary should now pay.[8]

Just over three years later Soskice was in a position to pay that debt when he became Home Secretary. Within months of taking office he made a complete volte-face and replied to a demand for a new enquiry by saying:

> I really do not think that an enquiry would serve any useful purpose, even if the innocence of Evans were established. I have no power to make an official declaration of it.

Eventually it was left to his successor, Roy Jenkins, to do what Soskice said he could not do and recommend to the Queen a posthumous free pardon for Evans.

Case 3: Nationalisation Compensation

In 1977 the Labour government nationalised the shipbuilding and ship-repair industries. Compensation was to be based on the "stock market valuation" in 1974. However, as most of the companies were not quoted on the stock exchange, figures did not exist and had to be invented. The artificial valuations appeared to undervalue the assets. The Conservative opposition was outraged and senior spokesmen, such as Sir Keith Joseph, Tom King, Nigel Lawson and Michael Heseltine, all later members of Mrs. Thatcher's cabinet, described the proposals as a "scandal" and "sloppy and ill-considered". The compensation terms were called "grossly inadequate", "confiscatory" and "not coming within light years of compensation". Feelings ran so high that on 27 May, 1976, in a now famous exhibition, Michael Heseltine seized the mace, the symbol of parliamentary authority, and swung it around his head. At the same time he gave "the clearest possible undertaking" to put right the compensation terms.

When the Tories gained power three years later "the clearest possible undertaking" became extremely muddy. Sir Keith Joseph (Secretary of State for Industry) decided he could not retrospectively alter the compensation terms. The companies took the UK government to the European Court of Human Rights. The Conservative government refused to consider any form of settlement. Not only did they defend the Labour government's compensation terms, they went even further and argued the government had total discretion to pay whatever it liked as compensation, no matter how unreasonable the terms.

A Complex Relationship

The sight of politicians doing an abrupt volte face on gaining power is not new. Charles Dickens in his lampoon of mid-nineteenth-century government – the Circumlocution Office – had already identified the phenomenon as commonplace:

> It is true that "How not to do it" was the great study and object of all public departments and professional politicians all round the Circumlocution Office. It is true that every new premier and every new government, coming in because they

had upheld a certain thing as necessary to be done, were no sooner come in than they applied their utmost faculties to discovering "How not to do it".[9]

The phenomenon also works in reverse, Time after time new governments reveal not only an ability to discover all the new-found difficulties but they also find themselves carrying out policies which they had not advocated, probably not even thought about, in opposition. Policies can be re-cycled as well as disposed of, some ideas emerge regardless of the party in power as proposals come up from the bureaucracy underneath. One example was the introduction of a scheme for the building societies rather than the Inland Revenue to deduct income tax relief on mortgages. This had been supported by the Inland Revenue since the 1960s as saving some 4–5,000 staff but was finally implemented by the Thatcher government. Similarly the major re-organisation of the British Army of the Rhine in 1975 (so disastrous that it had to be reversed within three years) had long been advocated by Army chiefs and was simply tacked onto the package that formed Labour's 1975 Defence Review.

It is too simplistic to explain the relationship between Ministers and Civil Servants only in terms of the domination of the politicians by the bureaucracy. Are civil servants telling them what to do, and what not to do, as well as how to do or not to do it? The alternative explanation is that many politicians are essentially duplicitous and will say anything in opposition to win popularity even if they have no intention of implementing the policies if they gain power. The thesis that politicans are mere tools in the hands of the Civil Service does not stand up to examination. Political will can and does dominate. If a Labour government wants to nationalise an industry, it is nationalised. If a Conservative government want to privatise a whole series of industries and public sector operations, they are privatised. If a Labour government wants to use the system of central government support for local authority expenditure (the rate support grant) to give more money to Labour-controlled councils in inner-city areas at the expense of Conservative-controlled rural areas, then that is how the system operates. Similarly a Conservative government is able to use the scheme in the reverse direction. If a Conservative government wants to cut the size of the Civil Service by a quarter then that is what happens. There can be no doubt that politicians are ultimately in control of the machinery of government. The Benn conspiracy thesis is clearly over-simplistic. So just what is the relationship between Minister and civil servants?

Ministers and Civil Servants

The classic statement of the role of the civil servant was made by Sir Brian Hayes (Permanent Secretary at the Ministry of Agriculture and later at Trade and Industry):

> The civil servant has no power of his own. He is here to help a Minister and to be the Minister's agent ... I think the job of the civil servant is to make sure that his Minister is informed; that he has all the facts; that he's made aware of all the options and that he is shown all the considerations bearing on those options. It is then for the Minister to take the decision. That is how the system ought to operate and that is how I think, in the vast majority of cases, it does operate.[10]

This paints a picture in which civil servants present, entirely objectively and dispassionately, a straightforward series of facts and options. Ministers on the basis of this rational and totally impartial advice then carefully consider this comprehensive range of material in order to arrive at the best possible solution in the interests of the country. But is government really this simple? If it were, it is surprising that governments so often seem to make bad decisions that carry little confidence and that Britain appears to be so badly governed. The image of a self-effacing Civil Service seems as unlikely and unhelpful as the Benn conspiracy thesis.

Politicians certainly would not describe the civil servant in the same way as Sir Brian Hayes did. After eighteen months in office Barbara Castle reflected on the roles of the civil servant and the Minister in her diary. Her picture has some of the same elements as Sir Brian Hayes's but it is more subtle, less black and white:

What fascinates me about a Minister's job is the difficulty in knowing when to stand out against official advice. Some of it (e.g. on technical problems) is invaluable, and civil servants are also the reservoir of knowledge about past parliamentary battles, the reaction of interested organisations, etc. Yet there are limits to the purely technical, and even these types of judgement overflow into, or are influenced by, political and economic attitudes. When you are pushed for time (as you always are) it is hard to stand out against a strong submission. You wonder if you are being unwarrantably pig-headed – yet, if you fail to back your own judgement, you are often left defending something about which you aren't happy.[11]

After a few months of government Richard Crossman was much less flattering about the entrenched Civil Service he was taking on:

The personnel is second-rate and unimpressive. They are extremely good at working the procedures of Civil Service. What they lack is a constructive apprehension of the problems with which they deal and any kind of imagination. Also they are resistant in the extreme to the outside advice which I think it is my job to bring in.[12]

The Wrong Question

There has been a long-running and inconclusive debate about who really governs Britain. Is it Ministers or is it civil servants? Just where do the boundaries lie between Civil Service power and Ministerial power? Some politicians have argued that the Civil Service has the real power. This argument is not the sole preserve of Tony Benn. Dick Crossman's diaries from the 1960s are obsessed with the question. Mrs. Thatcher and her closest associates have been worried by the power of the Civil Service and set out to reduce it.

A few years ago a journalist and a former politician and academic wrote a book about the Civil Service describing them as "Britain's ruling class".[13] Some politicians, such as Brian Sedgemore (an ex-civil servant and therefore gamekeeper turned poacher), have said that the Civil Service has invented a role for itself in governing the country, which he argued they do by keeping Ministers in their places by a number of devices such as delay, foreclosing on options in official committees, interpreting minutes and decisions in the way they want, slanting statistics, giving Ministers insufficient time to take decisions and taking advantage of Ministerial differences.[14]

Is the Civil Service really this united and self-conscious in working out a deeply-laid plot to keep all Ministers under control and implement instead some nebulous and ill-defined Civil Service policy? Perhaps Brian Sedgemore's complaints reflect a more basic dissatisfaction with the workings of the government machine itself.

The question of where power lies between Ministers and civil servants inside Whitehall can never be answered satisfactorily. The dividing line depends on so many things, the political strength and intellect of the individual Minister, the type of decision being taken, the amount of administrative detail involved, the level of political interest in the outcome of the decision and the personal relationship between the individuals. All these factors mean that boundaries of power are fluctuating continuously. We can however look at some basic facts.

At the top in Whitehall there are about a hundred Ministers and over half a million civil servants. Ministers normally only meet the 1,500 to 2,000 senior civil servants at the top in Whitehall. In this system the Civil Service is bound to have considerable power. They are the main channel through which information passes to Ministers. The Civil Service is permanent; politicians pass rapidly through Departments. The vast majority of decisions are relatively routine. Ministers have a limited amount of time and the Civil Service has often to decide which questions should be passed upwards for a Ministerial decision. The Civil Service also plays a vital role in supporting Ministers particularly in parliament in terms of questions, debates and legislation where so much depends on detailed facts and figures. The Civil Service is inevitably in a strong position even if ultimate authority always lies with politicians.

The Civil Service View

Because it is permanent and politicians are temporary residents in Whitehall the top civil servants can come to see themselves as embodying the continuing part of government regardless of who is in power. Incoming Ministers will be judged on the basis of what good they will be able to do for the Department. At the end of July 1945 the Foreign Office had to face the prospect of a new Labour government and the surprising choice of Ernie Bevin as Foreign Secretary. Sir Alexander Cadogan, just about to retire as Permanent Secretary, expressed in his diary the view that there was a continuing body called the Foreign Office which Bevin would lead temporarily:

> I think we may do better with Bevin than with any other of the Labourites. I think he's broad-minded and sensible, honest and courageous ... He's the heavyweight of the Cabinet and will get his own way with them, so if he can be put on the right lines, that may be all right.[15]

Twenty years later Labour came into power again. Dick Crossman was made Minister of Housing and Local Government with the formidable Dame Evelyn Sharpe as his Permanent Secretary. On his appointment as Minister he had agreed with Harold Wilson that the new Ministry of Land and Natural Resources under Fred Willey should take over the planning function of the Ministry of Housing. When Crossman explained this to Dame Evelyn she exploded:

> The Dame explained to me that what I had unconsciously done was to demolish the whole basis of her Department, because in her view – which I now suspect is correct – it's quite impossible to give physical planning, the land policy, to a new Ministry without giving it all control of housing. ... As soon as she realised this Dame Evelyn got down to a Whitehall battle to save her Department from my stupidity and ignorance ... I knew she had gone to the Head of the Civil Service, Helsby, and to Eric Roll, head of George Brown's new DEA. Regardless of anything Harold had said, she continued the war, capturing Fred Willey and putting him in a room by himself in our Ministry while she got hold

of his new Permanent Secretary, Mr. Bishop, and lectured him.[16]

This incident gives a superb insight into Whitehall at work. Dame Evelyn regards the Ministry of Housing and Local Government as *her* department; not one at the disposal of Ministers. The fact that the Prime Minister has made a decision is not regarded as final – it can be overturned by vigorous lobbying around Whitehall. The outcome might have been different if Dame Evelyn had not been so forceful, if Fred Willey had been stronger and if Harold Wilson had had more time to notice what was happening. Or indeed if Dick Crossman had felt any great desire to carry out his party's manifesto commitment to a strong Ministry of Land and Natural Resources.

What was the end result of this Whitehall in-fighting over the new Ministry? A small and largely powerless Ministry was left to carry out a manifesto policy with no support and indeed active obstruction from the more prestigious Ministry of Housing. Within a couple of years the new Ministry was wound up after it had achieved virtually nothing except the creation of the Land Commission which was itself abolished in 1970. The combination of Ministers and civil servants had between them managed to ensure that much time and effort had come to nothing.

The Real Question – Competence

Ministers and civil servants do not exist in two separate compartments. Together they form Whitehall, inseparable residents of the same tightly-knit village community. They operate closely together and although they have different interests they both participate in the same process. At meetings with Ministers it is often difficult to distinguish who is who. Civil Servants make suggestions about how to handle an issue in the most advantageous way politically and Ministers make suggestions about administrative matters. It is a sterile debate to argue about who has real power. Ministers and civil servants are inextricably interlocked in a single system of Government.

An analysis of how Whitehall works needs therefore to consider how the system that Ministers and civil servants have devised really operates. Who are the people in the system? How are decisions really taken? What are the real motives behind these decisions? Above all, it needs to address the question of whether the system produces competent government? Is it even a rational decision-taking machine?

Those who work in the system and many outsiders might be surprised that such a fundamental question should even be asked. While they might admit that not every decision had been proved right (it would after all be surprising if they were), they would have a picture of people honestly trying to cope with the complexities of governing a modern society, making difficult decisions, some of which will necessarily be unpopular, allocating scarce resources in the best way possible, all to provide a better society for their fellow citizens. The defenders of the system argue that inside Whitehall politicians and civil servants use the best modern methods to take decisions as they rationally debate, on the basis of carefully-argued papers and a large volume of background information, the relative merits of various options. Only at the last moment, if at all, will purely political considerations be taken into account; and even then only reluctantly.

The later chapters of this book will attempt to demonstrate that this view is grossly misleading in almost every respect about the way in which Britain is governed. Decision-taking in Whitehall is usually based on partial information, ill-argued papers, or papers that are simply telling Ministers what they want to hear. And the deicisons reflect deeply-entrenched departmental interests, the impact of strong pressure groups, and continuous inter-departmental conflict. When the decisions are finally taken – and often they are not taken at all because it is politically far easier to postpone a decision – they are dominated by short-term political interests on both a personal and party basis. In short, the system is a shambles.

How far do we have to look for the evidence that Whitehall operates in this way? The next part of this chapter investigates issues that raise real doubts about the quality and competence of British government, the way in which decisions are taken in Whitehall and the underlying priorities of the system. This section also introduces a number of themes that will be covered in greater depth in later chapters.

October 1964 – Labour decides not to devalue the £

In the autumn of 1964 Harold Wilson's newly-elected government faced a sterling crisis. It took a crucial decision not to devalue the pound from its then-level of $2.80. Three years later in November 1967 devaluation was forced on the government, but by then a series of Treasury-inspired packages of deflationary measures designed to defend the level of the pound had destroyed its economic policy, and as a result many of its social aims were to remain unachieved. One might expect that the initial fundamental decision of such far-reaching importance would only have been taken after a careful assessment of the balance of advantage and disadvantage, based on a clear view of the position of the British economy. The facts show it was very different.

The decision not to devalue was taken at 10 Downing Street late in the evening of the day Labour took office. It was taken by three men – Harold Wilson, George Brown and Jim Callaghan – with no officials present and with no papers in front of them about the state of the economy or the possible effects of the decision. The Ministers had just been appointed and were physically and mentally exhausted after a long and closely-fought election campaign. They met under cover of discussing the appointment of economic advisers in order not to alert the rest of Whitehall to what was happening.[17] The reason for the decision was not economic but political: having devalued the pound in 1949 the Labour party could not do so again. There were strong economic reasons for devaluing in 1964 but they were never discussed. Following the decision that evening, an edict was issued that there was to be no discussion of devaluation in any paper circulating in Whitehall.

The Cabinet never discussed the alternative courses of action over devaluation and they were left out in the cold on all the talks about the economic crisis that month. Crossman described the scene in one of the first Cabinet meetings of the new government:

It really was an absolute farce to have George Brown saying "Naturally you won't want to be told, for fear of the information leaking, how serious the situation is. You won't want to be told what methods we shall take but we shall take them."[18]

Whitehall Grapples with High Technology

Whitehall has to take decisions of fundamental importance about highly complex projects involving advanced technology such as nuclear power programmes, computers and aircraft. Its record is appalling. Ministers usually have little or no expert knowledge and are being advised by senior administrators who have no direct experience and little knowledge of the items under discussion. Further down the chain these civil servants are themselves being advised by scientists who are often strongly committed to the projects and who lack objectivity about the prospects for success. The top-level policy debate is chaotic and uninformed as the participants often have little idea of what they are discussing.

For example in late 1966 the Cabinet Committee on Science and Technology (set up by Harold Wilson to direct the famous "white heat of the technological revolution") was discussing the future of the Black Arrow rocket for launching communications satellites. Both the Ministry of Defence and the Department of Economic Affairs were in favour of cancelling the project, but the Foreign Office wanted to keep it going because of the European implications. The Committee originally decided to cancel. But Lord Zuckerman, Scientific Adviser to the Ministry of Defence, began lobbying to keep the project and wrote a new paper. The Committee discussed the subject again and this time agreed to keep it going. Modestly for once, Dick Crossman reflected on what happened:

The discussion showed how little any of us politicians can really understand these enormously expensive space enterprises. I was in favour of cutting it on the clear evidence of both the Defence Department and the DEA. Now Solly [Zuckerman] comes up with a paper giving a totally different account of what Black Arrow is. How can Cabinet come to a sensible decision when none of us have the vaguest idea what these things really are.[19]

This episode is also an illustration of one of Parkinson's laws that committees will spend hours discussing a cheap and simple project they can all understand and minutes discussing expensive high technology proposals they do not understand. For example the Labour government decided in 1969 to go ahead with the Tornado multi-role aircraft, which was to cost about £10 billion, after just two minutes' discussion in the Defence Committee.[20]

The most notorious example of all is of course the Anglo-French Concorde project: a brilliant engineering achievement but a financial disaster. The basic facts are well known. After development costs of over £1,100 million and production costs of about a further £1,000 million just fourteen aircraft were sold to British Airways and Air France. As state-owned airlines they could have their arms twisted to take the aircraft. Even then they had to be subsidised to operate them. By 1985 Concorde was reduced to flying charter pleasure flights round England and the scheduled London-to-Newcastle run when better aircraft were being serviced. It would have been cheaper never to have produced the aircraft even when development was completed and it would still have saved money never to have flown the aircraft once they had been made.

How did such a project ever get started and why, once the impending financial disaster was clear, was it kept going? The facts behind the project show that it was started not by the aircraft companies but by a small group of scientists inside government at the Royal Aircraft Establishment, Farnborough. In the mid-1950s after the Comet project failed to put Britain ahead of the much larger and commercially stronger US aircraft industry, Farnborough decided to make yet another effort by leapfrogging to the supersonic jet. This was the first disastrous choice; the US went for larger capacity jets culminating in the highly successful and commercially popular Boeing 747. In Britain a committee composed entirely of representatives from the Ministry of Aviation and the aircraft industry proposed building two types of supersonic aircraft at a total cost of £175m with estimated sales of 500 aircraft. The Ministry of Aviation, as sponsors of the aircraft industry, backed the idea with enthusiasm. They argued for two even more sophisticated designs which they said would, surprisingly, cost only half that of the less complex aircraft originally proposed. When offered the prospect of all this work by government the aircraft industry naturally fell into line. To ensure the success of the project, the Ministry of Aviation started lobbying in Whitehall. In mid-1960 the Minister, Duncan Sandys, put a paper to Cabinet explaining the real thinking behind the project:

> If we are not in the big supersonic airline business, then it is really only just a matter of time before the whole British aircraft industry packs up ... If we miss this generation we will never catch up again.

Unfortunately it was the wrong generation. The Whitehall departmental line-up was predictable. Aviation was strongly in favour, the Treasury was sceptical but the civil servants there had no detailed knowledge to back up any arguments with the "experts" in Aviation, who were not independent but highly committed. Transport was doubtful that the airlines (which they sponsored) could afford Concorde. The Foreign Office came out in favour once France decided to support the project because of the attempt to join the European Community. Defence was for it because the engine to be developed for Concorde would also power their pet project the TSR 2.

Harold Macmillan, a sceptic at the outset, set up a special committee chaired by an old crony from his days in the Ministry of Housing, Lord Mills. Already the technical and commercial case was deteriorating. Costs had risen to £200m, predicted sales had fallen to less than 200 and there were doubts about noise, the level of fares and the ability of the airlines to buy the aeroplane. But, as we have seen, the departmental line-up inside Whitehall was now favourable and that is what counted. By November 1962 when the Cabinet took the final decision the die was cast. There was only a few minutes' discussion and most of this was taken up by Harold Macmillan in reminiscent mood. He fondly recalled his great-aunt's Daimler which only travelled at 30 mph but which enabled passengers to wear their top hats. He appreciated however that nowadays people seemed to want to dash around more and, if so, he was inclined to think that Britain should "cater for this profitable [*sic*] modern eccentricity". Thus the decision was taken. It only needed a further decision a few days later in favour of an unbreakable treaty to stop the French leaving the project to complete the recipe for disaster. Two months later De Gaulle vetoed British entry to the Common Market and the political case for the project disintegrated.[21]

That Concorde would be a disaster was clear within months. Costs escalated rapidly, performance fell, likely sales fell and environmental doubts increased. The Labour government reviewed the project at least twelve times in Cabinet, or Cabinet committee, between 1964 and 1970. The line-up was always the same, with the Treasury in favour of cancellation, Aviation and the Foreign Office backing continuation and the crucial role falling to the Law Officers who usually advised that unilateral cancellation would not save money because of the way the Treaty was written and that the French would win any case at the International Court. Just once, in December 1969, the Strategic Economic Policy Committee agreed to cancel, after the Law Officers altered their advice. The timing of the announcement about cancellation was important on political grounds because of the forthcoming General Election. As Barbara Castle summed up the discussion:

> Most of us agreed that it was politically not on to cancel before the Election, though the aim should be to cancel immediately after.[22]

The Labour government never had to carry out this bold policy and cancel, and the incoming Heath government decided to keep the project going. No doubt entry into the EEC was a vital consideration. When Labour returned to power early in 1974 another review was started by Tony Benn, Secretary of State for Industry, and MP for Bristol where Concorde was built. The Whitehall line-up was the same as ever and when the Cabinet discussed the future of the project in June it agreed to build sixteen aircraft. "Wedgie wasn't to be deterred: we should be guided by 'simple common sense', he said, i.e. his constituency considerations I suppose," wrote a cynical Barbara Castle.[23]

A small group of interested government scientists had tempted the government into a financial disaster with promises of a great technological leap forward. An amateurish Civil Service had been unable or unwilling to identify the scale of the problems. The politicians had shown an inability to cope with high technology, and political considerations of one sort or another had always been uppermost in their minds. As Barbara Castle wrote in her diary:

> Harold has refused to do what I suggested a long time ago and tell the House plainly that we had been landed in a mess by the Tories' appallingly mismanaged treaty. His reason: Concorde might be a success and then we would want to claim the credit.[24]

Whitehall Tries to Plan: the Saga of London's Airports

If Whitehall has found it difficult to deal with high technology, has it done better in taking planning decisions? These decisions require the careful balancing of different interests and are tricky to handle politically. The saga of London's airports nevertheless showed an exceptional degree of incompetence.

The story is one of a government department determined to develop Stanstead as the third airport, forcing that decision through and defending it doggedly. It is also a story of endless independent enquiries whose recommendations were ignored or torn up. Late in 1984 the report of the latest enquiry chaired by Graham Eyre QC into the airport development was published. For a government enquiry it came out with a staggering indictment of Whitehall:

> The history and development of airports policy on the part of administration after administration of whatever political colour has been characterised by ad hoc expediency, unacceptable and ill-judged procedures, ineptness, vacillation, uncertainty and ill-advised and precipitate judgements.[25]

What had driven the chairman to such a conclusion?

In 1943 the government decided that Heathrow should be the site of London's airport and that construction work should start immediately after the war. The site was judged to be ideally suited because of the good communications to London that could be provided both by rail and tube. Yet, although both the main lines to Paddington and Waterloo pass nearby, no rail connection has ever been built and it took thirty years to extend the Piccadilly line the short distance from Hounslow. The 1943 Report identified the sludge treatment works as the main obstacle to any planned and logical expansion and recommended its removal. (By 1985 it was still the main obstacle although studies were yet again in hand on its removal!)

In 1953 a White Paper concluded that Gatwick would be the second airport although it was to have no scheduled services and only operate charter flights in the summer. (Once the airport was built that pledge was immediately forgotten.) Having secured the second airport at Gatwick, Whitehall then turned its attention to a third airport for London. In 1963 an Inter-Departmental Committee, composed entirely of officials from interested departments, concluded that Stanstead should be the third airport and the search was put in hand for a fourth airport. The case for Stanstead was based on the fact that the officials calculated that by 1972 Heathrow together with Gatwick (expanded to two runways) would be unable to cope with the projected level of traffic. This was to be a permanent obsession based on the continual over-assessment of traffic flows and thus the need for more runways, when the crucial constraint was passenger-handling facilities. Just how wrong the assessments were is shown by the fact that by 1985 Heathrow together with one runway at Gatwick was still coping with all the traffic.

The Cabinet agreed in 1963 to the development of Stanstead although Rab Butler was reluctant because it would interfere with the shooting on his country estate. The public objections were so strong that in 1965 the new Labour government had reluctantly to set up a public enquiry. Its report in 1966 effectively rejected Standstead and asked Whitehall, for the first time, to do some decent planning work. The government evidence, described as "most unsatisfactory", did not even consider access to the airport or the origin and destination of passengers, and was later described as "shot through with blatant shortcomings".[26]

Whitehall did not take this rejection lying down and decided to fight back. Another inter-departmental enquiry was set up because, it was argued, a full external enquiry would be "too time-consuming". Nevertheless the Whitehall study took a year even though it did not bother to consult the planning authorities involved. The 1967 White Paper predictably once again endorsed the Whitehall view that Stanstead was the right choice. This White Paper was described by the 1981–83 Enquiry in the following terms:

> It is the most extraordinary exercise I have ever seen in a document emanating from Goverment ... it is difficult to resist the conclusion that the purpose of the review was to discredit the opinions and calculations of the Inspector ... a lamentable piece of decision taking. Its content is entirely unconvincing.[27]

The storm of public protest following the White Paper led to the setting up of the Roskill Commission which after a two-year enquiry costing over £1 million chose a new site at Cublington in Bedfordshire. Another public outcry led to another decision, taken solely by Whitehall, without any outside consultation and later described by Graham Eyre as "unquestionably ill-advised and precipitate", to build the massive new airport at Maplin near the Thames Estuary. Again little thought had been given to various questions such as access and environmental problems. The new Labour government scrapped the scheme. Whitehall still did not give up and continued to press for Stanstead as the only choice, and by 1979 it was again the preferred option. In 1985 it was finally announced that Stanstead would be the third airport. Doubts must still remain since the need for a new airport is justified only by a predicted doubling of the number of passengers in fifteen years. All previous forecasts had said the same and been proved wrong. But, as this episode illustrates, once Whitehall had taken up a view it is tenacious in sticking to it regardless of the evidence or the objections. The end of this twenty-year-long saga of disastrous policy-making by Whitehall was that the gap was not just between the facts and the official conclusions, as was made clear by Graham Eyre in his 1984 report:

> A strong public cynicism has inexorably grown. Political decisions in this field are no longer trusted. The consequences are grave. There will now never be a consensus.[28]

Once again Whitehall had failed Britain.

Politics is About Presentation: Rhodesian Sanctions Busting

In December 1965 an embargo was placed on the supply of oil to the rebel régime in Rhodesia. Breaking the embargo was made a criminal offence. By 1967 it was clear from the success of the Rhodesian economy that sanctions were being evaded. In June 1967 the Minister at the Commonwealth Office, George Thomson, wrote to an MP that "we are absolutely satisfied that British oil companies are not involved in the supply".[29] In early 1968 Shell and BP realised that their subsidiary in Mozambique had probably been breaking sanctions for a long time by knowingly selling petroleum to an intermediary in South Africa who was then selling the oil to Rhodesia. The oil never physically left Mozambique until it was moved by rail direct to Rhodesia. This seemed to be a breach of British criminal law. To get round this problem, yet at the same time maintain their position in South Africa, Shell and BP made a swap agreement with the French company Total who in return for supplying Rhodesia would receive an equivalent amount of oil in South Africa from Shell and BP. Technically ingenious, this scheme was hardly in the spirit of UK sanctions legislation.

On 21 February, 1968 two top executives from Shell and BP went to the Commonwealth Office to put George Thomson in the picture. By chance the records of the meeting made by the companies and by George Thomson's private secretary are both available,[30] although they hardly seem to describe the same meeting. On the one hand the Shell/BP report deals with the technical details and there is exactly one sentence on how the situation will be presented. The official report, on the other hand, is obsessed with presentation. Ministers were not worried by the fact that UK companies had probably been breaking UK law by supplying Rhodesia with oil and that an elaborate subterfuge had been devised to enable this supply to continue. Nor did they take steps to make the sanctions effective. Instead they wanted to work out a public line that would enable them to refute allegations that British companies were supplying Rhodesia and somehow square this with the facts.

The paragraph in the official minutes on this tricky exercise is a masterpiece of Whitehall drafting:

> In discussion it was agreed that in any statements in the House of Commons or elsewhere, Ministers would be stating the position *with complete accuracy* if they used a formula along the lines "No British company is supplying POL [petrol and oil] to Rhodesia". If asked whether POL consigned to the Transvaal by the British companies was being diverted to Rhodesia, Ministers could *truthfully* say something along the following lines "We have of course looked into this possibility. We are satisfied that this is not happening".[31] (my italics)

It was as one oil company executive wrote at the time "pretty thin".[32]

As we can see words mean different things in Whitehall than elsewhere, and the idea of telling the *whole* truth never entered the discussion. The use of the phrase "with complete accuracy" is stunning: it sounds so much more palatable than "without telling a direct lie". The general impression that it is intended to give the public is that all is well, but in such statements it is the careful choice of wording that needs attention. The let out for the government is the new swap arrangement and provided the statement is confined to stressing only the *direct* role of British-owned companies and is expressed in the present tense (i.e. not what happened before February 1968) it is just about *technically* correct. Whether any unbiased observer would describe the statement as *completely accurate* must be very doubtful.

This is a good example of day-to-day dishonesty in Whitehall. Government is not about truth and it is in very short supply in Whitehall. By stretching words as far as they can go and putting great importance on every nuance, the Civil Service is able to "draft round" a political problem for

Ministers. And that inevitably means leaving out (or dressing up) any unpalatable facts. It becomes such a habit that the good civil servant will do what the politicians want, and its morality is never openly questioned or discussed. The public needs to know that no statement from Whitehall should be taken at face value.

Whitehall: a Preliminary Assessment

These examples have sketched Whitehall at work and shown some of the main characteristics of British government. They reveal a political class obsessed with presentation and short-term political requirements, assisted by an amateur Civil Service devoted to helping Ministers put across in public a presentational case that bears little relation to the full facts. The Civil Service emerges as highly skilled in writing elegant English designed to conceal problems. It has, however, little capability to manage complex problems, plan strategically (even if Ministers wanted to) or develop coherent integrated policies. The power structure inside Whitehall is one where departmental interests are dominant and often government policy is settled by crude trading between these special interest groups. The combination of these elements has produced a record of consistently bad government in Britain.

Why is Whitehall like this? The next part of this book sets out to analyse the Whitehall system by looking at it from a number of different perspectives. First, the principal actors in this play that is both tragedy and farce – Ministers and Mandarins. We need to investigate who they are, and their real motives and priorities. Then we can move on to examine in more detail how the system they have devised really operates.

The "Good Chaps" Theory of British Government

But first a short warning. Ministers and top civil servants will vehemently deny that Whitehall resembles in any way the portrait painted by this book. Naturally they have a vested interest in doing so. But there is a deeper reason that is fundamental to understanding Whitehall's mentality and outlook. Sir John Hoskyns, the former head of Mrs. Thatcher's policy unit at No. 10, described a powerful version of "Catch 22" that is designed to put Whitehall above criticism.

> No one is qualified to criticise the effectiveness of government unless he has first-hand experience of working in it. But if he has worked in it, then there is a convention that he should never speak about it thereafter, except in terms of respectful admiration.[33]

Although the influence of the clubs of St. James's has much diminished, the world of Whitehall still regards itself as a sort of club. Members of this club share certain beliefs and conventions. In this club policy is of secondary importance. Politics are mainly about personality and the ambition and rivalry of politicians in the same party for the top jobs, power and influence. For the Civil Service, a deeply conservative body, the institution of government is basically sound and satisfactory, subject to one or two minor improvements.

In this club people are judged not by what they achieve but by their behaviour. If you accept the rules of the club, are a "team player", then mistakes are accepted as part of life and not punished. The important part is to play by the rules and accept the traditions and attitudes of the club. However, the real rules are not written down. For example the code of conduct for the Civil Service simply states that "although the rules of conduct for the Civil Service are largely unwritten they are nevertheless well known". Translated, this means: "If you have to ask what the rules are then you're not a member of the club."

This principle of behaviour, not achievement, is fundamental to Whitehall and is at the heart of British government. Whitehall has a great reluctance to lay down rules about how things should operate or the relationships between different bodies. What really matters is to place a "good chap" in the right job. Then there is no need to define how something works. A "good chap" knows what to do within the accepted code of conduct and the unwritten rules of the Whitehall game, and, if not, a quiet word will soon put things back on the right lines. Success in Whitehall depends not on achievement and formal structures but on behaviour and who you know. Nothing upsets the deep inner confidence of Whitehall in the system it operates. As one of the characters employed in the appallingly inefficient Whitehall portrayed in Dickens' *Little Dorrit*, which bears a stricking resemblance to Whitehall today, says:

> Though I can't deny that the Circumlocution Office may ultimately shipwreck everybody and everything, still, that will probably not be in our time – and it's a school for gentlemen.[34]

But the signs now are that the shipwreck might be in our time.

CHAPTER TWO

Ministers

The only qualification necessary to become a Minister is to be a member of parliament or, more rarely, a peer. Increasingly, British politics has been dominated by the career politician, the person obsessed by politics and prepared to put them above family life and any other interests. This is fundamental to understanding why Whitehall operates in the way it does. Ministers have spent most of their careers in politics and only for a relatively short time do they find themselves in charge of a major department. All their experience and their instincts emphasise the day-to-day short-term political aspects of the job and not the more difficult task of managing a complex Ministry and taking long-term strategic decisions that may only bear fruit after they have left office. There has been much justified criticism of the top Civil Service as amateurs. But the real amateurs in government are Ministers.

Parliamentary Background

In the last twenty-five years MPs have been overwhelmingly male, middle-aged and upper middle class. The majority are aged between forty and sixty and three-quarters of them come from the top two socio-economic categories, particularly professional and business backgrounds. 60% of them are graduates and nearly half went to public school (nearly 80% in the Tory party). About 16% are lawyers. Over half of Conservative MPs are barristers, company directors, farmers or retired Service officers. In the Labour party almost a third of MPs are teachers or lecturers, and about 12% are trade union officials but they tend to be older and much less likely to become Ministers. Few of these jobs can be said to provide remotely adequate training for heading a major Department of State. Perhaps the most important factor in becoming a Minister is to have a safe seat. On average about 70% of the members of a government and 98% of the Cabinet are drawn from those MPs (two-thirds of the House) who have served more than three terms. On average it takes an MP fifteen years before he can expect to become a member of the Cabinet.[1]

Ministers are therefore above all professional politicians whose whole lives are dominated by politics and who will long ago have seen any limited experience outside parliament swamped by the demands of their careers. A politician learns his trade in the House of Commons with its arcane procedure, petty point-scoring and endless speech-making. The rules of political life are fairly simple. Progress up the political ladder of ambition has to be firmly based on loyalty to the party.

The House of Commons, and politics in general, is an adversarial system – constant opposition to whatever the other party proposes. The procedure of the House is built around this principle. We shall see in a later chapter that the fundamental problem in trying to achieve greater parliamentary control of the government is the adversarial system. Parliament does not act, as does Congress in the United States, as a check on the power of the executive. Instead, it is a debating chamber for the government and the official opposition where loyalty to the party overrides any loyalty to parliament.

British politics and the House of Commons in the twentieth century resemble the rotten borough of Eatanswill in *Pickwick Papers* and the endless conflict between the Blues and the Buffs:

> Now the Blues lost no opportunity of opposing the Buffs, and the Buffs lost no opportunity of opposing the Blues; and the consequence was, that whenever the Buffs and the Blues met together at public meeting, Town Hall, fair or market, disputes and high words arose between them. With these dissensions it is almost superfluous to say that everything in Eatanswill was made a party question. If the Buffs proposed to new sky-light [*sic*] the market place, the Blues got up public meetings, and denounced the proceeding: if the Blues proposed the erection of an additional pump in the High Street, the Buffs rose as one man and stood aghast at the enormity.[2]

Power and Ambition

Politicians are a mixed bunch. Some know their limitations and do not expect to rise far up the ladder to power. Some have genuinely-held principles and beliefs, though often formulated in a general and vague way. But, for most, ambition to rise to the top (not necessarily to become Prime Minister but certainly to reach the Cabinet) and the desire for power are the main motivating forces. Asquith once wrote to Lloyd George, the man who supplanted him as Prime Minister in the 1916 coup, about:

> the drudgery and squalor of politics, with its constant revelation of the large part played by personal and petty motives.[3]

Edward Gibbon put the same point in his more elegant eighteenth-century prose:

> History has accustomed us to observe every principle and every passion yielding to the imperious dictates of ambition.[4]

It is power that politicians really want, what Barbara Castle described as the "febrile, exacting and fulfilling world of power"[5]. Just before she wrote this Barbara Castle had had the revealing experience of looking across the chamber of the Commons at Margaret Thatcher on the day after she came top of the poll and ousted Ted Heath from the leadership. She mused on why Mrs. Thatcher looked so happy. "She is in love : in love with power, success – and with herself. She looks as I looked when Harold made me Minister of Transport."[6]

Power is only achieved when politicians gain office. As Dick Crossman wrote, "Now at last I was a Minister in charge of an important Department and I could take decisions, lay down the law, handle people as I wanted."[7] Just what sort of decisions politicians like taking Crossman made clear in an entry in his diary a few days earlier. He reflected on the affair of the *Torrey Canyon* – the oil tanker that had been shipwrecked off the Isles of Scilly – during which Harold Wilson had been dashing about, Ministers had decamped to Plymouth to run

naval operations, and bombing missions by the RAF had been
organised to try and sink the ship:

> This is the kind of politics politicians enjoy. They don't like
> sweating it out with papers and working out blueprints
> behind the scenes. They like being ostentatiously in
> command and being seen taking great decisions.[8]

Mrs. Thatcher went one better; she had a real war to command.
At the top of what Disraeli called the "greasy pole" the Prime
Minister is particularly susceptible to the delusions of power.
Lord Armstrong, a former Head of the Civil Service, mused
about the Prime Ministers he had known:

> Absolute power did corrupt him [Wilson], but not in the
> formal sense – bribes and so on. I mean folie de grandeur.
> The man who had it in a big way was Harold Macmillan.
> The sign of it is when the PM says to a Minister: "I'll take
> this on" when the Minister knows better how to do it, but the
> PM thinks his charisma will be enough.[9]

The same signs are already evident in Mrs. Thatcher's personal campaigns to stop the hard drugs trade and soccer
violence. Achieving power is not of course the same as changing the course of of events. Although Ministers can be said in a
sense to control events in Whitehall, their control over what
happens outside is very limited. A few, such as Joel Barnett,
Chief Secretary to the Treasury from 1974 to 1979, do leave
politics disillusioned – "My desire to give it all up stemmed . . .
from the recognition of how little one could achieve."[10] But
most never suffer from this experience. They remain devoted to
politics, power and getting into office.

Preparing for Power

Opposition parties spend most of their time trying to score off
the government in debates and at question time in the
Commons, and on various media appearances. In the background a little effort is put into sketching policies which it is
hoped will appeal to the electorate. Very little time is spent
working them out in detail or deciding how to achieve these
aims once they are in power. Oppositions make promises and

worry about carrying them out later. For example in the 1979 election campaign Mrs. Thatcher promised to implement the Clegg Commission pay awards for the public sector. They were to add 25% to the public sector wage bill in twelve months and help ruin the government's counter-inflation strategy. Why was such a promise ever made? One senior member of the Cabinet explained that "Margaret wanted to win that election as if there was no tomorrow".[11]

Just how unprepared for government opposition MPs can be is illustrated by Joel Barnett's experience on taking office after being a member of the Shadow Treasury team from 1970 to 1974:

> I have no doubt that I should have made much greater preparation for embarking on the job of Chief Secretary to the Treasury. My problem was that I did not know that I was going to be appointed Chief Secretary ... We in the Shadow Treasury team, however, did little or nothing about how much, or rather how little, total public expenditure would be available, and how it should be divided in terms of priorities. If Denis Healey had worked out a plan for a Parliament I am bound to say he kept it a secret from me. We naturally discussed the likely immediate economic situation we would face, but medium- and long-term planning on the allocation of resources rarely. It never entered into our thinking and discussions ... we had worked out no short-, medium- or long-term economic and financial policies.[12]

This lack of planning and preparation has disastrous results. In 1945 Labour had come into power committed to large-scale nationalisation but with no plans as to how it should be done or how the new industries were to be structured and controlled. There was not a single piece of paper at Transport House giving any guidance. By 1964 nothing much had changed. Dick Crossman, as the Minister of Housing, put rent control legislation at the top of his list of priorities:

> Characteristically enough, I find that though the Labour party has been committed for five years to the repeal of the Enoch Powell Rent Act, there is only one slim series of notes

by Michael Stewart on the kind of way to do it in the files at Transport House. That's all there is. Everything else has to be thought up on the spot.[13]

It was just the same in 1979 when the Tories came to power pledged to increase defence spending by 3% a year. They had no idea how the money should be spent and so it inevitably went on the pet projects advocated by the powerful Service lobbies. Even the limited amount of work done in opposition can come to nothing. Shadow spokesmen are often appointed to completely different Ministries from those they covered in opposition. Dick Crossman had this experience in 1964:

> Of course all through I've an underlying anxiety caused by my complete lack of contact . . . with the subjects I'm dealing with. It's amazing how in politics one concentrates on a few subjects. For years I've been a specialist on social security . . . Science and Education I had picked up in the months I was Shadow Minister. But I've always left out of account this field of town and country planning . . . all this is utterly remote to me and it's all unlike what I expected.[14]

No wonder the ideas and proposals made by the Civil Service can be a dominant factor inside Whitehall.

Who Becomes a Minister?

On gaining office the Prime Minister has the immediate and fraught job of selecting a government. Deciding who gets what post can be a delicate balancing act at Cabinet level. But at the lower levels there is a real problem. The Prime Minister does not know every backbencher and it is here that the Whips play a vital role. They act as a kind of personnel department putting up names of possible candidates. Their choices are very often based not on actual or potential administrative ability but on performance in parliament. Can he make a good speech, is he an effective debater?

Even so the pool of talent is limited, at most about 350 MPs. From this list they have to choose almost a third to join the government – about 22 in the Cabinet, 4 Law Officers, some 30 Ministers of State, another 30 junior Ministers and a dozen or so Whips. Inexperienced new MPs and old hands who have been tried and found wanting in government have to be excluded, together with those who do not wish to give up their lucrative outside jobs. The too obviously incompetent are normally also out of the running. The end result is that anybody who is even moderately competent is almost certain to get a job in order to make up the numbers. This is shown up most sharply at the level of junior Minister where the turnover is high and the general level of ability low. They tend to be the sorts of person described by Dick Crossman as: "People who should be given three years of fat Ministerial life as reward for services rendered but whom one shouldn't keep longer than that."[15]

The Civil Service does have a role to play in Ministerial appointments, especially at the very top where the Secretary to the Cabinet advises the Prime Minister on the allocation of Cabinet jobs particularly if security matters are involved. Even lower down their influence is felt. In February 1969 Dick Crossman needed a new junior Minister and Harold Wilson suggested Bea Serota, a Deputy Whip in the House of Lords. Crossman did not know her but his Permanent Secretary did and went away to "make some soundings", in typical Civil Service fashion. It was discovered that she had been the Home Office nominee on the Seebohm Committee on the organisation of social services. The Home Office thought she had been "first-class" and so she became a Minister.[16]

Higher up the Ministerial tree, jobs depend on performance, ambition and luck. As Aneurin Bevan said:

> There are only two ways of getting into the Cabinet. One way is to crawl up the staircase of preferment on your belly: the other way is to kick them in the teeth.[17]

Taking up Office

How Ministers get into office is not a particularly uplifting story, but what follows is even less so when viewed from behind the scenes. When the great moment has arrived and the politician has gained office and power the Whitehall machine moves smoothly into action. The Minister will be contacted by his Private Secretary and shortly afterwards will arrive at his new department. Few have made such a remarkable entrance as Lord Brayley, proprietor of the Canning Town Glass Company, large donor to Labour party funds and surprise choice as Army Minister in 1974. He arrived outside the Ministry of Defence in a Lamborghini and immediately apologised to his flabbergasted Private Secretary, "Sorry about the car but the Rolls is in being serviced." He later resigned when the Fraud Squad started to investigate the company.

If it is a new government taking office the newly-appointed Minister will find that all the files of the previous administration will have been removed. He will be handed the briefing papers written in the pre-election period and a document entitled "Guidance to Ministers". This is his introduction to the world of Whitehall. It sets down the established rules and precedents for the way government operates, from how to prepare Cabinet papers and consult other Ministers, to the fact that the Law Officers must be consulted before any Minister starts any personal legal action. The rules have gradually been added to over time and are always accepted by each incoming administration. The guidance emphasises the continuity of British government and the fact that Ministers hold power only temporarily in that world. It enshrines the view that there is an accepted way of conducting the nation's affairs which must be followed by each government. The embrace of the establishment has begun.

The Civil Service prides itself on making a smooth transition from one government to another as if this were a virtue in itself. As Dick Crossman noticed:

> The only operation to which I can compare the Whitehall drill for a change in Government is the hospital drill for removing a corpse from the ward and replacing it with a new patient.[18]

The Minister then has to get to know his Private Office which forms his link with the Department. The Private Office is run by bright ambitious young administrators. Their rank will depend on the grade of the Minister. A junior Minister only merits a young trainee who has been in Whitehall for two or three years, and the job is used as a way of giving him an early introduction to the way Whitehall works at the top. A Cabinet Minister normally has a Principal as his Private Secretary, though in major departments such as the Treasury, Defence and the Foreign Office the job is done by an Assistant Secretary normally in his mid- to late-thirties and marked out to go to the top. The Prime Minister has an Under-Secretary to head the Private Office, and this job is traditionally reserved for those intended to be future Permanent Secretaries or Secretaries to the Cabinet. The Private Office has to perform the difficult balancing act of trying to put over to the Department what the Minister really wants and at the same time putting the Department's views over to the Minister. But the Private Office is not a policy-making division, it is a paper-processing office. A good Private Secretary will not forget that the Minister is temporary and that his future career depends on how the senior officials in the Department rate his performance.

The Private Secretary has to work closely with the Minister (and often with the rest of the family). This is always a good source for gossip and stories for the rest of the Department. Sometimes the relationship can be fraught. George Brown's Private Secretary resigned seven times in three months at the new Department of Economic Affairs in 1964. Others, particularly Tory gentlemen of the old school such as Lord Carrington and Francis Pym, were much liked because, as one person who worked for both once said, "At least they know how to treat the servants properly." But the main job of the Private Secretary is telling the Department what the Minister really wants. The Minister rarely writes a minute to the Department, it is all done on his behalf by the Private Secretary. This can be difficult, as one Private Secretary to Denis Healey admitted:

> He would put an exclamation mark, or a cross, or "Bollocks" in the margin and we had to distil his comments into memos that said "The Chancellor has some doubts about your proposal".[19]

However the Civil Service has learnt to overcome such difficulties and turned the Private Office function into one great achievement. Five days after he became a Minister Dick

Crossman was still reeling from the impact Whitehall had made on him and the way in which he was made to fit into the machine:

> I realise the tremendous effort it requires not to be taken over by the Civil Service. My Minister's room is like a padded cell, and in certain ways I am like a person who is suddenly certified a lunatic and put safely into this great vast room, cut off from real life and surrounded by male and female trained nurses and attendants. When I am in a good mood they occasionally allow an ordinary human being to come and visit me ... It's also profoundly true that one has only to do absolutely nothing whatsoever in order to be floated forward on the stream.[20]

Many Ministers fall into the trap of believing that a smoothly operating Private Office is equivalent to good government.

Ministerial Life

As Dick Crossman found, Whitehall takes over a Minister and assumes that all his time is available for public business. The working day is long, crammed full of meetings and visits, and then in the evening there are receptions and dinners followed by more work from the ubiquitous red boxes, full of paper from the Private Office. Social life is built around the job and the few politicians who want a separate life in the evenings have to fight very hard to get it. The routine is ideal for workaholics and insomniacs, as Joel Barnet discovered to his dismay:

> I soon found that good health, and an ability to manage on little sleep – I am fortunate in only needing five or six hours – were invaluable assets ... Even with that amount of time spent working, it was often extremely difficult to read the papers adequately to brief myself for the host of meetings I had to attend ... the sheer weight of work gives one little time to sit back and just think about the way the job should be done.[21]

This is no new phenomenon and only a few Ministers are able to avoid this fierce pace of work, as Hugh Gaitskell observed in 1949:

I must say the technique of modern Government becomes almost intolerably difficult. On the one hand, the key Ministers are hopelessly overworked. Stafford [Cripps, Chancellor of the Exchequer] spends his time dashing between Paris, Brussels and London ... The PM [Attlee] is perhaps so successful because he is content to let others do the work. I noticed that he was at Lords on Saturday morning and Wimbledon on Saturday afternoon, and went down to Chequers for the weekend. Poor Stafford spent most of his weekend in bed writing his latest paper and in a state of complete exhaustion.[22]

Mrs. Thatcher is not like Clem Attlee and certainly tries to personally direct the whole of Whitehall and prides herself on her machismo style of regularly working to the small hours of the morning and needing very little sleep.

It is instructive to look at a short period, chosen at random, in the life of one Minister – Barbara Castle – to see the strain under which they operate. On Monday, 25 March, 1974, after a weekend spent working on official papers in her red boxes, she was able to get up late and leave her country cottage for a 10.30 meeting with officials in the DHSS to discuss expenditure negotiations with the Treasury. At 11.30 it was time for the Cabinet meeting to hear the details of the Budget. Lunchtime was spent eating sandwiches during a meeting with officials. At 3 pm she had to go to the House of Commons to make a major statement. This lasted till 4.30 pm and in the next two hours she worked in her room at the Commons and had more meetings with officials and junior Ministers. Before a reception and dinner at Lancaster House she was able to visit the dying Dick Crossman. At 9.30 pm it was back to the Commons to go through more papers, with a vote at 11.30 pm. She arrived home at midnight and worked till 1 am, but when another red box was delivered in the early hours she gave up and went to bed. The rest of the week was no better. On Tuesday she not surprisingly fell asleep in the Commons during the Budget speech, before attending a political dinner and returning to work at the Commons till the early hours. On Wednesday she was up at 6 am to tackle more boxes of papers. The day was taken up with meetings and speeches and she got to bed at 1 am. Up again at 6 am on Thursday, she had to attend a Cabinet meeting, make a statement in the Commons and appear on TV. She then went home to rewrite a speech for the next day but gave up and wrote in her diary, "By then I just didn't care what happened and headed for bed."[23]

Ministerial Behaviour

The constant pressure week after week takes its inevitable toll of Ministers. Nobody can expect to take sensible decisions on complex issues in this sort of atmosphere. The pace of Ministerial life coupled with the excessive workload is one of the main reasons for the poor quality of British government. But the strain begins to tell elsewhere as well. After adrenalin, alcohol is probably the major lubricant of Whitehall and some Ministers crack under the influence. Between them Dick Crossman and Barbara Castle record at least thirteen occasions when George Brown was so drunk that he was incapable of taking part in Ministerial discussions. According to Dick Crossman Harold Wilson was reduced at one stage to drinking whisky during Cabinet meetings in order to keep going[24]. Ministers are regularly falling asleep in crucial cabinet sessions.

Ministers also become subject to the prima donna complex as attention is lavished on them and teams of civil servants are at their beck and call. This nearly always manifests itself in detailed attention to their "life-style". Long and bitter arguments take place over the allocation of rooms, the standards of furnishing and who has the biggest car. Shortly after arriving in Defence John Nott decided he would have a radio telephone installed in his car. Soon all his junior Ministers were fighting hard to get telephones in their cars.

Ministers also revel in the outward signs of their status – the red boxes and the official car. On one occasion Dick Crossman used his official car to take his family to the circus, and wrote in his diary:

> We drove home from Banbury station in fine fettle that night. It was a splendid outing and the extra splendour of the Minister's car and the Minister's reserved compartment

made the children for the first time see the point of their father being a Minister.[25]

Matters of protocol become supremely important. When Harold Wilson reported to the Cabinet in February 1975 on his visit to the United States to see President Ford all he had to say on foreign policy was that relations with the United States were "as good as they have ever been". But the important point was that "the ceremonies of welcome went far beyond anything I have ever had before".[26]

Even small items of domestic protocol can affect the quality of government. Harold Wilson dates the decline of Attlee's government to the decision in 1947, as an economy measure, to stop smoking in Cabinet. As a result Ministers had to keep dashing out of the meeting to have a quick smoke in the ground-floor lavatory at No. 10.[27] At other times ministers do not even need this excuse to behave in a prima donna-ish way. Dick Crossman regularly used to walk out of Cabinet meetings if he was bored. In addition, in October 1966, Crossman attended the Defence Committee for the first time to discuss a paper he had written on Malta. But he was only invited to attend and was not a full member of the Committee. The result was that "I sat on my dignity, refusing to speak and merely listening to the debate".[28]

Relations Between Ministers

Although Ministers are all members of the same party and government they are often rivals and bitter opponents. Add to this the normal level of inter-departmental conflict and Whitehall can be riven by Ministerial enmities and disputes as they jockey for power, position and promotion. For example the degree of hatred between Margaret Thatcher and Francis Pym was almost tangible and could be felt all round Whitehall, whether he was in Defence or at the Foreign Office. Politics is a lonely profession generating few friends and many enemies. Often the Prime Minister is in the most isolated position of all. As Harold Wilson remarked to Barbara Castle about his Cabinet colleagues: "Do you really think there is anyone of them I can trust?"[29] A few weeks later Wilson carried out a major reshuffle of the government and explained the rationale to Dick Crossman:

> For the first time I can get rid of the people I took over in the Shadow Cabinet. When I became Leader I only had one person in the Parliamentary Committee who had voted for me and when I formed my first Cabinet in 1964 it contained only two or three of you who were my supporters. The rest were opponents. Now I shall be strong and need not worry about any debt I owe to my enemies.[30]

Margaret Thatcher found herself in the same position: her first Cabinet in 1979 contained many Ministers who were not her supporters. In the first reshuffle a few isolated opponents such as Norman St. John Stevas were sacked. It was not until 1981 that she was in a sufficiently strong position to dismiss some of her major opponents – Lord Soames and Sir Ian Gilmour – and to demote others such as Jim Prior. Francis Pym did not meet his fate until after the 1983 election.

In governments the hatreds and feuds between Ministers grow. By the middle of 1968 Harold Wilson could not stand Jim Callaghan. As he explained to Dick Crossman on two occasions:

> He is inordinately ambitious and inordinately weak. So weak that as Chancellor he used to weep on my shoulder and then go away and intrigue against me ... I showed a perfectly Christian mood ... by God, the time will come when I'll dig Jim's entrails out for what he did to me.[31]

Ministerial meetings can often degenerate into personal abuse and shouting matches. Barbara Castle describes two such scenes inside No. 10. The first took place in March 1968 after Roy Jenkins had replaced Jim Callaghan as Chancellor of the Exchequer:

> He [Callaghan] complained that some Ministers seemed to have political press officers to protect them – looking hard at Roy. It was all said as offensively as possible and Roy's face tightened with steely hate. "If you are thinking of John Harris," said Harold, "he is a civil servant." "If so," said Jim, he wanted to know why Harris had been moved from

his job at the Home Office without consulting Roy's successor [Callaghan] and what was he doing now at the Treasury? "It's none of your business, Home Secretary," said Roy viciously. He and Jim outstared each other across the table.[32]

The second incident, which also involved Jim Callaghan, took place in the Inner Cabinet to just over a year later during the row over the proposed Trade Union legislation, "In Place of Strife". Dick Crossman launched an attack on those trying to get rid of Harold Wilson:

> The plotters had better realise that it wouldn't work, four of the inner heart of the Cabinet couldn't and wouldn't serve under the supplanter. We would sink or swim together. "Sink or sink," interposed Jim. Dick rounded on him, how could he work with the rest of us when he believed the next election was already lost? ... "If my colleagues want me to go, I will," murmured Jim unctuously. Dick flashed back at him, "Why don't you go? Get out!" We all sat electrified until Harold intervened soothingly.[33]

Callaghan had the last laugh over Barbara Castle and those who had supported her over the proposed Trade Union legislation. He sacked her the moment he became Prime Minister in 1976.

Ministers in the same department often do not trust each other either. The relationship between Michael Heseltine and his junior Minister John Stanley who followed him from Environment to Defence was always intriguing. It was generally assumed that Stanley, utterly loyal to Mrs. Thatcher, was used to keep an eye on one of the main rivals to the Prime Minister. When Barbara Castle had Roy Hattersley as a junior Minister she was warned by Harold Wilson that he was "one of Jenkins' boys" (though Fred Peart was less polite, describing him as a "right-wing bastard"[34]). Castle was convinced that he was relaying information from the Department of Employment back to Roy Jenkins as Chancellor and was trying to set her up on one particular issue so that Jenkins could score a political success. Castle consulted Harold Wilson and on his advice deliberately arranged a meeting with Roy Jenkins.

Hattersley was made to attend and to defend the Department of Employment and its policy in front of Jenkins[35]. Hattersley is, of course, no longer "one of Jenkins' boys".

Ministers as Administrators

Beneath the world of feuding, back-stabbing, plot and counter-plot, which is the stuff of political life, how do Ministers see their roles as policy-makers and administrators? What are their real motivations? How much time do they have left over for administering anything? Ministers are first and foremost politicians and they see their jobs as heads of departments in political terms. How can they use their stay in the department to further their careers? How can they obtain maximum public exposure through the media? For them these are the absorbing questions. Administrative decisions and policymaking are subsidiary to this overriding concern.

On most matters Ministers will see the issue in terms of the political impact. How many votes may be affected? Will it influence a crucial marginal constituency? Can this decision be defended easily in parliament? If forced to take a difficult decision which may be unpopular the first reaction is to see whether the opposition can be blamed in some way. If not it may be possible to fall back on the argument that the opposition did just the same when they were in government.

The political process dominates the work of Whitehall. In practice, long-term planning in Whitehall means thinking about up to four years ahead when the next election is due. Ministers are virtually uninterested in what will happen after the next election. "Long-term" policy-making covers a shorter and shorter period. Policies have to be designed for an immediate impact – if not in the real world at least in political terms. Indeed, politicians believe that action in the political world is equivalent to action in the real world. Words speak louder than actions. The presentation of policies rather than substance is what matters. Whitehall is dominated therefore not by long-term strategic planning but by short-term political expediency.

As an election approaches this process becomes even more dominant and blatant. Policies must have an immediate impact, particularly in public relations terms. But a new phenomenon also emerges: the desire to fudge issues and put them off until after the election. The thinking behind the move is that if the election is lost the mess will be left for the new government to clear up.

The Dominance of Elections

The desire to win the next election is the driving force of all governments and everything is subordinated to this aim. The Budget is, of course, a major tool of political policy, as Jim Callaghan explained to Barbara Castle one night at the House of Commons in February 1965 during a particularly difficult period economically:

> So we had to make up our minds: either an election before the Budget or one immediately afterwards in which we could gamble by introducing a soft Budget for electoral purposes.[36]

The Thatcher government appears to be adopting the same policy for the election due in 1987 or 1988 with the planned tax cuts to be financed by selling off state assets. In early 1970 the Labour Cabinet discussed how to deal with the large pay rises recommended for the armed forces, nurses, teachers and post office workers. Predictably, the departmental Ministers argued in favour and the Chancellor opposed. Harold Wilson reminded them that they had to look at the problem politically:

> Timing was the essence of our problem, particularly as events now made a Spring Election impossible. We should aim to postpone the results of these claims as far as we could: he would rather win the Election and have a November budget than have July measures and lose the election.

The Cabinet agreed to phase in the increases and postpone some of them till January 1971, long after the Election. As Barbara Castle admitted: "It was all pretty crude."[37]

Such "political" thinking can backfire. Sometimes decisions are taken only for the Election date to be moved at the last minute with disastrous consequences. On 20 July, 1978 the Labour Cabinet had to consider the wage norm for the next round of pay settlements. They chose 5% but later Jim

Callaghan decided against an autumn Election. The 5% pay norm led on to the "winter of discontent" and the collapse of the Labour government. In July it had all seemed very different, as Joel Barnett explains:

> I was sceptical about its prospects and doubt if it would have been agreed so easily if we had not all been so certain of an Autumn election, before the pay round really got under way.[38]

Electoral considerations can affect even the most small-scale, routine and ordinary Whitehall decisions. Early in 1965 Tony Benn, then Postmaster General, had to decide whether to put up postal charges. The evening before the issue was to be discussed in Cabinet he spoke to Barbara Castle to get her advice. As a politician to her fingertips she had no doubts what to do:

> The real question was when the next General Election would be. If it was in a matter of months ... then it would be absolutely ridiculous to do the Tories' dirty work for them. Putting up postal charges would help them to win the Election, then they would inherit the benefit.[39]

The next day in Cabinet this argument was accepted but in typical Whitehall fashion a different reason was thought up as the public line and smokescreen:

> It was decided to postpone the increase in the letter rate, on the argument that the Postmaster General was engaged in an efficiency audit.[40]

In the same way, one of the most difficult political issues for Whitehall in the last few years has been dog licences. The Thatcher government decided that they would continue with a system, heavily criticised by the Public Accounts Committee, and under which the cost of collecting the fees from dog licences was far greater than the revenue received. The reason was that Ministers felt the possible political consequences of substantially increasing the fee were too damaging. A new scheme was only introduced after the 1983 Election.

Buying, or not losing, votes is the vital consideration in the run-up to elections. In July 1969 the Central Wales railway line was saved from closure because it went through three marginal seats. As Dick Crossman reflected:

> Here we are in the run-up to the Election and this was the third time we had overwhelming evidence that from now on this Cabinet is to be dominated simply and solely by the thought of losing votes.[41]

In the same way the Ravenscraig Steel Plant was kept open by the Conservative government before the 1983 Election.

The other side of the coin is that if policies do not bear immediate fruit then Ministers are not very interested, whatever the intrinsic merit of the scheme. The 1964–70 Labour government was committed to increasing civilian scientific, high-technology, research. Sir Solly Zuckerman, Chief Scientific Adviser, came up with a scheme to reduce military research and development and transfer it to civilian use. But the proposal was made in May 1969 and it was too near the next election. As Harold Wilson, the great exponent of the "white heat of the technological revolution", explained:

> I am afraid there is no political capital in this because nothing we decide will have any effect until years after the next Parliament gets going.[42]

By-elections

By-elections are the time for imaginative thinking in Whitehall and the quick political gesture. In March 1967 Willie Ross (Secretary of State for Scotland) wanted to announce the building of a container berth at Greenock before the by-election in the nearby Pollock constituency. The Ministry of Transport had to agree, which they did, and then get Treasury approval. With just two days to go before voting, rapid action was required. At a first meeting of officials the Treasury refused to accept the proposal. But, late in the evening in the House of Commons, Barbara Castle had a quiet word with Jim Callaghan, the Chancellor, who was better able to appreciate the political arguments and agreed to the proposal. Civil Servants in the Department of Transport hastily drafted a speech and the day before the by-election Barbara Castle made the announcement to Parliament. To appease her conscience, and to try to make the proposal look more reasonable, another container berth was agreed at Seaforth. Barbara Castle somehow managed to convince herself that she was not a party to what she described as "a squalid by-election bribe"![43] All the activity turned out to be fruitless because Labour lost the by-election. In similar fashion Michael Heseltine announced in June 1985, just before voting in the crucial Brecon and Radnor by-election, that an Army camp at Crickhowell, in the constituency and long scheduled for closure, would now be kept open. This ploy was also unsuccessful: the Tories lost the by-election and the Army was left with an uneconomic camp to run. Both of these cases show how politicians believe it legitimate to use public money for their own short-term political purposes.

Timing of announcements is also vital. Bad news must be suppressed before a by-election. Barbara Castle describes the scene inside No. 10 in October 1968 when the Labour Cabinet was discussing the introduction of new hire purchase controls:

> And so into Cabinet, where we turned to the question of when the new controls should be announced. Roy wanted to announce them tomorrow whereupon someone, I think it was Denis, exclaimed 'Not on the eve of poll at Bassetlaw!' Roy looked taken aback at this: the election implications just hadn't occurred to him.

There was a brief discussion and the usual quick Whitehall fix:

> Eventually it was agreed that the announcement should not be made till Monday 4 November, when it would appear a natural [*sic*] introduction to the economic debate.[44]

Just how over-sensitive and paranoid Ministers can become about announcements was shown by another episode six months later. Dick Crossman had to announce the results of an enquiry into abuse of patients by staff at Ely Mental Hospital, on the face of it a purely routine, administrative matter. The draft paper was discussed in Cabinet as Crossman described:

> They thought, "My God, another bloody scandal," but really the interest to the Prime Minister lay in the fact that it

was being announced on Thursday, the day of three by-elections ... Harold wondered how it was possible that one should ruin the chances of people voting Labour by having this terrible story blurted out on the 6 o'clock news that very evening.

As usual party political considerations, and not the interests of the Health Service, were uppermost in Ministerial minds as they focussed not on the issue but on presentation:

Colleagues were chiefly anxious about the blame which would attach to the Government and anxious that we should put it back on the Tories.

And so Dick Crossman went back to the DHSS and asked the civil servants to try and find as many damaging statistics as possible about the Tory government's record for his conference in the afternoon.[45]

But it is not just at times of elections that party political considerations together with the associated squalid manoeuvrings are at the heart of government inside Whitehall. This is a process which goes on all the time as the next two case studies show.

Party Politics and Whitehall: Development Areas

Selection of development areas and allocation of regional aid have been an irresistible opportunity for Ministers to use public money for party advantage. In 1969 a report by Sir Joseph Hurst on Intermediate Areas[46] recommended introducing a new category of areas for assistance, which would receive slightly less financial support than the development areas. It also recommended removing development area status from Liverpool. The report was considered in the Strategic Economic Policy Committee, chaired by Harold Wilson, MP for Huyton in Liverpool. His first act was to put Merseyside firmly back into the development areas. At the next meeting Crossman and his colleagues were left in no doubt about the main purpose of the exercise:

This morning he [Wilson] began again by saying that this

was a highly political subject, elections were coming up and we must look at this with open political eyes.

Crossman and Dick Marsh tried to argue for more aid everywhere on the grounds that there were lots of marginal constituencies outside the development areas. (They were MPs for Coventry and Greenwich respectively.) This idea went down like a lead balloon:

> We were pushed aside because according to our colleagues so many promises have been made in Blackburn or Humberside, in Yorkshire, in Derbyshire and Plymouth that all kinds of expectations have been built up.[47]

The day of reckoning came when, four days later:

> we got on with the pork barrel, sorting it out and sweating it round ... Part of the solution was a decision to build the Humber bridge ten years earlier than the traffic requirements justify. This was something Barbara and I promised in order to win the Hull by-election in March 1966 and, ironically, the money was found by deducting it from the Development Areas.[48]

So the areas most in need were to be deprived of money in order to try and buy votes elsewhere. This interesting piece of socialist economic planning fell apart when the subject came to the full Cabinet for approval three days later. Tony Crosland (President of the Board of Trade) announced that the "redistribution" formula would not work. Rather than start again, in typical Whitehall fashion it was decided to go ahead anyway and worry about where the money was coming from some other time:

> We were left with the appalling job of patching up a statement from Peter Shore so he could say that the whole cost of the new help to the grey areas would be financed out of the existing funds being spent on regional development, but not exactly how.[49]

The statement could not say how, because the Cabinet had no idea.

Party Politics and Whitehall: Parliamentary and Local Government Boundaries

Every fifteen years or so, an independent commission redraws the boundaries of the parliamentary constituencies. Because people have been moving out of the inner cities, this process normally benefits the Conservatives as a number of Labour inner-city seats are abolished and new seats in suburban areas are created. In the late 1960s Jim Callaghan, as Home Secretary, fought a long and ultimately successful campaign to stop the implementation of the new boundaries before the 1970 Election. In 1983 the opposite happened. The Tories had decided to have an early election to cash in on their post-Falklands popularity but not before the new constituencies were created. Civil servants in the Home Office worked long hours to produce a detailed plan for the rapid implementation of the new boundaries, and the Cabinet kept a careful watch on the proceedings to ensure that there was no slip-up. Fifteen years earlier when Dick Crossman was made Minister for Local Government in 1964 he found himself responsible for implementing the recommendations of an independent commission looking at redefining local government boundaries. Parliamentary constituencies have to follow local government boundaries as far as possible and so the decisions Crossman made would have important implications for the electoral chances of the Labour party. Crossman was in no doubt about his Ministerial mission as he wrote in his diary: "All I have to do is prevent thirty or forty Labour seats going to the Tories."[50]

During his tours round the country he talked with local Labour organisers and Transport House officials to assess the impact of the recommended changes on Labour seats. This was what he indulgently described as "one of those minor improprieties I allow myself"[51]. Harold Wilson kept a close eye on what was happening and at the end of March 1965 held a meeting in Downing Street, also attended by the Home Secretary, the Attorney General (no doubt to ensure that what Ministers did was at least legal), and the Leader of the House of Commons (for obvious reasons). Crossman summed up the Prime Minister's position:

Harold was obviously concerned to make quite sure that I was doing my job as a politician on the local boundary decisions, that no adjustment was politically disadvantageous to us.[52]

Wilson need not have worried, Crossman was well up to the task. In June 1965 he announced new boundaries in three areas, but only after a struggle with his civil servants. In Leicester he had had to fight a long battle with the civil servants in the Ministry of Housing and Local Government to reverse the recommendations of the independent commission by putting only the city-controlled housing estates (mainly Labour votes) into the new borough. His diary makes the motivation clear, and that he did not dare reveal his motives in public:

I realised that this solution would ... save the Labour seats in the next parliamentary distribution. This is the line I forced on the Department ... In the weeks of consultation I haven't bothered to conceal the political factor from my officials but I was careful not to mention it ... in my press briefing.[53]

After the various diary entries on this sordid saga comes one of Crossman's most remarkable passages. It reveals the essential duplicity of Ministers, the difficulty they have in recognising the truth and the way they conceal their motives even from themselves. Crossman's final words on the subject were:

It has been an anxious job because I have to be sure that no one can accuse me of gerrymandering the boundary for Party purposes.[54]

Politics is everywhere in Whitehall

Party political considerations are very powerful inside Whitehall and can dominate decisions from the very important to the trivial. Just how trivial can be seen from the fact that, under pressure from Barbara Castle, Roy Jenkins put traffic wardens in London under the control of the police rather than of the Greater London Council because the Tories had just gained control of the GLC[55]. In the mid-1970s The Scottish

National Party were a major force in Scottish politics. With so many Labour seats at stake, the Cabinet decided reluctantly on a policy of dispersing Civil Service jobs to Glasgow and devolution of power to a Scottish Assembly in an attempt to buy off nationalist support. Just how thin the degree of commitment to devolution as a matter of policy rather than political opportunism really was is illustrated by the all-day conference at Chequers on 16 June, 1975 after the Common Market referendum showed a low level of support for the nationalists.

> The significant thing about this meeting was the attempt of Denis, Roy et al to backtrack on the whole devolution idea on the grounds that the Common Market referendum result in Scotland showed that the Scots Nats. were a busted flush.[56]

We shall examine in a later chapter the close relations between politicians and the media. As can be seen from the honours regularly handed out by the politicians to Fleet Street, sympathetic control of the press by the right people is vital. In February 1970 the Cabinet Strategic Economic Policy Committee discussed the merger between IPC and the *Daily Mirror*. Barbara Castle proposed that it should be referred to the Monopolies Commission. Nobody else on the committee could see why she had made such a proposal.

> Harold launched into a great attack, saying this was political suicide. The *Daily Mirror* was the only paper likely to be loyal to us in the election and we must be political people, not mere runners of Departments. Surely it was clear that we should not refer this case and alienate the *Daily Mirror*.[57]

Exactly the same considerations may have been behind the decision by the Thatcher government not to refer the bid by Rupert Murdoch, a strong supporter of the government, for Times Newspapers to the Monopolies Commission.

Decision-taking in Ignorance

Many of the decisions made in Whitehall are taken in ignorance. Many different factors and pressures contribute to this state of affairs. Frequently, Ministers have not read the relevant papers before the meeting through pressure of work or laziness or lack of interest. The papers themselves are all too often written by civil servants who only have, at best, a partial appreciation of the facts. The final product will have been re-drafted several times and each time by someone further removed from any detailed knowledge or understanding of the subject. The pace of work inside Whitehall, the continual sense of panic and the hasty putting together of a paper for last-minute circulation before a meeting are not conducive to a cool appraisal of all the available facts. A state of ignorance can be, if not blissful, very convenient for Ministers who prefer to exercise their prejudices on a topic unconstrained by uncomfortable information and facts that might show that their political instincts or prejudices were unfounded.

The sheer volume of work coupled with the need to compress facts into a few paragraphs can have a devastating effect on the level of debate. The higher papers are passed up the hierarchy, the less those at the top will know about the problem under discussion: this can reach farcical dimensions. In November 1968 the Cabinet met in the Prime Minister's room at the House of Commons (in order to avoid the press) to discuss the traditional Treasury deflationary package for the economy. This time the proposals included a scheme for import deposits. Dick Crossman describes the ensuing fiasco:

> Perhaps the most remarkable thing was that when we asked about the details and machinery of the imports deposit scheme no one knew. Tony Crosland was in Vienna, the PM didn't know ... the inner group of six who had prepared the package didn't know what goods were covered by the scheme.

The Cabinet Secretariat scrabbled around outside and eventually a small note was brought in that answered some of the questions:

> It is fantastic that in this particular case there was no bit of paper giving the package or the reasons for it. It was all told us verbally and we have serious doubts whether a clear-cut plan had ever been worked out.[58]

In very complex subjects like the Rate Support Grant and the Common Agricultural Policy, Ministers do not even begin to understand the topic. In others their social background produces ignorance. A number of members of Mrs. Thatcher's Cabinet needed an explanation of what a mortgage was and how it worked before one meeting.

Decision-taking by Chance, Bargain and Personality

Even if Ministers do know what they are talking about the final result often owes as much to chance, political bargains and pure prejudice as to anything like objective and careful consideration of the facts.

In December 1967 by sheer coincidence the pay of London dockers and Scottish teachers were simultaneously on the agenda of the Cabinet Prices and Incomes Committee. Ray Gunter (Minister of Labour) advised giving in to the dockers, and the rest of the Committee agreed on the grounds that "we can't afford a dock strike in January". The sequel was almost inevitable:

> Having conceded to the dockers, the Committee felt it necessary to smack down poor Willie Ross when he tried to offer the Scottish teachers a decent wage. He hadn't a single person on his side and we all knew that the two cases had not been decided on their merits.[59]

In trying to get their policies agreed Ministers are quite willing to strike crude bargains with each other that bear no relation to the merits of the issues. In June 1968 Roy Jenkins was opposed to the rapid implementation of the Fulton Report on the Civil Service. Dick Crossman was trying to stop Jenkins cutting the social security programme and was also trying to save his proposals to reform the House of Lords. The two met late at night in the Commons:

> I was just leaving the room when Roy said "Now, Dick, let's be practical. If I agree with you about postponing the decision on Social Service cuts for a week will you give me your full support on Fulton?" "Yes", I said, "if you will support me on Lord's reform as well." And that, roughly speaking, was the deal we came to.[60]

Ministers are often bored with the subjects dealt with in their Departments and they see issues primarily in terms of whether they will project their public image and enhance their political status. Ministers regard the consequencs of such decisions as of minor importance. Michael Heseltine's decision to reorganise the Ministry of Defence in 1984 stemmed largely from political motives. He had a reputation, largely undeserved in the view of those who worked for him, as a manager of large departments. His predecessor, John Nott, had carried out a Defence Review which removed that avenue for gaining political visibility, and the nuclear issue was producing diminishing publicity returns after the 1983 Election. With no other obvious options open for staying in the public eye, Heseltine decided to "reorganise" the Ministry. Heseltine's priority was changes, with little concern about detailed structures, for the sake of projecting his image as a manager and reformer of Whitehall.

Tony Crosland was certainly bored as Secretary of State for Education. At different times he told his wife: "I'm not frightfully interested in the arts at this moment" and "I'm not frightfully interested in the public schools". This boredom and irritation would influence or even dictate his education policy, particularly if preceded by a bad meeting or a poor dinner. After one dinner arranged to discuss universities he returned home and vented his spleen:

> The Vice-Chancellors this evening went on and on as if their precious Universities weren't already rich and successful ... to be truthful, I'm not frightfully interested in the Universities ... Tomorrow I shall tell the Vice-Chancellors they can stuff themselves. "Enough of this niggling and nagging" I shall say. "I have other things on my mind than your petty preoccupations."

Crosland was in an even worse mood when he returned from a meeting with the four teachers' associations and announced his new carefully-thought out policy for schools:

> If it's the last thing I do, I'm going to destroy every fucking grammar school in England he said. And Wales. And Northern Ireland.[61]

It was prejudice to the point of perversity that committed the

Tory government to abolition of the GLC and Metropolitan Counties in 1983. Having failed to reform the rates, despite their Election manifesto promise in 1979, the government were anxious to find some way of demonstrating their concern, and their radical credentials, on the local government issue. A ninety-page report compiled by an inter-departmental group of officials was put to Cabinet just before the election was called. It showed that, even on the most optimistic assumptions, abolition would only save £20 million and on the most likely outcome would not save any money at all. In order to achieve this the most complex bill ever put to parliament would have to be drafted. Undeterred, the Cabinet, with the election imminent, decided to go ahead anyway. Although the bill was eventually passed the whole unproductive process took up a monumental amount of parliamentary time and effort with very little to show at the end of it.

Petty Decisions and the Talking Shop

Grand strategy and high policy affecting the future of the nation account for a surprisingly small amount of Whitehall's time and effort. Many of the items coming up for decision by Ministers inside departments are about the minutiae of administration. They reflect an inability on the part of Ministers to plan their time effectively and concentrate on the broad issues of fundamental importance. And it is not just in departments that this process takes place. At one Cabinet meeting there was a long discussion about whether the Prime Minister and the Foreign Secretary should send Christmas cards to the Russian ambassador.[62]

High-level attention does not guarantee that the subject is important or the results significant. In September 1966 Dick Crossman conducted a full-scale review of the Government Information Service. The terms of reference were agreed by the Cabinet, and the Secretary to the Cabinet, Burke Trend, was closely involved in all the discussions. Crossman spoke to every interested Cabinet Minister. The report was considered personally by the Prime Minister. What were the recommendations of this radical reappraisal of the information services? Crossman suggested one extra person working in No. 10 and one extra person in his own office. The Cabinet solemnly discussed and agreed to implement the report in November. The conclusion was even more farcical. Two months later the additional person at No. 10 had been removed. All this work for just one extra job in Crossman's office!

Given their training and background, it is not surprising that Ministers are great talkers. For them, talking is equivalent to action and generally preferable to decision-taking. Much of their time is spent talking each other into submission. Many issues, ranging from the weighty to the trivial, have to reappear time and time again on the Cabinet agenda before they are finally resolved or finally deferred. For example it only took twenty-six Cabinet meetings to resolve the discussions on the IMF loan in 1976. No wonder it is sometimes easier to put off a decision altogether. For as that great exponent of political pragmatism, Harold Wilson, once said: "A decision deferred is a decision made."[63]

Often, Ministers find it impossible to distinguish talking and deferring decisions from policy-making. In December 1968 there was a special all-day meeting of the National Economic Development Council at Chequers. Barbara Castle left full of enthusiasm. "Everyone agreed afterwards that it was the best meeting of Neddy that had ever been held." But when the record of what took place is examined the performance falls far short of its extravagant billing; all the meeting had accomplished was two long discussions reaching no conclusions and the commissioning of more studies. As Barbara Castle explained:

> We agreed we needed a deeper joint study and analysis of the nature of unemployment ... The afternoon was spent analysing the reasons why investment remained so low and here again we agreed that follow up studies were needed.[64]

If this was the best meeting it is difficult to imagine what a bad meeting would be like.

Jobs and Honours for the Boys

One of the major rewards of Ministerial life is patronage; the ability to hand out jobs and honours. Appointments to all the different areas that Ministers control – nationalised industries, advisory councils and committees, regional councils, etc. – are a powerful tool for rewarding the faithful, and influencing others. The biographer of Hugh Dalton, Chancellor of the Exchequer in the 1940s and MP for Bishop Auckland from 1935 to 1959, comments on how Dalton used this power to reward his constituency secretary, Will Davies:

> Will Davies ... would never have received the OBE in 1947, gained a place on the Board of Aycliffe Development Corporation, or acquired the somewhat surprising job of Welfare Officer for the West Auckland Clothing Company without Dalton's personal intervention.[65]

There was an illuminating conversation between Harold Wilson and Barbara Castle in the House of Commons shortly before one New Year's Honours list. Wilson wanted to give George Eddie, Castle's agent in the Blackburn Labour party and leader of the Labour group on the council, a knighthood. Castle's comments in her diary show first that the Civil Service has a scale against which honours can be awarded determined by the size of the borough not the service rewarded; and second the level of self-deception about their motives of which politicians are capable:

> The officials were trying to tell him [Wilson] that George couldn't get one [a knighthood] because Blackburn was not big enough. He was prepared to sweep aside nonsense like that to help his friends. His reformism consists of not altering the conventions like Honours, but in using them in unorthodox ways.[66]

Barbara Castle was not above using the Honours system in such a "reformist" way herself. In April 1970 her husband Ted was not re-selected as an Alderman on the GLC. He was very bitter and Barbara moved swiftly to try and compensate him. She went straight round to see Harold Wilson and demanded he do something. Wilson immediately offered a peerage. Unfortunately for Ted Castle, Wilson lost the 1970 election, but he got his consolation prize as soon as Wilson returned to power in 1974.[67]

In 1966 Wilson decided to abolish the special category of

political honours. How much of a cosmetic and public relations change this "unorthodox" move turned out to be is revealed by the account given by Dick Crossman of the meeting at No. 10 on 22 September, 1966 also attended by Tony Greenwood (Minister for Local Government) and the Chief Whip. Crossman pointed out that abolition of political honours would really only exclude party agents and regional organisers. Wilson was not bothered by this. "We'll include them all under public honours," he said. As Dick Crossman rightly commented, "But of course once you do this your announcement is merely a gimmick because you haven't cut out political honours." Mrs. Thatcher restored political honours in 1979 and the party faithful are now once again openly rewarded for their services. In addition retiring junior Ministers and long-serving backbenchers are rewarded with knighthoods.

As Ministers rise up the ladder of seniority the rewards they can expect increase. At Minister of State level membership of the Privy Council (with the additional status of using the prefix Rt. Hon) is automatic after a few years. At the top the rewards that Ministers can give themselves are that much greater. Senior Cabinet Ministers can expect, or even demand, a life peerage, as Barbara Castle found out when she was sacked by Jim Callaghan in April 1976. At the end of the painful interview the following exchange took place:

> "Do you want to go into the Lords?" said Jim. "Good God, no," I replied. "thank heavens," said Jim [it would have meant a by-election]. "Though I can't refuse it to you any time you ask for it."[68]

Other very senior Ministers, such as Willie Whitelaw, are now rewarded with hereditary peerages.

Conclusion

In this chapter we have observed the real way in which Ministers conduct themselves in Whitehall. Much of the evidence has, necessarily, been based on the Crossman and Castle diaries as the only even remotely honest accounts of political life. Most memoirs by politicians are bland and dissembling. The Diaries of Tory Cabinet Ministers have not yet been published. My own experience is that Tory Ministers are just the same, and in some ways worse, than their Labour opponents as the Westlands affair and the battles between Michael Heseltine and Leon Brittan at the end of 1985 and early 1986 show. The realities of Ministerial life are far from the reassuring image they try to convey to the public through the public relations machine and political memoirs. The conventional view that Whitehall and Ministers are selflessly working for the public interest is an illusion.

Inside Whitehall is a seedy world of half-truth, ignorance and botched decision-taking. It is a world dominated not by devotion to the public good but by personal ambition and short-term political interests, the desire of politicians to stay in power at any price. The instinctive reaction of most Ministers when confronted by an issue is not to think in terms of analysing a complex problem to seek out the optimum solution but instead to see it in political terms.

The questions they ask are: "How can this issue be exploited politically to maximum advantage?" "How can the party gain and how can we maximize problems for the opposition?" And finally: "Does this issue increase my political exposure and will it benefit my career?" In order to achieve these ends presentation is more important than facts.

The top of the Civil Service is deeply involved in this grubby atmosphere of Ministerial politics which it grandly calls "policy-making". We now need to look at the Civil Service as the other major component of Whitehall. We shall see here again that the reality of the Civil Service is very different from its public face.

CHAPTER THREE

Mandarins

The Civil Service is a highly developed caste society. It is divided into 38 general classes and about 500 departmental classes. Movement between these classes is rare and the whole system is run by a group of about a thousand – the mandarins. This élite has little or no direct contact with the other 600,000 or so civil servants, spends most of its time in the highly political world of Ministers, and believes that it is the Civil Service.

The Real Civil Service

The Civil Service is about 600,000-strong. Some 120,000, or 1 in 5, are industrial civil servants, working in dockyards, stores depots, workshops and research establishments. Most are employed either in the industrial enterprises of the Ministry of Defence supporting the Armed Forces or in maintaining the large array of government buildings. Of the rest, 50,000 are scientists and professional and technological civil servants. They work mostly in research establishments (again mainly for the Ministry of Defence), but their activities also embrace all the varied and complex tasks undertaken by government from the Road Research Laboratory to fisheries research. Then there are 30,000 tax inspectors, over 8,000 people working in Customs and Excise, and 50,000 people paying out social security benefit. The Civil Service employs over 25,000 typists and secretaries. There are also a number of smaller categories who are counted as civil servants as an historical accident – 17,300 prison officers and 1,700 driving examiners.

When all these different groups have been counted it leaves about 225,000 to make up the so-called administrative class, about a third of the Civil Service. But of these 146,000 (or 65%) are clerks, mainly responsible for looking after the vast quantities of paper in the system. There are then the major executive grades which account for nearly all the remaining 75,000. The top Civil Service, the mandarins who wait on Ministers in Whitehall, represent a tiny fraction. The top three grades of the Civil Service – Permanent Secretary, Deputy Secretary and Under-Secretary – amount to just 650 people or about 0.1% of the total. Even if everybody in the next two grades – Assistant Secretary and Principal – are included (and many of these are not located in Whitehall) they still account for less than 1% of the Civil Service.[1]

In this book the focus is on the Civil Service in Whitehall, what can truly be called the Mandarin class. But it is vital to remember that this is a very small, select group, the very top of the caste society. They are in nearly every way detached from the other 99.9% of the Civil Service; they have different values and in fact spend very little of their time looking after the interests of the rest of the Civil Service. But this élite is articulate and, increasingly in the last few years, it has ventured into the media to try and explain what the Civil Service does. On nearly every occasion they describe the functions of the Civil Service in terms of what the élite does – "policy-making" with Ministers.

The real Civil Service lives in a very different world from the corridors of power in Whitehall inhabited by the mandarins. No briefing of Ministers and writing of parliamentary statements; less chairing of meetings and hosting lunches. For the majority of civil servants the working environment is sordid and dispiriting: a world like the DHSS and Department of Employment offices at the Elephant and Castle in London where 10% of the staff leave every month because of appalling conditions and vandalism, where the funiture is screwed to the floor, where there is a steel turnstile instead of a main door, and where claimants attack the staff. Both staff and the public suffer in such conditions. The DHSS and Department of Employment are separate organisations. The distinction is maintained largely for reasons of departmental politics inside Whitehall. Claimants do not understand these subtleties and do not know which department to go to for help. If they go to the wrong one they can waste hours queuing again in the other department. The two departments, though in the same building, can only communicate by telephone, which is rarely answered. As one clerk in the Department of Employment commented:

> It is like Kafka's castle ... nobody knows what the other person is doing. If you asked me how the DHSS work or how housing benefit is worked out I could not tell you. There is no central authority where you can go to sort things out.[2]

Two final points about the real Civil Service. The public image of a male civil service working in London is wrong. About 270,000 (or 44%) are women. But they are not, as we shall see, anywhere near the levels of power. Overwhelmingly they are low-paid typists, clerks and cleaners. The vast majority of the Civil Service does not work in inner London. Indeed more civil servants work in Scotland, Wales and Northern Ireland than in central London. About 80,000 civil servants do work in inner London, but many of these do so in local offices, like the Elephant and Castle, and have nothing to do with Whitehall. The tiny group of mandarins is therefore wholly untypical of the rest of the Civil Service. It lives in an isolated world of its own, with its own customs and code of conduct. It strongly believes in its effortless superiority and recruits new members in its own image. It is a true ruling class.

The Origins of the Ruling Class

How did the British Civil Service come to be dominated by the mandarin élite? And why is that élite composed of Oxbridge-educated arts graduates? The origins of the system date back to the middle of the nineteenth century and the Northcote-Trevelyan report. This report was part of a process of administrative change following the fiasco of the Crimean War. The report recommended the replacement of the existing system of patronage in appointments to the Civil Service by a competitive examination. Appointments to the Civil Service would be in the hands of an independent commission. Merit, not good connections, was to be the test for entry and for promotion within the system. The new system took a long time to be fully operational and pockets of patronage persisted until the First World War.

It is generally assumed that the Northcote-Trevelyan report

was one of the great reforms of the nineteenth century, opening up power from aristocratic patronage to a new class based on merit. In fact, a more subtle process was at work. The newly-reformed public schools together with a reformed Oxbridge (led by men like Jowett at Balliol) were deliberately setting out to produce a new ruling class for Britain and the growing Empire based on the public school ethic. Northcote-Trevelyan was part of the process whereby the new élite came to dominate Britain. The real motivation was well described by William Gladstone, Chancellor of the Exchequer, and one of the main proponents of reform:

> One of the great recommendations of the change in my eyes would be its tendency to strengthen and multiply the ties between the higher classes and the possession of administrative power ... the separation of work ... into mechanical and intellectual ... will open to the highly educated class a career, and give them command over all the higher parts of the Civil Service, which up to this time they have never enjoyed.[3]

The new élite would be non-political, work for Ministers of any party and would take over the "intellectual" work, and would constitute the "administrators" in the "First Division". The "Second Division" was to undertake the "mechanical" work and in 1920 they were organised as the Executive class. The specialist grades – scientists, architects, lawyers, etc. – were not even recognised as Civil Service classes until 1945; until then they had only been employed by individual departments. The strength of tradition in the Civil Service is shown by the fact that the trade union for the top civil servants (Principal and above) is still known as the First Division Association.

The Domination of the "Administrators"

From the start of the modern Civil Service, therefore, it was assumed that there was such a task as "administration" that could be organised separately and undertaken only by a dedicated class. During the last century it has remained the fundamental organising principle of the Civil Service. This view has two major consequences. First, it assumes that the élite can be recruited on the basis of general qualifications (a well-trained mind), and second that it can then undertake any task in "administration", because these tasks are essentially the same. Mandarins believe that administering the prison service, controlling nearly £20 billion of defence expenditure, paying subsidies to farmers or creating a new policy for higher education can all be undertaken by the same sort of people. They are all problems in administration. They are not seen as specialist problems requiring specialist skills. Therefore the only training the administrator really requires is how to handle the machinery of government. Learning how to consult, how to draft minutes, chair a committee and deal with Ministers are the sole skills required, and training is best carried out "on the job" and acquired by experience and oral tradition.

This assumption might have been tenable in the late nineteenth century when departments were small and their functions limited. Administrators came from the same background in a relatively homogeneous ruling group that shared many assumptions regardless of the party in power. The idea of a non-political group advising Ministers seemed reasonable. The functions of Civil Service could be seen as working closely with Ministers, formulating policy in the small select world of Whitehall. For example in 1908 the Treasury had just 26 staff – 1 Permanent Secretary, 2 Deputies, 4 Principals and 19 clerks.[4] In 1913 the Home Office had only 28 staff – 1 Permanent Secreaty, 1 Under-Secretary, 2 legal Under-Secretaries, 6 Assistant Secretaries and 18 clerks.[5]

The twentieth century has seen a vast expansion in the executive responsibilities of government: the creation of the Welfare State, starting with the setting up of Labour Exchanges in 1909, and compulsory National Insurance in 1911, the emergence of whole new Ministries such as Health, Social Security, Transport and Industry. With this expansion has come a huge increase in the number of civil servants. Most of these civil servants are carrying out executive functions – paying social security benefits, collecting taxes, paying bills on government contracts and so on. But the top of the Civil Service, although increasing in numbers, has remained largely unchanged in the values it holds and the way it operates. It is still recognisably the same as the evidence given a century ago to the first Royal Commission to the Civil Service revealed:

> It is extremely desirable to have in the upper ranks of the Service men who have the esprit de corps of our public schools and our Universities, and who are able to hold their own, to speak what they consider to be the truth about their business; and able to deal with persons outside the office as gentlemen.[6]

Recruiting the Élite

To understand how the system works and how it has become self-perpetuating we need to look at recruitment policy and practice. The people at the top of the Civil Service are now recruiting the young graduates who will be the mandarins of the first decades of the twenty-first century. They were themselves recruited in the 1940s and 1950s under a system devised by those who had joined the Civil Service in some cases before the First World War. This explains much of the institutional conservatism of the Civil Service.

Until 1945 entry to the top of the Civil Service was through an examination system. This system was highly biased in that the examination subjects discriminated in favour of the public school, Oxbridge-educated arts graduate. For example as late as the 1940s medicine, architecture and engineering were excluded. The philosophy was that the competition should be "a test of general rather than highly specialised ability and education", and the basic premise was that "such subjects as language, literature and history are, on the whole and for the most part of young men, the best preparation for the Higher Civil Service".[7] The idea that qualifications or technical knowledge might be relevant to the work of the Civil Service was abhorrent. For example, papers on economic history, political organisation and public finance were given half the marks of the paper on Italian literature. The examination system was also socially biased since it required applicants to live in London for a month to take the exams but without any payment for living expenses.

The examination was followed by a fifteen-to-twenty-minute

interview which was awarded as many marks as the three
compulsory exam papers. It was at this stage that the obstacles
to a genuinely open entry on merit alone became glaringly
obvious. The interviewers were largely drawn from Oxbridge
on the "good chap" principle as explained by the man
responsible for their selection:

> We try to choose people who have broad sympathies ... you
> get the advice of your friends; you get people you know, and
> then people whose opinion you value recommended people.[8]

What sort of qualities were the interviewers seeking in the
candidates? The chief Civil Service Commissioner in the 1940s
explained that they were looking for "the intelligent man who
can turn his hand to anything". In order to do this:

> We take very great account, for instance, of references in the
> referees' reports on candidates to their home origins, the fact
> that their family have brought them up well and the fact that
> they have been persons well respected in their community.[9]

The interviews themselves concentrated on "general address,
good manners, brightness, interest in various things and
sympathy",[10] although the man in charge of the whole system
did admit to a personal preference for field sports rather than
games as a fruitful topic for interview questions.[11]

  This system of selection by examination and short interview
was not abolished until 1969, and it was still the route by which
the majority of the mandarins joined until 1957. The people at
the top of the Civil Service today are likely to have been chosen
through this process.

A New Way of Choosing the Élite

During the Second World War the Civil Service considered
how to recruit the large number of new entrants that would be
required after the war. The mandarins had doubts about the
examination system – not on the grounds that it was biased but
because it was not selecting enough "good chaps"; in other
words it was not biased enough. They were worried that too
many highly intelligent, grammar-school-educated, "scholar-
ship" boys were getting through. They wanted a recruitment

procedure that gave greater emphasis to "character".[12] They were impressed by the officer selection process in the Army, which naturally emphasised "character" and other "officer-like" qualities. With the help of Sir Cyril Burt (whose work in educational psychology has since been discredited as fraudulent), a new scheme based on a Civil Service Selection Board (CSSB) was devised. It is this system that now selects those intended for the top of the Civil Service. Knowing how this system works is fundamental to understanding the ethos of the higher Civil Service. The system itself says more about the way Whitehall works than is apparent at first glance.

Candidates are put through two days of tests by the Board and assessed by a panel of three – a senior retired civil servant, a psychologist and young civil servant who went through the process five or six years before. There are the standard set of interviews, one with each assessor, and a series of intelligence, literacy and numeracy tests.

The centrepiece of the whole process is a simulated problem in policy-making. Candidates have about two hours to read a file on a complex problem and recommend one of the options. Typically, they might be faced with how to provide the water supply for a new town. There are usually three solutions, none of them self-evidently right, each with drawbacks, e.g. one of the schemes may involve drowning a valley in a national park. The candidates have to write a brief for the Minister setting out the various arguments and recommending a solution.

This is an unintentional parody of the top of the Civil Service at work. In an impossibly short time you have to read a mass of papers on a topic about which you know next to nothing, write a succinct and coherent brief for the Minister, recommend a solution and find convincing arguments in its favour. In this exercise the fatal mistake is to make value judgements about what would be the right solution or to suggest that more information would be needed before making a decision. In Whitehall you have to learn that recommending any solution, as long as it is cogently presented and politically acceptable, is what is required.

There are two further exercises based on the story in the file. The first is drafting a diplomatic letter in the wake of some unfortunate incident. This is a test of the vital attribute required in the good civil servant – an ability to spot what answer is required and then produce the arguments to back it up. Most candidates do not do well at this exercise. They are not cynical enough. Some may even be sufficiently naive to try and explain what happened and apologise instead of making up a convincing excuse. A few years in the Civil Service will usually provide the right amount of training.

The other major test is the committee exercise; a simulated meeting where each member of the group is given thirty minutes to prepare to act as chairman and two minutes to prepare to act as a member. Candidates are marked on their ability as chairmen to get the rest of the group to reach a consensus, or failing that a compromise, and also on whether they can make a constructive contribution as a member of the committee. This is another introduction to the Civil Service at work – committees discussing topics about which they know little and under pressure to come to rapid agreement on any acceptable basis.

The assessors now have to decide how to mark the candidates. There are marks for each exercise but also eleven separate marks awarded for various personal qualities. These are not all added up to reach a total mark. Instead, the process is much more subjective. The assessors discuss the candidates and their performance and in some mysterious way agree on a final letter (from A to G) to be awarded. There is therefore plenty of scope for subjectivity and domination of the procedure by the views the assessors have of the "personal qualities" of the candidates.

The last stage is the Final Selection Board. This consists of one of the Civil Service Commissioners, some senior civil servants, a couple of professors and a representative of industry and of the trade unions. The interview lasts about fifty minutes but the CSSB marking is only rarely altered. The philosophy of the interview is simply to review the CSSB marking and confirm it is broadly correct.

The Qualities of a Successful Candidate

In the CSSB process there is a mixture of written and oral tests combined with an assessment of the candidate's personal qualities. But what qualities are the assessors told to look for? In 1976 the Civil Service made public the briefing paper for assessors. It is an illuminating document which shows how the Civil Service recruits in its own image, and what enormous scope exists for highly subjective judgements.[13]

As in the past the successful candidate should still have a "good all-round intellect" in which "penetration and judgement are of high importance". But there must also be "a commonsense appreciation of what is practicable or *likely to be politically acceptable*" (my italics). As judgement cannot be measured objectively, phrases such as "likely to be politically acceptable" simply mean that the assessors will judge candidates entirely subjectively against what the Civil Service already regards as "politically acceptable". The successful candidate must be able to "hold his own in discussion while maintaining good relations" and there is "no place for the man who must work on his own". Candidates must be ambitious, but not for power only for "responsibility". They must show "tolerance and humanity", "drive and determination" and "integrity". As a true élite in the making they must show "understanding of how their decisions will affect *ordinary* people". All of these qualities are entirely subjective and very difficult to assess even in two days. But they are undoubtedly the qualities prized by the Civil Service – a touch of greyness, ability to turn out work for any purpose, no strong beliefs and an ability to fit in amongst other "good chaps" in the Service. What is lacking in this catalogue of qualities is any suggestion that originality and concern would be acceptable. Indeed any hint of *commitment* makes the Civil Service very uneasy indeed.

Bias in Recruitment

The Civil Service selection system is highly biased. Given its operating procedures it would be surprising if it were not. Yet the Civil Service is extremely sensitive about this accusation and always insists that the system is the most fair and unbiased in the country. After similar criticisms of bias in the Fulton Report the Civil Service brought in an establishment figure – a deputy Governor of the Bank of England – to look at the system. He was able to make a reassuring report which said:

We found no evidence of bias in Method II [the CSSB process] itself, either in the procedures or on the part of the assessors.[14]

What the available evidence actually suggests is massive bias towards upper middle class male candidates from public schools and Oxbridge who have arts degrees.

Not surprisingly the Civil Service tends to reflect the fact that Britain is an unequal society and that those from middle class and professional backgrounds are likely to do better in the educational system and subsequently in their careers. About 80% of the Civil Service come from families in the top two socio-economic groups. The Civil Service also reflects a cultural bias in Britain about the desirability of certain types of career for different groups. Public schools educate less than 1 out of 15 children yet provide 4 out of 10 applicants for the Civil Service. The problem with the Civil Service is that the selection process *increases* the existing biases in society, as we shall see when looking at who applies and who succeeds, and how their sex, background, place of education and choice of degree subject influence the chances of entry.

The system is biased against women. In 1984 they made up 49% of the applicants but only 28% of the appointments. Amongst the male applicants and appointees the system is biased towards the top two socio-economic categories:

	% of applicants	% of appointees (1971–75)
Father's occupation		
Categories I & II (professional and management)	57.5	68.9
Category III (skilled)	33	24
Category IV (semi-skilled)	4	2
Category V (unskilled)	1	–

The system is biased towards the public schools:

(1973–75)	% of applicants	% of appointees
Public school/Oxbridge	29.2	34.6
Public school/non-Oxbridge	8.6	21.3

The ability of the assessors to spot the merits of a public school man even without the benefits of an Oxbridge education is clearly remarkable as the non-Oxbridge figures show. The system is, as we shall see in detail shortly, also heavily biased towards Oxbridge graduates.

The system is biased towards arts graduates. In 1971–75 they made up 42.5% of the applicants and 56.7% of the appointees. The other side of the coin is that the system actively discriminates against both social science and natural science graduates. In 1971 36% of the male applicants had social science degrees but they made up only 25% of those appointed. Similarly science graduates made up 17.4% of the male applicants but only 10.8% of the appointees.

In every respect therefore the Civil Service selection system is highly biased.

The Dominance of Oxbridge

The major bias in the selection process and the most important factor inside the top Civil Service is undoubtedly the dominance of Oxbridge. From the start of the century until the 1960s Oxbridge regularly supplied between 75% and 85% of the intake into the top of the Civil Service. The new scheme for graduate recruitment introduced in the early 1970s together with the emergence of the new universities had some impact and by the mid-1970s the Oxbridge share of new recruits fell to about 50%. But, very rapidly, the share has risen and by the early 1980s it was back to its historic level of 75%. In spite of the emergence of the new universities the dominance of Oxbridge is now greater than it has ever been in the last eighty years. At every stage the system is biased towards the Oxbridge graduate as the latest figures for 1984 show:

% of candidates from Oxbridge and other Universities passing each stage of the selection process

	Qualifying Test	CSSB	Final Selection Board
Oxbridge	39	43	75
Other	10	22	54

The effect of all these successive filters is that an Oxbridge graduate is *nine* times as likely to be selected as a graduate from any other university.

This dominance in the selection process is naturally reflected in the people at the top of the Civil Service, although it is perhaps more surprising to see the trends becoming more marked in recent years: 80% of the current Permanent Secretaries went to Oxford or Cambridge and this percentage has actually risen steadily since 1950. Oxbridge comes to dominate the ethos and philosophy of the Civil Service; it is seen as standing for all that is best in Britain and as naturally the main source of its recruits. One or two examples will give the flavour of these hidden cultural biases. Contemporary papers are not publicly available but those that are from the 1930s and 1940s show that the men who selected the people currently at the top of the Civil Service and who designed the current selection system were dominated by Oxbridge. Nothing much has changed in the intervening period.

In the 1930s there were, as today, complaints about bias in the selection system. Some suggested that science subjects should be given more weight in the examinations. Sir Warren Fisher, Head of the Civil Service, agreed to consult the Universities about the possibility but quickly added, "In the first instance consultation had better be limited to Oxford and Cambridge."[15] Two years later an MP queried why, in typical Civil Service fashion, everyday science was omitted from the list of compulsory examination subjects. It was explained to him that:

> on the question of consultation with representative bodies as to the desirability of this step the Civil Service Commissioners obtained the concurrence of the Universities of Oxford and Cambridge, whose considered advice may be taken as representative of general well-informed opinion.[16]

The Civil Service Commission, which recruits all civil servants, was not greatly interested in recruiting people from outside Oxbridge. In 1947 the Chief Commissioner admitted that in nine years he had visited a university other than Oxford and Cambridge just once.[17] Those candidates who did apply to join the Civil Service had to run the gauntlet of a selection system dominated by people from Oxbridge. In 1947 Oxbridge made up 65% of the University members who sat on the Final Selection Board. Even in 1977 they still constituted 47% of the membership.[18]

Though Oxbridge dominated, and still dominates, the Civil Service, some felt that they still missed the life of an Oxbridge college. In 1950 Lord Bridges, Old Etonian, Head of the Civil Service and former Secretary to the Cabinet, could lament the fact that the Civil Service was "unfortunately lacking those expressions of a corporate life found in a college", because it had "neither hall nor chapel neither combination room nor common room".[19]

Many Permanent Secretaries are however able to fulfil this dream when they retire, by becoming Heads of Oxbridge Colleges. Lord Trend, former Secretary to the Cabinet, went off to be Rector of Lincoln College, Oxford in 1973, and Sir Patrick Nairne became Master of St. Catherine's College, Oxford when he left the DHSS in 1981.

Joining the Civil Service

What sort of life faces the young graduates who have successfully passed through the Civil Service selection process? The first discovery is that they have not joined the "Civil Service" – they join a Department. And this Department will be their career. They will be initiated into its values and view of the world. Some may have one posting to another department, usually the Treasury or the Cabinet Office to "broaden" their experience slightly, but they will spend the bulk of their life in one area. They will meet people from other departments at meetings or on the occasional course at the Civil Service College, but they will be judged on their performance in the Department and promoted by the people at the top of their Department. Whitehall is itself a limited and closed world, and many civil servants only see a very small and fairly self-contained part of this world. The young graduate can express a preference but will be given little information or choice about the department he is allocated, and will just have to make the best of it. The chances of getting a transfer are small.

The young graduate will, as an administration trainee (or AT), usually work with a young Principal in his early thirties.

Apart from a small number of short courses at the Civil Service College, all his training will be given "on the job" (and this will often mean being given a lot of odd jobs to do). Such an approach reflects the great feature of the British Civil Service. Administration is not thought of as something that can be taught – it is something that is learnt by doing a job and by observing others. In the 1950s one senior civil servant tried to sum up "the Spirit of British Administration". He caught the mood brilliantly and the philosophy he set out still applies today. Administrators were, he said:

> intelligent amateurs who form their judgements on the basis of experience rather than as a result of a prescribed course of theoretical training.

Indeed some administrators who went abroad were naturally:

> shocked to discover that many countries were administered by men who read books about public administration. Such people were committing the crime of learning from books something one just does.[20]

The young AT will also be introduced at an early stage in the initiation process to another fundamental aspect of the Civil Service. He will learn that his essential contribution to the work of government is to be "administration". This does not require, indeed positively militates against, gaining specialised knowledge about a particular area. An administrator must be able to pick up any job quickly – his skill comes not from knowing anything about the job he is doing but by knowing how the departmental machine and the wider Whitehall machinery work. He must be capable of making the machinery work as smoothly as possible. He must know how to process paper, write the correct sort of brief or committee paper, and how to achieve a compromise between competing interests. The exact nature of that compromise matters far less than the fact that various groups have agreed and the well-oiled machine can continue. In order to get this sort of experience the young AT will be moved to a new job every six to eight months. Although, later in his career, this movement will slow down to about once every two years, the basic principle remains unchanged.

After two years the successful AT will become a Higher Executive Officer (Development) (HEO(D)). His jobs will bear little relation to the relatively tedious jobs of the normal HEO but the title was introduced in the 1970s to give a façade of equality. The HEO(D) is marked out for rapid promotion. There will be a job in a Minister's private office or with the Permanent Secretary. The HEO(D) does not make any great contribution, and his responsibility is limited. These jobs are educational. They are designed to show the young administrator life at the top of Whitehall so that the accepted ways of operating are passed on and the right values are learned at an early stage. After a year or so comes promotion to Principal and the first real job.

Moving up the Ladder

A Principal in a Whitehall job usually runs a small section of about half a dozen people, often less. He concentrates on a small area of policy and provides the first drafts of important papers, answers to Parliamentary questions, etc. He may have responsibility for a limited area of work and send papers direct to a Minister's office. But normally his work and role in policy-making is fairly circumscribed. This is still, to some extent, a learning grade. The senior Civil Service sometimes likes to encourage a degree of radical thinking at this level. It is often useful to be able to show Ministers that the Civil Service is capable of major policy re-thinks which then enables the senior people to show how difficult it would be to implement this sort of proposal. Also it can be tactically advantageous to let loose some radical thoughts about policies in other departments as part of the internal Whitehall battle.

The newly-promoted Principal usually starts in a relatively straight-forward job but performance here matters in order to get the right second job which is of vital career importance. Very early on the Principal will be aware of the career treadmill of the Civil Service and the importance of the annual report. As he spends only about two years in each job, the first annual report is vitally important since it is the major influence on the choice of the next job. Although the choice of job is usually made at the last moment by the senior staff involved, the most important factor is their perception of the young civil servant. Does he look like a candidate for the best jobs, is he a "high-flier" – the ultimate accolade in the Civil Service?

After the second job – and by now the Principal is probably in his early thirties – the important age of thirty-five is rapidly approaching. This is the earliest age for promotion to Assistant Secretary and three jobs is the usual minimum before this can happen. So it is vital to keep changing jobs every two years to get enough experience. Depth of experience is not important – width is the crucial factor. The last job as a Principal can be as Private Secretary to a senior Minister. To get such a job is virtually a guarantee of promotion at the end and is a sign of somebody marked out for the top.

Elevation to Assistant Secretary is the single biggest step up the promotion ladder and marks a major change in status. A Principal often has to share an office, relies on the typing pool and photocopying pool to get work done, whereas an Assistant Secretary has his own much larger office (with a fitted carpet and regulation issue hat-stand) together with a secretary who sits in the outer office, does all his typing and photocopying, makes phone calls and the coffee and tea.

An Assistant Secretary is definitely part of the senior management of the department. Normally they have two or three Principals working for them and a total staff of about twenty. The job is essentially one of linking together the area where the basic work is undertaken and the higher world of policy-making. Some work, such as the answers to Parliamentary Questions, has to be cleared at this level before it is passed to the Minister, and on many other occasions an Assistant Secretary will send papers direct to the Minister. The career pattern is much the same as that for a Principal. The ambitious Assistant Secretary will be looking to do three or at the most four jobs each lasting about two years before promotion to Under-Secretary in his early forties. Again, breadth of experience and not depth of knowledge is the most important factor.

Choosing the Top Civil Servants

It is worth pausing at this stage in our climb up the Civil Service ladder to examine how the top civil servants are chosen. In all departments, promotions to Principal are determined by the system of annual reports together with a promotion board which interviews and selects successful candidates. Some departments have promotion boards to Assistant Secretary, most do not. Above Assistant Secretary there are no annual reports, no selection boards, everything is decided by the personal assessment of those at the top of the department.

What qualities are required in the top civil servant? The standard annual report form makes fascinating reading and contains as many highly subjective elements as the Civil Service selection procedure – indeed many of the qualities to be judged are exactly the same. After a brief description of the job the form requires the person to be marked by their immediate superior on a scale from 1 to 6, "exceptionally effective" to "definitely not up to the duties". These extreme marks are hardly ever used and indeed most marks are graded 2 and 3, "more than generally effective" and "generally effective". In other words most people are marked as better than average! In 1983 this reached such a point inside the Ministry of Defence than an official reminder was circulated to all staff saying that more realistic marking was required.

The next section of the annual report is the largest and in it a number of qualities have to be marked on a six-point scale from A to F. Thus for "foresight" A means "anticipates problems and develops solutions in advance" and F means "handles problems only after they arise". Apart from "foresight" all the classic Civil Service virtues reappear – penetration, judgement, expression on paper, oral expression, relations with others, acceptance of responsibility, reliability under pressure, drive and determination. One of the most enlightening is the marking of judgement. A is gained for "his/her proposals or decisions are consistently sound". To be "sound" is the highest of all the Civil Service virtues, to be able to judge what those up the chain will find acceptable is the greatest of all gifts. This makes you a team player, a person who can be trusted. To be regarded as "unsound" is the most damning epithet in the Civil Service.

Two sections on training needs and the type of job to be given next follow. Both are usually treated as unimportant. Training is not taken seriously and everybody knows that the next job is decided not on the basis of the report but by those in charge of the department. Then comes a section on promotability with a three-point scale, well fitted, fitted and not fitted. Next there is an important section on long-term potential and then a "short and vivid pen-picture". A final section is completed by a second person normally two grades above the individual being reported on. He also provides a short picture and is supposed to hold an interview or "Job Appraisal Review" (JAR) to discuss the year's performance and how this can be improved in the year ahead. The idea of the JAR was part of the post-Fulton proposals to improve Civil Service management. In practice a JAR often does not happen, or if it does it is only perfunctory.

Even though the Civil Service has this elaborate reporting system most of the judgements and reasons for promotion or non-promotion depend on the personal views or idiosyncracies of those at the top of the department and their opinions of those under them. One of the great delights of the Permanent Secretary and his head of personnel is to sit late at night over a whisky moving people around the department. It is after all one of the few areas where they have almost total power.

The Top of the Civil Service

Below Permanent Secretary the two most senior grades are Deputy Secretary and Under-Secretary. But it is very difficult to define what they actually do. They are always both represented in the management chain, they both chair committees, sit on inter-departmental committees and attend meetings with Ministers. In some way they usually allocate the work between them but their exact responsibilities are never really defined and distinguished. In some large departments the Principal Finance Officer and Principal Establishment Officer are both Deputy Secretaries, in others, they are Under-Secretaries. The result is that there tends to be administrative confusion at this level with too much copying of paper and people doing each other's jobs. Much of the emphasis is not on executive responsibility but on co-ordination.

The bulk of Under-Secretaries are promoted from Assistant Secretary between the ages of forty-three and forty-eight, though a third will be promoted in their fifties and will probably go no further. The real "high-flyers", the people who will become Permanent Secretary, make Under-Secretary before forty-three. Most Deputy Secretaries reach the grade aged between forty-nine and fifty-one. The top two grades of the Civil Service are therefore composed of people between fifty and sixty who emerge from an exhausting series of high-pressure jobs, who have been assessed as good team-players and who, by the time they reach the top, have lost what little, if any, reforming zeal they might have had. They are simply content to operate the machine as it is.

The training of those at the top, so far as it exists, is incredibly introverted. They will have been in the Civil Service since their early twenties and apart from the odd job, entirely in one department. At present just two of the current eighty or so Permanent and Deputy Secretaries have had any experience at all outside the Civil Service. The Civil Service ensures that there is no way of joining aged about forty or forty-five with outside experience in management, finance or any other specialist skill. Only three out of the eighty did not join as fast stream graduates and have instead worked their way up through the promotion structure from the bottom. 80% of them went to Oxbridge and a third to public schools. Over a third belong to one of the recognised London clubs.

In view of this very narrow experience what happens at the top of the Civil Service structure is even more extraordinary. After a career spent almost entirely inside one department a Permanent Secretary is often expected to take over and run a completely new department for the last few years of his career. Seven of the current twenty Permanent Secretaries have never served before in the departments of which they are heads. This is Civil Service amateurism with a vengeance. It is a perfect illustration of the view that specialist knowledge of a subject is a handicap and that a top civil servant is really an expert in the peculiar art of "administration" or oiling the wheels of the Whitehall machine.

"Amateurism"

The word that has caused the greatest offence to the top Civil

Service was the basis of the Fulton critique – "amateur". The senior ranks of the Civil Service believe strongly that they are professionals – professionals in the art of government. But this means knowledge of how Ministers really operate; and this as we have already seen is a seedy and cynical world. The mandarins can only justify themselves on the basis that there is a separate function of operating the Whitehall machine in which knowledge detracts from so-called professional objectivity and is therefore positively harmful.

This is a bogus claim invented and sustained with great determination to provide a justification for the administrative class. It is encapsulated in the views of Sir Warren Fisher, Head of the Civil Service, to the Royal Commission on the Civil Service in 1930:

> Let us guard ourselves against the idea that the Permanent Head of a department should be an expert: he should not be anything of the kind. Instead he should be a man of such breadth of experience that he will soon find himself picking out the essential points; and remember, there is a great deal to be said for a fresh eye.[21]

Another senior civil servant described the work of the mandarin administrator as follows:

> [He] knows the construction of the whole machine, the position of his own and other departments as wheels of the machine and their relations to the other wheels, and the general principles of operation which must be observed if the machine is to work smoothly. Finally, and perhaps most important of all ... it is the business of the high official to know the men who for the time being are, like himself, important parts of the central and controlling mechanism.[22]

In other words the mandarins can be left to get on with oiling the wheels of government, confident in their arrogance that they can master any problem however complex or specialised and come to sound judgements, perhaps with the help of other "good chaps" they happen to know.

This "amateurism" has left an appalling catalogue of failure in Whitehall. At times its effects verge on the ludicrous as the following examples illustrate:

1. In 1976 the Head of the central Management Services Department for the whole of Whitehall had had no previous experience of management services work.[23]

2. Two out of the last three heads of the division in the Ministry of Defence responsible for the control of the £18 billion a year Defence Budget had had no previous experience of budgetary or financial work.

3. The Department of Education Planning Unit investigating the future needs of education in the UK contained no sociologist, no economist and no educational expert.[24]

4. Apart from some accountants in the Ministry of Defence's section responsible for internal audit (the examination of accounting procedures) Whitehall had no professionally qualified auditors to control expenditure of nearly £140 billion a year.[25]

5. In 1983 the Deputy Secretary, Under-Secretary, Assistant Secretary and Principal in the Ministry of Defence responsible for controlling the £18 billion a year Defence Budget and conducting all negotiations with the Treasury were all classicists who had read Greats at Oxford.

6. Until the early 1980s the Controller and Auditor General responsible to Parliament for auditing all government expenditure was always an ex-Permanent Secretary with no training in accountancy.

7. The trading activities of the Crown Agents, that were to cost the public £200 million in the mid-1970s, was controlled by one lowly-qualified accountant (before 1964 there were no professional staff) and until 1968 the accounts were kept on odd pieces of paper in the office and the basic device of double-entry book-keeping, known for over six hundred years, was not used.[26]

8. One of the newly appointed Directors of the Ministry of Defence's Information Technology Unit responsible for introducing new technology has never worked with computers before.

Attitude to the Rest of the Civil Service

The top mandarins have maintained their superior position by two devices which have helped to sustain the Civil Service caste system. First, specialists such as economists, scientists, accountants, architects and statisticians are employed in the Civil Service, but only in their own rigidly defined groups. This is justified on the basis that when they join they really want to be economists or scientists (otherwise they would have joined the administrators!). They spend the first part of their careers operating within their specialist areas. Later when they are more senior they can be kept out of the administrative jobs because, it is argued, they lack the necessary "broadening" experience of dealing with Ministers. These barriers are reinforced by creating separate organisations and hierarchies for the specialists. They work in separate divisions of their own. Administrators may ask them for their views but it is the administrators who will "co-ordinate" and present these views and it is the administrators who have nearly all the access to Ministers.

Second, the administrators have established a wide gulf between themselves and the lower grades – the executives. These are the people who join as Executive Officers, or as clerks, and have to work their way up through the chain of Higher Executive Officer and Senior Executive Officer to Principal. Promotion is slow and Principal is often not reached until the mid-forties. Although the administrative, executive and clerical classes were formally merged in 1971 following the Fulton Report this has made little difference in practice. Those from an "executive" background still get posted (by the administrators at the top) to executive-type management jobs and they rarely, if ever, get any rapid form of promotion at the higher levels of Whitehall.

The patronising attitude of the administrators to the executives was well set out by Sir Henry Hancock (Permanent Secretary at the Ministry of Food) to the Royal Commission on the Civil Service in 1955:

They are not asked to work out a new policy on any subject from the start. They are frequently consulted, and properly consulted, in fact consulted with great profit and value, on adjustments of policy ... but they are not asked to create a new policy, and, generally speaking, those people would not be in their element. In fact they might be completely lost if you set them down in Whitehall and said "Now we have got to legislate on food and drugs, what shall we do about it?" That is not their job. It would not be fair to say that to them, but they have a very responsible job in administering and managing a big block of staff and work.[27]

The idea that "policy" on food and drugs could sensibly be thought up quickly in a vacuum obviously did not cross Sir Henry's mind. This quotation also illustrates the secondary place given to management by the mandarins.

The Outlook of the Mandarins

The mandarins' contempt for management and executive work flows from their perception of their role. They see themselves as policy-makers and advisers of Ministers. They look upwards and not down to the 600,000 people who work under them. From the very start of their careers in the Civil Service they have been treated as the specially-selected élite that will form the superior caste at the top of the Civil Service. They rarely, if ever, move outside a narrow circle of jobs in the headquarters of each department in close contact with Ministers and Whitehall policy-making. They have little contact with, or knowledge of, the mass of executive work that goes on outside Whitehall. Indeed, they rarely leave the rarified atmosphere of Whitehall to see for themselves what happens. The world of Ministers is the world of the top mandarin. The one sure route to the top of the Civil Service is to be the Private Secretary of a senior Minister.

Management of large complex operations is not a skill that is learnt by the higher Civil Service, indeed it is not even considered to be important. A posting to a management job is regarded as a black mark in the promotion stakes. The closed world of the mandarin becomes apparent when they talk about the work of the few in Whitehall as though this constituted the whole of the Civil Service. For example, Sir Douglas Wass, ex-Head of the Civil Service, has written that:

a skilled civil servant will get a great deal of satisfaction from the correct reading of his Minister's mind, even in ambiguous circumstances.[28]

But what of the 600,000 civil servants who never see a Minister in the whole of their careers except on television?

Sir Patrick Nairne summed up the real values of a Permanent Secretary when he described their two main roles:

> The primary role of senior civil servants must be to share a responsibility with Ministers for formulating in detail and carrying into effect the policy commitments on which they were elected.

and:

> The most valuable legacy a Permanent Secretary can leave behind him is a series of well-judged promotions to Under-Secretary and above.[29]

Permanent Secretaries spend a great deal of time with Ministers, are closely involved in their political schemings and personal ambitions. For example Sir Donald Ferguson, the Permanent Secretary of the Ministry of Fuel and Power, when Hugh Gaitskell became Minister in October 1947, could set out the main tasks facing Gaitskell in a highly personal way. His minute detailed the main policy problems and then suggested "the best way of tackling them both in the national interest and in your own interest"; and added that success "would immensely strengthen your own personal position in the Party, Parliament and the country".[30] Few, though, have been as close to their Ministers as Sir Warren Fisher (Head of the Civil Service), who once wrote a short note to Neville Chamberlain:

> Neville Dear – I did enjoy getting a little note from you – It gives such a cosy feeling. Bless you. That's a truly delightful paper from Bullock, isn't it? But there's no escape from the consequences.
>
> with fond love
Warren.[31]

Even if senior civil servants are not always that intimate with their Ministers – and it is difficult to imagine Sir Robert Armstrong writing to Mrs. Thatcher in that vein – they are still obsessed with the world of high politics and the manoeuvrings and jockeying for position. They get a sense of power simply from knowing what is going on in Whitehall and observing with detached amusement the foibles of Ministers. Late one evening in February 1969 Barbara Castle was talking to Sir Burke Trend, Secretary of the Cabinet, after an appalling mock Cabinet meeting put on to impress the visiting President Nixon. "We had a natter about Cabinet affairs and then he said with impulsive jocularity, 'But it's all *great fun* isn't it?' "[32]

The Ethos of the Civil Service

Top civil servants have rarely spoken out about their beliefs but it is possible to piece together what they really think. Like all members of the British establishment they are essentially conservative. Not necessarily in a party political sense, but they have a deep-seated conviction that the processes of government in Britain are near perfection, that the system works well and that any change should be limited and gradual.

Some of these thoughts emerged in the Reith Lectures by Sir Douglas Wass in 1983. At the end he reflected on the strengths of Whitehall:

I am struck not by its deficiencies ... but by its strengths ... The evolutionary quality of our system of government reflects our pragmatic and cautious approach as a nation to change and reform. It is an approach I instinctively warm to ... When the authors of the American constitution prescribed the elaborate system of checks and balances, they knew that they were putting obstacles in the way of swift decisions and decisive action. But their instincts were right.[33]

It was all summed up by Sir Patrick Nairne when he wrote that "the principal responsibility of the Permanent Secretary [is] in simple terms, to keep the show on the road."[34]

There is therefore no point in expecting the top Civil Service to advocate reform or to implement it with any degree of enthusiasm. They are content with the system as it is – it is, in one of Whitehall's favourite phrases, "broadly on the right lines".

Indeed "enthusiasm" is a concept that is highly distrusted in Whitehall. As Sir Douglas Wass wrote, "I have my doubts ... about its place in administration: it can colour judgement and lead to unwise decisions."[35] The civil servant is trained not to see issues in terms of whether they are right or wrong. To make a value judgement about a question is one of the greatest sins a civil servant can commit. Any conscientious objection or moral qualm can be left to the high moral sense of Ministers. Civil Servants decide how a policy can be steered through the Whitehall machine. They are also expected to advocate the policies of whichever area they are working in, and they are trained to move rapidly from one area to another and equally rapidly to adapt to advocating a different policy.

This stress on detachment, reinforced by rapid changes of jobs, tends to breed a peculiar attitude amongst top civil servants. There is plenty of intellectual brilliance, indeed often too much for the quality of work involved. But it is intellectual brilliance in a vacuum, displayed for itself and not for any purpose. This leads many senior civil servants to see the whole of Whitehall as a game. Everybody plays by the unwritten rules and the only objective is to see whether a few points can be scored over colleagues in the same department or whether the department can win a battle against its rivals in the Whitehall machine. Ultimately, it leads to a high degree of cynicism about the whole process of government and an atmosphere where personal ambition is one of the main motivating forces inside the Civil Service.

Whitehall is an introverted world in which the senior civil servants have little or no experience of life outside the village community in which they spend their lives. This leads to a kind of Olympian detachment in which Whitehall is the centre of everything and, because it knows best, can lay down policy for the rest of the country. This élitist attitude is well illustrated in Dick Crossman's portrait of his Permanent Secretary at the Ministry of Housing, Dame Evelyn Sharpe:

> She is rather like Beatrice Webb in her attitude to life, to the left in the sense of wanting improvement and social justice quite passionately and yet a tremendous patrician and utterly contemptuous and arrogant, regarding local authorities as children which she has to examine and rebuke for their failures. She sees the ordinary human being as incapable of making a sensible decision.[36]

This is the attitude that hides behind the CSSB criterion that top civil servants should understand how their decisions can affect "ordinary people".

Life in the Civil Service

Much of the life of the Civil Service is physically squalid. The staff are poorly accommodated in badly decorated buildings, with inadequate typing and photocopying facilities, and surrounded by petty regulations. In the Ministry of Defence until the early 1970s the "modern" invention of the roller towel was unknown and an old lady with a trolley used to come round once a week distributing new towels and pieces of cheap gritty soap. The canteens are all too often depressing places tucked away in the basement, generally justifying their nickname of the "Greasy Spoon".

But much of the work even at the top of the Civil Service is equally depressing. The amount of personal responsibility is very limited. An individual rarely takes a decision on his own partly because as the work gets divided up into smaller and smaller units the degree of overlap increases. The job of a senior civil servant is not to take decisions but to consult others, to co-ordinate views, to produce pieces of paper which are agreed by everybody. The invention of the photocopying machine has reinforced this tendency with a vengeance. Now everybody who has even the slightest interest in any aspect of a subject will receive a copy of a paper and will in turn send copies of his comments, often only of marginal interest, to everybody else. So the mountain of paper accumulates.

The watchword is caution and the avoidance of failure. This system does however have one great advantage for the participants. It makes it very difficult to allocate responsibility to an individual when something goes wrong. But, even if it were possible, the ethos of the Civil Service is against openly allocating blame. That is contrary to the rules of the club, although the club does, of course, have discreet ways of dealing with the individual who it is decided should take the blame, as Sir Ian Bancroft, former Head of the Civil Service, explained:

> If the advice was, as I assume it must have been, honestly given on the facts available ... I don't think I myself would

want to see a large label hung round that man's neck for the rest of his career, saying he gave the wrong advice on a particular subject. It will be apparent to his peers that he had given the wrong advice, and the grapevine in the Civil Service ... is a fairly powerful one.[37]

The work of the top Civil Service is always conducted in unfailingly polite terms. No instructions are ever issued, instead they are couched in terms like "I should be grateful if ... " The idea that Whitehall is just one big game is reflected in the language used. Civil Service prose is scattered with cricketing terms such as "straight bat", "googly", and comments on a draft are normally required by "close of play". One Deputy Secretary sitting on a departmental promotion board once described a young administrator as "not Test standard; but a good county player". He was promoted. Other sporting analogies are slightly less common, though "par for the course" and "own goal" are quite popular. Latin phrases occur fairly regularly, though the excessive use of French is limited to the Foreign Office where the tradition of elegant dispatches finding the mot juste to describe the *démarche* dies hard.

The Civil Service is a job for life. Unless performance is catastrophically bad nobody is sacked. In 1983 just 0.1% of the non-industrial Civil Service were retired early. The numbers in senior grades are even lower. Each department usually has a quota of jobs where people who are well over the top can be posted and where it is hoped they will do little damage to the work of the department. But the pay is the same, the job undemanding and life is pleasant.

The Civil Service has gradually become more ossified. In 1920 Sir Warren Fisher was made Head of the Civil Service at the age of forty, and a few years later Sir Horace Wilson was Permanent Secretary at the Ministry of Labour at the age of thirty-nine. It is now rare for anybody to be made a Permanent Secretary below fifty. Promotion times have become slower. Before 1945 the majority of Assistant Secretaries took less than fourteen years to reach that grade. Now 83% take more than fifteen years. Similarly before 1945 22% of Under-Secretaries had taken less than nineteen years to reach the grade. Now only 6% do so. Promotion is a matter of slowly working up the ladder, waiting your turn, with the pace depending on the rate of retirement. The modern Civil Service sees this as a positive virtue, as Sir Ian Bancroft said:

> Of course one's got to have some general pattern, otherwise the able characters, not absolute fliers but the able characters, who ought to be able to expect a reasonable career in the Service would constantly get overtaken by the young fliers.[38]

The result is predictable. The safe, unimaginative people, those lacking originality and new ways of looking at things, move steadily up the ladder. The idea that somebody young and brilliant could be promoted out of turn is anathema, as Barbara Castle found out in 1974 when she discussed with Sir Douglas Allen (then Head of the Civil Service) who might replace Sir Philip Rogers as her Permanent Secretary at DHSS. Castle suggested one or two names of younger people she had known in the Department of Employment. Allen at first reacted favourably. "Then he had second thoughts and wonders whether the older people in my department might not resent being put under someone so young."[39]

Women in the Civil Service

Women are second-class citizens in the Civil Service. At the top it is overwhelmingly a male organisation. Before 1946 no married woman could remain and therefore only those like Dame Evelyn Sharpe, who were devoted to their careers, could get to the top. Obvious discrimination has now been removed. The marriage bar ended in 1946 and equal pay was introduced in 1961. But women remain mainly in the lowest paid jobs. 48% of the non-industrial Civil Service were women in 1982 but there is only one woman in the top two grades. Only 7% of Principals, yet 80% of the clerical assistants are women. Promotion rates are lower than for men and some discrimination remained until very recently. Until 1971 no fast-stream female graduates were allowed to join the Ministry of Defence. It was felt that the Armed Forces would not like having to deal with women.

As long as the Civil Service is dominated by the concept of the continuous fifty-year career, women will have little chance of reaching the top. If they leave to have children there is, unless they only take short maternity leave, no right to reinstatement, in their grade. They also suffer from the tendency of the top Civil Service to promote in their own image; under the present structure there is little prospect of breaking the virtual male monopoly at the top.[40]

Honours in the Civil Service

Twice a year in Whitehall a curious ritual takes place after the Birthday and New Year Honours Lists are announced. The top civil servants who are on the lists receive hundreds of letters congratulating them on the achievement and on their work that has merited such distinction. Nobody dares mention that the awards are not given for merit but are automatic. A Deputy Secretary will receive a CB and a Permanent Secretary will receive a KCB. A Permanent Secretary who serves long enough will get a GCB. The Secretary of the Cabinet gets a peerage on retirement. There is a queue because the number of awards allowed in each list is limited and the quota cannot be exceeded. But there is a special arrangement for ensuring that each person receives his due award before retirement even if it means jumping the queue.

The top mandarins take the issue of honours very seriously and there is an elaborate system to allocate the awards to themselves and to others. There are separate committees for industry, education, science, together with the arts committee which is always referred to, in true Oxbridge classicist style, as "Maecenas". Elaborate charts are produced twice a year of those in the running, and then the richly rewarding task takes place of putting the list together. This is the opportunity for the establishment to reward the "good chaps", both inside and outside, for their services to the system. The whole procedure is presided over by the Main Honours Committee chaired, at the moment, by Sir Robert Armstrong (Secretary to the Cabinet), and including the Prime Minister's Private Secretary and the Private Secretary to the Queen, together with other Permanent Secretaries. Although the final list is selected by the Prime Minister the real power to determine who gets honours lies with the Civil Service.

The Career Goes On and On

The career of a top civil servant does not end at sixty. Many remain available to be chosen by their old colleagues as one of the "Great and Good" to head enquiries and sit on committees. The list is endless: Lord Croham (ex-Head of the Civil Service) as chairman of Britoil and then of an enquiry into the University Grants Committee; Lord Hunt (ex-Secretary to the Cabinet) as chairman of an enquiry into the future of Cable TV; and Lord Trend (ex-Secretary to the Cabinet) to conduct an enquiry into whether Sir Roger Hollis, Head of MI5, was a Russian spy. Sir Patrick Nairne became a Privy Councillor and sat on the Franks Committee enquiry into the origins of the Falklands conflict. Sir Geoffrey Wardale from the Department of the Environment worked at CSSB, chaired an enquiry into the chain of command at the top of the Civil Service and another into corruption in the Property Services Agency. Sir Ewan Broadbent, a second Permanent Secretary at MOD, and responsible in that job for the MOD Police, came back immediately after retirement to head an enquiry into the MOD Police.

All of this activity ensures that the "good chaps" remain in a dominant position. "Independent" enquiries are set up but they are run by people who understand the values of the Whitehall system and they can be relied upon not to rock the boat by suggesting any radical solutions or reaching uncomfortable conclusions. The system is also a useful way of supplementing the inflation-proofed pensions.

Although the mandarins have been adept at ensuring that the Civil Service remains closed, where virtually nobody is able to join with any outside experience, they have taken a very different view about civil servants accepting outside jobs after retirement. In the last few years there has been a veritable flood of senior civil servants taking lucrative jobs, and many of these moves have been highly controversial. Sir Fred Kearns, Permanent Secretary at the Ministry of Agriculture, accepted a senior post with the National Farmers Union. Sir Frank Cooper, Permanent Secretary at Defence, took a job as chairman of a major defence contractor. Sir Brian Tovey, head of the GCHQ code-breaking centre at Cheltenham, took a job with a major supplier of GCHQ – Plessey.

In all, about half the retiring Permanent Secretaries take outside jobs after retirement. Some like Sir Peter Carey (Department of Industry) and Sir Douglas Wass (Treasury), collect a number of directorships. Others are offered jobs in the gift of the government often unrelated to their experience inside Whitehall. Sir Anthony Rawlinson (Treasury) went off to head the Gaming Board, Sir Louis Petch (Customs and Excise) became chairman of the Parole Board. All of this is achieved through the "old-boy" network, as Lord Hunt explained when he described how he moved from being Secretary of the Cabinet to Chairman of the Banque Nationale de Paris in London. Hunt "was summoned by the Governor of the Bank of England ... and to my surprise he said that the Banque Nationale de Paris were looking for a new Chairman and he would like me to consider it ... and he expressed the view himself that he hoped I would take it".[41]

As the flow of senior civil servants to lucrative post-retirement jobs has increased in the last decade there have been continual calls for tighter controls.[42] These have been rejected by Whitehall which has insisted on maintaining the current system of a scrutiny committee. In the normal Whitehall way this committee has no formal powers but relies instead on the "good chaps" playing by the unwritten rules. The committee naturally consists of trusted members of the establishment who will take an understanding view of an application. Virtually none is rejected.

Conclusion

This survey has demonstrated that the top Civil Service is run by an amateur élite, deeply conservative and conventional, highly resistant to change and complacent about the way in which Whitehall works. Coupled with a political class of low quality, the Whitehall system has given Britain decades of poor government. We have examined the main characters in the tragedy and farce of Whitehall and we now turn to look at the way in which these are played out. The investigation will reveal a worrying picture of incompetence; a picture that is normally concealed behind a veil of secrecy and misinformation.

CHAPTER FOUR

Power in Whitehall

Whitehall presents a monolithic face to the world. It tries to portray itself as a single smoothly-operating machine where everybody is on the same side working harmoniously together towards an agreed goal. The reality is very different. Behind this façade Whitehall is divided by fierce rivalries, constant battles and long-running rows. Within each department there are competing interests and much of the life of Whitehall consists of major inter-departmental conflicts. One of the major weaknesses of British government is that there is no strong mechanism for controlling this conflict. The central direction of Government policy is weak and vacillating and the inevitable result is confused policy-making and patched-up compromises. This state of affairs is made worse by the various vested interests and pressure groups which surround Whitehall and fight long and hard to get their policies accepted by the Whitehall machine.

Inside Departments

Whitehall departments are not homogeneous. They consist of various groups which, in large departments, can develop into self-contained empires that are difficult to control centrally. Instructions may be issued by the Permanent Secretary but they will not always be carried out and it is usually impossible to know, at the centre of the department, what is really going on. Within the Ministry of Defence, for instance, there are two areas – contracts and the Royal Navy Supply organisation – that are virtually autonomous units. They have separate personnel departments, people have careers almost entirely within these departments and they have their own philosophy and values different from those of the rest of the department.

How are departments controlled? Most Permanent Secretaries have a weekly meeting with their senior staff to discuss topics of current interest but largely in terms of top policy-making rather than management of the department. Instructions often percolate down through the machine in an informal way and people get on with doing their job with little interference from above. Some Ministers such as Peter Walker in DTI in the 1970s, Barbara Castle in DHSS from 1974–76 and Michael Heseltine in both Environment and Defence have daily meetings with their Ministerial team usually without officials present. But these meetings are not about controlling the department, they are about the day-to-day handling of political issues. Other Ministers such as Francis Pym and John Nott in Defence and Tony Crosland in Environment did not bother with such meetings. Much depends on personal style. For example, Francis Pym when he was in Defence liked to use the formal body known as the Defence Council, made up of all the top civilians and military together with Ministers, to take important policy decisions. His successor John Nott preferred smaller informal meetings and the Defence Council met only once when he was Secretary of State.

Which civil servants can submit papers to Ministers is strictly controlled in some Departments. In the Home Office all papers for the Home Secretary have to go through the Permanent Secretary. Michael Heseltine tried to introduce a system in Defence where only members of the Defence Council could send papers direct to him and everybody else had to send the papers through a junior Minister. This broke down as soon as a crisis occurred and was then quietly forgotten. Even so there is still one interesting piece of protocol inside Defence. Only Deputy Secretaries and above can address a paper direct to a Minister. Everybody lower down the ladder has to, at least formally, send papers to the Private Secretary even though they all finish up on the Minister's desk.

The most divided department in Whitehall is Defence; which still has the character of the original three separate Ministries – one for each Service – and a small group in the middle trying to control what goes on. The rivalry between the Services, mainly for money but also for power and prestige, is bitter and continuous, although it only surfaces publicly during highly contentious affairs like John Nott's Defence Review in 1981. Every year there are bitter wrangles over the splitting up of the Defence Budget, ofen reaching the ludicrous situation where one Service would rather see money wasted than being spent by a rival. The worst battles are between the Royal Navy and the RAF and no issue is ever too old not to be raked over to try and score points off a rival. In 1984 there was a furious exchange of correspondence lasting over a month about whether the Navy or the RAF could claim the credit for sinking the German battleship *Tirpitz* during the Second World War. These endless conflicts also involve the civil servants in the Ministry who for instance if they are working in the Navy Department are expected to adopt a pro-Navy attitude and take on their colleagues in other areas of the Ministry on behalf of the Navy.

In 1984 Michael Heseltine was one of many Defence Ministers to try to end this continual wrangling by introducing a more coherent central planning staff in the Ministry. The Chiefs of Staff fought long and hard to preserve the independence of the Services and to stop the reorganisation, but they lost the campaign. However, they were able to win many tactical battles on the subject of how the new staff was to be organised. Much of the independence of the Services remains and military personnel serving in the central staff will only be posted there for a short while from their Services where they will spend the rest of their careers. Their loyalty will always be to their own Service. It is very unlikely that the reorganisation will make any real difference.

The Character of Departments

Every department in Whitehall has its own character and ethos. Much of this stems from their size, tasks and history. In terms of numbers Whitehall is dominated by Defence – 180,000 (almost a third of the Civil Service). The vast majority work in dockyards, stores depots and research establishments, but even the headquarters element at about 15–20,000 is large by Whitehall standards. The DHSS has about 90,000 staff but most of these are in local offices paying social security benefit. The same is true of Employment where the majority of the 30,000 are paying unemployment benefit. The only other large department is the Home Office, just over 35,000, but most of these are involved in running prisons or the immigration service.

In the middle are departments such as Agriculture (MAFF), Trade and Industry, Transport or the Scottish Office, about 10–14,000 strong and many of these in regional organisations outside London. At the other extreme are small departments like the Treasury and Education and Science, both just over 2,000 strong. They are purely concerned with 'policy' and have no executive functions. There is also a collection of miscellaneous departments like the Law Officers or the Privy Council office employing only 20–30 people.

Inevitably the character of the departments is influenced by the job they undertake. The Home Office for example has a reputation, even within Whitehall, for being deeply conservative, partly because it deals with groups like the police and the prison officers who see society from an authoritarian viewpoint. The social security side of DHSS has, on the other hand, always prided itself on its radical approach to social problems and deprivation. The Department of Employment used to attach importance to its close and sympathetic relations with the Trade Unions and its intermediary role in disputes, but the loss of the conciliation service (ACAS) has altered the image of the department. Other departments have turned into little more than spokesmen for the industries with which they deal. This is particularly true of MAFF which has an almost incestuous relationship with the National Farmers Union and the food industry. Similarly the old Ministry of Aviation and then the Department of Industry were often merely sponsors for the aircraft industry. Indeed one of the reasons why so much public money has been poured into both farming and the aircraft industry is that they have their own departments to speak up for them in the Whitehall battles.

The Treasury

The Treasury is a special case. It is the most Olympian and detached of all departments and encapsulates in dramatic form the weaknesses of the Mandarin élite. It is the most Oxbridge-dominated of all departments and because of its small size (about 350 administrators) it has an informal and egalitarian atmosphere – rather like a good Oxbridge college. It fosters the cult of the amateur at its most extreme as arts graduates with no economic or financial training move from working on defence to housing to social security to international finance every two years. The pressure of day-to-day work is intense and there is little time for any long-term planning.

It is of course absurd to expect the ten people (including clerks) that the Treasury employs to 'control' the social security budget to have any deep knowledge or expertise about the programme. They are employed, in the true generalist role of the administrator, to ask intelligent questions. In fact the Treasury does not attempt to control public expenditure in detail. Its methods are much cruder. The whole philosophy of the Treasury is built around hostility to public expenditure. It is not interested in what public expenditure buys in the real world, it is simply interested in the total amount of public expenditure. Whatever the economic problems facing the country – falling pound, rising pound, balance of payments crisis, inflation, rising oil prices, falling oil prices, falling or rising unemployment – its remedy is always the same: cut public expenditure. To crisis after crisis the Treasury response over the years has been to put together the usual deflationary package.

This philosophy goes back at least as far as Gladstone and his belief in the extravagance of the public sector and his desire to save the 'candle-ends'. It is a philosophy that permeates the whole Treasury and is quickly absorbed by newcomers. Sir Leo Pliatzky (later Permanent Secretary at the Treasury) wrote of his experience on joining in 1950: "I took naturally to the austere Treasury ethos towards the use of public money."[1] This atmosphere of detachment from the hard world of real public expenditure decisions is reinforced by the domination within the Treasury of the views of the City of London, transmitted through the Bank of England, and also of the international financial institutions. They pay more attention to the exchange rate, interest rates and the stock exchange than to measures of the real economy – output, unemployment, etc.

Although the Treasury employs a number of economists, an atmosphere of genuine intellectual debate is lacking. Politics dominate the Treasury as they do every other department in

Whitehall. It was interesting to watch Treasury economists who had long been Keynesians suddenly espousing monetarist doctrines after the election of the Thatcher government in 1979. Similarly it is impossible for the Treasury to publish any forecasts for the economy that are not consistent with government policy. If the figures will not fit, then they have to be manipulated until they do, as one senior Treasury economist admitted:

> if Ministers feel that the Treasury forecasters . . . are putting forward a view which is perhaps rather pessimistic relative to the average public forecast, they may well say that they would prefer to see something more optimistic.[2]

Conflicts Between Ministries

Much of the work of Whitehall is institutionalised conflict between the competing interests of different departments. Each department will defend its own position and resist a line that, while it might be beneficial to the government as a whole or in the wider public interest, would work against the interests of the department. Large-spending Ministries fight the Treasury for more money, but also fight each other for the biggest possible share of public expenditure. The Treasury knows that it cannot win every fight and much depends on the political complexion of the government. It is always safe to attack the housing programme under a Tory government and the defence programme under a Labour government. Some of these conflicts are encouraged by inconsistent political commitments. For example, the Tories came into power in 1979 pledged to cut public expenditure and at the same time increase defence expenditure. The result was a long-running battle for two years until the politicians decided which pledge would have priority.

Other conflicts continue regardless of the party in power. For example, unemployment benefit is paid separately from social security benefit. This causes major administrative problems and often appalling difficulties for claimants. The reasons why the benefit system is split in this way lie in the Whitehall battles between the Departments of Employment and of Social Security. If Employment loses the unemployment benefit offices then most of its staff will go and its long-term future as an independent department will be jeopardised. Other conflicts are battles over resources. The Home Office is responsible for civil defence planning but has very little money to spend. The Ministry of Defence has a huge budget but gives a very low priority to civil defence and resists all attempts by the Home Office to try and get control of some of this money. Other battles reflect the differing interests of the groups that departments sponsor. Both the shipbuilding and shipping industries are in decline. But if the Department of Industry suggests that British shipowners should buy UK ships in order to support the industry the Department of Transport will, with the strong support of the General Council of British Shipping, fight any such proposal.

Some conflicts can be extraordinarily complex as several different departments try to promote their differing interests. For example, defence of the North Sea oil and gas fields and fishery protection is provided by the Navy and RAF but partly paid for by other departments. The Navy and RAF see this as a convenient way of maintaining more ships and aircraft but as usual everything they do is very expensive. The Scottish Office run their own Fishery Protection Fleet, MAFF are keen to do the same because it would be cheaper and increase their independence. Energy are worried that if MAFF pull out they will have to pay a bigger bill to defend the oil fields. The Welsh Office and Northern Ireland Office also have to pay their share of the costs. At the end of all this confusion a new government policy emerges. It emerges not after a careful assessment of the national interest but after a balancing of various Whitehall interests.

Some of these battles take predictable lines. A good example is a proposed arms sale. Within Defence there is usually a conflict between the sales divisions, who are obviously all in favour, and the Services who have often to divert some of their equipment overseas to meet tight delivery dates and who may also be worried about compromising security by selling new weapons. If Defence is in favour then the Whitehall line-up takes shape. Industry will be in favour together with Employment because of the extra work and jobs. Trade will be in favour because of their general support for exports. The

Foreign Office will probably support the sale as long as the weapons are not destined for a particularly brutal régime or obviously capable of being used for internal repression. The problems arise with the Export Credits Guarantee Department who may be asked to give a cheap loan and the Treasury who will automatically be against any subsidy from public funds.

All of these conflicts eventually affect Ministers. They are enlisted by their departments to carry on the battle through correspondence and if necessary in Cabinet committees. In many ways Ministers are simply acting as arbiters in long-running and anarchic Whitehall conflicts that go on regardless of the party in power.

What are the mechanisms for ensuring that this conflict is controlled and resolved and that a coherent government policy is imposed and followed through? It is here that one of the major weaknesses of British government is revealed. While there are mechanisms for canalising Whitehall conflicts within accepted Whitehall procedures there is no way of ensuring that a coherent and agreed policy is settled and carried through. There is a hole in the centre of British government.

The Hole in the Centre of Government

The institutions at the centre of Whitehall are small-scale and act not as strong central policy-makers but as co-ordinators of the powerful Whitehall departments. Whitehall has a federal structure and real power lies with individual departments. They are determined to ensure that there is no strong central direction that would interfere with their own autonomy.

Many of the institutions at the centre of Whitehall have been ephemeral. The Civil Service Department was set up in 1969, following the Fulton report, but it never had power to direct departments to do anything; it could only cajole and advise. The CSD was broken up in 1981 when the Treasury re-acquired the manpower control divisions that it had lost twelve years before. The Central Policy Review Staff was formed in 1970 to try and provide some central and strategic briefing for the Cabinet as a whole on the development of government policy. For a time, up to 1974, it carried this out and produced briefings every six months. Then it was diverted into 'one-off' studies looking at specific issues, and went into a decline. Ministers of both parties did not like being brought face to face with the long-term implications of their policy and Whitehall regarded the CPRS, in the words of Sir Douglas Wass (Permanent Secretary at the Treasury), as a "meddler in departmental business". Mrs. Thatcher disliked the CPRS intensely. After a series of politically damaging leaks about long-term public expenditure trends she nevertheless tried to claim the credit for having the CPRS.

> You may have heard leaks that we have a CPRS and a Policy Unit. That is because this Government has not stopped thinking.

Less than three months later after the 1983 election it was announced that:

> The Prime Minister has decided, after consultation with her Cabinet colleagues, that the purposes for which the CPRS was set up are now being met satisfactorily in other ways and it should therefore be disbanded at the end of July.[3]

The one institution that has survived since 1916 is the Cabinet Office. But this is not a policy-making body; its role is simply to co-ordinate the business, circulate papers and take the minutes at the Cabinet and the numerous Cabinet committees both Ministerial and official. The staff is tiny and consists entirely of people seconded from departments for a tour of about two to three years. As Sir John Hunt, Secretary to the Cabinet, once admitted the system was structured in this way in order to stop the Cabinet Office developing a view of its own.[4] Civil servants posted to the Cabinet Office know that their future lies with their departments and they are expected to protect the interests of their departments during their tour. Which posts are filled by each department is based on a long-standing convention: for example the Ministry of Defence always supplies the Under-Secretary who acts as Secretary to the Overseas and Defence Committee. But this body does not act like the National Security Council in the United States and co-ordinate the policies of the Foreign Office and Ministry of

Defence. It is merely the group that take the notes at the meeting where the two departments have their arguments.

There are other parts of the Cabinet Office which have a recognised existence, such as the Joint Intelligence Committee chaired by the Intelligence Co-ordinator in the Cabinet Office. The JIC has under it a network of Current Intelligence Groups that put together analyses of various problems. But again it co-ordinates the outputs of the various intelligence agencies, it does not direct their operations. There is a Civil Contingencies Unit for peacetime civil emergencies such as co-ordinating the response to strikes. But the title unit is only a glorified name for the usual Cabinet Office committee. Similarly for terrorist emergencies there is the Cabinet Office Briefing Room (COBR). However, the departments involved were careful to ensure that this is only a room where co-ordination and briefing take place. Executive authority still rests with Whitehall departments.

At the top of the Cabinet Office structure is the Cabinet itself and the network of Ministerial and official committees. We now need to examine how they work, explore their strengths and weaknesses, and discover why in the end they are unable to provide any strong central direction to British government.

Cabinet Procedure

The Cabinet normally meets in the Cabinet room at the back of No.10 with windows looking out over Horse Guards Parade. It is a long, thin, slightly shabby room with a table covered with a green baize cloth on which stand silver candlesticks, ink stands, tumblers and water jugs. The Prime Minister sits facing the window, in front of a restored eighteenth-century fireplace, with the Secretary of the Cabinet seated to her right. Ministers at the top of the Cabinet pecking order sit in the middle of the table with the others at the extremities. This ranking of Ministers is important because the acoustics in the room are so poor that those at the ends of the table cannot hear all that is being said. If the Cabinet meets in the Prime Minister's room in the House of Commons the accommodation is even more spartan and cramped and there is not enough room for all twenty or so members to sit round the table.

Normal Cabinet meetings follow a set procedure. The first two items on the agenda are a statement on foreign affairs by the Foreign Secretary and a discussion of Parliamentary business. Only then are other papers discussed. The proceedings are formal. Although all the members of the Cabinet know each other well, Christian names are not used and everybody is referred to by the title or the office they hold. It can be so formal that one hot day in July 1967 Harold Wilson had to inform members of the Cabinet that they could remove their jackets.[5] Barbara Castle described in her diary the atmosphere inside Cabinet and the way in which this artificiality influenced the proceedings:

> Once again I was struck by the hypnotic effect of Cabinet meetings. The whole procedure is designed to dull the political edge of argument. Politics seems positively indecent in that almost disembodied atmosphere.[6]

Nevertheless although the superficial niceties may be preserved there are plenty of rows in Cabinet as Ministers battle for their own personal prestige and ambition and act as spokesmen for the rival Whitehall departments they represent. Before Mrs. Thatcher became Prime Minister she naively assumed that all this bickering would stop: "It must be a conviction government. As Prime Minister I could not waste time having any internal arguments."[7] But like every other government the Thatcher government has seen fierce and bitter rows in Cabinet. This is inevitable: Whitehall is structured that way.

Cabinet Policy-making

Asking twenty-three politicians to provide strategic leadership is a vain task. Whatever the theory may say, in practice the Cabinet is not the supreme policy-making body in British government. Much of the real power is spread amongst the Cabinet committees and other informal groups of Ministers. Under Mrs. Thatcher the Cabinet has been utilised less and less and the number of papers coming onto the agenda has dropped as more informal methods of decision-taking are used.

The level of debate is often appallingly low as Ministers are not usually briefed by their departments on matters of general policy which do not affect the department. Even when they do read the briefs the results are not much better, as Hugh Gaitskell found:

> Sometimes Cabinet meetings horrify me because of the amount of rubbish talked by some Ministers who come there after reading briefs which they do not understand ... I believe the Cabinet is too large. A smaller Cabinet, mostly of non-Departmental Ministers would really be able to listen and understand.[8]

Within a couple of months of joining the Cabinet, Dick Crossman found that the Cabinet was not dealing with strategy:

> Again I had the uneasy feeling that we weren't grappling with central problems ... in our case all that happens is that twenty-three of us come, each with his particular pressures and problems, trying to get what we want. And we do avoid any collective discussion of general policy ... on the essentials of the home front there doesn't seem to be any general discussion at all – general issues just aren't raised.[9]

Crossman found the same lack of genuine collective grip the next day in Cabinet Committee. This episode is a very good illustration of the way in which Whitehall works, the domination of departmental interests and the difficulty, often impossibility, of getting any wider coherent strategy implemented. Crossman had asked the Public Sector Development Committee for an extra £20m for the rate support grant. The Treasury was, as usual, opposed but the other members supported Crossman. Jim Callaghan, the Chancellor, gave in and said he would not take the issue to Cabinet. The reason was almost certainly that the discussion would take place when Harold Wilson was in Washington and the meeting would be chaired by George Brown, Callaghan's arch-rival, who would almost certainly oppose the Chancellor. Crossman mused on what had happened:

> The more I reflect on it the more uneasy I become. Of course, I shouldn't have been allowed to win. In a sense I

had a strong case, but if there had been a collective Cabinet policy I wouldn't have stood a chance. Yet ... I felt no sense of responsibility for the general Cabinet policy and just pleaded my departmental case as well as I possibly could. In fact I was not the least concerned about the good of the country. I was solely concerned with looking after my department.[10]

Unfortunately, knowledge of the problem does nothing to prevent endless repetition. The real Whitehall problem is that there is nobody whose role it is to define and implement a government policy. Once again it is either tragic or farcical, depending on your viewpoint. Policy emerges *ad hoc* through a series of compromises between departments headed by powerful Ministers with their own ambitions.

Ignorance in Cabinet

Over a whole range of issues Cabinet does not discuss policy and is kept in ignorance about the facts. An ordinary Cabinet Minister can find it impossible to influence policy when its formulation is divided up in committees and *ad hoc* groups, as Barbara Castle experienced:

Another thing which strikes me is how limited "cabinet responsibility" really is in practice. I have been watching the Rhodesian developments on TV without having the slightest idea of what the government is planning or doing because I am not a member of the special Committee on Rhodesia. No doubt when we face a major crisis on this I shall be consulted – but by then it may be too late to influence events.[11]

Six months later, Castle suspected Wilson was trying to do a deal on Rhodesia inconsistent with the agreed line:

I then asked my Private Office to obtain copies for me of the weekend cables to and from the Governor and was informed by No.10 that they were for "restricted circulation only". How can you get collective responsibility that way?[12]

At other times, Prime Ministers simply refuse to discuss things with Cabinet. After one visit to Moscow and discussions with Brezhnev, Harold Wilson reported:

> The Russians were very tough on Vietnam but things were going on in that field which it was better not to discuss in Cabinet.[13]

After one of Wilson's visits to Washington Dick Crossman made a careful note of what he told the Cabinet, compared it with accounts of the visit in the *New Statesman* and *Sunday Times* following briefings from No.10, and came to the conclusion that "Harold told nothing to the Cabinet which hasn't been told to the Press".[14]

This sort of attitude can reach high farce as it did in June 1974 after Harold Wilson announced that there had been a nuclear warhead test (the arrangements had been made by the previous Tory government). There was a fierce row in the parliamentary party and Jim Callaghan (then Foreign Secretary) privately denied any knowledge of the test. Michael Foot raised the question of why the Cabinet had not been consulted only to be slapped down by a mysterious Wilson:

> It has always been the convention of Cabinet that certain things are not discussed in Cabinet ... I could not consult Cabinet because a leak of any kind would have very serious effects for reasons I can't give now.[15]

Much the same can happen in Cabinet Committees. The Overseas and Defence Committee does not even discuss all defence issues. In 1968 when Barbara Castle asked Wilson about links with the United States on chemical warfare, Wilson refused point-blank to discuss the subject in committee.[16] Similarly, as we shall see, this committee does not discuss policy on nuclear weapons, the single most important defence issue.

There are other ways in which the Cabinet can be kept in a state of ignorance. Papers can be circulated late in order to minimise the risk that Ministers might read them or be briefed on them before the meeting, or they can be presented as a virtual *fait accompli*. White Papers and other important papers for debate are often only circulated the evening before a

Cabinet discussion or even later. On other occasions there is no paper at all and the Cabinet is simply presented with no alternative. The financial crisis of July 1966 was dealt with by a small group – Wilson, Brown and Callaghan – and then sprung on the Cabinet, as Barbara Castle found:

> When I arrived at Cabinet at 9.50 expecting a short meeting as we only had one item (Post Office reorganisation) ... to deal with, Tony Greenwood asked me what I thought of the proposal to lop £100m off overseas government expenditure. It was the first I had heard of it. Yet apparently this was to be a key meeting in beating a new crisis.[17]

Similarly, in 1977, the Cabinet was told the terms of the Lib-Lab pact (to extend the life of the Labour government) only on the morning of the crucial no confidence motion in the Commons and was simply invited to agree to take the consequences.[18] When individual Ministers put a paper of their own to the Cabinet they will usually not give options to the Cabinet on policy issues. They take a decision on the policy they prefer within their department and the Cabinet is then invited to agree to it. The aim is to avoid a free-ranging debate. This naturally makes it impossible for another Cabinet Minister to develop an alternative policy.

Tactically, a Cabinet Minister is wise to get the agreement of the Prime Minister first in an informal discussion if the issue is likely to be controversial. With such powerful support, discussion in Cabinet is normally a formality. Only very rarely is there a Cabinet revolt. One of the most sensational happened in May 1967 during the deepening Arab-Israeli crisis before the Six Day War. When President Nasser of Egypt announced the closure of the Straits of Tirana, the Prime Minister, Foreign Secretary and Defence Secretary met and agreed to issue a declaration by the major maritime powers to ensure the right of innocent passage which would almost certainly have eventually led to UK military intervention in order to enforce this right. A few hours later the Cabinet met and Denis Healey (Defence Secretary) changed his mind, following advice from the Chiefs of Staff, and came out against the operation. Most of the Cabinet were opposed, particularly Jim Callaghan, Chancellor of the Exchequer. After a fierce debate he shouted at

Wilson, "Some of us won't have this policy," and Wilson shouted back, "Some of us won't have this constant obstruction." But the power of the Prime Minister and Foreign Secretary could not prevail on this occasion and they had to accept a humiliating rebuff.[19]

Cabinet Committees

Cabinet Committees have a long history. One of the first was the Committee of Imperial Defence set up in 1903. But the real growth started in the Second World War and blossomed in the Attlee government from 1945 to 1951. Now, every government relies on a network of these committees – often over 200 – to decide policy. The Prime Minister decides what committees are set up, under whose chairmanship and which Ministers will serve on them. The power to choose the members of the committee is of course often equivalent to being able to determine the outcome of the discussions. Other important committees (such as Overseas and Defence) are chaired by the Prime Minister. This puts enormous power into the hands of Prime Ministers, something which they exercise to the full. In 1979 a majority of the Cabinet were probably opposed to the vigorous monetarist policy favoured by Mrs. Thatcher. But she was able to choose the membership of the key economic committee and pack it with her supporters. Economic affairs were then kept off the Cabinet agenda. Barbara Castle once had the temerity to ask in Cabinet who would be on a key committee to discuss economic policy:

> To our surprise Harold said tartly that it was not customary to discuss membership of Cabinet committees at Cabinet (the first I've heard of that) and that the usual notice would be circulated.[20]

Under every government some key committees are always set up – Overseas and Defence, H (Home Policy Committee), an Economic Policy Committee (E under Mrs. Thatcher, SEP or Strategic Economic Policy under Wilson), QL to decide the content of the Queen's speech and the legislative programme, and L to scrutinise bills before they are introduced in parliament. The variation occurs in the *ad hoc* committees set up to deal with particular topics as they arise. These are given the title GEN (for General) or MISC (Miscellaneous), followed by a number, the prefix being changed with each new government.

Whitehall tries to pretend in public that most of these committees do not exist. The confidential document, "Questions of Procedure for Ministers", encapsulates the Whitehall view:

> The method adopted by Ministers for discussion among themselves is essentially a domestic matter and is no concern of Parliament or the public.

If the system of committees were made public then it would be clear just how fragmented and divided power is within Whitehall and the way in which Ministers really take decisions. This causes a tremor of fear to run through the system as "Questions of Procedure" makes clear:

> The growth of any general practice whereby decisions of the Cabinet or Cabinet committees were announced as such would lead to the embarrassing result that some decisions of government would be regarded as less authoritative than others.

And even worse:

> Critics of a decision ... could press for its review by some other committee or by the Cabinet.

The Emperor would indeed be seen to have no clothes.

Cabinet Committees in Action

Cabinet Committees vary in size from two or three members to the extraordinary Strategic Economic Policy Committee which under Wilson in the late 1960s consisted of twenty one out of the twenty four members of the Cabinet. Even a key committee like Overseas and Defence has a membership of a dozen. Although Attlee used this committee to direct British involvement in the Korean War, both Eden and Thatcher used much smaller groups during the Suez and Falklands conflicts.

Eden set up an 'Egypt Committee' which was essentially a

group of his close political supporters. Rab Butler (Leader of the House of Commons) was originally excluded but simply turned up at one of the meetings, was allowed to stay, and became one of the key members in negotiating the agreement to collude with Israel and France to attack Egypt. For the Falklands, Mrs. Thatcher set up what was officially a sub-committee of the Defence Committee to direct the conflict. But the main committee never functioned and the whole Cabinet was only consulted over policy on three occasions. Two members of the sub-committee (known as OD (SA)) chose themselves, Pym as Foreign Secretary and Nott as Defence Secretary. Whitelaw as deputy Prime Minister was an almost automatic choice. The fourth was less obvious, but Parkinson, a keen supporter of Thatcher, was included to give her enough support in the committee if Pym and Nott decided to take a conciliatory line. He was also to run the public relations aspects.

In one area, nuclear weapons, virtually every government has restricted decision-taking to a very select group. The exception was Churchill who held three discussions in Cabinet in 1954 on whether Britain should develop an H-bomb. The Attlee government made the equally momentous decision to start the preliminary work for the A-bomb in a committee known as GEN 75 consisting of just seven Ministers. But the final decision to produce a British A-bomb was made in an even smaller group – GEN 163.

In the last twenty years or so, decisions on nuclear weapons have been kept to a small group consisting of those holding particular appointments and regarded by the civil service as reliable enough to receive the information. It is the same group regardless of the party in power – Prime Minister, Foreign Secretary, Defence Secretary and Chancellor of the Exchequer. The Overseas and Defence Committee is not consulted and Cabinet is only invited to ratify decisions made elsewhere. And if this combination of Ministers is in favour there will be no real opposition in Cabinet. It was this group of Ministers – known as MISC 7 under Mrs. Thatcher – that took the decision to go for Trident. Similarly under Labour back in 1974 it was the same group that decided to endorse the Chevaline programme to improve the Polaris system. It is instructive to see how much information was later given to the Cabinet in November 1974 when the proposal was agreed. It was slipped in as part of Roy Mason's Defence Review and Harold Wilson simply said, "Though we would keep Polaris and carry out certain improvements at a cost of £24 million, there would be no 'Poseidonization' and no MIRV." There was some opposition from Michael Foot and Barbara Castle, none from Tony Benn.[21] This series of 'improvements' costing £24 million, though Wilson may have meant £24 million a year for ten years, was actually a major programme to enable Polaris to penetrate Soviet ballistic missile defences. It went disastrously wrong and eventually cost over £1,000 million. Yet the whole project was nodded through Cabinet with virtually no debate and no information about what was really involved.

Cabinet Minutes

Until 1916 there were no records of Cabinet discussions apart from a short weekly letter from the Prime Minister to the monarch. There are occasionally unofficial records like the letters Asquith used to write to his lady friends during Cabinet meetings. The absence of minutes posed problems not just for historians of the period, but at the time it made running the government very difficult, as is illustrated by the letter the private secretary to Lord Hartington wrote to the private secretary to Gladstone (the Prime Minister) in 1882:

> Harcourt and Chamberlain have both been here this morning and at my chief about yesterday's Cabinet proceedings. They cannot agree about what occurred. There must have been some decision, as Bright's resignation shows. My chief told me to ask you what the devil was decided for he be damned if he knows.[22]

In 1916 when Lloyd George became Prime Minister, Maurice Hankey, an ex-Royal Marine Officer who had been secretary of the Committee of Imperial Defence, set up the Cabinet Secretariat. Hankey remained Secretary to the Cabinet till 1938. His records of the discussions are almost verbatim accounts of what took place and it is possible to find out which Ministers were in favour of a proposal and which against. By the late 1940s the system had been taken over by the Civil Service and the modern style of Cabinet Minutes had been imposed. They are useless as historical records and designed to conceal, even within Whitehall, what really takes place.

The minutes follow a set formula and bear little relation to what happens at the meeting. They start with the accepted phrase "Introducing his paper the Secretary of State for ... said". Then follows not what the Minister said but a Civil Service précis of the paper he submitted and therefore what he should have said. Then follows the formula "In discussion the following points were made ..." These are not attributed to individuals and are phrased in bland tones to disguise any hint that there might have been a row. At the end come the words "summing up their discussion the Prime Minister said the Cabinet were agreed that", followed by a summary and a list of items for further action. The summing up and the conclusions reached will rarely have been that coherent and the Civil Service usually has to judge roughly what was the consensus of the meeting and translate this into firm decisions.

The minutes are circulated round Whitehall on a strictly limited basis and item by item so that hardly anybody sees a complete record of the meeting. Since the mid-1970s each copy is marked diagonally in red letters "Ministry of ... copy of a Cabinet Document", to try and stop leaks or at least make them easier to trace. This method failed and by the early 1980s an even more restricted circulation of politically sensitive documents was introduced – CMO or Concerned Ministers Only. This meant that the documents are normally not allowed out of the Minister's private office and civil servants have to go there to read them.

The minutes are not written by the Secretary to the Cabinet himself but by a Deputy Secretary from the Cabinet Office who sits at a separate table at the end of the room. The minutes are not agreed by the Prime Minister before they are circulated[23] Not every discussion at Cabinet is minuted,[24] some are so sensitive they are kept separately, and on other occasions the Secretary may even be instructed not to record some of the furious rows between Ministers.[25] The system was well summed up by Sir Burke Trend when he was Secretary to the Cabinet in 1965. Dick Crossman had complained that one set of minutes included a particularly sensitive phrase about German nuclear re-armament, attributed to Harold Wilson, but which he had never used. Trend explained:

> Ah, of course he never said it, we never do give verbatim what people say. We précis the sense and give the substance of what they say.[26]

The Diffusion of Power – Public Expenditure

We have seen how the structure of power inside Whitehall produces no strong central direction and a system where powerful departments bargain with each other over policies and resourcs. This is well illustrated by the problem at the centre of British government and one which takes up a vast amount of time and effort inside Whitehall – the control of public expenditure. The failure of Whitehall to grapple with this issue over the last twenty years has been central to the failure of many of these governments. The processes adopted inside Whitehall to control public expenditure illustrate many of the failings of the British system of government: debate restricted to a small group of officials and Ministers inside the system, the amateurism of the top civil service, the crude manoeuvrings and bargaining between departments, the inability of Ministers to devise a coherent system for deciding on priorities or subordinate their short-term political interests to achieve a longer-term strategy.

Setting up the System

Until about 1960 Whitehall controlled the allocation of public expenditure by the methods of the nineteenth century. As Sir Leo Pliatzky wrote;

> If a reincarnated Gladstone had returned to the Treasury in the 1950s he would have found himself perfectly at home with the traditional procedures governing the Consolidated Fund and supply estimates.[27]

There was little attempt at any forward planning and, although the idea of a three- or five-year defence plan had been

common since the 1930s, the introduction of major new prog-
rames on the domestic front, such as the start of the National
Health Service, a major series of nationalisations and a new
system of social security, made no difference. In April 1950 Sir
Norman Brook (Secretary to the Cabinet) wrote complacently
to Sir Edward Bridges (Permanent Secretary at the Treasury)
in a Memorandum entitled, astonishingly, 'Classes of business
not regarded as appropriate for Cabinet discussion':

> It is curious [*sic*] that in modern times the Cabinet though it
> has always insisted on considering particular proposals for
> developments of policy and their cost, has never thought it
> necessary to review the development of expenditure under
> the Civil Estimates as a whole.[28]

By the late 1950s, with the government already responsible for
allocating and spending about a third of the nation's wealth,
even Whitehall agreed that this ramshackle system could not
continue. An "independent" committee, chaired by Lord
Plowden, was set up to recommend a new system. In typical
Whitehall fashion the committee consisted of Plowden (an
ex-Treasury civil servant), five other civil servants and four
"outsiders" who all just happened to be ex-civil servants. The
whole of the report was too secret to publish and only a
summary was made available as a White Paper.[29]

The proposals left unchanged the nineteenth-century system
of accounting (which still flourishes today), but imposed upon
it a new superstructure for estimating growth in national
wealth up to five years ahead and then planning the allocation
of resources and total public expenditure over the same period.
This process was entirely carried out in 'constant prices'; that
is, no account was taken of inflation. One of the main pro-
tagonists of the system, Sir Richard (Otto) Clark (Permanent
Secretary of the Treasury), set out the basic aim the system
had to meet:

> The point at issue . . . was whether the Treasury and then the
> Government could develop a rational public expenditure
> policy (in this most "political" of all fields of government).[30]

The system evolved during the 1960s, the methodology
became more complex and by 1969 annual White Papers were

produced. By 1973 Samuel Goldman, in charge of public expenditure at the Treasury, could proudly claim that:

> After many vicissitudes we have evolved a system for managing the public sector which despite many deficiencies is probably superior to that found anywhere else in the world.[31]

The reality was very different. Just how great the "many deficiencies" really are we now need to investigate.

The Failure of the System

The essential point about the system that evolved after the 1960s is that it was a peculiar mixture of the highly technical and the highly political. The Treasury developed an elaborate accounting system that became ever more sophisticated. Involved tables, computer returns, statistical analyses all added to the comforting illusion that a complex methodology was equivalent to control. But control over the system was exercised not through forms or the Treasury computer but by the politicians. And inevitably they exercised it in a political way.

Realistic assumptions about future expectations are a vital ingredient in successful planning. It was, however, always too tempting to assume that faster growth in the economy would somehow magically happen and allow the politicians to spend what they wanted to spend and avoid difficult choices about priorities. Instead of long-term planning of resources Whitehall was soon reduced to the old yearly exercise of last-minute cuts consisting of a package put together in a hurry to meet arbitrarily-imposed Treasury targets. The system was also marked by that strong Whitehall tendency not to look back and analyse what had gone wrong but instead to stagger on from one crisis to another and from one expedient to the next. By the mid 1970s the system was breaking down. The introduction of cash limits on spending increased Treasury control and began the process of devaluing any debate about the realities of public expenditure (what it bought in the real world) in favour of a simple strong financial control. This process was completed by the Tory government in 1981 when it decided to stop any attempt to plan rationally future public expenditure by shifting the system from constant prices to cash planning where it is impossible to work out in advance what particular levels of public expenditure will provide.

The failure of the system was massive. It did not control public expenditure, which rose steadily. Some of its inadequacies, in particular its arbitrary nature, can be illustrated very quickly.

1. The coverage of the system was inconsistent. Housing expenditure by local authorities was included and therefore regularly cut. Mortgage tax relief to owner-occupiers was not included because it only reduced revenue to the Treasury. It was left untouched.

2. Ministers often realised their decisions were being moulded by the way the PESC (Public Expenditure Survey Committee) system operated and defined "expenditure" but did nothing to alter the system.[32]

3. The artificiality of the system was shown in 1976 when the existing way of defining public expenditure meant that it amounted to nearly 60% of the gross domestic product. This was thought for political reasons to be too high. So the definition was simply altered and public expenditure suddenly made up only 46% of the gross domestic product. But nothing had changed in the real world.

The system could reach complete farce on crucial exercises, such as the discussions over the IMF loan in 1976, which were later shown to be a waste of time because of inadequacies of the system. The planned cuts in public expenditure almost split the Labour Cabinet that year. Yet when the money came to be spent it was found that the estimating was so bad that twice as much money as that cut in the IMF exercise was saved simply because it was not needed. The whole long-drawn-out crisis had been entirely unnecessary.

How the System Works

The expenditure system follows a ritual pattern every year. In the spring the Treasury lays down guidelines for Whitehall departments who then work out the cost of their programmes in great detail, originally for five, but now for three, years ahead. All these contributions make up the "red book" or report by the Public Expenditure Survey Committee (PESC), which is chaired by the Treasury and composed entirely of officials. Ministers usually do not read this lengthy report but instead have a simpler paper from the Chief Secretary. This is normally discussed in Cabinet in July and at this stage only a global figure for total public expenditure is agreed. Bids from departments always add up to more than this. The crucial decision is, however, to set the global figure because this determines how difficult the next stage, reducing the bids to the agreed level, will be.

This stage begins after the summer holidays, with a series of "bilaterals" between the Chief Secretary and the individual spending Ministers. Total agreement is rarely reached and any strong and determined Minister will fight on to the next level. In some administrations (Wilson, Heath, Callaghan), the final arguments took place in Cabinet. Mrs. Thatcher introduced a slightly new approach in October 1981 when Willie Whitelaw chaired a group known colloquially as the "Star Chamber" and officially as MISC 62. It did not meet in the autumn of 1982 but has met every year since. The aim is to try and conciliate between the Treasury and the spending departments. It works at a frantic pace over a couple of weeks and usually only a handful of items are left to be resolved by the Cabinet in November. This fits in with the style of the Thatcher government which is to avoid substantive discussions in Cabinet and instead to sort out problems in small *ad hoc* groups.[33]

How Decisions are Made

In the autumn of 1984 the House of Commons Treasury and Civil Service Committee was questioning the Chancellor, Nigel Lawson. He was asked the fundamental question: "How do you make decisions in Government about various priorities within public expenditure?" This completely floored Lawson, who could only reply, "I do not think that the procedure can be as scientific as you imply." That, as we shall see, was a major understatement. The PESC system does not involve a rational assessment of priorities but is instead the result of hard bargaining between rival groups within government. As Joel

Barnett, Chief Secretary in the Treasury from 1974 to 1979, explained:

> Expenditure priorities were generally decided on often out-
> dated and ill-considered plans made in opposition, barely
> thought through as to their real value, and never as to their
> relative priority in social, socialist, industrial or economic
> terms. More often they were decided on the strength of a
> particular spending Minister, and the extent of the support
> he or she could get from the Prime Minister.[34]

If the Minister is trying to maximise his budget the worst tactic he can adopt is to try and negotiate reasonably. In 1975 Fred Mulley (Secretary of State for Education) agreed a cut of £580 million in his bilateral with the Treasury. Encouraged by this success, the Treasury promptly reneged on the agreement and demanded another £124 million in savings. As Mulley complained to the Cabinet, "Those who offered the most were penalised the most."[35] The same year, Tony Crosland (Secretary of State for the Environment) tried a slightly more sophisticated tactic. He actually volunteered a cut of £1 billion on roads and other areas of his budget if the Treasury could agree to leave the high priority housing programme alone. Once again the Treasury pocketed the proffered £1 billion and then asked for cuts in the housing programme. The rest of the Cabinet, delighted to find another Minister offering cuts and thus saving their own programmes, joined forces with the Treasury and cut the housing programme.

After this fiasco Tony Crosland pondered his tactics and discussed them with Joel Barnett, who told him that "if he could have been as unreasonable on every penny of his programmes as Barbara Castle certainly would have been, he might well have got away with smaller cuts".[36] Barbara Castle was indeed renowned for fighting every inch of the way. But she understood how illogical the whole system really was:

> There is always an enormous waste of time over these public
> expenditure exercises. I spend hours mulling up this statistic
> and that and preparing my case, but in the end Cabinet
> decides these things on a kind of hunch. A bias builds up
> against this programme or that. If the tide is with one, one
> wins. Rational argument has little to do with it.[37]

For example, any semblance of rational assessment of priorities reflecting agreed Government policy disappeared when
Fred Mulley reluctantly acceded to cutting another £50 million
off the education programme. Wilson quickly intervened with
his personal prejudices:

> Of course Harold insisted that the Open University must
> not be touched, because it is his brainchild, but whether this
> overriding priority can be justified on grounds of social
> policy, compared with the things we are ready to give up, is
> another matter.[38]

The final requiem for the attempts by Whitehall to operate any
rational public expenditure planning system should be the
scene inside the Cabinet room on Thursday, 11 November,
1976. The Treasury had as usual opened the exercise by asking
for far greater cuts than they actually thought necessary – £200
million when, as Joel Barnett admits, "I would have been quite
happy to settle for £100 million'. Then something went wrong.
Ministers began offering up cuts and very rapidly the £100
million figure was passed and the total began to be near £200
million. Joel Barnett describes the inevitable farcical result.

> It turned out that John Morris, Secretary of State for Wales,
> was the luckiest Minister in that we did not reach his
> programme until late in the proceedings. I asked for £30
> million but, because we were so near our target, Jim
> [Callaghan] asked John for an offer. He said £5 million, and
> to his astonishment, had it promptly accepted.[39]

Changing the Lay-out of Whitehall

Politicians have, particularly in the last twenty years or so,
deluded themselves into believing that by changing the lay-out
of departments real changes can be made in the way Whitehall
works. This is an illusion because the new departments are just
like the old, manned by the same sort of people, and operating
within the same set of rules. Titles have been changed, areas of
work have been shifted about, "new" Ministries like the giant
Ministry of Technology in the late 1960s have been created
and abolished, and the world of Whitehall has continued in the
same old way.

For example in 1964 the new Labour government created the Department of Economic Affairs to try and reduce the influence of the Treasury. It did not work. Little was changed in the real world. By the autumn of 1967 Harold Wilson clung to the belief that if he personally took over running the DEA he could succeed in transforming the British economy, as he explained to Dick Crossman:

> If I can't run the economy well through DEA I'm no good. I was trained for this job and I've now taken powers to run the economy.[40]

In November 1968 Wilson could describe the DEA in the House of Commons as "a permanent, continuing and essential part of the machinery of modern government". Less than a year later he abolished it. In the autumn 1985 reshuffle Mrs. Thatcher moved one Minister and about thirty civil sevants in the Small Firms Unit of the Department of Trade and Industry to the Department of Employment in the vain hope that this would transform the British economy. It was this sort of behaviour that drove Lord Armstrong (Head of the Civil Service) and a technocrat to comment:

> There are some general principles of organisation, but the application of them is constantly interrupted by short-term political considerations. In my experience politicians have a contempt for good organisation.[41]

Apart from any presentational value, politicians do indeed have another motive for tinkering with the Whitehall machine – the need to change departments around to meet short-term political needs. Thus, although the DEA may have been created to reduce the role of the Treasury, it was also a very useful manoeuvre to meet Wilson's major party political problem – what to do with George Brown, the deputy leader of the Labour Party, when Jim Callaghan became Chancellor and no other job was suitable. Similarly the embryo Department of the Environment was set up in the autumn of 1969 partly because Wilson was getting tired of Tony Crosland's dissent on economic policy. As he said to Barbara Castle, "it will stop him [Crosland] interfering so much in economics."[42] In September 1965 Wilson considered transferring responsibility for immigration policy from the Home Office to the Ministry of Housing and Local Government simply because the Home Secretary, Sir Frank Soskice, was incompetent.[43]

It is impossible to find any underlying pattern or logic in the way Whitehall has been reshuffled apart from the recurring need in every government to balance the Cabinet and find suitable jobs for particular politicians. For example, Overseas Development has been, at various times since 1964, a separate Ministry with a Cabinet seat, a separate Ministry without a seat in the Cabinet, part of the Foreign Office without a Minister in the Cabinet, and part of the Foreign Office with a separate Minister in the Cabinet. After the second change in status inside a year Barbara Castle wrote in her diary:

> It is this kind of behaviour that makes one despair of him [Wilson]. He subordinates all considerations, not only of principle but of administrative effectiveness, to his balance of power manoeuvrings.[44]

The story is even worse elsewhere in Whitehall. In 1964 the Labour government set up the new Ministry of Technology. Over the next six years it gradually took over other departments – Aviation, Fuel and Power, and parts of the old DEA. By 1970 under Tony Benn it was a major department in Whitehall. It was broken up by the new Tory government later that year and the pieces reshuffled into the Department of Trade and Industry. This lasted three years before a separate Department of Energy was hived off. Two months later the rest of DTI was broken up into different departments of Trade, Industry, and Prices and Consumer Protection. Behind this move was Wilson's desire to stop Tony Benn from having control of a massive department and also to find a Cabinet job for Shirley Williams (Prices and Consumer Protection). In 1976 a separate Department of Transport was created to give Bill Rodgers a Cabinet job. In 1979 Transport remained separate but without a Minister in the Cabinet. Prices and Consumer Protection was less lucky and became part of the Department of Trade again. In 1983 the pack was reshuffled once more. Transport came back into the Cabinet and gained the shipping and aviation parts of Trade in order to provide a job with sufficient status for Tom King who had just been moved from Environment, Trade and Industry were amalgamated again to provide a suitable amount of status for Cecil Parkinson who had masterminded the successful 1983 election campaign.

This elaborate game of musical chairs has little or nothing to do with good administration, most to do with the personal ambitions of politicians. It has only a marginal effect on the balance of power in Whitehall and, apart from creating temporary disruption, no lasting effect on the way in which Whitehall works.

The setting up of a new Ministry is a fraught time in Whitehall but it has its compensations for the bureaucracy. It is an opportunity for every Permanent Secretary to get rid of his incompetent and burnt-out staff, which does nothing to improve the chances of the new Ministry. (Most Permanent Secretaries keep a special list of the staff who are always available for transfer.) Simple domestic arrangements can be difficult enough. When the DEA was set up in 1964 the new Ministry started with only a handful of staff and just one chair – used by George Brown; the rest sat on the floor. There were no typewriters and no notepaper. The new Secretary of State only received a brief because his Private Secretary purloined a copy of the Chancellor's brief. And this was the new department trying to deal with the challenging problems of the latest economic crisis and to regenerate the British economy through the National Plan!

The Fringes of Whitehall

All round Whitehall are clustered large numbers of bodies which have dealings with Whitehall and are able to exert leverage on the machine. There is constant tension between the desire of these bodies to appear to the public as independent, yet at the same time be part of the Whitehall decision-taking process. The politicians and Civil Service want to see the right sort of people running these organisations to ensure that they are not too disruptive. This is the area where the "good chaps" theory of British government operates. The exact relationship between Whitehall and these fringe bodies is not defined. Instead the system relies on having the right man in the right job. Both the Arts Council and the University Grants Committee are responsible for paying out large sums of money from the government, but Whitehall always claims that the policies they adopt are entirely for them to decide. They are "independent". Yet the membership of both organisations is chosen by the government! They remain nominally independent, Whitehall can continue to claim that it is not responsible for their policies, yet the "good chaps" do what is required. This delightfully informal system is the basis of much of British government.

Just how useful it can be to have the right people as Governors of the BBC was shown in July 1985. The Home Secretary chose not to use his powers of direction but instead requested the Governors to ban a documentary about Northern Ireland. No direction or order was ever issued but the end result was the same. In 1965 Lord Normanbrook (ex-Secretary to the Cabinet), chairman of the Governors, was able to anticipate the need for any overt move. Disturbed by the film about nuclear war, *The War Game*, he went round and saw some of his old colleagues in Whitehall, sounded out the right people and then banned the film.[45] The Overseas Service of the BBC is nominally independent yet it is entirely funded by the Foreign Office and receives daily a collection of Foreign Office telegrams as "guidance".[46]

Choosing the "Good Chaps"

The Civil Service controls the list known as the "Great and the Good", those who are judged suitable people to head enquiries and quangos and sit on committees. Technically, it is possible for any member of the public to nominate himself for the list although this fact is not widely advertised. Instead, the system relies on informal contacts and recommendations from other "good chaps". Whitehall exercises an enormous amount of patronage through this machine – about 9,000 paid posts and 30,000 unpaid posts. Exactly how people are chosen is not disclosed, nor how their performance is judged once they have the job.

Only really "sound" people get the most important jobs, and it is particularly helpful if their views are known beforehand. In July 1967, at the height of a row over D-Notices,

Wilson was under pressure to hold an enquiry that would enable the chairman of the D-Notice Committee, Colonel Lohan, to rehabilitate himself following Wilson's refusal to accept the report of an independent enquiry. At a meeting in his room in the House of Commons Wilson made it clear what he would do if he was forced to have an enquiry:

> Harold's main point was that he wanted to appoint Helsby, the ex-Head of the Civil Serice, because he knew in advance what his report on Lohan would be.[47]

In February 1985 accusations were made by an ex-MI5 employee that MI5 had been tapping telephones illegally. Lord Bridges, the chairman of the Security Commission, was asked to investigate. In just a week, including two days sitting full-time in the House of Lords, he was able personally to examine 6,129 warrants signed between 1970 and 1984, decide on the merits of each warrant and conclude that not a single warrant had been improperly authorised.

Appointed people are rarely very independent of those who appoint them, as Barbara Castle concluded after she met the regional chairman of the National Health Service:

> I get the feeling that these appointed bodies are like a fifth wheel on the coach. They neither speak as elected representatives nor do they have the expertise of their own officials. And their attitude to the Secretary of State and the department is necessarily pretty subservient – they want to keep their jobs.[48]

How the heads of nationalised industries are removed and chosen is made clear in a succession of entries in Barbara Castle's diary when she was Minister of Transport. By the middle of 1967 she was fed up with Sir Stanley Raymond of British Rail, though she had earlier got him his knighthood, and wanted to replace him with Peter Parker. She thought about what to do with Raymond:

> I have come to the conclusion it would be altogether too cruel – as well as too risky – just to sack him outright. In any case I have no power to do so. I would have to blackmail him into resigning.[49]

The nature of the blackmail was made clear when she talked to Harold Wilson about the problem during the Labour Party conference at Scarborough. "If it will help, Raymond can have a peerage," said Wilson.[50] Everything in the plot was going well until one of Castle's colleagues, Ray Gunter (Minister of Labour), leaked the story to the *Daily Mail*. When Castle found out they were going to publish the next day she had a few hours to fix something:

> I must now offer him [Raymond] the chairmanship of the Freight Integration Council in order that we could present the story as one of transfer, and *not* sacking.

This was cleared rapidly with Harold Wilson and then Raymond was called in and told what was going to happen to him. Next day:

> The press stories are just what I wanted. Raymond offered new job.[51]

The rest of the operation did not go smoothly. One candidate was ruled out because he gave Castle breakfast in a freezing cold room and Peter Parker turned down the job when the Treasury refused to increase the salary of the chairman (he accepted when it was offered again a few years later). Eventually having lost the candidate she wanted and given Raymond a job she did not want to give him, Castle had to settle for the only candidate left – a career British Rail man – as the next chairman.

Pressure Groups

Whitehall is surrounded and in many cases penetrated by powerful pressure groups trying to influence the government machine. Some are regarded by departments as legitimate groups who should be consulted about policy. They are the well-established and "respectable" groups such as trade associations, the CBI, the British Medical Association and other professional groups. Other more radical groups are seen as being outside the system, wanting major changes and therefore largely to be ignored. For example on prison policy the Home Office regularly consults NACRO (National Association for the Care and Resettlement of Offenders), a government-sponsored quango, and the Howard League for Penal Reform because they are seen as safe groups. The more radical PROP (Prisoners Rights) is ignored.

Departments deal with these pressure groups on a day-to-day basis and departments can soon come to see the world in much the same way as these powerful groups. Some departments finish up by becoming in effect spokesmen for these groups within Whitehall. For example, in nuclear power policy there is a tight group of quasi-official organisations – UKAEA and CEGB – together with the powerful GEC company who dominate policy within the Department of Energy and through them the rest of Whitehall. Environmental groups who dissent from the pro-nuclear power stance are excluded from the process and their views discounted. Similarly the Road divisions of the Department of Transport have very close links with the main lobby groups – British Road Federation – and road-building gains a powerful voice within Whitehall.

Perhaps the most powerful pressure group is the National Farmers Union (an employers' organisation not a Trade Union). They are lucky to have a department firmly devoted to their interests. This has produced a bizarre situation. Farmers now receive a direct subsidy of £2 billion a year, equivalent to 40% of the total production of the industry. This compares with so-called inefficient industries such as British Rail and the National Coal Board which receive subsidies of 33% and 10% respectively. In addition farmers are exempt from both VAT and rates (worth about £500 million a year) and from most planning controls. Because of the way the support is structured the consumer also pays an additional £1½ billion a year through being unable to buy on the cheaper world market. This vast amount of subsidy has been directed at large farmers and investment trusts that have increasingly come to own farms for tax purposes, while employment in the farming sector has fallen from 450,000 in 1957 to 140,000 in 1983.

But the farmers have an additional source of strength inside Whitehall apart from the devoted help of MAFF. A large number of Ministers own farms and therefore take a sympathetic view of the "problems" farmers face. For example ten members of Mrs. Thatcher's 1979 Cabinet owned substantial farms or estates – Lord Carrington (1,200 acres), Willie Whitelaw (a share in a large farm company), Francis Pym (500 acres), Michael Heseltine (400 acres), Jim Prior (380 acres), John Nott (130 acres), Ian Gilmour (married into the largest landowning family in the country), Michael Jopling (a farm in Westmoreland), Peter Walker (200 acres) and George Younger (a family farm). Other members of the government such as Alick Buchanan-Smith, Earl Ferrers, Lord Mansfield, Sir Hector Monro and the chairman of the Tory party, Lord Thorneycroft, were also farmers. Adam Butler, himself a farmer, was the brother of the President of the NFU. A previous President, Sir Henry Plumb, is a Tory Euro-MP.

But it is not only in Tory Cabinets that Ministers are farmers. Dick Crossman owned a 500-acre farm near Banbury and regularly used to brief the NFU behind the backs of his Cabinet colleagues. In 1970 he advised Henry Plumb about how the MAFF-Treasury negotiations were going and suggested ways in which the NFU could successfully lobby for more money. The Treasury as usual wanted to keep down public expenditure and Crossman helpfully pointed out that "the Treasury would much prefer to help the farmers at the expense of the housewife and the cost of living".[52]

An even more extraordinary scene took place three years earlier over the annual farm price review and the increase in support for milk. MAFF asked for 2d a gallon, the Treasury had originally started at ½d a gallon, but in the Agricultural Committee chaired by Patrick Gordon-Walker had "compromised" at 1½d. Crossman spoke to his farm manager who thought 1½d was "very good if the farmers could get it". So much for the "compromise"! Crossman, who owned a large dairy herd, and therefore stood to gain directly from this generous settlement, not surprisingly spoke up in Cabinet for helping the farmers and did not tell them what he knew about the "compromise". Crossman describes the inevitable conclusion:

At this Harold Wilson intervened, "Why don't we just let through the compromise [i.e. 1½d a gallon] which Gordon Walker had so admirably provided?" he asked, and sure enough Cabinet assented. No one knew that the compromise was a very generous concession to the farming industry.[53]

This example says much about the negotiating tactics of MAFF (asking for more than the farmers really needed in order to get a good deal); ignorance in the Treasury, and total ignorance in the Cabinet. It is also an interesting comment on Crossman's personal morality. But other members of that Labour Cabinet were also farmers. Jim Callaghan owned a 200-acre farm in Sussex and Barbara Castle summed up the whole system in her description of the annual debate in Cabinet, this time in 1969:

> Most of Cabinet was spent on our annual wrangling over the agricultural price review, on which Labour Ministers of Agriculture are always more pro-farmer than their Tory counterparts – heaven knows why. We cheerfully clobber everyone else but are seized with a kind of holy awe when we talk about agriculture – everyone that is but the Chancellor. Roy [Jenkins] was as tough as Jim Callaghan used to be, but this time Jim Callaghan has become a weekend farmer and argued as passionately for generosity as he used to resist it.[54]

We have seen the way in which Whitehall operates and the way in which power is distributed inside Whitehall. Not surprisingly Whitehall tries to keep this unedifying spectacle secret. How it does so is the theme of the next chapter.

CHAPTER FIVE

Secrecy, Propaganda and Accountability

The traditional attitude of the British governing class to the dissemination of information has had a lot in common with the ancient public school attitude to sex. Ideally, it does not happen. If it turns out to be unavoidable, it should be carefully controlled and regulated, like some form of disease. How it is in fact done should never be mentioned in public; and, if anyone goes too far and breaks the gentleman's code of practice, he should be expelled immediately.[1]

Secrecy is at the heart of the way in which Whitehall works. We have already seen how Whitehall resembles a small village community, introverted, with its own set of values. This attitude is reinforced by the wall of secrecy around Whitehall. Secrecy makes Whitehall even more inward-looking and ready to argue that "policy-making" should be restricted to the small group of insiders who have access to all the best information. People outside the magic circle need not be involved because they do not see the really important information kept inside Whitehall, and the public at large is not to be trusted with this information. Instead, Whitehall issues a large amount of publicity material, government statements, White Papers and background documents which mask the real level of secrecy. This is not "information", it is public relations material designed to back up the political interests of the government. It is of no benefit to the government to provide genuine information, particularly if this could be the basis for real and detailed criticism. Governments only publish information that supports what they want to do. Even the monthly and annual sets of statistics that have to be published are doctored as much as possible. All of this is backed up by a compliant news media fed by a well-oiled Government machine and largely content to play by the rules set by Whitehall.

The Official Secrets Act

The legal basis for all government secrecy in this country is the Official Secrets Act, and in particular Section 2 of that Act. Its introduction was as disgraceful as its content is disastrous for genuine democracy. Section 2 in its present form dates from 1911. A few years before, the Liberal government had become alarmed by the amount of official information being published in the newspapers and its inability to stop this flow. A special group of the Committee of Imperial Defence decided that legislation would be needed but, following the failure of the earlier attempt to introduce legalised press censorship, it felt that a more cautious approach was needed. A bill was drafted in secret but it was not to be introduced until a suitable opportunity, and then it would be claimed that the new powers were needed for national defence.

The opportunity came in the summer of 1911 in the middle of a spy scare and the growing possibility of war with Germany. The bill was introduced, as part of the long-laid plot, by the War Office to give the right flavour of national security. Late on the morning of 18 August, long after MPs would have preferred to be on the grouse moors, the new Official Secrets Act passed through all its stages in the House of Commons in just forty minutes. There was no debate at all about the provisions of Section 2.

Despite disingenuous disclaimers from the government the change in the law was major and intended to be so. The Official Secrets Act has remained essentially unchanged since 1911 and the Act has become one of the fundamental constituents of the Whitehall system.

How the Official Secrets Act Works

Section 2 of the 1911 Act makes it a criminal offence, punishable with up to two years in prison, for any Crown Servant to pass any piece of information to an "unauthorised person". There are other provisions making it an offence to receive the information. The important part of this section is that it not only covers "classified" or "secret" information, as many people believe; it involves every single piece of information inside Whitehall. It is therefore a criminal offence to give anybody outside Whitehall any information about what goes on inside the government machine.

Obviously government could not continue to function if the Act was applied rigorously and there is an exception to the general non-release of information. Disclosure is acceptable when it is "authorised". What this actually means is far from clear. Many people might think that in a bureaucratic world like Whitehall there must be a form which is filled in and sent up through the machine for signature at the appropriate level, and the release of information is then "authorised". There is no such procedure.

In practice what happens is that Ministers, at the top of the machine, authorise themselves to release whatever information they like including material classified Confidential and Secret. We shall see that this process is at the heart of the "lobby system" where Ministers feel free to tell journalists what went on inside the Cabinet room. In practice senior civil servants and others in the upper echelons of Whitehall also feel free to tell the media highly selected items of information from inside the machine. Occasionally they step over the (unmarked) line – for example Admiral Sir Henry Leach's public attack in 1981 on the government for cutting the Royal Navy whilst he was still First Sea Lord. But people at this level are too powerful to suffer more than a light rap over the knuckles. Only when a less powerful civil servant "leaks" information embarrassing to the government is there a prosecution under the Official Secrets Act.

The Official Secrets Act is therefore a very convenient tool. It enables Whitehall to keep secret all the pieces of information that might damage the government or reveal what really happens inside the machine, whilst also enabling it to deliberately "leak" a large amount of highly slanted and tendentious material that backs up the general public relations effort.

Every person who joins the Civil Service is brought up against the Official Secrets Act right at the start of his career. They are asked to "sign" the Official Secrets Act. This is the form known as E74, and the whole process is very revealing about the world of the Civil Service. First, the form itself is irrelevant. Everybody is bound by the law whether they "sign the Act" or not. Second, its content is grossly misleading. The front, the only part most people read, where they sign, is about the duty not to publish any material about Whitehall and the Civil Service without official permission and without submitting two copies for approval well in advance of publication. This has nothing to do with the Official Secrets Act but it is a convenient way of giving the impression that this purely administrative code is in some mysterious way part of the criminal law.

This form is a blanket measure applied to everybody in the Civil Service, not just the Mandarins in Whitehall. It is signed by cleaners, who might disclose what floor polish is used, by cooks, who might talk about the menu in government canteens with "unauthorised" people, and by gardeners who might reveal the secrets of the flowers planted in the Royal Parks. The form is also signed by anybody outside government who has any dealings with the Whitehall machine. Consultants brought in to sit on committees and eminent academic advisers all have to sign it.

Secrecy Inside Whitehall

Inside Whitehall, secrecy is an obsession. Everybody who joins the Civil Service, or any outsider who comes into contact with Whitehall, whether as a consultant or adviser, is subjected to "negative vetting". This involves a security check through the MI5 and Special Branch archives and the Criminal Record Office computer. Anybody in Whitehall who has regular access to highly classified information is also subject to "positive vetting". This involves detailed checks into their background – every address where they have ever lived, financial situation, political beliefs and sex life. It is normally carried out by a dismal man in a grubby raincoat and trilby, often a retired colonel, whose political and social views atrophied in the 1940s. This elaborate process has never caught any of the professional spies or real security risks such as Geoffrey Prime at GCHQ or Michael Bettany in MI5 and it wastes a lot of time and effort inside Whitehall.

Whitehall has its own elaborate system for classifying pieces of paper on their alleged sensitivity. The official definitions about their release are:

Restricted: undesirable in the interests of the nation
Confidential: prejudicial in the interests of the nation
Secret: serious injury to the interests of the nation
Top Secret: exceptionally grave damage to the nation

In addition there are a number of other subsidiary classifications such as "Management-in-Confidence", "Commercial-in-Confidence", and "Honours-in-Confidence".

The problem is that nobody in Whitehall knows what these definitions really mean. There is no objective set of criteria, and the definitions are particularly meaningless outside the area of national defence. The classification of a piece of paper is decided by the person writing it and he will have to decide on the right category by a mixture of intuition, guesswork and experience from seeing other pieces of paper. There is an inevitable tendency to overclassify documents "just to be on the safe side". This creates a vast amount of unnecessary work because the higher the classification the greater the amount of effort involved in sending papers by special mail, in double envelopes and recording movement in special registers.

Inevitably, the system is regularly abused. Secrecy is used not to protect national security but to prevent political embarrassment; and papers that show the fallibility of government policy or the deviousness or duplicity of Ministers can be, and frequently are, highly classified. For example an internal DHSS paper in 1985 on how to cut £120 million a year from the poorest people claiming Supplementary Benefit, how to get the proposals through the independent Social Security Advisory Committee without advance warning, how to start a campaign to "reduce public expectations and prepare the way for a more restricted social aid scheme" despite the fact that the Minister, Norman Fowler, had earlier pledged that there would be no cash losses, was classified "secret".[2] Although the political embarrassment involved is obvious it is difficult to see how disclosure would cause "serious injury to the interests of the *nation*." Similarly in 1984 at the height of the *Belgrano* cover-up, John Stanley, the junior Defence Minister, said that he would be quite prepared to classify information which all his advisers

– military, intelligence and Civil Service – told him was unclassified and could be made public.

The weight of classified information inside Whitehall provides another effect rather like tunnel vision. Because the information is classified it is seen as more important and reliable than information from outside the machine. This can have disastrous consequences in intelligence assessment but also in every other field where it warps the decision-making process and leads to poor decisions based on inadequate and bad information. A subsidiary consequence is that it increases the self-esteem of those inside the system. Because they have access to this information that seems to be so special they come to see themselves as important people in privileged positions.

Some positions are more privileged than others. Information is not freely available inside Whitehall. As we have seen, decision-taking is split up into a vast number of tiny units. Information is treated in the same way. Whitehall works on the "need-to-know" principle. Individuals should only see papers strictly related to their work and they should not see or find out about what is going on elsewhere in the machine. The processes of government and also individual departments become highly fragmented, and virtually nobody is able to fit all the various parts of the jigsaw together.

Gerald Kaufman spent a number of years working with Harold Wilson inside No. 10 and also as a Minister in the 1974–79 Labour government. He saw the whole Whitehall system of secrecy as ludicrous. His view of the way Whitehall abused the classification system was that:

> According to my own private system of classification Restricted was the kind of thing no newspaper would bother to publish, Confidential was interesting enough to warrant a couple of paragraphs in the *Daily Mail*, while Secret would rate an Insight story in the *Sunday Times*.[3]

But there is a more serious side to the whole problem. The level of secrecy inside Whitehall protects the position of the Civil Service. "Official" information is what counts and the Civil Service is the exclusive channel for the flow of information to Ministers. That is why, or is one of the reasons why, as we shall see, the Civil Service has fought long and hard not to reform the Official Secrets Act and to stop the introduction of any form of Freedom of Information. Secrecy also produces a situation where knowledge of mistakes is kept within a restricted group who will judge any lapses by their own code of conduct not by any criteria which might be supported by the public at large. It is a cosy atmosphere in which one of the rules of the club is that everybody must join together to repel any external criticism, since it is in all their interests that they should continue to run the club in their own way.

As Sir John Hoskyns, once Head of the No. 10 Policy Unit under Mrs. Thatcher, has said:

> The Official Secrets Act ... by hiding peacetime fiascos as though they were military disasters, protects Ministers and officials from embarrassment.[4]

Government Information Machine

We have already seen that the Official Secrets Act allows Whitehall to control the flow of "information" to the outside world – a product more aptly described as government propaganda. The idea that the government information machine is about non-political public service announcements, like foot and mouth disease warnings after *The Archers* on the old Home Service, has long since passed. The Whitehall machine is constantly engaged in putting out material to the press, much of it very little different from party propaganda. For example in early 1983 before the General Election a special unit, known as DS19 and staffed by civil servants, was set up inside the Ministry of Defence, to write anti-CND propaganda. This was close to party propaganda at public expense.

Each department has its own public relations office manned mostly by a special class of information officer. The quality is generally low; often recruited from among failed journalists and they are kept out of the mainstream of departmental affairs. Most civil servants in Whitehall rarely deal directly with the media. They provide press releases and background information for the press office but it is the information officers who deal directly with the media. Only rarely do administrators serve in public relations posts. The head of the Foreign Office press department is always a career diplomat and the Treasury press office is often headed by an administrator. They are both allowed into policy meetings and so actually understand the background to the information they are giving. Elsewhere the relationship is much more at arm's length. Defence has occasionally had an administrator in charge of public relations but he is still kept well away from policy-making. This deliberate separation only reinforces the idea that information is something that has to be "processed" before being allowed outside Whitehall.

Whitehall departments go their own way in public relations, usually dealing with the specialised set of journalists who cover defence or health or environmental matters. Many people have tried to co-ordinate Whitehall publicity, from Dick Crossman in the 1960s to Angus Maude in the Thatcher Cabinet. All of them have failed. The latest to try is the formidable and irascible Bernard Ingham, Press Secretary to Mrs. Thatcher. He chairs a weekly meeting of departmental information officers, known as MIO, which meets every Monday afternoon in the Cabinet Office to plan a strategy for the week's press releases and public statements. At the lowest level it is able to ensure that two Ministers with positive things to say do not speak on the same day. It is also able to co-ordinate the old trick of swamping embarrassing reports with other material. For example on the day the Foreign Affairs Committee report on the *Belgrano* affair was published in July 1985 co-ordination ensured that the Home Office released the report of the enquiry by Judge Popplewell into safety at football grounds. Departments can be left to themselves to manage traditional gambits like making controversial statements on the last day of parliamentary sessions to stop questioning, e.g. a by-pass through the Dartmoor National Park was announced on 26 July, 1985 as the Commons went into recess for three months.

The Lobby System

The Whitehall system of deliberate "leaking" of information by politicians and "background" briefings of journalists could not function without the tame acquiescence of the national press and television through the lobby system. For the system to work, the media have to agree to play by the Whitehall rules and in almost every case they do so.

The "lobby" started a century ago as a group of journalists who hung around the lobby of the House of Commons collecting political gossip. Since then it has developed into a sophisticated system for collective briefing of the media. The golden rule of the lobby is "non-attribution". Officially, none of the briefings ever takes place and the sources for the briefings are never disclosed but disguised by phrases like "senior Whitehall sources", "sources close to the Prime Minister" (both of which mean the No. 10 Press Secretary) or "widely seen at Westminster" (one Minister has been talking to the lobby).

There is a formal structure to the official lobby briefings. The No. 10 Press Secretary holds two briefings a day. The first at 11 a.m. is for the provincial evening papers and at 4 p.m. there is another for the national dailies. In addition every week when Parliament is sitting there are additional political briefings. The two leaders of the Alliance brief at 4.45 p.m. on Wednesdays, and on Thursdays at 4.15 p.m. the Leader of the House of Commons gives a general political briefing, usually drawing on what took place in Cabinet that morning. He is followed at 5.15 p.m. by the Leader of the Opposition. The Thatcher government has introduced a new briefing by Lord Whitelaw on government strategy on Fridays at noon. On Friday afternoons there is the special session by the No. 10 Press Secretary for the Sunday papers. The stories that are given to the journalists at these briefings are then repeated in the press, the sources always slightly disguised in order to protect the lobby system and as though the journalists had found the stories themselves. The Labour MP Austin Mitchell illustrated the insights that can be gained in the game of "spot the lobby briefing":

It takes a certain sophistication to know that anything which appears in the Friday papers about the Opposition comes directly from its leader, that "some Ministers are believed to disagree with the Prime Minister" meant when Francis Pym was Leader of the House that he thought it was time Thatcher went, "complaints voiced" means a blazing row, and "PM trounces critics" means that she lost but got her story in first.[5]

Few people have the time or patience to cross-check all the pieces in the press and on TV, and the lobby system can survive with "stories" that are nothing more than deliberate plants by politicians.

As part of this system of regular briefings there is a well-tried arrangement for handing out to journalists advance copies of White Papers and other official documents. In order to protect the myth that parliament is always informed first, the journalists are given what is known as a "Confidential – Final Revise" of the document. This is the paper as it will be published, but it pretends to be a late draft in order to protect the proprieties. Copies are handed out a couple of days before publication to give time for the media to work up the story and to enable the government PR machine to see that the right "colour" is given to the story. In addition, most government departments are now covered by a group of "specialist" correspondents who are given regular briefings – the Defence correspondents get one a week on Thursday mornings – on a lobby basis. These chosen few are also given various "facilities" such as interviews with the Secretary of State, background briefings from Ministers and trips to interesting places. It is easy to see what a close and convenient arrangement this can become.

Apart from all this regular briefing there is still the "lobby" of the Commons where MPs mix with correspondents and give them stories – always on a "non-attributable" basis. Stories starting "Friends of X say" means that X had to plant the anecdote himself. Here, too, the system works well so that the media get their stories and the politicians get the publicity they so desperately seek. But the system is sordid and corrupting; Anthony Howard, now Deputy Editor of the *Observer*, once described the scene in the lobby of the Commons:

> It's almost like Piccadilly before the Wolfenden Report. There stand the Lobby Correspondents waiting, soliciting for the politicians to come out. They treat them as if they were their clients and you know, in some ways, I think the fact has to be faced that Lobby Correspondents do become instruments for a politician's gratification.[6]

The media get their easy stories and they appear to be in the know about what is going on inside Whitehall but they are only printing what the politicians and Whitehall want them to print. This is not "investigative" journalism and far from what a genuinely "free press" could and should achieve. Political correspondents come to accept Whitehall on its terms and are drawn into that system. They, too, become obsessed by the short-term manoeuvrings between political rivals and the internecine warfare of Whitehall. As Barbara Castle wrote after a lunch with the lobby:

> They're just not interested in hearing factual stuff about the Department and I've come to the conclusion that the lobby are a pretty illiterate lot on everything but political in-fighting.[7]

How Politicians use the System

All politicians use the lobby system to their own advantage, hiding behind the "non-attribution" rule. One of the masters of the art was Harold Wilson and he used it at every level as part of his political tactics. In March 1965, when the Tory opposition were contemplating removing Sir Alec Douglas-Home as leader (a move that Wilson thought would be to his disadvantage), he interrupted a lunch with the Israeli ambassador to call in his press secretary (a civil servant) to spread a deliberately untrue story.

> I told him to spread abroad the fact that I have no speaking engagements between the end of April and early June. This will inevitably lead everyone to expect a May election and, as long as the Tories are expecting that, they won't get rid of Sir Alec.[8]

The press religiously printed the story. In September 1985 the day before the autumn Cabinet reshuffle the lobby were told that Cecil Parkinson would not be rejoining the Cabinet. This was done to stop that news dominating the actual reshuffle and the expected publicity bonus.

Politicians also use the lobby to signal messages around the establishment. In February 1965 there was growing discontent inside the Labour government about the role of the Governor of the Bank of England, Lord Cromer. Dick Crossman wrote a letter to Harold Wilson protesting about Cromer's attitude. Seeing a good opportunity, Wilson called in David Wood, political correspondent of *The Times*, and showed him Crossman's letter. Wood produced a piece saying that Ministers were against Lord Cromer. Nothing was done about the real problem. As Crossman reflected:

> This is typical of Harold's handling of politics. He still thinks he can settle problems just by talking to the Press.[9]

The lobby is a marvellously convenient way of briefing against Cabinet colleagues. In May 1965 George Brown appeared to break with Cabinet policy by offering concessions to the Labour rebels over the renationalisation of the steel industry. Wilson and Crossman discussed what to do. Wilson said that:

> he intended to hold a Lobby conference that day in which he would explain how George Brown had done it entirely on his own and how he himself had nothing to do with it.[10]

Similarly in early 1982 Francis Pym made a very pessimistic speech about Britain's economic prospects. Mrs. Thatcher was angry but in the Commons she took the public line that it was "an excellent speech". Whilst she was saying this her press secretary, Bernard Ingham, was upstairs in the Commons briefing the lobby about what she really thought. The *Daily Mail* the next day got the story right and used the right attribution for Ingham – "Senior Whitehall sources said that Mrs. Thatcher was furious."[11]

Individual Cabinet Ministers regularly brief the press about their own policies and how well they are doing in Cabinet disputes. Every October and November the papers are full of accounts about the battles over public expenditure as each Minister deliberately leaks selected details of the negotiations in an attempt to strengthen his negotiating hand. There are so many, almost daily, examples of this sort of behaviour in every field of Whitehall activity that it is almost impossible to follow any story in detail. Two examples will give a flavour of what goes on. In April 1985 there was an all-day meeting at Chequers to discuss reform of the rates. One of the possible reforms was introduction of a poll tax, but it was strongly opposed by the Home Office. On 8 April Ian Aitken (*Guardian* lobby correspondent) wrote a piece saying that "Ministers who attended the Chequers meeting on rates reform earlier this month were astonished by the strength of the opposition launched by Mr. Leon Brittan" (then Home Secretary). The article went on to describe in detail the conclusions of the meeting, together with details of the paper from the Home Office that was discussed at the meeting. This account can only have come from one of the Ministers present at the meeting – no prizes for guessing which one! Similarly on 26 June, 1985 the *Guardian* carried a long account of the meeting held two days earlier at Chequers to discuss public expenditure. The article concentrated on the strong opposition from four Cabinet ministers – Michael Heseltine, Norman Fowler, Peter Walker and George Younger – to the proposals from the Treasury for the usual round of cuts. Details of the Treasury paper and the summing up by the Prime Minister were also included in the story. Again the source can only have been one of those present, probably one of the four dissidents.

The motivation for Ministers in all this leaking to the media is pretty clear – to help fight internal Whitehall battles, to increase their public standing and also to keep in with their press contacts. Dick Crossman frankly admitted his reason for showing a memorandum he had written for the Prime Minister (on how to reorganise local government) to the *Economist* was simply "because I wanted to curry some favour with the *Economist*."[12]

The Two-faced Attitude

Ministers all believe that their deliberate "leaks" to the press of the details of Cabinet discussions and papers and of any other "official secret", great or small, are "authorised" (as the Official Secrets Act defines it) and the (unwritten) justification for all this is, presumably, that background briefing is of great value to the nation, and themselves. However, if any civil servant leaks information he or she is liable to be prosecuted, and in the case of Sarah Tisdall sent to jail. In other cases similar double-standards apply. In May 1965 Dick Crossman left Cabinet papers in an exclusive West End restaurant, but nothing happened to him.[13] In 1982 Robin Gordon-Walker, who worked for the Central Office of Information, left some Foreign Office papers on a tube to Heathrow. They were printed in *City Limits* and were mildly embarrassing because they showed that the public line taken by the Foreign Office on the Israeli invasion of Lebanon and on Nicaragua was not the same as its internal views. He was prosecuted under the Official Secrets Act and fined £500.

Opposition politicians find leaks useful in attacking the government. Once in government their attitude changes radically. Prime Ministers particularly dislike their Cabinet colleagues leaking stories, wanting to see the "official" line given to the press through their own press secretary. In January 1981 Mrs. Thatcher exhibited these double standards. On TV she sanctimoniously condemned leaks:

> They should not happen ... It doesn't make for efficient Cabinet government. I think people are very much aware of the damage they have done.

Two weeks later she called in the lobby correspondents of *The Times*, *Financial Times*, *Daily Telegraph* and *Guardian* and told them the details of the budget weeks before Budget Day.[14]

The diaries kept by Dick Crossman and Barbara Castle record an unending stream of complaints by Harold Wilson about the number of leaks from Cabinet. But they all knew that Wilson was always doing what he condemned in others – "briefing" the press. The results of this two-faced attitude can reach farcical proportions. The worst example came in December 1967 during a huge Cabinet confrontation about the possibility of restarting arms sales to South Africa. Over the weekend there were major leaks from Ministers in favour (mainly George Brown) on why sales should be resumed and how isolated Wilson was in opposing the policy. Wilson reacted violently in the Cabinet meeting early on the Monday morning:

> The discussion began with a tremendous personal attack delivered from the chair against all the people who had leaked to the press over the weekend ... I've never heard

anybody publicly scourged as George Brown was scourged by Harold this morning.

That afternoon Wilson made a statement to the Commons saying that the Cabinet was united behind the old policy of no sales. A few minutes later Dick Crossman came across Wilson talking to the press in the lobby. He stopped to listen to what Wilson was saying:

> On my best calculation there were sixteen members of the Cabinet who explicitly wanted me to make the Statement I made this afternoon. – Then he told them it was a lie that there ever was a majority in favour of selling arms ... After this he went on to describe what had happened in Cabinet this morning.

Dick Crossman summed up the attitude of all politicians when he commented on Wilson's behaviour:

> He really and sincerely believes that as far as he is concerned he only briefs the press and never leaks.[15]

D-Notices

There is only one area where Whitehall tries to directly limit the freedom of the media – through the issue of D-Notices asking the media not to give details of particular aspects of the defence programme. The whole system is a marvellous example of the "good chaps" principle at work. The government has no statutory power to issue the notices and they are only "guidance". It is assumed that editors will play by the rules and accept the system (thereby no doubt improving their chances of receiving an honour). The scheme was introduced after the failure of a proposal in 1906 to establish press censorship, and the whole "good chaps" principle was well set out by the Director of Naval Intelligence when he suggested the idea:

> A simple method worthy of trial, is to put the press on their honour in the schoolboy sense of the term, prior to any experiments which the [Admiralty] Board may wish to keep secret, by issuing a communiqué to the Press Association

stating what is going to be carried out and asking them to co-operate in the public information likely to be of value for foreign countries.[16]

D-Notices now cover a vast range of defence information from details of nuclear weapons to showing pictures of GCHQ at Cheltenham. But after they were introduced Whitehall tried to use the system in ways unconnected with national security. In 1923 a D-Notice was issued to try and stop publication of a story about a scandal in the Royal Family. In 1961 Whitehall tried to get a notice accepted that would have prohibited publishing anything but official information on weapons projects. This would have stopped all criticism of the scandalous cost escalation, delays and overcharging by contractors then beginning to become public. The press refused to accept these attempts to cover up stories. Now D-Notices are ignored by an increasing number of journalists who have realised that they are entirely voluntary and do not, contrary to the Whitehall line, have anything to do with the Official Secrets Act. But the system is still in operation and Whitehall still tries to use them to cut down the amount of comment about defence issues.

Accountability

We have seen that Whitehall puts up an elaborate smokescreen of secrecy and propaganda to protect itself. Information is power and Whitehall tries to keep as much information, and therefore power, as possible in its own hands. Information, or more correctly propaganda, is given out, but this is always to serve a purpose and is not intended to encourage genuine public debate about the government's policies and performance. In this attitude Whitehall is supported by the media through the lobby system. They accept the rules as set by Whitehall and become players in the same game. If the public is denied access to information and the press regularly carries the government line how good is parliament at getting at the facts? How accountable is British government? One of the great myths of the British constitution is that Ministers are personally accountable to parliament for every action of their department. In theory if a civil servant makes an error the

Minister must take the blame and, if necessary, resign. The last Minister to do so was Sir Thomas Dugdale, Minister for Agriculture, in 1954 over the actions of his civil servants in the Crichel Down affair. The latest papers now available in the Public Record Office suggest that this was not so much a noble gesture as a quick political fix by Winston Churchill to appease angry Tory backbenchers and find a suitable scapegoat. Having reluctantly accepted this role, Dugdale retired to his large estate in Yorkshire and was suitably rewarded with a peerage. More recently this principle seems to have been abandoned altogether. Jim Prior, Secretary of State for Northern Ireland, for example, refused to resign when there was a mass break-out of IRA prisoners from a top security jail, once he had established that he was not *personally* responsible, although there had been failures elsewhere.

Even if resignation is now unusual Ministers are still thought to be accountable to parliament which is itself still supposed to act in its historic role as a check on the powers of the executive. In support of this view it is argued that Ministers appear regularly to make statements and take part in debates, they answer questions both oral and written, and they appear before Select Committees. In addition civil servants now also have to appear before these committees who are investigating what happens inside departments. Superficially, this provides a comforting picture of parliament acting as a check on the power of Whitehall. We shall see that this is not the case and that Ministers and civil servants are largely unaccountable. In nearly every case parliamentary control is more apparent than real.

Parliamentary Debates and Questions

There are regular debates in parliament on matters ranging from general policy issues to the details of legislation and the interests of individual constituents of MPs. In this process the scales are tilted heavily in favour of Whitehall. One of the most crucial reasons is that nearly all of the important information is kept inside Whitehall and is only available to Ministers. The opposition is usually content to make general political points rather than detailed criticisms which need the detailed information they lack. In addition, most MPs do not have research assistants who could at least go some way towards balancing the unequal contest.

In any appearance in the House, a Minister will be supported by a phalanx of officials who squeeze into the cramped official box with its hard wooden benches by the side of the Speaker's Chair ready to draft instant replies to awkward questions. The Minister's opening speech will have been carefully prepared beforehand and notes for the closing speech already produced in advance of the debate. The Minister's private secretary will have a huge file of background material on any topic which Whitehall thinks might be raised. Other civil servants will be "on call" at home to give immediate advice if an unexpected topic is raised. With all this support behind him the Minister should have no problem dealing with any topic raised by the opposition.

Once a month each department in turn is top of the list to answer questions for about forty-five minutes at the start of the parliamentary day. On this "Top Day" only the first ten or twelve questions are answered orally by Ministers and the rest will appear in Hansard treated as normal written questions. The MP who asks the question is allowed one supplementary question and there are normally also two or three supplementaries from other MPs. The questions are known for about a fortnight before so that the Civil Service has plenty of time to provide material for the Minister – the answer to the question, answers to the supplementaries that are likely to come up, and a note summarising the relevant background. This whole process is a ritualised combat with the scales again weighted heavily in favour of Whitehall. Question time is not an occasion for probing enquiries or searching attempts to understand the complexities of a problem. It usually degenerates into the traditional exchange of well-known party positions or the raising of local issues designed to give the MP some publicity in the local press. As Dick Crossman wrote, "what most questions usually reveal is the capacity of a Minister to evade an issue".[17]

In addition to oral questions there is a regular daily stream of written questions for answer. Some of these are purely factual and only a few raise any really difficult problems. They are passed down from the Minister's office in special files and take priority over other work. Quite often they are given to young graduate trainees as a good introduction to the world of Whitehall. At first they often make the perfectly natural mistake of either answering the question or even worse answering the question the MP really wanted to ask but which he missed because of a slight mistake in the drafting. They have to learn from their more experienced colleagues that answers are designed to give away as little information as possible. The wording of the question is absolutely vital and if there is the slightest nuance that means that the Minister can get away with not answering any difficult part of the question it is gratefully accepted. Even if it is quite obvious what the MP really wants to know, if he has not asked exactly the right question he will not get the information. Only when it is politically convenient will the Minister provide more than the bare essentials.

Even if an MP gets the wording of his question right, he will not automatically get an answer. First the Table office in the House of Commons has to vet the question. On a number of topics MPs are not allowed to ask questions, and the list of censored topics does not just include security and intelligence matters but ranges from the makes and numbers of cars recalled because of defects through forecasts of future levels of unemployment to the activities of the White Fish Authority. If the question reaches the department there are other ways of not answering. The information can be "not readily available" or only "available at disproportionate cost" (currently defined as more than £200), or as a last resort the answer can be refused on the simple grounds that "it is not our practice to disclose such information". The chances of an MP discovering anything really embarrassing about the activities of Whitehall through parliamentary questions is therefore remote.

Just how easily Whitehall can step over the thin dividing line from routine dissembling and prevarication to deliberately misleading parliament was shown by an episode in 1973. The Minister who was caught in the act (owing to a set of coincidences) was Michael Heseltine later to be a central figure in the *Belgrano* cover-up. He was then Minister for Aerospace and responsible for financing, through the National Research and Development Corporation, a research programme on tracked hovercraft. After spending over £5 million the NRDC decided on 24 January, 1973 to wind up the project. Five days later the Department of Trade and Industry accepted this decision to end the project. On 8 February the Commons Select Committee on Science and Technology decided to enquire into the project and to take evidence from Heseltine on 14 February. Then two days before the appearance, and a fortnight after the decision to abandon the project, Heseltine had to answer a written question from David Stoddart on future financial assistance for the project. Heseltine's answer was:

> The question of the government's providing financial assistance for the continuation of this project is still under consideration. I shall make a statement shortly.[18]

No doubt that was the line he intended to take with the Select Committee – it was the easiest way of dealing with the problem rather than defending the decision to cancel. Unfortunately he could not take this line because the evidence given by the NRDC the very next day revealed that a decision had already been taken at the end of January to end the project. At the Select Committee, Heseltine's evasive defence of his deliberately misleading answer to David Stoddart was:

> It was a difficult situation to know the way in which, as the Minister responsible for these matters, I should reveal information to the House of Commons and to the Select Committee.

Difficult or not, the Select Committee could only conclude that

> Mr Heseltine's answer to the Stoddart Question on 12 February was therefore untrue.[19]

Similarly in March 1984 the junior Defence Minister, John Stanley, asked for two drafts of a reply to the Shadow Cabinet from the Prime Minister about the *Belgrano*. One gave the correct information, one did not. Ministers wanted to choose which one to send. This time they drew back and reluctantly sent the right answer.

The whole contest between Whitehall and Parliament is an

unequal one. Ministers and departments do not feel that they are under consistent and detailed scrutiny from MPs and there is no real parliamentary control of the activities of Whitehall. After two years in office Dick Crossman reflected on the whole relationship between Whitehall and parliament:

> How effectively does Parliament control him [a Minister]? How careful must he be in his dealings with Parliament? The answer quite simply is that there is no effective parliamentary control. All this time I have never felt in any way alarmed by a parliamentary threat ... I can't remember a single moment in the course of legislation when I felt the faintest degree of alarm or embarrassment and I can't remember a Question Time, either, when I had any anxiety.[20]

Select Committees

It was partly to redress this obvious imbalance that over the last twenty years the system of specialised parliamentary Select Committees has been developed, although it was not until 1980 that each Whitehall department had a committee to monitor its activities. All through this long-drawn-out process Whitehall has continually obstructed their development. Once in power Ministers lose interest in parliamentary investigations into Whitehall and senior civil servants have never liked the concept. Burke Trend lobbied strenuously within the Wilson government to try and stop the idea of investigative select committees from getting off the ground, and Sir Douglas Wass, summing up the Whitehall attitude to the risk of increased exposure posed by the new committees, said that his colleagues:

> viewed the development with concern, because we expected the committees to delve into matters which, for apparently good reasons, had been kept confidential.[21]

In April 1967 the Labour Cabinet had to decide whether Ministers could be called to give evidence before the Committees. Jim Callaghan described the idea as an "outrage" and Michael Stewart went even further.

[He] couldn't understand how any socialist could propose to limit the powers of the Government by creating specialist committees to poach on their preserves.

In true Whitehall fashion the minutes of that Cabinet Meeting are more circumspect and merely record that the idea of specialist committees:

> should be advantageous to members of the opposition but it was doubtful whether it was compatible with good government.[22]

Just what Whitehall means by "good government" is made clear in the rules issued to all civil servants who have to give evidence to a Select Committee (the Osmotherly Rules, named after the Department of the Environment Under-Secretary who drafted them).[23] The rules get off to a good start:

> The general principle to be followed is that it is the duty of officials to be as helpful as possible to Committees, and that any withholding of information should be limited to reservations that are necessary in the interests of good government or to safeguard national security.

This promising start is quickly qualified. Select Committees usually publish the evidence given and the public may even read it. Therefore it is necessary to be very careful in giving out even innocuous information:

> Once information has been supplied to a Committee it becomes "evidence" ... The risk of publication ... must be taken into account in deciding what it is prudent to make available even within authorised categories.

The true Whitehall attitude is revealed in the use of the phrase "the *risk* of publication".

What is kept from a Select Committee in "the interests of good government"? The list is long and includes:

1. Advice given to Ministers
2. Information about interdepartmental exchanges
3. The level at which decisions are taken
4. The way in which a Minister consulted his colleagues
5. Cabinet committees and the decisions they make

6. The way in which a subject would be reviewed within Whitehall.

This reflects the usual Whitehall attitude that the workings of government are not a suitable subject for study by outsiders, whether parliament or the public, and that the impression must always be given that Whitehall is a single well-oiled machine. Everything must be done to stop Committees prying into Whitehall. For example it is normal practice to announce the setting-up of official Committees that have outside members. But Select Committees might then get to hear about them and ask questions so:

> these implications need to be taken into account in deciding how much publicity should be given to the establishment of Committees of this kind.

Select Committees do not normally have access to Whitehall papers. Instead they are given specially-written papers that are of course designed to provide the minimum of information and protect the Whitehall position. In July 1984 one civil servant in the Ministry of Defence had to prepare a memorandum for the Foreign Affairs Committee. If the questions posed by the Committee were answered they would reveal the *Belgrano* cover-up; he therefore consulted his colleagues about what to say, "lest I have departed inadvertently from the public line and risked a breach in our united front".

How effective have the new Select Committees been? They have certainly not caused any great tremor of fear to run through Whitehall. They bear little resemblance to the powerful Congressional Committees in the United States. They are still composed of politicians who in the last resort will give their loyalty to the party. The party whips decide who should be members, many of the Committees are made up of safe old party hacks, and the government has a majority on each Committee. Each Committee only has a few specialist advisers to do the research necessary if the Committee is to be well enough informed to deal with the mass of information inside Whitehall. When dealing with relatively uncontroversial areas the Committees have produced some good reports but when they investigate highly political issues the system breaks down and the members retreat into their respective party positions.

For example the Foreign Affairs Committee investigation into the sinking of the *Belgrano* actually produced two completely different reports, one justifying the government position, one disagreeing in almost every respect. They only agreed on the fact that there had been a cover-up.

The Public Accounts Committee

The senior parliamentary investigating committee is the Public Accounts Committee, set up over a century ago. Permanent Secretaries, as Accounting Officers, have to appear before the Committee, normally every year, and defend the record of their departments in spending public money.

The process starts months before when the National Audit Office begins an investigation into a particular project or item of expenditure. They have the right to look at departmental files and they then write a detailed history finishing up with a list of questions and explanations required. This is not a process of joint investigation but a contest where from the start the department is on the defensive, determined to justify itself and reject criticism. The aim of the department is to come out of the process with as little blame as possible. If the final report is referred to the Public Accounts Committee the Permanent Secretary will have to give evidence as he is, in theory, personally responsible for all spending. He will also have to read a massive pile of detailed briefing and hold interminable meetings in order to familiarise himself with the details of what may well be some relatively obscure area of the department's activities.

The whole process is not one of joint investigation aimed at agreeing improvements in the public interest. It is a battle; what Sir Patrick Nairne (Permanent Secretary at DHSS) has called the "annual gladiatorial contest with the premier committee of Parliament". And how did Sir Patrick approach the contest?

As champion, in effect, of the Department's and the NHS's financial performance. I was often placed in [*sic*] the defensive – more concerned on occasion to show that the criticisms were unjustified or exaggerated than to demonstrate how the planning and management were being, or could be, improved.[24]

In practice much of the work of the PAC is sterile. It is investigating decisions taken five or more years earlier. It is looking back over systems of accounting and recommending improvements to try and stop the same mistakes being made again. Only recently has it even begun to look at whole areas of activity and ask how they are organised and how they could be made more efficient. The results inside the Civil Service are also unproductive. The idea of the Accounting Officer is important to the Civil Service because it boosts the position of the Permanent Secretary inside the department. He, and not the Minister, is formally responsible for spending public money. As Accounting Officer he has the right to ask the Minister to give a specific direction if he believes that a decision to spend money cannot be justified. This can be a powerful bargaining tool inside departments but it has rarely been used. In the Department of Industry in 1974 Tony Benn wanted to spend money on workers' co-operatives, but his Permanent Secretary objected, demanded and obtained a specific power of direction which he later used as a defence in front of the PAC.

The fear of a PAC investigation induces the Civil Service to be even more cautious than it would otherwise be. It leads to more rules and regulations and less efficiency. Sir Derek Rayner, who spearheaded the drive for greater efficiency, saw the reality beneath the preservation of constitutional niceties in Whitehall:

> The concept of a simple accounting officer who can be held responsible for a wide range of activities, even though it is impossible for him to have proper knowledge of or ability to influence them, is an absurd illusion, which does little to promote efficiency but leads to more rules, procedures and monitoring activities, thus fostering the tendency within government to issue new general instructions because of events in particular cases even though the total effect may be to raise costs rather than reduce them.[25]

Conclusion

British government is conducted behind a screen of secrecy
and propaganda. The secrecy is designed to conceal exactly
what goes on inside Whitehall and the propaganda, mas-
querading as information, to paint a false picture of what is
taking place. Whitehall is not, in any real sense, accountable
for the way in which it works. For Whitehall, government to be
good must be confidential. Indeed it does everything it can to
ensure that the "mysteries" of government are not revealed, so
that Whitehall can continue in the same, unchanged, un-
trammelled way.

CHAPTER SIX

Behind the Scenes in Whitehall

So far we have examined the main features of Whitehall and the British system of government. We have looked at Ministers and civil servants, their values, priorities and methods of operating. We have also seen how power is fragmented inside Whitehall and how the whole system is protected by a smoke-screen of secrecy and propaganda. Now we shall explore what happens when this mixture is brought together.

This chapter investigates activities behind the scenes in Whitehall – the world that is usually kept well away from the eyes of the public. Four examples have been chosen to illustrate different themes and to show what happens at various levels and in different parts of Whitehall.

The first concentrates on strategic policy-making at the centre of Whitehall as the Thatcher government dealt with the Falklands problem in the period before the Argentine invasion. It is a story of policy failure and lack of clear political direction from the top. The second example takes us into the fringes of Whitehall where a little-known body – the Crown Agents – managed to lose £200 million of public money mainly through property speculation. It illustrates the inability of Whitehall to produce a coherent policy, the "good chaps" theory of government at its most extreme and the amateurism of the Civil Service élite. The third example enables us to sit round the Cabinet table at Chequers and listen as Ministers try to deal with the long-term problems facing Britain. It is a study in the failure of the political class. The last example takes us inside a major Whitehall department – Defence – to examine the setting up of a Defence School of Music. It illustrates the role of powerful pressure groups within the system, the obstacles in the path of the drive for greater efficiency and the role played by the political interests of Cabinet Ministers.

These case studies are typical of Whitehall, but the record of incompetence and failure inside Whitehall, though long and tragic, is usually hidden from the public even though the price for that failure has been paid in many fields, usually by people well outside the Whitehall system. This chapter will show why Whitehall is in urgent need of reform.

1. Whitehall Grapples with Strategy: Disaster in the Falklands

From the mid-1960s until early 1982 the question of what to do about the Falklands was on Whitehall's list of outstanding foreign policy problems but it was always relegated to the fringes of Whitehall's strategic thinking. Like the rest of the country Whitehall saw the Falklands as a remote set of islands inhabited by a handful of people, one of the last remnants of a declining Empire. For over fifteen years British governments of both parties tried to achieve a diplomatic solution based on an eventual transfer of the islands to Argentina even though fiercely opposed by the Falkland Islanders and their support-ers in Britain. Britain maintained a tiny garrison on the islands together with occasional visits by the Antarctic patrol ship HMS *Endurance*. Although the rest of Britain could afford to view the problem with indifference it was Whitehall's job to assess the situation correctly, in particular the strength of Argentine opinion, and take the necessary action. Failure to do so produced an unnecessary war with its equally unneces-sary deaths. The Whitehall tradition was to play for time and hope the situation might solve itself. In October 1969 the Labour Cabinet discussed the possibility of allowing an American company to drill for oil in the Falklands. The Foreign Office was strongly opposed to this idea and simply wanted to keep the Falklands problem as quiet as possible. Jim Callaghan suggested using the scheme as a way of opening negotiations with Argentina. The Foreign Office objected strongly to this move as well. Dick Crossman des-cribes what happened next:

> In the end we universally settled for a suggestion of George Thomson's. "We don't want to go into this in the year before the election," said he, "let us play for time this year." With his brilliant words ringing in my ears I rushed out back to my car.[1]

Whitehall continued to "play for time" throughout the 1970s.[2] Some minor agreements were made with the Argentines but the basic question of the future of the islands was avoided as far as possible. The only firm action was taken by Jim Callaghan as Prime Minister when he sent a small naval task force into the Atlantic late in 1977 in case negotiations broke down. It is unlikely, though, that Argentina ever knew this took place.

Thatcher takes office

By 1979 the situation was becoming serious. Most of the possible solutions to the problem had failed and only one option for a long-term settlement was left: the islands would formally pass to Argentina but there would be a "lease-back" for a period of years with continuing British administration before a final Argentine take-over.

The leisurely pace of work that was characteristic of Whitehall's approach to the Falklands between 1979 and 1982 was apparent from the start of the Thatcher government. They took office in May 1979 but it was not until late September that the Foreign Secretary, Lord Carrington, circulated a note about the problem to the members of the Overseas and Defence Committee (OD). He discussed this note with the Prime Minister and in mid-October circulated a full OD paper. This was eventually discussed three and a half months later at the end of January 1980. Preliminary talks started with Argentina and in July 1980 OD agreed the "lease-back" option. Over a year after taking office the Thatcher government accepted an option already agreed by the previous Labour government. Again nothing much happened for four months until November 1980 when OD agreed to a visit to the Falklands by Nicholas Ridley, a junior Foreign Office Minister. On his return in early December he made a statement in the Commons about "lease-back" but faced a very hostile reception. Resistance from the Falklands lobby might have been expected but the Labour Party, which had accepted the lease-back option when in office, now bitterly attacked Ridley for advocating it. This unexpected parliamentary resistance was discussed by OD the next day when it was agreed that the government would have to approach the whole problem even more cautiously.

Over the next fifteen months before the invasion this caution was to be turned into inaction. From the beginning of 1981 until the Argentine invasion in April 1982 OD never met to discuss the Falklands and the government never attempted to have any full-scale review of the problem.

Whitehall Faces the Problem

The events of June and July 1981 show that the government was fully aware of the deteriorating situation. On 30 June there was a major meeting in the Foreign Office attended by Ministers, senior officials, the Ambassador in Buenos Aires and the governor of the Falklands. The conclusions of the meeting were the same as at almost every previous Whitehall meeting on the subject. The "immediate aim should be to play for time with Argentina".[3] The poor level of government co-ordination of policy was made clear the same day, when it was announced that HMS *Endurance*, the Antarctic patrol ship, was to be withdrawn from service.[4] This decision was taken as part of John Nott's 1981 Defence Review in which the bulk of the cuts had fallen on the Navy who had in any case never given a high priority to keeping HMS *Endurance* in service. (Scrapping it did not save much money but it was a high-profile cut and the Navy thought it might be rejected as the previous Labour government had always rejected it. Nott, who had little time for the Falklands Islands lobby, did not fall for the Navy tactics and accepted the cut.) The decision was to be seen by Argentina as a signal of a clear lack of interest in the Falklands.

The Argentine position was correctly analysed by the Joint Intelligence Committee in an assessment circulated on 9 July. It said that "the overriding consideration would be Argentina's perception of the Government's willingness to negotiate genuinely about, and eventually to transfer sovereignty", and concluded that if Argentina felt there was no hope of a peaceful transfer of sovereignty then there was a high risk of a full-scale invasion without warning.[5] It was to be the last assessment before the invasion nine months later and its implications were never followed through.

Initially, there was an attempt to act on this warning. Ten days later Nicholas Ridley wrote to Lord Carrington proposing a full-scale review by OD in September. His view was that lease-back was the only possible solution and that "if Argentina concluded, possibly by early 1982, that the Government were unable or unwilling to negotiate seriously, retaliatory action must be expected". The only solution was seen to be an education campaign on British and Falkland Island opinion over the lease-back option.[6] At the end of July Argentina sent a formal note to Britain registering "serious concern at the lack of progress" and saying that the next round of talks had to be the decisive stage in resolving the dispute.

The Crucial Meeting

On 7 September, 1981 a crucial meeting took place in the Foreign Secretary's elegant wood-panelled room overlooking St. James's Park. It was attended by Nicholas Ridley, Ian Gilmour, the deputy Foreign Secretary who was about to be sacked by Mrs. Thatcher in the autumn reshuffle, and Lord Carrington. Decisions taken at that meeting were to lead to his resignation seven months later.

The situation in front of the meeting was clear. Argentina's patience was running out; British intelligence assessed that if they thought Britain would not negotiate they would probably take action. The only negotiating option was lease-back but this was unpopular with both the Islanders and the House of Commons. Ridley proposed an education campaign or in other words an attempt by the government to take the lead, act in the wider national interest and try to resolve the problem. He also stressed the "increasing urgency of finding a solution".

The Foreign Office, in typically discreet fashion, does not keep a record of Ministerial meetings. However, it has been possible to piece together what took place. A draft paper for the OD Committee was tabled by Ridley but rejected by Carrington who also turned down the idea of any OD discussion at all. He further rejected Ridley's idea of an education campaign because "such a campaign would not have been agreed to by his colleagues".[7] This probably meant that Mrs.

Thatcher had already made it clear informally that she did not like this option.

There was no OD discussion on the Falklands, just a short note from Carrington to his colleagues saying that the situation was difficult but there might be some chance of more negotiations. Reassured, Whitehall continued as normal.[8]

The Slide to Disaster

What Ministers failed to recognise or admit was that, in adopting the line of least resistance, they had now adopted the position of greatest danger. They had no real negotiations to offer and were only prepared to go through the motions. Their own intelligence assessments showed that when the Argentines realised this they were likely to take action, rapidly and without warning. After Ministerial inability to devise any policy the second failure came here: no recognition of the true exposed position and no precautionary measures taken against possible Argentine action. As the Ambassador in Buenos Aires wrote to the Foreign Office at the beginning of October 1981, "The decision was to have no strategy at all beyond a general Micawberism."[9] The problem was that nothing did "turn up".

Officials in the Foreign Office recognised the dangers. The Head of the South American Department wrote in February 1982 that the lease-back option was "effectively dead", that the islanders wanted a "Fortress Falklands" option and that "we are left with no alternative way to prevent the dispute moving sooner or later to more open confrontation". A month later the Under-Secretary in charge of policy in the Foreign Office wrote to the Governor of the Falklands, "We are now perilously near the inevitable move from dialogue to confrontation."[10]

The position inside Whitehall may have been uncomfortable but the external position was worsening. At the end of January 1982 Argentina sent a formal note emphasising the need for a rapid resolution of the dispute and suggesting a permanent negotiating commission meeting once a week for a year. Clearly they were getting increasingly impatient with the lack of progress and Britain's reluctance to negotiate. In the middle of February Carrington circulated another note saying that there should be a further round of talks but that there was no hope of a solution. Mrs. Thatcher wrote that in the negotiations the wishes of the islanders were to be paramount, thus giving an effective veto to such negotiations.[11] Brave words, but the inevitable consequence was that without real negotiations Argentina might take action. Nothing was done to back up these words. No military preparations were put in hand and no intelligence assessment was made of Argentine intentions.

Talks with Argentina in New York at the end of February ended with an agreement to set up a negotiating committee. But when Argentina issued a unilateral and very tough communiqué the danger signs were obvious. Early in March Ministers and officials met in the Foreign Office. They agreed that as a response to the hardening Argentine position there should be a series of diplomatic messages and an OD paper "fairly soon". After the Permanent Secretary had been consulted Carrington was informed about the action of the Labour government in 1977 in sending a small task force to the South Atlantic. Carrington decided to take no action.[12] Three days later the Prime Minister saw a telegram from Buenos Aires reporting press comment on the hard line communiqué and wrote, "We must make contingency plans".[13] But the leisurely pace of life in Whitehall continued unchanged. The Foreign Office and MOD agreed that there might be an OD meeting some time in April and the early drafts of the paper were prepared. Nothing else happened.

This somnolent existence was rudely interrupted by the South Georgia incident on 19 March when Argentine scrap metal merchants landed without permission. Suddenly British government indolence was replaced by over-reaction. With little or no force available (only the ice patrol ship HMS *Endurance*) the government decided to escalate the dispute, demand the withdrawal of the scrap metal merchants and threaten to use force to remove them. From this point events rapidly got out of hand and left the government in disarray in trying to co-ordinate any response. John Nott was away in the United States, the Chief of the Defence staff was in New Zealand. Thatcher and Nott later flew to Brussels and Carrington was in Israel. Submarines were sent but by then it was all too late to deter Argentina and stop the invasion, Carrington and the junior Defence Minister Peter Blaker were advising the Prime Minister against sending surface ships as such a move would be too provocative.

Conclusion

This whole saga illuminates the inability of Whitehall to plan any coherent long-term policy and the reluctance of Ministers to face up to unpleasant news, difficult options and the need to take decisions. The basis position was clear: continued unwillingness to negotiate would drive the Argentines to take action. The Thatcher government refused to negotiate and allowed the islanders to have a veto over British policy and then would not face up to the consequences of that policy: the need to defend the islands against likely Argentine aggression. Instead of coming to terms with realities Ministers just hoped that something would turn up. Nothing did and the crisis slid into disaster. It was this appalling mismanagement and incompetence that the Thatcher government tried to put right by military success in the Falklands, that would lead to political success at home. Lord Carrington and his colleagues at the Foreign Office did the decent thing and resigned.

II. The Fringes of Whitehall: The Crown Agents Affair

The Crown Agents were one of those peculiar bodies that occupy the fringes of Whitehall. They had begun as purchasers of British goods for Colonial governments and had continued to act for a number of these countries after independence. They had no knowledge of or expertise in banking or financial operations. In the late 1960s they started a major expansion of their activities using first their own money, then the money they held that belonged to other governments. In effect they set up a fringe banking operation with interests in property companies and other loans. In 1974, during the fringe banking crisis, borrowers defaulted on the loans and the whole ramshackle structure collapsed. The government had to intervene and eventually over £200 million of public money was used to put right the ensuing mess. The Tribunal of Enquiry that investigated the affair summed up the activities of the Crown Agents:

They drifted into acting on their own without themselves properly appreciating what was involved, without adequately considering the risks, and the reserves available to cover them, without resolving the question of ultimate liability, without consulting the Ministry, without taking expert advice and without laying down rules for the control of the new activities.[14]

But the failings were not just in the Crown Agents. The affair deeply involved both Whitehall (the Ministry of Overseas Development and the Treasury) and the Bank of England.

The Crown Agents

The Crown Agents seemed to be part of the public sector but nobody could define their exact status. They had no legal or corporate status and had simply been set up as an executive act. They were not a government department and the staff were not technically civil servants (though many of them were civil servants by background and they were paid at civil service rates). The Minister for Overseas Development answered the occasional Parliamentary Question about them but since they did not receive any public money the ODM exercised no financial control and only a vague general responsibility for their actions.

In the 1960s the Crown Agents developed a conviction (without any hard evidence to support it) that they should now operate on their own without government support. But they made no attempt to clear up the constitutional confusion over whether, in the end, the government would have to be responsible for their activities.

The Chief Crown Agent from the late 1960s, and throughout the affair, was Sir Claude Hayes. He had been appointed in the true "good chaps" tradition. A career civil servant, Oxbridge arts graduate, ex-Treasury and ODM, he was an austere, aloof figure who, once appointed, jealously guarded his own independence and that of the Crown Agents. He spent a great deal of time travelling abroad and took little interest in the day-to-day management of the Crown Agents and its increasingly complex financial affairs. As the Tribunal reported he had:

No experience of or expertise in commercial or city finance. Most of the other members of the Crown Agents Board were similarly ill-equipped to supervise the work of the Finance Directorate.[15]

Ironically, what was happening in the Crown Agents was spotted very early on during an investigation by the Exchequer and Audit Department. In September 1969 they took the unusual step of writing to the Treasury about the scope of the Crown Agents' activities and the liability to public funds that could be involved. The focus now turns to Whitehall and it is worth noting the scale of the liability as part of the background to the Whitehall discussions. The Crown Agents' financial liabilities expanded from £38 million in 1968, to £127 million when the report first alerted the Treasury in 1969, to £184 million by the end of 1970, and to £472 million by 1973. The 1969 liabilities were already a hundred times larger than the reserves. The Crown Agents were gambling heavily both with other people's money and with borrowed money.

Whitehall

Inside Whitehall each department involved had only a partial and incomplete picture of what was going on and each assumed that one of the other departments was grappling with the problem. Although the Crown Agents were their nominal responsibility, ODM had no powers of control and relied on the informal relationships of the "good chaps" principle. The problem was that Sir Claude Hayes would only deal with Ministers and not mere ODM officials. The officials anyway lacked the expertise to cope with the complex financial operations now underway.

The Treasury had no direct responsibility and dealt with the Crown Agents through the ODM. To make life more difficult responsibility within the Treasury was split between two divisions. The Treasury thought the Bank of England was responsible for supervising the banking system, and in some informal way the Crown Agents as well. As Sir Douglas Wass told the Tribunal of Enquiry:

The Treasury expected the Bank to keep some sort of an eye on what they [the Crown Agents) were doing but not to be familiar with the details of their business or to study their balance sheet.[16]

The Bank of England did not think it had this responsibility, did not regard the Crown Agents as a bank and actually thought the Crown Agents were a public sector body controlled by the government. They exercised a general overseeing of the financial system and occasionally the Crown Agents drifted into their field of vision and then out again.

Danger Signs

Apart from the report by the Exchequer and Audit Department in 1969 there were other signs that all was not well with the Crown Agents. In January 1970 the Bank of England told the Treasury that the Crown Agents were infringing the foreign exchange control rules. Sir Alan Neale, a Treasury Deputy Secretary, told the Bank that his instinct was to leave the whole subject well alone.[17] Five months later during an informal meeting the Bank again expressed concern to the Treasury about the Crown Agents. While the Bank felt this was a clear warning of the need to do something, the Treasury kept no record of the meeting and did not view it in that light. Further "warnings" from the Bank came in December 1970, again ignored by the Treasury.

There were articles in the press about some of the investments made by the Crown Agents and one or two questions in Parliament. It was the latter, in true Whitehall fashion, rather than the financial evidence, that stirred ODM into some sort of action. The Permanent Secretary wrote a personal letter to Sir Claude Hayes and had lunch with him to pass on an informal note of caution. It had no effect. Whitehall decided on the old standby – a committee of enquiry. But the pace of preparatory work was slow. A first draft of a paper for Ministers was ready in July 1970 but was only submitted six months later after endless inter-departmental discussion. This submission shows many of the usual Whitehall faults. It concentrated not on the financial problem, which Whitehall was ill-equipped to understand, but on the much easier to comprehend uncertain constitutional position of the Crown Agents and the risk of political rather than financial embarrassment. The generally relaxed and uncomprehending attitude in Whitehall is encapsulated in the startling minute by the Foreign Secretary (Sir Alec Douglas-Home) agreeing to set up the committee of enquiry:

> It would be a pity to clip the wings of a body which seems to show, unlike so many ventures, enterprise and profit.[18]

This was at a time when the financial position of the Crown Agents was already extremely dubious.

Committee of Enquiry

It took another six months to set up the committee and even then its members did not start work for another month. In keeping with the "good chaps" theory of government it was chaired by a retired Permanent Secretary, Sir Matthew Stevenson, from the Department of the Environment, who had no previous experience of this sort of problem. It was not clear what the committee was supposed to achieve and, although its establishment may have defused the immediate political problem by giving the impression of action, it had the unfortunate effect that neither Whitehall nor the Bank of England made any further enquiries into the Crown Agents whilst the committee was sitting.

The proceedings of the committee were amateur in the extreme. There were few background papers, most of the evidence was oral and there were no detailed written submissions from either the Crown Agents or the ODM. Everything depended on whether the members of the committee, who had little relevant experience, could first identify and then ask the right questions. Even then the right people were not there to answer. The only formal evidence from ODM was a half-hour session by two junior officials who were given less than a day's notice in order to prepare. The first contribution from the Treasury was made over lunch with the Chairman and the formal evidence was provided by a senior official who had never dealt with the problem before and who was given no co-ordinated brief by the Treasury staff. The Bank of England gave evidence but did not tell the committee about its earlier concerns and warnings over the Crown Agents' trading activities. The evidence from the Exchequer and Audit Department, who had first identified the growing crisis, consisted only of an informal discussion over lunch, and their offer of help to the committee was never taken up.

The committee imagined that the Bank of England felt that all the trading activities of the Crown Agents should be kept together in one organisation. If the Crown Agents were going to act as a bank then they ought eventually to move to the private sector. The Bank, however, did not think this because it knew the private sector would not finance such an operation. The Treasury, after it had given its limited and inadequate evidence, eventually decided the dubious trading activities should stop. By the time it had made up its mind it was too late for the committee had reported.

The Committee Report

The committee reported in March 1972 but, in typical Whitehall fashion, the report was not published until 1977, after the collapse of the Crown Agents. The committee recommended keeping all the trading activities together and proposed four possible models for future status, only one of which (minority government shareholding in a private company) would remove the ultimate liability of the government for all the now considerable debts of the Crown Agents.

Having set up a committee of amateurs, Whitehall now treated its report as holy writ. Although the investigation had been anything but thorough – it had for example hardly touched on the trading activities – the report was regarded as complete, giving the Crown Agents a clean bill of health. At one meeting Sir Matthew Stevenson, when asked to justify the view that all the trading activities should continue, said that it was based on "discussions with informed and experienced people". Similarly, Whitehall said it felt unable to reject the report because it came from people with "significant experience in relevant fields". The "good chaps" principle was at work again.

For the next two years, until the collapse of the Crown Agents, Whitehall was to think about implementing the Stevenson report. Nothing was actually decided and the only achievement of the period was to produce a piece of paper that was supposed to be a new agreement between ODM and the Crown Agents but was only a triumph of Whitehall drafting in avoiding the real issues. The top officials involved were unable to see what was happening. The Permanent Secretary in charge of ODM was an ex-diplomat with no experience of complex financial matters and Sir Claude Hayes at the Crown Agents continued in his autocratic and independent way. He hardly supervised the financial operations yet in November 1972 could still claim that the trading activities had been "amazingly successful".[19]

Avoiding the Problem

It took four months from the delivery of the Stevenson Committee report before the government made a public statement. This was done, as so often, in a rush just before the end of the parliamentary session in July 1972. Even then the statement only gave general approval for the report and explained the need to look in more detail at the constitutional position. Discussions on the future went on for the rest of the year. There was a general agreement in Whitehall on the need for a new long-term structure but nobody knew what this should be and no proposals were ever made. By the end of 1972 nothing had been achieved except that the Stevenson Committee recommendations had been dropped because the options for the future all involved too many difficult decisions. The first five months of 1973 were taken up with internal discussions in ODM which by June had reached the Foreign Secretary when his agreement was obtained to the idea that there should be no new structure, just an "improvement" of the existing system.

Whilst the financial affairs of the Crown Agents continued to deteriorate Whitehall had spent three years getting nowhere. A committee had been set up after the laborious process lasting a year. The enquiry had taken a year and it took Whitehall another year to ignore it. They now decided that the "improved arrangements" would be in the form of a letter to

Sir Claude Hayes, although he would of course, again in true Whitehall style, be given the opportunity to approve the letter before it was officially sent. The idea that any solution could be imposed by the government was obviously anathema. ODM did not bother to consult the Treasury about the new arrangements but what they do show is the skill of ODM in constructing phrases that mean different things to each side. ODM could believe it would provide greater control whilst the Crown Agents could equally reasonably believe that it left them to carry on just as before. The important parts of the letter, with the key phrases that avoid all the fundamental problems of objectives and accountability italicised, are:

3. The Crown Agents will keep *in close touch* with the Minister on *major* matters ...
4. Financial business on the Crown Agents' own account will *in general* be conducted on the basis of the trustee analogy, but other investments which are *prudent* and consistent with the *name and standing* of the Crown Agents would *not be excluded*.
5. The Crown Agents will maintain a *prudent* level of reserves ...[20]

Everything would depend on how phrases like "prudent" or "in general" or "major" were interpreted in practice. The onus to act in these carefully unspecified ways was firmly placed by ODM on the Crown Agents. Whitehall did not want to take control.

Disaster

This virtuoso piece of drafting had taken another six months until late 1973. It was complacently regarded by ODM as "a useful step forward". By then the "good chaps" principle had come into operation again. Sir Claude Hayes was to retire early in 1974 so it was agreed that it would be better and easier to leave any further discussions till his successor took over.

Before that could happen the Crown Agents were in financial difficulties. The fringe banking crisis started and a number of property companies ran into trouble. The Bank of England then encouraged the Crown Agents (as a semi-government body) to go on giving support: action which only dragged the

Crown Agents into more trouble. The Crown Agents refused to provide ODM with any detailed information but at a meeting at the Treasury in May 1974 following the collapse of the Stern Group the worrying situation at the Crown Agents was apparent for those who wanted to see. But that meeting concentrated on the immediate presentational aspect, a statement to be made in parliament by the Chancellor. The Crown Agents did produce a balance sheet that would have shown an accountant that their solvency was in question. But there was no accountant at the meeting and none of the administrators present understood the significance of the information and were in any case more interested in the wording of the parliamentary statement. There was no action to investigate the true position of the Crown Agents. As usual everybody thought that somebody else was responsible. It was not until October 1974 when a businessman, Sir John Cuckney, was put in charge of the Crown Agents that any action was taken. After just fifteen days he realised the seriousness of the situation, called in independent auditors, and within two months negotiated £85 million of government assistance. Over the next few months the enormity of the losses, amounting to nearly £200 million, finally emerged.

Conclusion

This sorry saga is an indictment of the Whitehall system. As the Tribunal of Enquiry concluded:

> No one comes out of the story with much credit. Activities ... would have brought down the whole organisation had not the Government provided financial help. The Government had known about the activities since 1969 and had realised, at least from early 1970, that it would have a responsibility to stand behind the Crown Agents if the activities went badly wrong, but by 1974 it had failed to take any effective action to investigate or control the activities.[21]

Apart from the amateurism and incompetence of the Crown Agents it was the Whitehall system that was at fault. The ODM was nominally in charge but had no expertise to deal with financial problems. The Treasury left it to them and relied on the Bank of England who in turn left it to Whitehall. The Civil Service administrators concentrated on the constitutional position but never solved that problem and instead relied on the "good chaps" principle to ensure that everything was all right.

The conclusions of the Tribunal of Enquiry could stand as an epitaph for the whole Whitehall system:

> The result of these relationships was that there was a great deal of activity, with many papers passing to and fro, which only concealed the fact that nothing was being achieved. Many meetings, both departmental and inter-departmental, were called with no defined purpose and ended without anything having been decided and no course of action having been agreed.[22]

III. *Politicians Guide the Destiny of the Nation: Chequers, Sunday, 17 November, 1974*

We have already seen that one of the aims of the Central Policy Review Staff was to try and make Ministers think about long-term strategy, and that this is an uphill task under any government. At the core of the process was a regular six-monthly briefing for the Cabinet by the CPRS on where the government was heading and the issues that needed to be tackled.

The November 1974 briefing was likely to be gloomy. Britain was still trying to cope with the impact of the massive oil prices following the Arab-Israeli war a year before, together with the miners' strike, rapidly rising inflation and major industrial unrest. The task before the Cabinet was clear; to devise a strategy to enable the country to cope with this difficult period and construct a long-term policy for recovery. The Wilson government had been narrowly re-elected a month earlier and it seemed unlikely to last the full five-year term of a parliament. Nevertheless Wilson was confident about his government's ability to rise to the challenge. As he wrote later:

> I was not exaggerating when I called the 1974 Cabinet the most experienced and talented this century, transcending even the Campbell-Bannerman Administration of 1905.[23]

That was a bold claim since the Campbell-Bannerman government included three future Prime Ministers – Asquith, Lloyd George and Churchill – who rank among the greatest of the century and other eminent figures such as Sir Edward Grey and Lord Haldane.

The quality of the Wilson government in action can be judged from the notes kept by Barbara Castle in her diary.[24] As a trained shorthand writer she took down some of the contributions verbatim, which gives us an unrivalled picture of the modern Cabinet at work. The resulting picture of the "governance" of Britain is a depressing portrait of the low level of the political class in Britain. Many of the interventions are anecdotal, none rises above the level of platitude and all show a complete inability to understand, let alone grapple with, long-term issues, strategic planning or any of the real problems facing Britain. It shows politicians with nothing much to contribute, no special expertise or powers of leadership. The top Civil Service can do nothing but ask questions the politicians do not want to try to answer. The whole session rarely rises above the level of a saloon bar conversation.

Castle started by noticing the amount of redecoration at Chequers during the Heath period but then the meeting began.

As the discussion unfolded, revealing problems of almost insurmountable gloom, I had the quiet feeling that so much expertise, sense and conviction of purpose must enable us somehow to win through. Though CPRS had drawn up an agenda in four parts, starting with our relationship with the external world, we soon found ourselves in the middle of a second reading debate over the whole field. Ken Berrill, head of CPRS, introduced the discussion succinctly, setting out the problems (the threatening world slump, the petrodollar crisis, etc.) rather than attempting to answer them. Harold Lever then spoke to his own paper. "We have only a 50 per cent chance of avoiding world catastrophe," he told us. Getting some international machinery to recycle the petrodollars was the only hope. Everything else, like petrol rationing, was only "frolics at the margin". We should broadly back the Americans. Denis [Healey] admitted that it was very unlikely we could close the whole of the balance of payments gap by 1978–79, even if things went well. But unless we improved our competitiveness our balance of payments position would become disastrous. There was a strong case for an energy conservation programme, if only on psychological grounds.

Then Roy Jenkins intervened with a few platitudes:

"Your memory is better than mine, Prime Minister, but I believe it is ten years ago to this very day that we sat in this room discussing the Defence Review. The world has changed out of all recognition since then." He then talked about the changes in the power blocs, adding that those like himself who had expected the coherence of Europe to develop strongly had found the reality "disappointing". The Middle East situation was full of menace and he believed a preemptive strike by the USA was possible.

Eric Varley tried out a few anecdotes and:

talked about energy extremely competently, though he insisted that looking for major energy savings was likely to be "extremely disappointing". He was "very opposed" to petrol rationing and maintained that rota cuts, organised systematically, would be the only effective method – and they were out of the question. The only hope was to move to energy self-sufficiency. But the miners' attitude was frightening. He had been speaking only a day or two ago to a miners' meeting attended by what he called the "Scargill Mafia". When he told them that the Government could have used more oil at the power stations this summer and so built up coal stocks for the winter against a possible strike, but hadn't, they had merely retorted, "More fool you", and thanked him for letting them know how strong their position was. He concluded sadly: "Don't let us frighten the oil companies away." We needed their investment.

Next came the contribution from the guru of the left, Tony Benn, who brought the discussion nearer home but scarcely down to earth when he argued that:

we had got to look at the problem in domestic as well as international terms. A devolution of power had also been going on at home and all our policy must take account of it. "We cannot win consent to a technocratic solution. We must redistribute power in this country by peaceful means. Beyond the slump must be the perspective of a better society." He did not believe the solution lay in bigger and bigger units: he had been immensely struck by the emphasis which Jim laid on devolution in his paper. "We must show what sort of Government we are." Were we going to go for impersonal macro-solutions, or were we going to realise that the people were looking to us as their leaders to provide an answer to their difficulties? To them their leaders seemed utterly remote. "Without consent no solution we work out round this table will have a chance."

After a couple of interventions from Michael Foot on the need to develop a contingency plan for world catastrophe and from Roy Mason on the danger of war in the Middle East the Cabinet was feeling dispirited. Still, Jim Callaghan could always be relied on to make the atmosphere worse:

> When I am shaving in the morning I say to myself that if I were a young man I would emigrate. By the time I am sitting down to breakfast I ask myself "where would I go?"

Following an outburst of laughter Callaghan continued in pessimistic vein. If Britain moved to a siege economy democracy probably would not survive. The US probably would not intervene in the Middle East but Britain was on the way steadily downhill.

> One prospect is that we shall lose our seat on the Security Council. Jim concluded gloomily that in his view we should go on sliding downhill for the next few years. "Nothing in these papers makes me believe anything to the contrary. I haven't got any solution. As I said, if I were a young man, I should emigrate."

Barbara Castle intervened more chirpily next and said, in a way typical of politicians, that "presentation was the key". But the only practical suggestion she could make was to have a "popular" version of the public expenditure White Paper. Then came Denis Healey in his usual knockabout style saying that Britain could not keep intervening everywhere: "It's no good ceasing to be the world's policeman in order to become the world's parson instead." (This was an old joke that he had first tried out in Cabinet in 1968.) He countered Callaghan's gloom and doom by saying that "If we do join the Third World it will be as a member of OPEC". In his view there was also no point in planning for catastrophe, the great power blocks were breaking up and "international communism has as much or as little significance as the Commonwealth".

After these sparkling and incisive contributions it was time for lunch. Wilson summed up the meeting by saying that the discussion had been first class; "the best I have ever heard in this type of gathering." If this really was the best, the worst is unimaginable.

The conclusions at the end of all of this hot air were neither profound nor imaginative. Wilson decided to tinker with the Whitehall machinery: he would be setting up another Cabinet committee, this time on overseas economic policy.

After lunch the Cabinet re-assembled in the library and began with another series of intellectual platitudes, this time from Ross, the deputy head of the CPRS, as Castle records:

> There was, he said, no surefire recipe for economic growth. There was a role for general incentives and also one for selective assistance. We needed to find a balance between them and help the regions to help themselves.

After this tour de force on economic policy, Ken Berrill, the Head of the CPRS, posed some questions:

> The Government ... was more likely to be judged by inflation than by the standard of living. And he believed that was right. Inflation was a straight wage-price-wage problem. What policies will impinge at the point of the wage bargain? How do you break into it? Was index-linking the answer?

The civil servants could pose the questions and look to the politicians for the answers. The politicians had no solutions to propose and hoped the Civil Service would tell them what to do.

At this point of total sterility Tony Crosland, the supposed economic genius of the Cabinet, the philosopher of social democracy and the man many thought should have been Chancellor of the Exchequer, intervened. He had nothing positive to contribute and his sophisticated economic analysis was that:

> We didn't know how our relative decline had taken place. All we can do is to press every button we've got. We do not know which, if any, of them will have the desired results ... Curing inflation was more important than economic growth ... All we could do was grit out teeth till the oil flows.

The discussion rambled off into a debate about the social contract. At last the politicians were back on something they could understand – how to get through the next couple of months. A discussion of wage controls versus unemployment got nowhere and everybody agreed to think about it again in the spring. The purpose of the meeting – long-term strategy – had long been forgotten and it was now nearly 5 p.m. and the Cabinet wanted to go home. A quick dash through "presentational policy", including Castle's gimmick of a "popular" version of the public expenditure, and it was all over.

What had been achieved? Just one new Cabinet committee. The Civil Service had contributed nothing but questions. Ministers had provided no answers and their contributions to the debate were no wiser than might have been expected from the average man in the street. Still politicians love talking and they left Chequers in an optimistic mood:

> We broke up, congratulating ourselves on a valuable day. The problem, as always, will be whether we have the time to follow our own lessons through.

Exactly what those lessons were Barbara Castle does not make clear. The importance of this day at Chequers is that it was the last attempt even to look at the long-term future. It was the last presentation by the CPRS to the Cabinet, and Ministers could now settle back to short-term policy-making and political fixes without having to confront, even twice a year, the implications of their decisions in the long term. It was the end of a short-lived and doomed attempt to introduce at least a little long-term strategy and rational planning into Whitehall.

IV. Politics and Efficiency: The Defence School of Music

The Thatcher government came into power determined to improve the efficiency of the public sector, cut out waste and get better value for money. The creation of the Defence School of Music is a good illustration of what happens when these general desires come up against the political interests of Ministers. It also demonstrates the power of vested interests – in this case the Armed Forces – inside government. When these two elements combine they produce a mixture that has little to do with good government.[25]

The Inefficient System

In the autumn of 1981 John Nott, Secretary of State for Defence, decided to follow up his Defence Review with an attack on waste in the Armed Forces and in particular their massive training organisations. He had no specific ideas on what to do, just a general conviction that too much money was being wasted. I was asked to set up a series of studies ranging from the training of cooks, through engineers, drivers and computer operators to musicians.

The first report on musician training had to be ready in four months and the first job was obviously to go and look at the existing organisation. The idea of a common school for musician training had been around for about twenty-five years but the three Services had always managed to block any attempt to change the system, under which they each had their own independent organisations and did exactly what they wanted. The Army School at Kneller Hall, in Hounslow, was the most prestigious and had been founded back in the 1850s. By the 1980s it was run-down and decaying. The old house needed repair, the barracks accommodation was spartan, music practice facilities were almost non-existent, there was no concert hall, and worst of all it was directly under the flight path to Heathrow with large jets passing overhead every few minutes. It was just about the worst possible place to put a music school but it did have the advantage of providing free parking for the Army top brass for rugby internationals at Twickenham. The Army had neglected it for years, spending very little money on it, but the moment it was under threat they were to start a long campaign, using every possible trick, to try and preserve their independence.

The RAF had a tiny training school, as part of the large RAF complex at Uxbridge, a few miles from Kneller Hall. Although it was a modern building the roof leaked and the music rooms were not sound-proofed. The Royal Marines school was at Deal in a nineteenth-century barracks built to hold a thousand men and now occupied by about 120. No maintenance had been carried out for years and the whole site was slowly crumbling. The Marines had long wanted to leave Deal and move to the old barracks at Eastney near Portsmouth where they had one of their headquarters and the regimental museum.

Battles Inside the Ministry of Defence

I sent the first report to the junior Defence Minister, Jerry Wiggin, at the end of March 1982 after six months of obstruction and dissent from the Services. It showed that the three existing schools were working well under capacity and very uneconomically. Large sums of money could be saved by combining them and the report recommended a study on where this new school should be sited. The report landed on Jerry Wiggin's desk the day Argentina invaded the Falklands and we all had other things to do until June. When Wiggin did consider it he decided on one of the standard ploys of the Thatcher administration: don't rely on what the Civil Service tells you, call in an outside expert. Wiggin asked an old friend of his, John Gale, to do a study of musician training. His report, in September 1982, agreed that there should be a single integrated school and that the musical training of the three Services needed to be radically overhauled to improve standards. At the same time I had done some more work on costs which showed that setting up a new Defence School of Music at Eastney would be the cheapest option, by about £4 million.

With the odds now stacked against them the Services

decided to fight back. They demanded that a military officer should look over all the ground already covered by the outside consultant. This obvious attempt to sabotage the operation backfired when the military report said it would be feasible to implement the changes suggested by the outside consultant. By April 1983 the Services had been pushed into a corner and at a meeting with Jerry Wiggin they were forced to agree "in principle" to the setting up of a new Defence School of Music. The next study was to concentrate on where the school should go. Its location was subject to one important point. The school was not, Ministers said, to go to Deal because the facilities were inadequate.

What the three Services meant by agreement "in principle" became apparent during the next stage. The decision by the Minister made no difference to their total opposition. They concentrated on obstruction, putting forward unreasonable demands for massive new facilities, arguing over every single point, and particularly over the crucial issue of status – which Service would command the new school. Nevertheless by the autumn of 1983 the position was clear. A new Defence School of Music could be built and it would provide much better facilities than anything that currently existed. Not only that, it would actually save money. With Deal ruled out by Ministers because it would be too expensive to modify, only three sites remained: Kneller Hall, which was unsuitable because there was no room to build the facilities needed, Woolwich, which was very expensive, and Eastney. Eastney was the obvious choice, it would save £4½ million in capital costs and about another £250,000 every year in running costs.

The Army fought hard against the proposals. They would appear to accept the detailed financial appraisal carried out by the independent management accountants but then advise their Generals to disown the figures they had previously agreed. At the same time the local MP for Twickenham, Toby Jessel, was lobbying Ministers about the closure of Kneller Hall. In doing so he was remarkably well briefed on details and able to quote from the internal Ministry of Defence studies to support the Army's position. Ministers suspected what was going on but never started a "leak" investigation.

Ministers Take a Decision

The final report recommending Eastney was considered and agreed by the new junior Defence Minister, Lord Trefgarne, who had replaced Jerry Wiggin, and by John Stanley, the Minister of State. After two years' hard work and intense opposition from the three Services it at last looked as though a new Defence School of Music would be set up, since the main objective set by Ministers – saving money – had been met. We had not reckoned with Michael Heseltine. Most papers sent to him stayed in his "in tray" for a long time without any action but this time we were lucky and it only took about five weeks to set up a meeting at 7 p.m. on the night before Christmas. The meeting lasted exactly three minutes. Heseltine as usual lounged on his sofa, idly flicking through the papers. Before any discussion he announced his decision: "I'm fed up with all these bases in the south-east. You can go anywhere you like as long as it's north of Birmingham." He gave no reasons for his decision and when Lord Trefgarne tried to explain why Eastney had been chosen Heseltine brusquely dismissed us and we all trooped out of his room. This was obviously Heseltine in his "Minister for Merseyside" role.

Still, at least we had a "policy" decision. Deal had already been excluded by Ministers and now the rest of Southern England was also ruled out. Early in 1984 the search started for sites elsewhere. By February we had found a potential site in Edinburgh. Suddenly the Army shifted from total opposition to the Defence School of Music to tremendous enthusiasm. The reason was that the site in Edinburgh was part of an Army complex and the various moves that would be involved would be beneficial to the Army. At the same time the Royal Marines began to lose interest in the project now it was unlikely to save an old Royal Marines barracks. The first financial estimates for moving to Edinburgh showed that it would be more expensive than the preferred move to Eastney.

Ministers Reverse their Decision

Heseltine never had to face the choice between Edinburgh and Eastney because suddenly a new factor in this power struggle emerged – Peter Rees, Chief Secretary at the Treasury, and the man in charge of cutting public expenditure. But Rees was also MP for Dover which included Deal within the constituency boundary. In March 1984 he asked Lord Trefgarne to go over to the Treasury to see him. Presumably he asked for the Defence School to go to Deal and Rees was a powerful Minister in Cabinet battles over spending. The very next day instructions were issued to find a use for Deal. A rapid financial appraisal was carried out which still showed that Deal was far more expensive than Eastney and instead of saving money would actually increase costs.

Heseltine was now faced with a real problem. Eastney was the cheapest option, Deal the most expensive. But Heseltine had already said that the new school had to go "north of Birmingham". However, a powerful Cabinet colleague wanted it at Deal. Heseltine showed his real priorities when he decided to make a U-turn on his decision at the Christmas meeting, and spend an extra £2½ million of public money rather than save £4 million, and thus placate his colleague Peter Rees by moving the new school to Deal. The Ministry of Defence had to admit that the decision was taken for "other than financial reasons". The final irony was to announce the decision in the 1984 White Paper about improving the efficiency of decision-taking inside the Ministry of Defence.

One problem still remained. The Permanent Secretary, Sir Clive Whitmore, was worried about the decision to spend public money rather than to save it in order to put the school at Deal. How could he justify this decision before the Public Accounts Committee? He wrote to Heseltine asking for a "power of direction", in other words a direct order from Heseltine to spend the money. Heseltine, obviously aware of the problems such a direction could cause him if the Public Accounts Committee investigated, refused to issue the direction. Whitmore was left in a difficult position and asked officials to do some more work. Some "creative accounting" was required and by juggling most of the costs at Deal on to other projects the figures were reworked so that Deal conveniently came out slightly cheaper than the alternatives. Ministers were happy and the Civil Service could carry on with the task of putting the new school at Deal. Latest indications are that costs have continued to rise and no work has started on converting the site. In December 1985 Sir Clive Whitmore admitted to the Public Accounts Committee that the decision to go to Deal was entirely political.

Conclusion

After three years' work originally intended to save money and improve efficiency the Ministry of Defence ended up with a plan to spend more money to put a new school, disliked by all three Services, at a politically convenient location that had originally been rejected by Ministers. This example, though only a minor incident in the day-to-day life of Whitehall, illustrates many features of the system: the length of time taken to reach any decision, the strength of powerful vested interests within the system, the illogical ways in which Ministers take decisions, and their real values and attitude to spending public money when crucial choices have to be made. Political expediency dominates everything else.

CHAPTER SEVEN

Whitehall Defeats the Critics

Over the past twenty years there have been numerous attempts to reform the way in which Whitehall works. At different times the focus has been on the organisation of the Civil Service, the level of secrecy, and on efforts to improve efficiency. All of these attempts have failed to produce fundamental change and the Whitehall system has remained unaltered in its essentials. The rhetoric may have changed, lip service may be paid to modernising the Civil Service or to better management and greater efficiency, but the underlying reality is unaffected. The ability of the system to withstand these outside attacks demonstrates its inherent strength and its capacity to neutralise those who want change. The top Civil Service has never had any desire to fundamentally alter the system, indeed to do so would remove much of its power. It has been adept at the old Whitehall arts of agreeing change only "in principle", arguing about practicalities, slowing up the pace of decision-taking and dividing up fundamental issues into a vast number of small questions so that the overriding strategic question is forgotten. In this process the top Civil Service has been assisted by the politicians who have been unable to devise a long-term strategy or remain interested in a subject for more than a few months at a time.

This chapter will demonstrate the enormous difficulties facing any future government determined to reform Whitehall. The first part deals with the attempts to reform the structure of the Civil Service, in particular the Fulton Report and why it was never implemented. The second part looks at the attempts to reduce the level of secrecy and introduce some form of freedom of information. The third part investigates the attempts to improve the efficiency of the Civil Service and examines in particular the policy of the Thatcher government towards Whitehall.

I – Reforming the Whitehall Structure

The Fulton Committee

In 1966 Harold Wilson decided to call in an old crony from his wartime days as a temporary civil servant – Lord Fulton, now Vice-Chancellor of Sussex University – to head an enquiry into the Civil Service. The idea of reforming Whitehall fitted in with the image that Wilson liked to project – the moderniser of Britain's institutions. There had been a growing chorus of criticism of the top Civil Service, particularly from the left, exemplified in a 1964 Fabian pamphlet from Lord Balogh which castigated the "dilettantes of the administration class" with their "jejune amateurism".

The work of the Fulton Committee was hamstrung from the start in two crucial aspects. First, and more important, its terms of reference deliberately excluded any consideration of the structure of government. As Harold Wilson said when announcing the setting up of the Committee:

> The Government's willingness to consider changes in the Civil Service does not imply any intention on its part to alter the basic relationship between Ministers and Civil Servants.

This meant that any serious look at how Whitehall functioned was impossible and that the report was bound to be restricted to suggesting limited structural reforms within the Civil Service. This was the first important victory for the mandarins, who had drafted the terms of reference, and who clearly hoped in this way to limit the scope for real change.

The second limiting factor was the presence on the Committee of four senior civil servants. This was the first time that civil servants had been allowed to sit on a committee or Royal Commission investigating the Civil Service. They were bound to act as a brake on the work of the Committee and trim back the more extreme recommendations. The Secretary of the Committee, who would draft much of the report and the crucial recommendations, was also a civil servant. Apart from Lord Fulton, the key figure on the Committee was Dr. Norman Hunt, an Oxford politics lecturer who was close to Wilson and was later to serve in the 1974–76 Labour government as Lord Crowther-Hunt.

The Report of the Fulton Committee

The report of the Fulton Committee is a paradoxical document in that its findings are not matched by its recommendations. The signs of a compromise are clear. The first chapter is a scathing attack on the administrative class, and it is this radical section that attracted most public attention. The civil servants on the Committee were obviously prepared to agree to this because the rest of the report is much more conservative and the actual recommendations at the end of the report are even less controversial.

The Report started with bold statements about the need for reform:

> The Home Civil Service today is still fundamentally the product of the nineteenth-century philosophy of the Northcote-Trevelyan Report. The tasks it faces are those of the second half of the twentieth century. This is what we have found; it is what we seek to remedy ... the structure and practices of the Service have not kept up with changing tasks. The defects we have found can nearly all be attributed to this ... the Service is in need of fundamental change.[2]

It then went on to identify a number of inadequacies in the Civil Service but included a general criticism that was to cause high blood pressure among the mandarins – "the service is still essentially based on the philosophy of the amateur". This was a severe blow to the self-esteem of the mandarins who regarded themselves as "professionals" in the "art of government". It meant that much of the reaction to the report was emotional rather than rational. Fulton continued by describing this amateurism in more detail:

> The ideal administrator is still too often seen as the gifted layman who, moving frequently from job to job within the Service, can take a practical view of any problem, irrespective of its subject-matter, in the light of his knowledge and experience of the government machine.[3]

In Fulton's view domination of the Service by the administrators brought grave disadvantages:

> The present system of classes in the Service seriously impedes its work ... many scientists, engineers and members of specialist classes get neither the full responsibilities and corresponding authority, nor the opportunities they ought to have.[4]

The ethos of the Civil Service also produced damaging effects:

> Too few civil servants are skilled managers ... (administrators) tend to think of themselves as advisers on policy to people above them, rather than as managers of the administrative machine below them ... civil servants are moved too frequently between unrelated jobs, often with scant regard to personal preference or aptitude ... there is not enough contact between the Service and the rest of the community.[5]

Fulton had correctly identified the basic weaknesses of the Civil Service, but these radical criticisms were not followed through into radical recommendations for change. The administrative class was not to be abolished, but modified. Fulton proposed that the administrative class should continue, but grouped into two categories, and administrators would specialise in either economic and financial jobs or social administration. They would receive appropriate training and be recruited only to do a specific range of jobs in a particular area of work. On recruitment the majority view was that preference should be given to a relevant degree. Predictably the mandarins on the Committee dissented from this recommendation. To improve training, a Civil Service College should be set up which would also have a research function in public administration. Inside the Civil Service there should be a fundamental change in structure involving formal abolition of all classes and introduction of a single grading structure. The old division between administrators and the rest would go. There should also be much greater movement in and out of the Civil Service with short-term appointments and people joining in mid-career. The level of secrecy was also to be reduced. To oversee all these changes a new Whitehall department – the Civil Service Department – was to be established.

The Cabinet Discusses Fulton

The Fulton Report was ready in June 1968. Before it was considered by the Cabinet, Fulton and Norman Hunt saw Wilson and secured his agreement to some of the main proposals. However, the Cabinet when it discussed the report was much less enthusiastic. Barbara Castle left the meeting to keep a more important lunch appointment with the editor of *The Times*[6] and Roy Jenkins, Denis Healey, Michael Stewart and Dick Crossman were all opposed to accepting the main recommendations. Crossman wrote in his diary:

> All the support Harold got was from Wedgy Benn and Peter Shore, his two hirelings. He was so upset that at this point he stopped the meeting and asked that it should be resumed later. I'm pretty sure that the reason he [Wilson] has committed himself to this report so early and so personally is partly because he thinks this way he can improve his image as a great moderniser.[7]

Five days later the Cabinet took up the discussion again. This time there was little opposition, and little interest in the Report; as usual a presentational success was more important than a carefully thought out administrative reform:

> Harold started on the Fulton report, where we gave him a very easy time. It's a second-rate report written in a very poor style by Norman Hunt ... However, it's been a success with the press and the public. Harold needed a success for himself and Cabinet consented to his getting it with a Statement tomorrow.[8]

Wilson's statement generally accepted the report and announced the setting up of the Civil Service Department and Civil Service College. This however was only the first and easiest stage. The most difficult part, ensuring that the Fulton reforms were actually implemented, lay ahead. This process would be very largely in the hands of the Civil Service and the top mandarins. The way in which they refused to implement

Fulton, apart from a few cosmetic changes, is an object lesson for all those who believe that the Civil Service is interested in reform and a warning of the obstacles in the way of genuine reform of the Whitehall system.

The Civil Service View of Fulton

The Fulton Report posed a major problem for the top mandarins. They were deeply offended by the criticisms and the use of the phrase "amateur", yet some reform was obviously going to be needed following the government's acceptance of the report. For them the important point was to preserve the essentials of the existing system even if it had to be superficially modified.

Creation of a new Civil Service Department could easily be accepted – it would after all be staffed by civil servants and it would operate within the existing Whitehall system. The reaction of Sir Leo Pliatzky, later Permanent Secretary in the Treasury, was typical and also revealing of the mandarins' contempt for "management" jobs.

> I thought the Fulton Report a loaded piece of work in many respects, but I approved of this measure [the creation of CSD] since, like many other Treasury people, I was relieved not to be at risk any longer of being shifted back on to Establishments work as my next posting in the Treasury.[9]

Similarly, creation of the Civil Service College posed few problems. It would be under Whitehall control and indeed the Treasury had already proposed the establishment of such a college a year before the Fulton Report.[10]

Abolition of the class structure inside the Civil Service was however seen as a threat to Civil Service civilisation as the mandarins knew it. The administrative élite can only survive as long as it controls the top jobs and keeps out others (the "specialists"). If the recruitment system is changed or if there is free movement within Whitehall, the long-term future of the administrators is bleak. In any opening up of the system the movement is bound to be all one way – "specialists" take over jobs from administrators and not the other way round. Sir William Armstrong was clear about this when he said to Wilson during their first discussion of the Fulton Report:

It isn't practicable, and if you give me a chance I would hope to be able to demonstrate it. I'm with you on getting rid of unnecessary obstacles from bottom to top. But it isn't on for doctors, lawyers or engineers to become administrators. The traffic would be all one way.[11]

It is instructive to look at what the mandarins thought should happen to the structure of the Civil Service. When the Treasury gave evidence to the Fulton Committee it had suggested its own reforms. They had proposed that the separate Administrative, Executive and Clerical classes should be abolished and be replaced by a single group. This was acceptable to the administrators because it would still keep the "specialists" outside these jobs while opening up the possibility of more movement from bottom to top within the new group. Naturally the administrators would still be in charge of the system and would be able to determine the rate and type of movement and control the chances of executives getting to the top three grades of the Civil Service (Under-Secretary and above). This theoretical opening up posed no problem to the administrators because by the time people reached these grades all their training and experience would only fit them for certain types of job and there was no real threat of "specialists" taking over "administrative" posts. The effect of these changes recommended by the Treasury would be essentially cosmetic; the power of the administrators would remain.

The Fulton Committee appreciated the limitations of such an approach and saw exactly what the mandarins were trying to achieve in recommending it:

> The operation of the present structure has bred over a long period of years, attitudes and practices that are deeply ingrained. Therefore we do not believe that it is sufficient to leave the structure basically as it is; incorporate in it some modifications; and then expect the Service to operate it in a fundamentally new way. This is in essence what the Treasury have proposed ... In our view this partial reform is inadequate.[12]

What is most instructive is that the changes that were actually implemented were those proposed by the Treasury (the man-

darins) and not the recommendations of the Fulton Committee. How the Civil Service, and in particular the Head of the
Civil Service, Sir William Armstrong, achieved this result is
the theme of the next section.

Implementing Fulton

The way in which Fulton was implemented, or in practice not
implemented, is a superb example of the top civil servants'
ability, whilst paying lip service to the concept of the Fulton
Report, to subtly redefine questions in ways favourable to the
administrators. They argued that discussion should concentrate on "practicalities"; they played for time whilst the
politicians lost interest in all the details that would determine
whether Fulton's recommendations would be successfully
carried out.

The degree of concern felt by the administrators at the threat
posed by Fulton is illustrated by the unprecedented step taken
by Sir William Armstrong at the very start. He decided to
involve the Trade Unions and staff associations in working out
the process of implementation. Normally in Whitehall Trade
Unions are kept well away from policy-making and only
consulted after decisions have been made. He stopped
Wilson's statement on 26 June, 1968 from specifically endors-
ing the abolition of classes. Instead it said that there would be
"consultations with the Staff Associations ... so that a practicable system can be prepared for the implementation of the
unified grading structure". This may have looked reasonable
but Armstrong knew that there were irreconcilable differences
between the Unions representing the administrators, executives and clerks on the one side and those representing the
"specialists" on the other. These differences would help to
ensure that Fulton was not implemented.

Armstrong chaired a Committee of the National Whitley
Council (the main negotiating forum with the Unions) which
consisted of eleven generalists and just two specialists. The
problem before them was how to time the removal of the main
barriers to movement within the Civil Service. The first was
the barrier between the administrative, executive and clerical
classes. The Unions representing the latter two groups

favoured removal to create more opportunities for their members. The only chance of implementing what Fulton wanted would be to make implementation of this proposal conditional on the removal of the barrier stopping movement from the specialist to the generalist classes. The executive and clerical Unions were bitterly opposed to these barriers coming down, because it would open their members to competition from the "specialists". The process of unpicking Fulton began with the first report of Armstrong's Committee in February 1969. It rejected as "impracticable" one single radical change to a classless Civil Service with a single unified grading structure though it still, for presentational reasons, subscribed to the aim of getting there eventually. Such a change would have been difficult but not impracticable. When the government accepted this recommendation, the way was open for partial reform, even though all concerned still formally subscribed to the "eventual" achievement of the complete abolition of classes.

Two months later an internal committee on future structure, run by the Treasury, had subtly redefined the problem. The objective now was presented in highly diluted form:

> In particular, professionals need greater opportunity than they now have to manage within their own sphere, to assist in the formulation of policy and to enter general mangement.[13]

This was the antithesis of what Fulton wanted. The Fulton Report sought to end the very idea of separate classes "with their own spheres" and the idea that specialists might merely "assist" in policy formulation. In other areas too the process of diluting or deviating from Fulton was at work. On unified grading Fulton had proposed that it should apply throughout the Civil Service whereas in its evidence to the Committee the Treasury had proposed it only for the top three grades down to Under-Secretary. In 1969 an internal paper on "implementing" Fulton proposed:

> to start at the top of the Service, where it is already proposed to introduce a common grading structure, and to see how far down it can and should [*sic*] be extended.[14]

In November 1969 Sir William Armstrong explained to Wilson what "reforms" would be implemented. The outcome was to be exactly what the Treasury, and the top administrators, had always wanted. There would be unified grading down to Under-Secretary but only "studies" on going further. The Administrative, Executive and Clerical classes would be merged into a single group and there would be similar mergers to create the Scientific and Professional and Technological Groups. This improved mobility within the Groups, but did absolutely nothing to deal with the fundamental proposal by Fulton that there should no longer be such groups. Although the proposals were dressed up for public presentation as the first "practicable" steps towards the Fulton idea, their practical effect would only be to set in concrete the existing divisions within the Civil Service.

In June 1970 the Labour government lost power. What little driving force there was behind the Fulton Report went with it. The Heath government had its own ideas for restructuring Whitehall departments and took little interest in the Fulton proposals. The administrators, having secured their position in the post-Fulton battles, could now concentrate on maintaining this position and gradually winning back some of the concessions that had been forced on them in the late 1960s.

The Reformed Civil Service?

In 1976 and 1977 there was a major investigation into the Civil Service by the House of Commons Expenditure Committee under the Labour MP Michael English. In its comments on the report of that Committee Whitehall said glibly that "acceptance" of Fulton had resulted in "a number of radical changes in the organisation and management of the Civil Service".[15] All the available evidence suggests that there had been virtually no significant change at all in the period since 1968 and that the old-style Civil Service dominated by the administrative amateur still flourished.

1. Fulton recommended that "administrators" should specialise in either social policy or financial and economic policy, and be recruited and trained accordingly. An internal study (never published and conducted entirely by

administrators in charge of personnel policy) concluded within six months of the Fulton report that jobs could not be divided in that way and the old style of recruitment and training of generalist amateurs should continue. Thus within six months of the Fulton report this fundamental recommendation had been rejected.

2. Fulton recommended the abolition of all classes within the Civil Service. Before the report there were 47 general service classes and 1,400 departmental classes. Ten years after the report there were 38 general service classes and 500 departmental classes.

3. Together with the abolition of classes Fulton recommended an "open structure" for employing people within the Service, designed to increase the influence of the "specialists". This was only introduced down to Under-Secretary level and covered just 850 posts out of a total non-industrial Civil Service of 570,000. It was not until 1984 that it was extended down to the next grade – Assistant Secretary.

4. Whitehall argued that 40% of these posts in the Open Structure were held by specialists but neglected to mention that exactly the same percentage was held by specialists before Fulton because the "open structure" includes automatically posts at the top of the specialist career structure for solicitors, scientists, actuaries etc.

5. A new group of "open opportunity" posts was introduced that could be held by either specialists or administrators. This covered exactly 0.2% of the jobs in the Civil Service and half of these were filled by administrators anyway.

6. A new scheme to train specialists in "administration" early in their careers was introduced in 1972. (Yet again the opposite of what Fulton wanted.) Its impact was minimal since it only involved twenty-five people a year.

7. Fulton wanted a massive expansion of recruitment in mid-career to open up the Civil Service to able outsiders with relevant experience. A very limited scheme was introduced but quickly dropped under convenient pressure from the Trade Unions as Civil Service numbers were reduced.

8. Fulton wanted a powerful highly-trained group of

accountants in the Civil Service. It took three years from the Fulton Report to commission another study on the subject which was not completed till 1973. It then took another two years to appoint a head of the accountancy service. A year before the Fulton report there were just 309 accountants in the Civil Service. By 1979 there were 364.

9. Fulton wanted to amalgamate the two functions of staff inspection and organisation and methods (O & M) to create a single powerful group that could improve efficiency inside Whitehall. The Civil Service did not like this idea as the Head of the Civil Service (Sir Douglas Allen) explained to the English Committee:

> In the discussions which took place in the two or three years after the Fulton Committee reported ... the Service [*sic*] felt that it was best to leave things as they were.[16]

10. Fulton suggested a committee with "one or two eminent people from outside the Service" to advise on appointments at Permanent Secretary level. The Committee was set up but it has never had any outside members.

In virtually every area Whitehall paid lip service to the Fulton ideas, claimed in public that they were being implemented, but in practice ensured that they were not. Two further examples – the creation of the Civil Service College and the recruitment of young mandarins – illustrate the methods used to bring this about.

The Civil Service College

Fulton had two aims for the Civil Service College. First, to radically improve the level of training and expertise of the Civil Service and in particular the top administrators. Second, to provide a body, like a university, that would undertake academic research in public administration. The top mandarins distrusted both aims. Training had never been taken seriously and experience "on the job" had always been thought to be more important. The idea that academics might investigate the workings of Whitehall was also anathema.

The Civil Service College was set up but placed under the

close control of the Civil Service Department. Academics were appointed but all on short-term contracts. Posts at Assistant Secretary level and above were held by administrators who decided on the teaching programme and syllabus for each course. There was no assessment of students on courses and the academic lecturers were therefore left with a minimal role. As one of them described the position to the English Committee:

> academics find themselves increasingly in the position of specialist advisers to be called on at the discretion of generalist administrators.[17]

Not surprisingly in these circumstances, the general quality of the academic staff was low.

No coherent research programme on public administration was ever devised and in the few studies that did take place the Civil Service Department had strong objections to publication of the results. To make assurance doubly sure the administrators also controlled the College through an Advisory Board which met twice a year and ensured that the College was kept "on the rails".

The teaching programme at the College remained a motley collection of courses ranging from training administrators in basic economics and statistics, to data processing and language training. Ninety per cent of Civil Service training continued to be undertaken within individual departments and, of the ten per cent that the Civil Service College was responsible for, one-fifth was specialist computer training. The College quickly lost any sense of coherence as an investigation five years after it was established reported:

> It is as though the same institution were expected to combine the roles of All Souls and an adult education centre, with some elements of technical education and teacher training thrown in for good measure.[18]

In the late 1970s the volume of training, particularly of young administrators, declined. This trend was reinforced by the Thatcher government when the College was instructed to charge departments for training their staff. The enthusiasm of departments to send their staff away to be trained, which had always been strictly limited, waned even further. Instead of fulfilling Fulton's idea of a reforming and academic institution, the Civil Service College was left as a quiet Whitehall backwater.

Recruiting Young Administrators

In the wake of the Fulton report the recruitment process for young administrators was altered. The existing biased selection system at CSSB (described in Chapter 3) would be maintained but from 1971 the minimum standard would be lowered and about three times as many candidates would be passed. They would then be tested for about two to three years in various jobs within departments. Those "fast-streamed" would follow the old administrative path with rapid promotion to Principal in their late twenties and Assistant Secretary at about thirty-five. Those "main-streamed" would join the old executive grades as Higher Executive Officers and might make Principal by their mid- to late-thirties. More candidates from inside the Service would be encouraged to go through the CSSB process with its subsequent chance of "fast-streaming". In practice the system discriminated against people inside the Service trying to join administrators. About 85–90% of the external candidates passed by CSSB reached the fast-stream but only 50% of the internal candidates. Internal candidates were moreover only a small proportion of those passed each year by CSSB (often as low as 12%).

Even these limited changes were disliked by the mandarins. The broader selection system threatened to undermine the élitist administrative class. In 1977 a Committee was set up to review the new scheme. Its composition shows the domination of Whitehall by the administrators and their ability to determine their own future. The Committee had twelve members, one academic, one ex-personnel director from a clearing bank and ten administrators. The result was predictable. The Committee noticed that as the graduate job market had become more difficult the proportion of graduates joining as Executive Officers (the bottom of the executive class) had risen from 5% in 1965 to 48% in 1979. These people they argued, in true élitist fashion, could fill "middle management posts". But there should also be an "improved development procedure" for executive officers. This spectacular advance might mean that about 1% of them could move into the fast stream. Having thus dismissed the bulk of the Civil Service, the Committee recommended that recruitment through CSSB to the administrative class should revert to its old pattern. Numbers would be cut back to their former level and all would be virtually guaranteed a future in the fast stream as the new élite of the Civil Service. So within ten years the administrators had re-established the historic system under which they had themselves been recruited and ensured the continued domination of the public-school, Oxbridge-educated élite.[19]

Political Advisers

In the past twenty years Ministers have turned increasingly to the use of political advisers in an attempt to reduce the power of the Civil Service within the Whitehall machine, and to reform the structure of Whitehall. Yet again the result has been all too predictable. A few scattered advisers seeing papers at the last moment as they are submitted to Ministers have been unable to influence the policy-making process within the Civil Service. Their impact has been marginal.

The Civil Service has been ruthless in excluding political advisers from positions of real power. Under Harold Wilson, Marcia Williams, his political secretary, and Tommy Balogh, the economic adviser to the Cabinet, fought long-running, and in the end unsuccessful, battles to gain access to papers coming from the Civil Service to Ministers. In 1974 Labour came into power with a number of political advisers to Cabinet Ministers; and, at the same time, the political staff at No. 10 was expanded into a Policy Unit under Bernard Donoughue. Mrs. Thatcher carried on the role of the Policy Unit, although the first choice to head the Unit – Sir John Hoskyns – resigned over what he saw as the failure of the government to tackle the entrenched position of the Civil Service. This small band of political advisers has been able to act as a link between the Ministers and party thinking but, not unexpectedly, a mere handful of people has been powerless to change the way in which Whitehall works.

How has the Civil Service viewed such a development? At first it seemed alarming. Outsiders would be trespassing on the one area reserved for the top administrators – "policy advice" to Ministers. This might be the thin end of the wedge for the position of the administrative class. After this initial concern the mandarins soon realised that they could absorb this new threat and largely neutralise it. Political advisers were excluded from the details of departmental work and left to act virtually as extra members of the Ministers' private offices. By the early 1980s Sir Patrick Nairne could dismiss their role as giving "a kind of extra edge, a sort of extra tang when it came to speech writing".[20] If this is the role of political advisers then it poses no threat to the long-term position of the administrative class.

II – Breaking Down Whitehall Secrecy[21]

The Fulton Committee, as well as attacking the entrenched position of the administrators, also attacked the cult of official secrecy. Its analysis of the way in which Whitehall worked was devastatingly accurate:

> The increasingly wide range of problems handled by Government, and their far-reaching effects upon the community as a whole, demand the widest possible consultation with its different parts and interests ... It is healthy for a democracy increasingly to press to be consulted and informed. There are still too many occasions when information is unnecessarily withheld and consultation merely perfunctory ... It is an abuse of consultation when it is turned into a belated attempt to prepare the ground for decisions that in reality have been taken already.

Whitehall reacted predictably to this criticism. In 1969 there was a White Paper, "Information and the Public Interest". It enshrines the complacent introverted Whitehall view that has remained unchanged ever since. The White Paper had been prepared, it was proudly claimed, "on a wide inter-departmental basis", but there had been no consultation with outside interests and Whitehall had reassured itself that everything was satisfactory because more "information" was being published. But, as we have seen most of the information given out by Whitehall is really propaganda designed to back up decisions already taken in secrecy within the bureaucracy. On every occasion since the late 1960s Whitehall has repeated the view that information is what Whitehall chooses to release to the public and not what the public may want to know.

The Franks Committee

As we have seen the Official Secrets Act is at the heart of Whitehall secrecy. After an unsuccessful prosecution of Jonathan Aitken and the *Sunday Telegraph* in 1971 for publishing an official report on British assistance to the federal government in the Nigerian civil war, the government announced a full-scale enquiry into the operation of Section 2 of the Official Secrets Act.

The Committee was composed of the usual collection of the "great and good", headed by Lord Franks. Its report was surprisingly blunt:

> We found Section 2 a mess. Its scope is enormously wide. Any law which impinges on the freedom of information in a democracy should be much more tightly drawn. The drafting and interpretation of the section are obscure. People are not sure what it means, or how it operates in practice, or what kinds of action involve real risk of prosecution under it.

The Committee proposed that Section 2 should be replaced by a new Official Information Act. This would restrict the use of the criminal law to information classified "secret" or higher; in other words information that genuinely affects the security and interests of the country. Any civil servant who "leaked" information with a lower classification would be dealt with under disciplinary rules. These proposals were far removed from any concept of "freedom of information" or the right of people to know what was going on inside Whitehall. They were more in the nature of an administrative tidying up of a confused piece of legislation.

Nevertheless the very idea that the system of official secrecy might be reformed has been strenuously opposed by Whitehall. The prospect of freedom of information causes even greater alarm. Reform of the existing system would undermine the position of the Civil Service and its ability to restrict debate to a small circle of insiders. That is why it has fought long and hard to stop any change. In this it has been aided by politicans who, once they are inside the system, reject any idea of letting the opposition have freer access to information that might be useful. Whatever its views in opposition each new administration operates the Whitehall system to its own advantage and wants to keep it that way.

Freedom of Information?

The Heath government did nothing to implement the Franks Report before it lost the February 1974 election. The new Labour government was committed not only to reform of the Official Secrets Act but also to freedom of information. As the October 1974 election manifesto put it:

> We shall: Replace the Official Secrets Act by a measure to put the burden on the public authorities to justify withholding information.

That promise was never carried out.

In late 1974 Wilson set up a Cabinet Committee (MISC 89) chaired by the Home Secretary, Roy Jenkins, to decide what to do. After a visit to the United States which apparently supported the Civil Service view that freedom of information would be costly and difficult to administer, work continued in the Committee but with a growing lack of enthusiasm. Ministers were doubtful and the top civil servants did everything they could to encourage these doubts and hesitations. Although the Queen's Speech still promised legislation, nothing more happened before Wilson resigned in April 1976 and was replaced by Jim Callaghan. Callaghan was well known for his lack of enthusiasm for any reform in this area. He set up another Committee (GEN 29) to work on more proposals. The first result was that, although reform of the Official Secrets Act, as proposed by Franks, was still promised in yet another Queen's Speech in 1976, freedom of information was officially dead. Instead, there was to be a new voluntary policy of disclosure by Whitehall of information it thought might help public debate. But Whitehall was to be judge and jury in deciding what to release and, as Callaghan himself said, in a classic understatement:

> The cost to public funds is a factor here and we should like to keep that cost to a minimum. Therefore, arrangements will not be of a luxurious nature.[22]

The Croham Directive

The tepid enthusiasm within Whitehall for even this limited move is demonstrated by the fact that it took six months to issue any instructions about the new policy. These were contained in a letter from Sir Douglas Allen (later Lord Croham), the Head of the Civil Service, to all other Permanent Secretaries.[23] In true Whitehall fashion this was an internal document and only became publicly available when it was leaked to the press.

The letter set out at length every conceivable objection to the new policy, including obscure subjects such as Crown Copyright. The new policy was that background papers, provided they were unclassified, could now be made public, if Ministers agreed. But, as the directive made clear, "the initial step is modest", and Ministers would still decide exactly how much information would be released. This was little more than the old policy under a new guise to make it look more respectable. The main aim was to avoid moving to freedom of information. The hidden consensus behind the draft is made clear in the choice of certain phrases in the document:

> There are many who would have wanted the Government to go much further (on the lines of the formidably burdensome Freedom of Information Act in the USA). *Our* prospects of being able to avoid such an expensive development...

The prospects for the new policy were not good if even this letter could not be published. Within a year the new arrangements were shown to be a farce. On two occasions, Peter Hennessy, the Whitehall correspondent of *The Times*, asked to see the background papers behind White Papers. The first coincided with the response to the Expenditure Committee report on the Civil Service and the second with the July 1978 White Paper on reform of official secrecy. Hennessy was told that there were no background papers in either case. This was obviously untrue as no White Paper can be written without background papers.

The only impact of the Croham Directive was that the scale of government propaganda was stepped up. Genuine information was not released but instead specially prepared material designed to back up decisions that had already been taken inside Whitehall was increasingly produced under the guise of "information". Little else happened for the rest of the life of the Labour government. Promises were continually made that the Official Secrets Act would be reformed but no proposals were ever put forward. The two manifesto commitments in 1974 were never implemented.

The Thatcher Government

As we have seen in Chapter 1 the Tories in opposition were prepared to make political capital out of Labour's failure to reform the Official Secrets Act. Mrs. Thatcher had made her own views plain during her visit, as Leader of the Opposition, to the USA.

Asked whether Britain had anything to learn from the greater openness of American government her surprising response was:

Nothing at all; our system is much more open than the American one.

And on reform of the Official Secrets Act she added:

It should be reformed, but only to make some of its provisions against the unauthorised disclosure of official information stronger, not weaker.[24]

On gaining power in 1979 the Tories did introduce a bill to reform the Official Secrets Act. This was what the Civil Service had always wanted. The title – The *Protection* of Official Information Bill – said much and, although it did adopt the Franks recommendation that criminal sanctions should only apply to the unauthorised release of information classified secret or higher, it also contained startling new, and highly restrictive, proposals. Even to discuss some topics, such as the existence of MI5 and MI6 or the possibility of phone tapping, would be a criminal offence and it would not be a defence in law to show that the information had already been published.

The Bill generated such a storm of protest that it had to be withdrawn. This was all that Whitehall needed to ignore the subject altogether. Ministers were content with the existing system and never had any intention of introducing Freedom of Information. Instead, they used the Official Secrets Act more and more in a vain attempt to stop "leaks" of information embarrassing to the Government. The top mandarins in Whitehall had no interest in reforming the Official Secrets Act and were also content to leave the system as it was. Once again the entrenched Whitehall system had beaten off demands for reform.

The Crossman Affair

Official secrecy and accepted Whitehall traditions came under strong attack from another quarter. As we have seen, Dick Crossman kept a detailed diary of his time as a Cabinet Minister from 1964 to 1970. He had done this deliberately, with the knowledge of his colleagues, with the aim, as the historian of the whole affair put it:

> to blow apart the tradition of secrecy in British government and destroy the conventions which had rendered innocuous or misleading, or both, the writings of most former Cabinet Ministers about their time in office.[25]

Crossman regarded the diaries as his great legacy and was determined they should be published. He had agreed with Harold Wilson that they would not be published before the 1974 Election and, when he died, the onus was on his literary executors.

The diaries were submitted to Sir John Hunt, Secretary to the Cabinet, for clearance, as Crossman had always intended. Crossman, and later his executors, was prepared to take advice on genuine matters of national security but nothing else. Hunt immediately rejected outright any possibility of publication.

He argued that "in the public interest" rules had "evolved" and been accepted – which meant that Ministers were "entitled to put their own version of events on record", but this had to be done in such a way that it did "not endanger good government". Under pressure to define what he meant, Hunt set out what he called four "parameters", which encapsulate the Whitehall view of good behaviour and suitable reticence. There could be no material that disclosed "blow-by-blow" accounts of Cabinet meetings, or advice by the Civil Service or discussion of Civil Service appointments; and no record of private discussions between Ministers, or between Ministers and civil servants. Acceptance of these conditions would have neutered the diaries, but preserved the convenient myth of the smoothly-oiled Whitehall machine that should not be exposed to the profane eyes of the public.

The problem for Hunt was that there was no clear law on the subject, none of these conventions was written down, and everything depended on the acceptance of unwritten rules by the "good chaps" inside the system. After a great deal of abortive bargaining with Hunt, the *Sunday Times* started serialisation of the diaries. The government decided against using the Official Secrets Act and instead proceeded under civil law with an injunction to stop a breach of confidence.

The trial took place before the Lord Chief Justice, Lord Widgery, in July 1975. It was a fascinating battle between the establishment conventions of Whitehall and the claims of the outside world. The basis of the government case against publication was that there were certain rules of behaviour to protect "good government". As these did not exist, they had been invented – Sir John Hunt had to admit that, unfortunately, they had not been written down before the Crossman case, and that other publications such as Harold Wilson's own account of the 1964–70 government and the Lloyd George and Churchill war memoirs breached these "rules". What in essence the Whitehall establishment was saying was that everybody inside the system knew what life was really like in Whitehall, but that there was a general agreement that the public should not know until all those concerned had left public life, with their reputations intact; in other words, a record of events should be delayed until it was solely of academic interest to historians.

Surprisingly, and to the consternation of Whitehall, Widgery found in favour of Crossman. He agreed about the need for collective responsibility and the confidentiality of Cabinet discussions but felt that eleven years after the events the publication of Crossman's diaries would not affect the way government was conducted in the late 1970s.

The Establishment Strikes Back

Immediately after this judgement, a Committee was set up to review the rules on Ministerial memoirs and to try to prevent any more Crossmans. It was chaired by a well-known Conservative Judge, Viscount Radcliffe, and other members included Lord Franks, the former Head of the Civil Service Lord Armstrong, and various senior retired politicians.

The Committee report, published in January 1976,[26] first of all attacked Lord Widgery. Their findings:

> do not lead us to think that a Judge is likely to be so equipped as to make him the best arbiter of the issues involved. The relevant considerations are political and administrative.

The Committee accepted all Sir John Hunt's "parameters" and then devised a new fifteen year rule against publication. Ministers would have an "obligation" to follow such a rule, consult the Secretary to the Cabinet and "listen carefully" to what he said, even though the rule had no legal force. The Committee concluded with a superb statement of the establishment ethos:

> There can be no guarantee that, if the burden of compliance is left to rest on the free acceptance of an obligation of honour, there will never be an occasional rebel or an occasional breach; but so long as there remains a general recognition of the practical necessity of some rules and the importance of observing them, the Committee do not think that such transgressions, even though made the subject of sensational publicity, should be taken as having shattered the fabric of a sensible system.[27]

In other words, there may be the odd cad or bounder like Crossman but the "good chaps" will ignore him and continue to play by the unwritten public school rules, and stick together in true "team spirit" because they all have a lot to lose.

III – Efficiency and Thatcher's Whitehall

From the mid-1960s an increasingly important theme of the critics of Whitehall has been the inefficiency of the Civil Service. The response of the top Civil Service to these criticisms has been to admit that everything may not be absolutely perfect, but then to argue that there are a number of special factors making it very difficult for the Civil Service to be ultra-efficient. One or two new techniques are introduced, and for a short while are regarded as a panacea, but they are soon absorbed and neutered by the Whitehall machine. The mandarins pay lip-service to the idea of improving efficiency but, as we have already seen, they are not genuinely interested in management problems, regard them as of secondary important to "policy-making" with Ministers, and proposals for radical change are rarely implemented.

Staff Inspection and Management Reviews

The standard Whitehall system for assessing the number of staff needed to do a job is staff inspection. Each department uses civil servants temporarily deployed to investigate an area and by some mysterious rule-of-thumb procedure work out how many staff are needed to do the job. In 1947 the Treasury had asked each Whitehall department "to develop an efficient system of staff inspection". In 1964 a Parliamentary Committee found this remit had never been carried out and asked for every post in the Civil Service to be reviewed every three to five years. Ten years later two further reports concluded that not a single department had an effective system of staff inspection. The scale of the problem was illustrated by one report on the Driver and Vehicle Licensing Centre at Swansea which found that about a third of the posts could be abolished and that "much of the staff's time is spent sitting around for work to arrive".[28]

Even where staff inspection was carried out, the basic flaw was that no solution could be imposed. Nobody was obliged to implement the report, and endless time was spent arguing about individual posts, usually resulting in a compromise where one or two jobs at most would be abolished.

Similarly, the teams who advised on management methods were only called in by heads of division if they thought they had a problem, and even then the reports were still advisory. The teams were not allowed to pick the more obviously inefficient areas, carry out an investigation and impose a solution. Civil Service rules are too gentlemanly to allow such conduct. A third separate organisation – internal audit – existed to look at the efficiency of departments. They too had little power and were often disorganised. For example, the DHSS Statutory Sick Pay Scheme was subject to investigation by six different organisations because of overlapping responsibilities.

Following the Fulton Report, Whitehall introduced a new form of investigation – the Management Review. As with all such schemes it was greeted in public with a flourish as a panacea for reforming Whitehall, but the actual results were minimal. The review of departmental organisation was chaired by the Permanent Secretary and carried out by officials of the department concerned with the Civil Service Department taking part in each review as "outsiders". There were rarely any professional management and organisation specialists on the teams. The reviews concentrated on questions of departmental organisation rather than efficiency. Basic questions were seldom asked. For example, the Inland Revenue review did not even consider the fundamental question of how much it cost to collect different taxes.

In 1976 there was a Management Review of the Ministry of Defence. It lasted almost a year, masses of evidence were accumulated, eight separate teams investigated different areas of the department. The impression was given of a major and fundamental review. Yet the results were mouselike in their insignificance: one or two jobs abolished, and one or two minor changes in the organisation. This pattern of vast effort, the impression of fundamental analysis and review followed by minimal changes, is typical of Whitehall. The mandarins are not interested in management or in radical change in traditional organisation, but they realise that occasionally they have to be seen to go through the motions and at the end implement a few relatively minor changes just to show willing.

"Your Disobedient Servant"

In 1978 an ex-Assistant Secretary in the Property Service Agency, Leslie Chapman, published a book *Your Disobedient Servant* about his attempts to improve efficiency in one area of its work.[29] In 1967 Chapman was in charge of the Southern Region of PSA and started an investigation into whether every job really needed to be done. In the usual Civil Service fashion he was assured by everyone under him that the system was working as well and as efficiently as possible. He was suspicious and set up small teams to investigate what was really going on. The first study was of the Army Stores depot at Bicester. They found that the grass was cut to lawn standards even under pipes and cables, that empty warehouses were heated to office standards and that inter-city standards applied to the depot railway. Every other study revealed the same pattern, with potential savings of 30% in expenditure and 40 to 50% cuts in staff employed.

Naturally, full of enthusiasm to see this cost-cutting success repeated elsewhere, Chapman suggested that other regions should take up his ideas. None did. Successive Ministers were also enthusiastic when they heard of what had been achieved and asked for this new technique to be applied everywhere, but they were rarely in the job for very long and were not able to keep up the pressure on the mandarins to make sure the ideas were implemented. The top Civil Service did not share the enthusiasm for eliminating the obvious waste in the organisation, and after continually pressing for his ideas to be implemented Chapman resigned from the Civil Service. When he resigned he sent a full dossier on the whole affair to the Head of the Civil Service, Sir William Armstrong. He received a reply from Armstrong's private secretary couched in a typically dismissive style that shows the lack of any desire in the top Civil Service for an efficiency drive:

> I write to acknowledge your letter and enclosures of 20 December to Sir William Armstrong. These have been read with interest.[30]

No other action was taken. Chapman left the Civil Service to take up farming and became an independent adviser on "efficiency".

Enter Sir Derek Rayner

Chapman's book did, however, have an influence on the Conservative opposition and on Mrs. Thatcher. The Tories had always been suspicious of the public sector and under Mrs. Thatcher this suspicion had grown into real concern about the ability of the Civil Service, with its desire for outdated consensus politics, to thwart a radical government. Chapman's book fuelled all these feelings and the determination of Mrs. Thatcher to improve the efficiency of the public sector. Despite a number of meetings between Chapman and Mrs. Thatcher, it was Sir Derek Rayner of Marks and Spencer, who had also worked in Whitehall on the reorganisation of defence procurement under the Heath government, who was chosen to lead the new efficiency drive. In June 1979 Rayner was put in charge of a small Efficiency Unit reporting directly to the Prime Minister.

Each department was asked to choose one young Principal to work with Sir Derek and to investigate a particular area of activity. The investigation was to take just two months, and basic questions were to be asked about whether the work should be done at all and, if so, how it could be streamlined. The reports would go direct to a Minister in the department and to Sir Derek, without interference from the top civil servants in the department or those responsible for the area investigated.

I was given the task of looking at how the Armed Services obtained all their food. When the studies were complete Rayner held a two-day seminar at the Civil Service College at Sunningdale. The results were fascinating. Every study and every area investigated had shown major inefficiencies and defects in administration. It was after this seminar that I was asked, together with Norman Warner, who had run the DHSS study, to accompany Sir Derek when he saw the Prime Minister to report on his investigations into Whitehall efficiency. Norman Warner and I told the Prime Minister about the details of our studies and, full of enthusiasm, she asked us to repeat these presentations to a full Cabinet Meeting later in the week. At this, the Cabinet proved equally keen as we described the inefficiencies of Whitehall. This was just what they wanted to hear and confirmed their strongly-held suspicions about the public sector. The Rayner strategy was endorsed as the way to bring about lasting change in Whitehall and its philosophy.

Implementing Rayner

Sir Derek Rayner was well aware that the cupboards and filing cabinets of Whitehall are full of reports advocating radical change, nearly all of which have never been implemented and have simply been left to gather dust. His idea of getting round this problem was the "action plan" for implementing the report which he was to agree personally. Nevertheless, he underestimated the ability of Whitehall not to implement reports that were disliked for criticising the accepted ways of working. The classic Whitehall response follows a fairly predictable sequence. The department will generally welcome a report, argue that a detailed study is required, and then set up a committee to report on possible implementation of the proposed changes. Those responsible for the existing, criticised system will be well represented on this committee and psychologically opposed to major changes. After a few months a report is produced saying that some, but not all, of the proposed changes should be workable but need further study. A number of sub-committees are convened to look at all these detailed areas. Each report takes a long time, Ministers may have moved on, or become interested in other areas, there are difficulties about implementation and possibly more studies are needed. After a couple of years or so everything has been so much reduced to questions of detail that the general problem has been largely forgotten. A few minor changes can be implemented as the "first steps" towards the full reform package. Gradually the whole process grinds into the sand of bureaucratic inertia and little, if anything, is achieved. By this time also, it is possible to argue that developments elsewhere mean that the proposed changes have been overtaken by events or those working in the area have been studied so much that they need a "period of stability to get on with the job"; and that further studies should be abandoned.

It is worth looking at the two studies presented to the Prime Minister and the Cabinet to see what happened even to those reports that had backing at the highest level. Norman Warner investigated the way in which social security benefits were paid and in particular the use of the Post Office. He had recommended savings worth £66 million a year and a major reduction in the role of the Post Office. This was known to be politically difficult because a number of local offices might shut. Nevertheless Mrs. Thatcher had assured Warner that the government was determined to take difficult decisions to improve efficiency.[31] Three months later, after a parliamentary row, Mrs. Thatcher told the House of Commons that retirement pensions would continue to be paid weekly, thus immediately losing 40% of the planned savings. An internal Whitehall group was set up to look at the future of the Post Office and the House of Commons Social Services Committee investigated the new scheme. As a result the planned savings were reduced further to £38 million. Eighteen months after the Warner study the scale of savings had been cut again, to £32 million or less than half that originally proposed. As the new procedures were being established the Social Security Advisory Committee looked at them and reduced the savings yet again, to £29 million a year. By the time the new and much altered scheme actually started it would save just £10 million a year. All the main features of the previous system had been retained minus one or two minor administrative changes.

It was the same story on my own study into the supply of Food to the Armed Forces.[32] I had found glaring examples of waste and inefficiency everywhere – warehouses full of food that was stored for years, three separate distribution organisations, and nobody in charge of the system. It even took two months to answer a basic question such as the cost of running the system. My report suggested immediate savings of about £12 million and annual savings of about £4 million. A committee was set up, it took six months to report and offered one or two minor concessions before suggesting further work to be carried out by those responsible for operating the existing system. It took another nine months to complete the next stage, and the statistics on the cost of different operations were dubious in the extreme since they had, again, been produced by those in charge of the existing system. Another year of fruitless arguments went by, and another Minister who had not long been in the department was persuaded to end the studies with no changes of any consequence made to the existing, inefficient, system. As he wrote to the Treasury:

> There is much to be said for letting people get on with their jobs now, dispelling the uncertainty which has long hung over this whole area of business.

Shortly after this, Sir Derek (now Lord) Rayner left Whitehall and returned to Marks and Spencer. He had introduced a new system, and some small victories had been won, but Whitehall had absorbed Raynerism, as it had all the other schemes for reform and improving efficiency. In 1985 a report of the Efficiency Unit summed up what had been achieved since 1979:[33] only half the planned savings had been made and even then they had taken twice as long as expected. Officials have been actively opposed to carrying out the studies, and the so-called action plans have usually only been little more than a timescale for taking decisions in the future with no commitment to change anything. Whitehall has seen the whole process as one of "damage limitation", implementing as little as possible but just enough to avoid the accusation of outright obstruction. As one official wrote to the man in charge of an area subject to a Rayner Study:

> I have cleared the action plan, I think it is the minimum we are likely to be able to get away with, and I hope you will feel it is something you can live with.

Thatcher and the Civil Service

The new Conservative government in 1979 did not just intend to improve the efficiency of the public sector. There was a deep antipathy to the Civil Service and the top mandarins and their attitudes. High on the list of the objectives of the new Policy Unit at No. 10 was the attempt to "de-privilege" the Civil Service. This was part of an attitude of Mrs. Thatcher's which was once described by the Tory MP Julian Critchley as: "she cannot see an institution without hitting it with her hand-bag."[34]

The first assault was on the pay system for the Civil Service. This had evolved through two Royal Commissions in 1931 and 1955.[35] The Priestley Royal Commission in 1955 had recommended a pay system in which there was a "fair comparison with the current remuneration of outside staffs employed on broadly comparable work, taking account of differences in other conditions of service".[36] In 1956 an independent Pay Research Unit was set up to make these comparisons between pay in the outside world and Civil Service rates. In general the system worked well and, as the Vice-President of the Royal Statistical Society wrote in 1982 after investigating the system:

> Given the objectives, and the time and resources available, it is difficult to see how a better system could be evolved. No alternatives are readily available.[37]

In October 1980 the Thatcher government unilaterally withdrew from the pay negotiation process and in early 1981 refused to agree to any form of arbitration. This deliberate attack on the twenty-five-year-old pay system accepted by all previous governments, which had not led to Civil Service pay being ahead of the private sector,[38] brought about the longest ever Civil Service strike, from March to July 1981. The strike was not successful because the bulk of civil servants refused to take radical action. The government however was determined to win. When Lord Soames, the Minister responsible for the Civil Service, suggested a compromise he was defeated in Cabinet and then sacked by Mrs. Thatcher in the autumn 1981 reshuffle.

Following the strike, an independent committee was set up to consider a long-term pay system for the Civil Service. It concluded that "it is not possible in the long term to impose pay and conditions of service by fiat".[39] Under pressure from the government, the committee had to recommend a different system from that which had existed from 1956 to 1981. But they still suggested an independent board to undertake pay comparisons with the outside world, and bargaining between government and trade unions over the results of that work, but with greater weight given to the government's ability (or willingness) to pay. The Thatcher government's attempt to introduce a radically new pay system had not succeeded. Instead, they preferred to concentrate on annual negotiations with no agreed long-term solution.

Another area that came under attack was Civil Service index-linked pensions. Public attention was concentrated on the relatively few large pensions of top mandarins and not on the large number of small pensions for lower-paid civil servants. In May 1980 an enquiry was set up to look at the value of the pensions. Its report was a disappointment to the Thatcher government when it argued that the private sector should attempt to emulate the public sector.[40] The government considered whether to attack the system regardless of the report's findings. However, at this stage other, more political, considerations were important. Once it was realised that Civil Service pensions were part of a common system in the public sector also involving favoured groups like the armed forces and the police, and once the numbers now drawing pensions, or expecting to do so, plus their families were added up, the electoral disadvantages of radically altering the system were obvious. The Thatcher government settled for minor alterations to Civil Service pensions.

Cutting the Civil Service

The Thatcher government was, nevertheless, determined to reduce the size of the Civil Service. In May 1979 it decided to go about the process rationally. Each Whitehall department was asked to say how it would cut 10, 15, and 20% of its staff. The result was exactly what any cynic schooled in Whitehall battles would have expected. Departments put forward a few relatively easy cuts at the lowest possible levels and then immediately suggested that major, and highly public, cuts would have to be made to meet the targets in full. For example the Department of Energy said that it would have to end its energy conservation role, and MAFF indicated it would have to virtually stop inspection of horticultural produce. After protracted battles, cuts of just 40,000 (or 5.5%), spread over three years, were agreed. Many of these so-called cuts came from functions such as running Exchange Controls and the Metrication Board that had just been abolished.

Thatcher decided that this was not good enough. She picked an arbitrary target – the Civil Service should by 1984 be the smallest since the Second World War – and imposed it, regardless of the many intervening changes in the role of the public sector. This meant a 14% reduction from 732,000 to 630,000. The global figure was set first and Whitehall departments were then left to argue about who should be cut. When the decision was taken, Ministers had no idea what the cuts would entail. There was no strategy, just a general hack of Civil Service numbers. When in 1984 the 630,000 target was met it was decided to carry on the reductions to 593,000 by 1988, again with little idea of how this would be achieved. Some Ministers like Michael Heseltine tried to improve their image by forcing even lower targets than those imposed on their departments by the Treasury.

What has been the effect of these cuts, and have they really achieved the objective of greater efficiency and reduced public expenditure? One of the basic problems in counting the Civil Service is that there is no agreed definition of what is a civil servant. Until the mid-1960s all Post Office employees were civil servants but then changed their status. Teachers in Britain (unlike France) and employees in the National Health Service do not count as civil servants, whereas prison officers do. Just one example shows how arbitrary the system can be – the changing status of the staff of the National Economic Development Committee (Neddy). In 1968 they were a separate group of civil servants, in 1969 they were part of the Department of Economic Affairs, in 1970 part of the Cabinet Office, in 1971 they were a separate group again, and in 1972 they were hived off and no longer part of the Civil Service.[41] All this time they were doing exactly the same job.

Many of the reductions under the Thatcher government have been achieved in the same arbitrary way. Staff of certain museums have ceased to be civil servants. Kew Gardens' staff of 425 no longer count as part of MAFF, similarly the 400 staff of the Historic Monuments and Ancient Buildings division of the Department of the Environment and the 100 staff at Chelsea Hospital formerly run by the Ministry of Defence are no longer classified as civil servants. But this has been a book-keeping exercise relying on anomalies in the definition of a civil servant: the pay of these groups has stayed the same and they are still doing the same jobs. Getting numbers down has been the sole consideration regardless of the effects and the reductions have often saved little, if any, money. 43% of all the reductions between 1980 and 1984 were made by the Ministry of Defence and none of these has contributed to a saving in public expenditure. MOD has a single block budget so that all the savings on civilian manpower are used up elsewhere in the Defence Budget on such things as buying new equipment.

The reductions in the Civil Service have been achieved not by a planned programme of early retirement but simply by cutting back on recruitment which has fallen by 30% since 1978.[42] As posts have been trimmed and older staff have stayed on, the wait for promotion has become longer and longer and morale has fallen as a consequence. The administrators have been in charge of the whole process and have ensured that the upper echelons of the Civil Service have been less affected than those at the bottom. For example between 1979 and 1983 there were 14,700 redundancies among industrial staff but only 3,200 among non-industrials. Even within the non-industrial category most of the reductions have fallen at the bottom of the ladder. Inside the Ministry of Defence between 1979 and 1983 the number of administrative and executive staff fell by 9.6%. The number of clerks fell by 19.7%.[43]

The Civil Service is therefore smaller than it was when Thatcher came into office in 1979 but there is little evidence to show that it is more efficient, that the reductions have been made in the areas where there was over-staffing, or that there have been major financial savings as a result.

Civil Rights in the Civil Service

The Thatcher government has taken a much more restrictive view of civil rights in the Civil Service than any previous government. The most obvious example has been the removal of the right to union membership among staff at the Government Communications Headquarters (GCHQ) at Cheltenham who work on signals interception and code-breaking. This move was justified as the basis that there had been disruption during the 1981 Civil Service strike and was announced without consultation at the end of January 1984. Staff were offered £1,000 to give up statutory protection under certain employment legislation. A month later the Trade Unions offered a no-strike and no-disruption agreement to the government which met the government's declared objective in banning Trade Unions. This offer was rejected. When the ban was declared invalid by the High Court in July 1984, the government appealed to the House of Lords and completely changed the basis of its case to one of the overriding requirements of national security. The House of Lords gave a majority ruling in favour of the government but the Unions have now taken the case to the European Court of Human Rights. The general hostility to Trade Unions in the Civil Service was also shown by the new 1985 edition of the booklet given to all new recruits which removed references that urged staff to join a Trade Union.[44]

In April 1985 the government also introduced a new purge procedure into the Civil Service. The original system, which allowed the dismissal of those who belonged to communist and fascist organisations, had been dormant since the 1950s. The new system introduced sweeping new powers. Firstly, civil servants could be "purged" for belonging to any "subversive organisation", and these organisations were not defined – it was entirely up to a Minister to decide which groups should be included. Secondly, it was no longer necessary actually to join one of these ill-defined groups to be dismissed from the Civil Service but only to be deemed "sympathetic to or associated with members or sympathisers of such organisations or groups".[45] Thirdly, anybody accused under this procedure does not have the right to be told the evidence against him and, although there is a panel of three advisers (the usual collection of the "great and good"), the Minister can ignore their advice. In other words, a Minister can now act as prosecution, judge and jury. He has powers to dismiss a civil servant, without producing any evidence, simply for associating with sympathisers of unknown groups decided upon by the Minister without giving any reasons.

"Is He One Of Us?"

Mrs. Thatcher has taken a close interest in appointments at the top of the Civil Service. She has not been content like many of her predecessors to accept the recommendations of the mandarins, but has instead looked for candidates she believes are sympathetic to her general aims. She dislikes the quiet, detached mandarins who have dominated the Civil Service. In 1981 the Head of the Civil Service, Sir Ian Bancroft, and his deputy Sir John Herbecq were retired early in what was generally regarded as a snub to the Civil Service. Mrs. Thatcher has promoted people like Sir Peter Middleton to the Treasury and her ex-private secretary Sir Clive Whitmore to the Ministry of Defence, in an attempt to place sympathetic people in key positions. The vital question she is supposed to ask of any civil servant is: "Is he one of us?"

One appointment that certainly met that particular test but caused major controversy was that of Peter Levene as Chief of Defence Procurement at a total salary of £107,000 a year (over twice what a civil servant would be paid for the job). He was an industrialist working in the defence field, chairman of United Scientific Holdings and vice-chairman of the Defence Manufacturers Association. This appointment raised real questions about the Thatcher government's attitude to the Civil Service and "political" appointments. There was also controversy about the move of Sir Frank Cooper, ex-Permanent Secretary at MOD, to replace Levene as chairman of USH.

The decision was announced by the Secretary of State for Defence, Michael Heseltine, on 19 December, 1984. The Permanent Secretary, Sir Clive Whitmore, had been told the day before and argued strongly against. All five of the independent Civil Service Commissioners responsible for Civil Service appointments considered resigning because the rules about Civil Service appointments appeared to have been broken.[46]

In March 1985 Mrs. Thatcher explained how the original appointment had been made. It had, she argued, been by "secondment" and therefore outside the procedures controlled by the Civil Service Commissioners which demand open and fair competition for all Civil Service appointments. However, legal advice only sought in March 1985 considered that this was not in fact possible and that therefore the original appointment had been illegal. Mrs. Thatcher went on to say that the Civil Service Commissioners had "in these wholly unusual circumstances" nevertheless agreed to the appointment. Mrs. Thatcher made her statement on 18 March when she also said that it "would be very difficult, if not impossible to undo" these new arrangements.[47] A week later she had to admit that the "arrangements" had only been made on 18 March.

The appointment was already controversial. It was made more so when Levene was appointed for five years, or beyond the next general election. No other "political" appointment had been made for such a period. Also, because he had interests in firms which had contracts with the Ministry of Defence, special arrangements had to be made so that he did not see files dealing with these contracts even though he was the Accounting Officer and formally responsible to parliament for expenditure. The Public Accounts Committee's reaction was scathing, particularly in view of the justification for appointing Levene in the first place – saving money:

> The effect of the Government's decision is precisely to reduce the responsibility of the Accounting Officer to one of form without substance ... we regard the arrangement as a serious breach of the principle of personal financial accountability to Parliament.[48]

Survival of the System

The fundamental institutions of Whitehall have survived the Thatcher government intact. Although there has been a good deal of rhetoric about changing the culture of Whitehall, in practice little has been achieved. The government has been neither a good manager, nor a good employer. The Civil Service is certainly smaller but many of the cuts have been made by cosmetic changes and the bulk have fallen outside Whitehall and away from the élite at the top. Pay has fallen compared with that outside the Civil Service, except for the top three grades who received massive rises, up to 45%, in 1985. Morale is also poor. There is no evidence that efficiency has been improved. Half the reductions recommended by the

Rayner efficiency drive have never been implemented and Whitehall has absorbed and neutered the attempt to change the culture and make it more "managerial".

The Thatcher government has been truly conservative in its approach to the institutions of Whitehall. The Whitehall machine of inter-departmental battles and committees still works in exactly the same way, the top of the Civil Service is still recruited in the old manner and its training is little altered. The people at the top are still the same mandarin type.

CHAPTER EIGHT

Transforming Whitehall

Economic and Political Decline

Britain is a nation in long-term economic and political decline. The major failure of the political class in this century has been its inability either to devise policies to reverse that decline or to adjust to the reality of decline. The Whitehall system of government has been a major contributing factor to that failure.

Britain was the first country to industrialise and it was inevitable that its nineteenth-century predominance would be lost to the emerging super-powers, Russia and the United States. But, in the twentieth century, Britain has also suffered in comparison with other medium-sized powers such as Germany and France with similar resources. There has been economic growth in Britain but it has been patchy and consistently lower than in the rest of Europe or Japan. Britain's share of world trade has fallen steadily and major industries such as textiles, shipbuilding and motor-cycles have collapsed in the face of foreign competition. By the last quarter of the twentieth century Britain was one of the poorest countries in Western Europe with consistently higher levels of unemployment and inflation. The major bonus of North Sea oil has not been used to transform the economy.

Poor economic performance has been the background against which every government since the Second World War has had to operate. The major political problem has been to reconcile public expectations, often fuelled by politicians eager to be re-elected, about the level of services that should be provided by the public sector such as health care, education, housing and pensions, with the failure of the economy to produce the wealth to pay for these services. Politicians, reluctant to face unpalatable facts, have provided the services (though often at inadequate levels) by increasing public expenditure and putting up taxes to pay for it; or, when taxation has become too high for electoral popularity, by more short-sighted policies of using North Sea oil revenue to finance current rather than capital expenditure, and then selling off state assets.

In parallel with economic decline has gone political decline. This political decline has taken place steadily throughout the twentieth century. On a strategic level it has been manifested in the difficulty of defending with very limited resources an Empire that stretched round the world and then, after the Second World War, in a determination to maintain the trappings of world power on an inadequate base. For decades governments of both parties clung to the illusion that Britain was a major world power and therefore had to maintain an expensive defence and foreign policy to support this image of itself. Such a policy involved a world-wide chain of military bases until the mid-1970s, interventions in many areas including the disaster at Suez in 1956, and the maintenance of other symbols of national greatness such as the independent deterrent. This attachment to the symbols rather than to the reality of world power is equally apparent in other fields, for example in the desire, until the early 1970s, to continue the role of sterling as a major reserve currency. This involved the constant sacrifice of the real economy through repeated deflationary packages in a doomed attempt to maintain the value of the pound at artificially high levels and avoid devaluation.

The prospects for Britain for the rest of this century and beyond look bleak. Unemployment is likely to remain high and there are few, if any, signs of a major and sustained improvement in Britain's economic performance. For the first time in more than 200 years Britain now imports more manufactured goods than it exports. The peak of North Sea oil production will soon be reached and, when tax revenue from that source starts to decline, the problem of financing current levels of public expenditure will become serious. One-off sales of public assets are not a long-term solution only a short-term political palliative.

Administrative Failure

Whitehall is not solely responsible for Britain's economic decline though it has been unable to respond to the challenge posed by that decline. It shows no sign of being able to cope with the massive problems that lie ahead. But Whitehall's failure has not just been on the economic side. There has been an inability to provide successful and consistent administrative policies. We have had the twenty-year fiasco of London's Third Airport, the creation of the Greater London Council by one Conservative government in the 1960s and its abolition by another Conservative government twenty years later; the major, and widely disliked, re-organisation of local government by the Heath government in the early 1970s with the creation of the Metropolitan councils abolished by another Conservative government ten years later; the re-organisation of the Health Service in the 1970s that had to be undone within a few years; the failure to produce a consistent and agreed policy on state pensions; the chronic deterioration of relations between central and local government. The examples could be multiplied endlessly.

During the twentieth century Britain has continued to be governed by the methods of the nineteenth. There has been no attempt to overhaul the system of government and there has instead only been a series of piecemeal and minor reforms all within the general consensus accepted by a conservative establishment that the existing model of government is fundamentally sound. Parliament is still run within the framework of its historic traditions and has made little effort to grapple with the complexities of modern government and control the power of the executive. The structure of Whitehall, its way of taking decisions and the relationship between Ministers and civil servants, is still based on the model devised in the nineteenth century when the functions of government were limited and Whitehall departments were small policy-making units without vast executive functions. The top of the Civil Service is still recruited under a scheme devised 130 years ago and remains a predominantly Oxbridge and public school-educated élite with arts degrees, no specialist knowledge and little, if any, experience of the techniques required in modern government.

This system has failed to cope with Britain's problems for the last seventy-five years and there is no sign that it will suddenly be able to deal with the even graver problems of the near future. The Whitehall system has been powerful enough to block any of the major proposals for reform in the last twenty years and those inside the system show no desire to adapt their comfortable life and complacent attitudes to the harsher reality of the world outside Whitehall.

Transforming Whitehall

The ability of the existing powerful "establishment" within Whitehall to block piecemeal reform has been amply demonstrated. The scale of the problems facing Britain and the need to provide a greatly improved system of government mean that partial and haphazard reform is no longer adequate. There is an immediate and overwhelming need to transform the British system of government by a series of radical and wide-ranging reforms in every area. Nothing else will be sufficient.

The first course of action is to get rid of the carefully cultivated myth that the small group of about 1,000 Ministers and civil servants at the top of Whitehall are uniquely qualified to govern Britain free from outside "interference". Why should the rest of the country accept this condescending view that they are only entitled to learn about decisions taken in their name long after it is possible to influence those decisions? Reform will require freedom of information to provide both the basic right to know and the tools for informed public debate.

The second area for action is the structure of Whitehall itself and the myth that Ministers are, and should be, in personal control of every aspect of their departments. This only produces massive overloading as they attempt to deal with a multitude of detailed administrative problems and lose sight of important strategic questions in the process. Large parts of the Whitehall executive machine do not need to be part of the Whitehall policy-making function and their performance would be much improved if they were separated from Whitehall and became independent agencies.

The third area that requries major reform is the top of the Civil Service. The idea of the amateur administrative élite must go, the Civil Service needs to be opened up to much greater outside influence in terms of experience and training, and new people with new ideas need to be brought in. Career structures within the Service must be radically altered and its roles and duties need to be defined in much greater detail.

The fourth, and most difficult aim, is to improve the quality of the political class in Britain and to reduce the amount of short-term political thinking and decision-taking that has been a major part of the failure of every British government to grapple with the deep-rooted long-term problems facing the country. At the same time, the ability of parliament to act as a real control on the exercise of power by Whitehall and as a real investigator of what is going on inside Whitehall needs to be radically improved.

Freedom of Information

Information is power. As long as Whitehall continues to control information, and only allows out of its possessive grasp those pieces of knowledge which support what it has already decided to do, so long will real power continue to lie with the small group of Ministers and civil servants at the top of the Whitehall machine. Their opposition to freedom of information is based on the knowledge that its introduction would undermine their power base and their ability to take decisions in a small secretive circle away from the gaze of the public and any effective scrutiny by parliament.

Reform of section 2 of the Official Secrets Act, although an important measure that could stop abuse of the Act, by trying to conceal information embarrassing to the government, will not of itself mean freedom of information. A new Act would be necessary to give the public a right to know information held by the government subject to certain exceptions such as information dealing with genuine national security and confidential discussions with other governments. Advice to Ministers on how to present policies would also be excluded but all other background information and statistics would be included within the general right to know.

The new system would be relatively simple to operate. In order to allow access to government information, every department in Whitehall would have to keep a register of its papers and the register would be available to the public. Any member of the public could, without having to give a reason, ask to see any departmental paper. If the requested papers did not fall into the excepted categories then they would be made available on the payment of a small fee. If, however, the department felt the papers requested were in this category then it could refuse to release them. At this point it would be essential to provide the right of appeal to an independent tribunal. The tribunal would have the right to see the papers in dispute and would then rule whether the department had correctly withheld them. If the tribunal felt that the papers had not been withheld justifiably then they would have the power to order their release. An independent tribunal with these powers would be essential to ensure that Whitehall departments did not act as judge and jury in deciding which papers to release.

Such a system would obviously involve additional expenditure and extra staff. Experience in other countries suggests, however, that these costs would not be very great and the price would in any case be worth paying to obtain the benefits of freedom of information. Whitehall normally only uses finance as a pretext for not implementing policies which it dislikes on other grounds.

The benefits of freedom of information would be enormous in improving the quality of British government and reducing some of the appallingly bad decision-taking that has been related in this book. Such decision-taking will only continue as long as nearly all the available information can be restricted to a narrow circle within Whitehall, and the wider public is denied access to material which would show the insubstantial basis on which so many decisions are taken. Fear of public exposure would have a major impact on Ministers and civil servants engaged in the sort of sagas chronicled in this book. It would make it much more difficult for Ministers to suppress inconvenient information and pretend that the decision they have taken is the only possible one. The Whitehall attitude to decision-taking and public debate is well illustrated by Sir Douglas Wass, when he wrote:

Its [a government's] advocacy of its chosen policy could be

materially undermined if it were known to have entertained quite different choices, and to have placed weight on arguments it subsequently wished to play down.[1]

This is a very immature way of looking at the difficulties of policy-making in a complex democratic society. Decision-taking would be much improved if there were greater debate before decisions were made, involving not just Whitehall but those outside experts and interested groups who also have something to contribute. They cannot contribute fully unless they have access to the necessary information. In a mature democracy there would be no need to pretend that governments were uniquely capable of finding the one possible solution. Why should they not admit that choices were, as they always are, very difficult, but that on balance they have decided to go for one particular option and then argue why? Admittedly under this sort of system life would not be so simple inside Whitehall. No longer would the Civil Service be able to control almost totally the advice reaching Ministers, and they would not always be able to keep debate about options within narrow and decorous limits acceptable to Ministers and the bureaucracy. But this more complicated life in Whitehall would bring significant benefits to those outside the Whitehall system who have, so often, to suffer from the results of Whitehall's decision-taking.

Freedom of information would also help to transform the role of the media. They would be less dependent on the "information" (or propaganda) given out by the government through the lobby system. There would be much greater scope for investigative journalists to root out stories that the government did not want to publicise, and to a much greater extent journalists would not have to accept the agenda of items for discussion set by Whitehall. Freedom of information would also reduce the number of "leaks" from government because much of the information would then be publicly available. More effort could be concentrated on guarding genuine national security. It would also reduce the pressure on civil servants who at present are some of the few people who know what is going on in Whitehall and whether Ministers are not telling the truth, or the full truth, in their public statements.

Britain is now one of the few Western democracies that does not have a legally enforceable right to know. The United States and Western European countries all have such legislation. It is often argued that freedom of information is not necessary or perhaps even incompatible with Westminster-style democracy in which Ministers are accountable to parliament and members of parliament are able to ask questions and enquire into the activities of the executive. We have already seen in Chapter 5 that the much-vaunted authority of parliament is largely a myth, that Ministers are only accountable to parliament in the most general way, and that MPs have great difficulty in finding out the really important pieces of information or what is actually going on in Whitehall. In the last few years the other Westminster-style democracies – New Zealand, Australia and Canada – have all introduced successful freedom of information measures without damaging the accepted constitutional conventions. Freedom of information is not incompatible with parliamentary accountability but would instead improve it. Greater access to information would provide the basis for more intelligent questioning by parliament of the activities of Whitehall.

The Structure of Whitehall

The present structure of Whitehall, the demarcation lines between departments and the scope of those departments, has been arrived at by a process of historical precedent, ad hoc decision-taking and chance. The structure has not been radically altered this century yet it is responsible for some of the major failures of Whitehall.

We have already seen how the division of responsibilities within Whitehall, such as the distinction between DHSS which runs the social security system and the Department of Employment which operates the unemployment benefit system, causes real problems outside Whitehall. In addition, Whitehall departments are themselves a peculiar mixture of functions ranging from high-level policy-making with Ministers to a wide range of routine executive functions. The Ministry of Defence for example is responsible for a miscellany of areas such as nuclear weapons policy and running large industrial enterprises such as dockyards and maintenance depots which have little to do with each other. Some of these departmental structures are themselves inconsistent. For example, the DHSS is directly responsible for running and staffing the social security benefit system with its network of regional and local offices, yet the National Health Service is run by an entirely separate group of bodies whose staff are not even civil servants, although DHSS is still responsible for overall policy. This confusion of responsibilities has led to confused government.

These complex and enormous departments are still run by the methods of the late nineteenth century. Four or five Ministers will attempt somehow to control the day-to-day functions of up to 200,000 staff because they feel that they can be held politically responsible for everything that happens within that department. In practice this is clearly an impossibility, and the end results is an unhappy mix of crisis management and dilettante dabbling. A model of government designed for a time when a handful of civil servants and Ministers worked in Whitehall as a small policy-making Ministry with no executive functions has been dragged unmodified into the complexities of late twentieth-century government. Not surprisingly, it has failed.

One of the consequences has been an acute overloading of Ministers. They are in the position of having to make decisions and answer questions about what are relatively insignificant parts of the departments' activities. Their time, and the time of Cabinet committees, is spent to a large extent on the minutiae of public administration. In order to cope with this work-load, Ministers have to work long hours, often to the point of exhaustion, and even then important papers are left unread and discussions take place in ignorance. Physical and mental exhaustion in itself leads to bad decision-taking. The pace of work and the obsession with detail have enabled Ministers to avoid subjects they dislike such as strategic policy-making and long-term planning.

A few desultory and limited attempts have been made to alter the structure of Whitehall. In 1970 the Conservative government was keen on setting up "agencies". These included the Property Services Agency (responsible for looking after government offices and property) and the Procurement

Executive (responsible for the military equipment pro-gramme). But neither of these bodies was genuinely independent and both remained an integral part of their departments – the Department of the Environment and the Ministry of Defence respectively – and subject to detailed Ministerial control. All the other changes in the lay-out of Whitehall have, as we have seen, not altered the way in which Whitehall works and were mainly inspired by short-term political motives.

The Fulton Committee in the late 1960s was excluded from looking at the structure of Whitehall yet it felt that the organisation that had endured in such a confused and unplanned way was not ideal. They came to the conclusion that:

> We see no reason to believe that the dividing line between the activities for which Ministers are directly responsible, and those for which they are not, is necessarily drawn in the right place today.[2]

A New Structure for Whitehall

The Fulton Committee were "much impressed" by their study of the Swedish model of government.[3] There, small Ministries of just over a hundred staff are responsible for policy and legislation. They are headed by three officials – the Permanent Secretary responsible for administration, an Under-Secretary responsible for policy (normally a political appointment) and a Chief Legal Adviser. Administration is the responsibility of autonomous public boards which are outside the day-to-day control of Ministers and the scrutiny of parliament, but they are publicly responsible for all their activities. The relationship between the Ministries and the autonomous boards is closely defined by legislation: in general Ministers can publicly issue specific policy directives and the boards are responsible for carrying out these directives. Similarly the boards can publish the proposals they make to the Ministry for new policy initiatives and also their budget proposals. Such a system can only work where there is freedom of information, public accountability of the boards and a strong Ombudsman to oversee their activities. Civil servants are recruited as specialists to fill specific jobs within Ministries and promotion is then rapid. Those at the top are aged about forty, and still interested in new ideas; they then leave at about forty-five to fifty in order to take up senior positions on the autonomous boards. The boards obviously also recruit their own staff.

This system provides a model for how the structure of Whitehall might be genuinely reformed and the performance of British government radically improved. The first step would be to set up the agencies that would carry out the bulk of the functions of government departments. An obvious example is the social security system which would become independent of the DHSS and responsible for paying benefits. DHSS would decide the policy that the new organisation would implement. In the Home Office, for instance, responsibility for running the prison system would be transferred to a new agency, as would the system of immigration control. In the Department of Industry regional aid and assistance to industry would be similarly transferred to a separate agency. In order to emphasise the fundamental difference between the Ministries and the Agencies the latter would be moved from London. Across the whole of Whitehall this new system would transform the process of government into true policy-making.

The benefits would be great. The workload on Ministers, and senior officials, in Whitehall would be drastically reduced, leaving them more time to concentrate on important issues. The new Agencies would have freedom from direct political interference and would not be accountable to Ministers. They would have the ability to develop management structures, financial controls and staffing policies that were not constrained by the current rigid Whitehall system. They would have a much greater incentive to produce a service that met public demand since they would be accountable to the public. They would be accountable for their activities not only through a greatly-enhanced Ombudsman to investigate administrative failures but also through freedom of information which would ensure open administration within the Agencies. Policy instructions issued from Whitehall to the Agencies and their responses, together with Agency proposals, reports and budgets would be published and freely available.

With or without such changes there is a desperate need for much greater central control and direction of government. At the moment the Cabinet and its system of committees, both Ministerial and official, is essentially a system for arbitrating between departments and vested interests. The Cabinet Office is staffed mainly to run those committees and not to develop independent policy initiatives. The staff at 10 Downing Street, both Civil Service and political advisers, are no more than an extended private office for the Prime Minister. What is needed is much stronger central administration of British government. This might consist of a radically-revamped Cabinet office and Prime Minister's department staffed to take policy initiatives that would then be implemented by departments (or the new Agencies). On the foreign policy and defence side there is, for instance, a need for an integrated policy rather than reliance on what emerges from interdepartmental disputes between the Foreign Office and the Ministry of Defence. In addition there needs to be a central department that would take over all the public expenditure functions of the Treasury, leaving the remainder as a true Ministry of Finance dealing with the banking and financial systems both national and international. The role of the Treasury with its constant dedication to financial considerations, such as the level of the pound, has had a damaging effect on the real economy. There needs to be a separate department responsible for planning the vast resources (45% of the nation's wealth) controlled by the government. Another vital role at the centre would be met by creating a department based on the Central Policy Review Staff, but much larger, to undertake critical analysis of government policy. This should certainly be staffed by a high proportion of outsiders in order to avoid the cosy, complacent and uncritical attitude of many civil servants.

With a transformed and greatly reduced Whitehall the bulk of the Civil Service would become employees of the new Agencies, and inevitably the Civil Service would also be radically different. But reform of the Civil Service itself is urgent, whether or not Whitehall is restructured. How this can be done is the theme of the next section.

Transforming the Civil Service

For the last 130 years the Civil Service has been based upon two pillars: a non-political Civil Service at every level below ministers, and the domination of the service by the Oxbridge educated arts graduate who is a non-specialist amateur. Both of these concepts are now out-dated.

We have seen that the mandarins at the top of the Civil Service are a self-conscious élite who see their role as "policy advisers" to Ministers rather than managers of the complex operations run by the vast majority of civil servants under them. The mandarins do not have any expertise in the subjects with which they deal and specialise only in the arts of presenting the policies of Ministers in the most favourable possible light, oiling the machinery of Whitehall and processing paper through that machinery. The top of the Civil Service is an introverted world of safe jobs till retirement at sixty; the mandarins have little or no outside experience and those with a successful background in other fields cannot join the top of the Civil Service in mid-career. If the quality of British government is to be improved this cosy world needs to be broken open.

The first myth that needs to be tackled is the non-political nature of the top civil servants. Although they are not party loyalists they nevertheless hold deeply political jobs as the intimate advisers of Ministers. We have looked into this somewhat disreputable world where political opportunism and personal ambition predominate yet civil servants grandly call this "policy-making". They are in the position where, within a day, they may have to switch their loyalties from one party to another on a change of government. This may not have been a difficult intellectual feat when there was much greater political consensus between the main parties than there has been for the last ten years. As politics become more polarised that feat of objectivity is going to become increasingly difficult. And even if it can be achieved, what sort of person is going to be able and willing to serve equally well governments with radically different political philosophies? Those that stay the course are likely to have to become amoral and cynical or else be ruthlessly ambitious careerists – neither of which is healthy for running government. As Professor Ridley of Liverpool University said in a recent address to the Royal Institute of Public Administration:

> As politics become more polarised, it is harder to accept the comfortable tradition that civil servants can serve whatever kind may rule and remain honourable men.[4]

The dividing line between political appointments and the non-political Civil Service is drawn much higher up the administrative hierarchy in Britain than in almost any other country. Political appointments are confined to Ministers and a handful of political advisers. There is no logical reason why the line has to be drawn at this level particularly when the jobs immediately around Ministers, now filled by civil servants, are in practice highly political. As William Plowden, the Director of the Royal Institute of Public Administration, said when advocating more political appointments at the top of the Civil Service:

> The myth of the totally dispassionate, totally effective administrator should now be consigned to the dustbin of history with other comforting but outmoded myths.[5]

If there were to be more political appointments, how might the system work? One possibility would be to retain the present structure but allow Ministers to choose civil servants who are politically sympathetic to the government. We are perhaps already seeing the start of such a system under the Thatcher government with the political appointment of men like Peter Levene to jobs previously held by civil servants. But this policy would give the worst of both worlds. It would undermine one of the strengths of the current Civil Service – its formally non-political nature – but without replacing it by a fully-thought out and defensible new system. In other words it represents a typical Whitehall fudged solution. It would be politicisation via the back-door.

A second option would be to introduce the Ministerial "cabinet" system found in many continental countries. This would really only amount to more political advisers around the Minister, taking over the function of the existing Civil Service-manned private office. The "cabinet" would provide a political filter between the Civil Service and the Minister and increase the political influences on him at the expense of the bureaucratic. This might well give Ministers more political purpose but it does not tackle the real problem, which would still remain: the overwhelming influence of Civil Service advice from within the department. Nor does it tackle the problem of how to radically reform the Civil Service. Political advisers have been tried in the past, on a small scale, and they have not made an impact on the existing system. There is no evidence to suggest that the same experiment on a larger scale would be any more successful.

Under the third, and most radical, option the top three grades of the Civil Service – Permanent Secretary, Deputy Secretary and Under-Secretary – would become openly-advertised five-year appointments. Ministers would have the final say in all these short-term appointments. Some of those appointed to particularly sensitive jobs in policy formation might be political appointments. In other areas there would scope for outsiders with relevant experience – businessmen, financiers, academics, local government officials, trade union officials – to bring new ideas and greater expertise into the bureaucracy. Some of these jobs might be filled by career civil servants if they were the best candidates.

This solution would break the grip of the administrative class of the Civil Service on the top jobs, inject outside experience and bring in younger and more radical people who had a real contribution to make. Above all it would break open the introverted world of Whitehall. It would enable Ministers to appoint sympathetic individuals to key posts without losing expertise in other vital management areas that were less political in content.

In this new system the career Civil Service would stop at Assistant Secretary level; it would still provide the bulk of the administrative and executive staff and undertake the detailed and factual work of the department. There would still be opportunities to rise into the top three ranks, but there would no longer be any need to recruit an administrative élite specifically designed to fill the top jobs. The main level of recruitment would be as Executive Officer, and promotion would be by performance on the job. The idea of the non-specialist administrator should go. People should be recruited with particular skills to fill particular jobs and the Civil Service would have an open structure without some jobs reserved for people of particular classes or professional groups. At the same time the idea of a career till sixty regardless of performance should not apply at every level of the Civil Service. At the top there should be a system whereby, unless promotion to certain grades had been achieved by a particular age, then the career would come to an end.

It is this third option that provides a way most likely to transform Whitehall and improve the quality of British government.

A Code of Ethics

The British system of government is largely dependent on unwritten codes of conduct. One of these is that the government will behave legally and democratically and not attempt to ignore or subvert the rules if they become inconvenient. But what does the civil servant do if he finds the government is breaking these rules? One of the most flagrant breaches of the unwritten rules was the highly-organised deception and deliberate lying by the Eden government in 1956 before the invasion of Egypt, involving secret collaboration with Israel and France to provide the "justification" for the invasion, a collusion that was hotly denied at the time. Sir Leo Pliatzky, later Permanent Secretary at the Treasury, wrote of this episode early in his career:

> This was the only occasion in my time in the government service when I had to reflect how the British civil service, with its commitment to work for the government of the day, irrespective of its policies, differed from officials in Hitler's Germany who had helped to carry out the Nazi atrocities.[6]

But at the time was it seen in moral terms by the top civil servants concerned? There were a few minor protests inside the Civil Service – Sir William Armstrong wore a black tie for a few days – but the only person to resign was William Clark, Eden's press secretary, and he was not a career civil servant. In the end Pliatzky was able to rationalise his doubts:

> Even the Suez situation did not invalidate the concept of a civil service working for the government of the day on the

basis that, if its policies were wrong, it was for the democratic process to change either the government or its policies.[7]

This may be all very well in theory but what happens in practice if the government is deliberately lying and withholding information so that parliament and the democratic process cannot function? Twenty-five years later I found the same problem over the government-organised *Belgrano* cover-up. When I sent papers to a Member of Parliament revealing this cover-up, I was prosecuted under Section 2 of the Official Secrets Act. One of the consequences of that unsuccessful prosecution was that the idea of a Code of Ethics for the Civil Service was debated.

The Civil Service is probably one of the few professional organisations that does not have a written code of ethics. After my acquittal Sir Robert Armstrong, the Head of the Civil Service, issued guidance on the duties of civil servants. This note essentially said that the civil servant must be absolutely loyal to Ministers at all times and that if he found he was asked to do things which he thought were wrong he should talk to his Permanent Secretary and "transfer the burden of conscience" to him. This is a convenient and cynical concept. In the last resort Sir Robert Armstrong recommended that the civil servant should resign. Why the civil servant unable to suppress or pass on moral qualms should be expected to give up job and career simply because of wrong-doing elsewhere is unclear. And even if he does resign the civil servant cannot make public the reasons because he would still risk prosecution under the Official Secrets Act.

This Armstrong code is an inadequate and disgraceful document. The trade union for top civil servants – the First Division Association – has already proposed an alternative which contains two significant provisions. First, the civil servant does not, in the final resort, owe his loyalty entirely to Ministers. In certain circumstances there can be a higher loyalty to parliament or the public interest. Second, if the civil servant cannot obtain satisfaction from within the system then he has the right to appeal to an outside body, either an Ombudsman or a specially-constituted tribunal that could require the Minister to correct deliberately misleading or incorrect statements. Such a provision is now also recommended by Sir Douglas Wass, the ex-head of the Civil Service.[8]

The major obstacle to introducing any code of ethics is getting the government to agree provisions that might interfere with their own political requirements. Another problem is protecting the position and career of any civil servant who exposes government malpractice. The United States Civil Service Reform Act passed in 1978 could provide a model for a new British system. This Act imposes a duty on civil servants to reveal:

> mismanagement, a gross waste of public funds, an abuse of authority, or a substantial and specific danger to public health or safety.

The Act also provides a tribunal with legal powers to protect the job and career of any civil servant who follows the requirements of the Act.

Improving the Political Class

All of the proposals so far in this chapter have concerned the structure of the Whitehall system and the nature of the Civil Service. There is one further area that is just as fundamental to any improvement in the quality of British government, the quality of the political class. I have used the term "political class" deliberately because all politicians of whatever party share a devotion to doing whatever is necessary to get into power, and, once in office, to staying there.

Once in the government, they behave in exactly the same way, putting short-term political objectives above everything else and operating the system in the way we have seen in this book. There is what amounts to a tacit agreement between the politicians of all parties about how the political game should be played. Although one group may be temporarily out of power they can expect to regain it at some stage and therefore it is to their advantage to keep the rules of the political game unchanged. The quality of people in the political class is not high and the public has rightly become cynical about the motives of those who govern us. Increasingly over the last few decades politics has come to be dominated by career politicians who frequently have little experience outside politics and whose life is given over to their political ambitions. These are not the sort of qualifications required to ensure competent and decent government in a complex society facing the serious and deep-seated problems of a nation in decline.

The need for an improvement in the quality of both politics and politicians is acute. How this can be achieved, however, lies well beyond the scope of this book which has concentrated on the system within which the politicians and civil servants operate.

The Future

The problems facing Britain are serious and fundamental and stem from a long history of failure. No government has so far been able to deal with those problems successfully. One of the major reasons for the failure of Britain has been its system of government which has failed to rise to the challenge. It is still run by a short-sighted political class and an amateur Civil Service élite, with tools devised in the nineteenth century. This failure has for too long been obscured by the complacent view of a Britain governed by the immaculate mother of parliaments and the introverted clinging to outdated traditions and myths about the way in which Whitehall works.

There has been no serious attempt to reform British government this century. If Britain is to cope with its current and future problems, Whitehall must not only be reformed, but transformed. The deeply-entrenched interests of those who run the current system have so far managed to block reforms that would jeopardise their survival, and the omens for change are not good. There is little sign of any willingness to tackle the root and branch reforms that are needed. Without them the tragedy and farce of Whitehall will continue and Britain will continue to suffer from the consequences.

Bibliography

Command Papers

Cmd 3909	Royal Commission on the Civil Service (1929–31)
Cmd 9613	Royal Commission on the Civil Service (1953–55)
Cmnd 3638	The Civil Service (Fulton Report)
Cmnd 4156	Report on the Method II System of Selection for the Civil Service
Cmnd 4506	The Reorganisation of Central Government
Cmnd 5322	The Dispersal of Government Work from London
Cmnd 6386	Committee of Privy Councillors on Ministerial Memoirs
Cmnd 6524	Royal Commission on Standards of Conduct in Public Life
Cmnd 7117	Government Observations on the Eleventh Report from the Expenditure Committee (The Civil Service)
Cmnd 7797	Report on Non-Departmental Public Bodies
Cmnd 8147	Inquiry into the Value of Pensions (Scott Report)
Cmnd 8293	Efficiency in the Civil Service
Cmnd 8590	Inquiry into Civil Service Pay
Cmnd 8787	Falkland Islands Review: Report by a Committee of Privy Councillors
Cmnd 9465	Government Observations on the Eighth Report from the Treasury and Civil Service Committee

Parliamentary Papers

1947–48	Ninth Report of the Select Committee on the Estimates
1972–73	Third Report from the Select Committee on Science and Technology (Tracked Hovercraft) HC 420
1976–77	Eleventh Report from the Expenditure Committee "The Civil Service" HC 535 3 Vols.
1977–78	First Report from the Select Committee on Procedure
1982	HL 149/HC 364 Tribunal of Enquiry into the Crown Agents Affair
1983–84	Eighth Report from the Treasury and Civil Service Committee "Acceptance of Outside Appointments by Crown Servants" HC 302

Other Official Reports

Civil Service Commission	Annual Reports

Civil Service Commission	Report of the Committee on Selection Procedure for Recruitment of Administration Trainees 1979
Civil Service Department	Report of the Administration Trainee Review Committee 1978
Civil Service Department	Career Patterns in the Higher Civil Service 1976
Civil Service Department	Report on Civil Service Training 1974
Civil Service Department	Chain of Command Review: The Open Structure 1981
Efficiency Unit	Consultancy, Inspection and Review in Government Departments 1984
Foreign and Commonwealth Office	Report on the Supply of Petroleum and petroleum products to Rhodesia 1978
Management and Personnel Office	Equal Opportunities for Women in the Civil Service 1982
Management and Personnel Office	Report on the Selection of Fast Stream Graduate Entrants 1983
HM Treasury	Management Training in the Civil Service 1967
HM Treasury	Civil Service Pay: Government Evidence 1982
HM Treasury	Civil Service Pay: Factual Evidence 1982
HM Treasury	Civil Service Statistics 1984

The Airports Enquires 1981–1983 Report by Graham Eyre QC

Books

A. Barker (ed.). *Quangoes in Britain* London 1982
J. Barnett. *Inside the Treasury* London 1982
Lord Bridges. *Portrait of a Profession* London 1950
J. Bruce-Gardyne and N. Lawson. *The Power Game* London 1976
B. Castle. *The Castle Diaries* 1965–70 London 1984
B. Castle. *The Castle Diaries* 1974–76 London 1980
L. Chapman. *Your Disobedient Servant* (Penguin ed) 1979
R. A. Chapman. *Leadership in the British Civil Service* London 1984
Sir R. Clarke. *Public Expenditure, Management and Control* London 1968
M. Cockerell, P. Hennessy and D. Walker. *Sources Close to the Prime Minister* London 1984
S. Crosland. *Tony Crosland* London 1982
R. H. S. Crossman. *Inside View* London 1972
R. H. S. Crossman. *Diaries of a Cabinet Minister* 3 Vols. London 1975–77
H. E. Dale. *The Higher Civil Service in Great Britain* London 1941
G. K. Fry. *Statesmen in Disguise* London 1969
G. K. Fry. *The Growth of Government* London 1979
G. K. Fry. *The Administrative Revolution in Whitehall* London 1981
S. Goldman. *The Developing System of Public Expenditure Management and Control* London 1973
R. Gregory and P. Hutchinson. *The Parliamentary Ombudsman* London 1975

H. Heclo and A. Wildavsky. *The Private Government of Public Money* (2nd Ed) London 1984

P. Hennessy. *What the Papers Never Said* London 1985

C. Hood and A. Dunsire. *Bureaumetrics* Farnborough 1981

G. Kaufman. *How to be a Minister* London 1980

W. Keegan. *Mrs. Thatcher's Economic Experiment* Harmondsworth 1984

P. Kellner and Lord Crowther-Hunt. *The Civil Servants* London 1980

D. Marsh (ed). *Pressure Politics: Interest Groups in Britain* London 1983

C. Mellors. *The British MP* Farnborough 1979

J. Pellew. *The Home Office 1848–1914* London 1982

Sir L. Pliatzky. *Getting and Spending* Oxford 1982

C. Pollitt. *Manipulating the Machine* London 1984

C. S. Ponting. *The Right to Know* London 1985

H. Roseveare. *The Treasury* London 1969

Royal Institute of Public Administration. *Policy and Practice: The Experience of Government* 1980

M. Rush. *The Cabinet and Policy Formation* London 1984

A. Sampson. *Changing Anatomy of Britain* London 1982

C. H. Sisson. *The Spirit of British Administration* London 1957

F. Stacey. *The British Ombudsman* Oxford 1971

S. A. Walkland and M. Ryle. *The Commons Today* Glasgow 1981

Sir D. Wass. *Government and the Governed* London 1984

P. M. Williams (ed). *The Diary of Hugh Gaitskell 1945–56* London 1983

H. Young and A. Sloman. *No Minister* London 1982

H. Young and A. Sloman. *But Chancellor* London 1984

H. Young. *The Crossman Affair* London 1976

Articles

R. A. Chapman. Administrative Culture and Personnel Management *Teaching Public Administration* Vol. IV pp. 1–14

Sir J. Dunnett. The Civil Service: Seven Years After Fulton *Public Administration* No. 54

G. K. Fry. The Development of the Thatcher Government's "Grand Strategy" for the Civil Service. *Public Administration* Autumn 1984 pp. 302–335

G. K. Fry. The Attack on the Civil Service and the Response of the Insiders *Public Administration* Vol. 37 No. 4

P. Hennessy, S. Morrison and R. Townsend. Routine Punctuated by Orgies: The Central Policy Review Staff 1970–1983 Strathclyde Papers on Government and Politics No. 31

C. Hood. The Crown Agents Affair *Public Administration* Vol. 56 pp. 297–303

Sir J. Hoskyns. Conservatism is Not Enough *Political Quarterly* Vol. 55 No. 1 pp. 3–16

S. Jenkins. The Star Chamber, PESC and the Cabinet *Political Quarterly* Vol. 56 No. 2 pp. 113–21

D. Jessel. Mandarins and Ministers *Listener* 11 December, 1980

A. King. The Rise of the Career Politician *British Journal of Political Science* Vol. 11 pp. 249–285

R. Lowe. Bureacracy Triumphant or Denied? The Expansion of the British Civil Service 1919–39. *Public Administration* Autumn 1984 pp. 251–310

L. Metcalfe and S. Richards. The Impact of the Efficiency Strategy: Political Clout or Cultural Change? *Public Administration* Winter 1984 pp. 439–454

Sir P. Nairne. Managing the DHSS Elephant *Political Quarterly* Vol. 54 No. 3

P. Neville-Jones. The Continental Cabinet System: The Effects of Transposing it to the United Kingdom *Political Quarterly* Vol. 54 no. 3

A. Palmer. The History of the D-Notice Committee (in C. Andrew and D. Dilks (ed) The Missing Dimension: Governments and Intelligence Communities in the Twentieth Century. London 1984)

C. Seymour-Ure. British "War Cabinets" in Limited Wars: Korea, Suez and the Falklands *Public Administration* Summer 1984 pp. 181–200

N. Summerton. A Mandarin's Duty *Parliamentary Affairs* Vol. 33 No. 4 pp. 400–421

N. Warner. Raynerism in Practice *Public Administration* Spring 1984 pp. 7–22

Sir D. Wass. The Civil Service at the Crossroads *Political Quarterly* Vol. 56 No. 3 pp. 227–241

D. West. Taking the Axe out of Storage *The Times* 26 June, 1985

M. Wright. The Responsibility of the Civil Servant *Public Administration* Vol. 23 No. 4 pp. 362–95

Notes

Chapter One: *The Misgovernment of Britain*

1   J. H. Elliot *Imperial Spain 1469–1716* Penguin ed London 1970 p. 382
2   H. Young, A. Sloman *No Minister* London 1982 p. 20
3   Quoted in D. Jessel Mandarins and Ministers, Listener 11 December, 1980
4   Ibid
5   Hansard 15 June, 1978 Cols. 1270–5
6   Hansard 15 June, 1978 Cols. 1256–1261
7   Hansard (House of Lords) 5 November, 1979 Cols. 608–616
8   L. Kennedy *10 Rillington Place* London 1982 (reprint) pp. 7–8
9   Charles Dickens *Little Dorrit* Chapter 10 Penguin edition p. 145
10 H. Young, A Sloman *No Minister* p. 21
11 B. Castle *The Castle Diaries 1965–70* p. 114 (8–17 April, 1966)
12 R.H.G. Crossman *Diaries of a Cabinet Minister* Vol. 1 p. 115 (3 January, 1966)
13 P. Kellner and Lord Crowther-Hunt *The Civil Servants: An Inquiry into Britain's Ruling Class* London 1980
14 Minority Report to Eleventh Report from the Expenditure Committee 1976–77 "The Civil Service" HC 535 HMSO 1977
15 *The Diaries of Sir Alexander Cadogan* ed. D. Dilks London 1971 p. 776 (28 July, 1945)
16 *Crossman Diaries* Vol. 1 p. 25 22 October, 1964
17 Susan Crosland *Tony Crosland* p. 124–5 see also H. Wilson *The Labour Government 1964–70*
18 *Crossman Diaries* Vol. 1 p. 26 22 October, 1964
19 *Crossman Diaries* Vol. 2 pp. 125–6 15 November, 1966
20 *Crossman Diaries* Vol. 3 p. 479 8 May, 1969
21 See J. Bruce-Gardyne & N. Lawson *The Power Game: An Examination on Decision Making in Government* London 1976
22 *Castle Diaries 1965–70* pp. 738–9 10 December, 1969
23 *Castle Diaries 1974–76* p. 124 27 June, 1974
24 *Castle Diaries 1965–70* p. 625 24 March, 1969
25 The Airports Enquiries 1981–1983 Report by Graham Eyre QC Conclusion 1
26 Ibid para 6.47
27 Ibid paras 6.50, 6.52, 6.58
28 Ibid conclusion 1
29 Report on the supply of Petroleum and Petroleum products to Rhodesia (Bingham Report) HMSO 1978 para 6.33
30 Bingham Report pp. 256–8 and 259–61

31 Bingham Report p. 257 Official record of meeting 21 February, 1968 para 7
32 Bingham Report p. 270
33 Sir J. Hoskyns Conservatism is not Enough *Political Quarterly* Vol. 55 No. 1 pp. 3–16.
34 C. Dickens *Little Dorrit* Chapter 26 Penguin ed p. 358

Chapter Two: *Ministers*

1   A. King The Rise of the Career Politician. *British Journal of Political Science* Vol. 11 p. 249–285
    M. Rush *The Members of Parliament in The Commons Today* ed. S. A. Walkland M. Ryle Glasgow 1981
    C. Mellars *The British MP: a socio-economic study of the House of Commons.* Farnborough 1979
2   C. Dickens *The Pickwick Papers* Chapter 13 Penguin ed pp. 237–8
3   J. Grigg *Lloyd George: From Peace to War 1912–1916* London 1985 p. 255
4   E. Gibbon *Decline and Fall of the Roman Empire* Vol. 1 Everyman ed. p. 104
5   *Castle Diaries 1974–76*, p. 409 9 June, 1975
6   Ibid p. 303 5 February, 1975
7   *Crossman Diaries* Vol. 2 p. 293 27 March, 1967
8   Ibid p. 289 23 March, 1967
9   Susan Crosland *Tony Crosland* p. 205
10 Joel Barnett *Inside the Treasury* London 1982 p. 2
11 W. Keegan *Mrs. Thatcher's Economic Experiment* Penguin Harmondsworth 1984 p. 110
12 Joel Barnett *Inside the Treasury* p. 15
13 *Crossman Diaries* Vol. 1 p. 28 22 October, 1964
14 Ibid p. 23 22 October, 1964
15 *Crossman Diaries* Vol. 2 p. 761 3 April, 1968
16 *Crossman Diaries* Vol. 3 p. 378 23 February, 1969
17 RH Crossman *'Inside View'* London 1972 p. 46
18 Ibid p. 13
19 Peter Kellner & Lord Crowther-Hunt *The Civil Servants* p. 152
20 *Crossman Diaries* Vol. 1 p. 21 22 October, 1964
21 Joel Barnett *Inside the Treasury* pp. 16–19
22 *Gaitskell Diaries* p. 117 28 June, 1949
23 *Castle Diaries 1974–76* pp. 49–50
24 *Crossman Diaries* Vol. 2 pp. 564–5 9 November, 1967
25 *Crossman Diaries* Vol. 1 p. 107 18 December, 1964
26 *Castle Diaries 1974–1976* p. 305 6 February, 1975
27 Harold Wilson *The Quality of Cabinet Government* BBC Radio 3 27 June, 1985
28 *Crossman Diaries* Vol. 2 pp. 70–1 12 October, 1966
29 *Castle Diaries 1964–70* p. 379 23 February, 1968
30 *Crossman Diaries* Vol. 2 p. 722 19 March, 1968
31 *Crossman Diaries* Vol. 3 p. 180, p. 166 4 September, 1968, 31 July, 1968
32 *Castle Diaries 1964–70* p. 414 28 March, 1968

33　Ibid p. 647 8 May, 1969
34　*Crossman Diaries* Vol. 3 p. 215 5 October, 1968
35　*Castle Diaries 1964–70* pp. 437–9 6–8 May, 1968
36　Ibid p. 10 10 February, 1965
37　Ibid pp. 761–3 12 February, 1970
38　Joel Barnett *Inside the Treasury* p. 163
39　*Castle Diaries 1964–70* p. 4 27 January, 1965
40　Ibid p. 7 28 January, 1965
41　*Crossman Diaries* Vol. 3 pp. 603–4 31 July, 1969
42　*Crossman Diaries* Vol. 3 p. 486 12 May, 1969
43　*Castle Diaries 1964–70* pp. 232–3 7–8 March, 1967
44　Ibid p. 541 29 October, 1968 see also *Crossman Diaries* Vol. 3 pp. 241–2
45　*Crossman Diaries* Vol. 3 pp. 427–8 23 March, 1969
46　Cmnd 3998
47　*Crossman Diaries* Vol. 3 pp. 443–4 17 April, 1969
48　Ibid pp. 448–9 21 April, 1969
49　Ibid pp. 452–3 24 April, 1969
50　*Crossman Diaries* Vol. 1 p. 132 16 January, 1965
51　Ibid p. 127 13 January, 1965
52　Ibid pp. 188–9 30 March, 1965
53　Ibid p. 240 2 June 1965
54　Ibid
55　*Castle Diaries 1965–70* p. 251 2 May, 1967
56　*Castle Diaries 1974–76* p. 418 16 June, 1975
57　*Crossman Diaries* Vol. 3 pp. 810–11 10 February, 1970
58　*Crossman Diaries* Vol. 3 p. 270 22 November, 1968
59　*Crossman Diaries* Vol. 2 p. 615 20 December, 1967
60　*Crossman Diaries* Vol. 3 p. 98 17 June, 1968
61　Susan Crosland *Tony Crosland* pp. 147–8
62　*Crossman Diaries* Vol. 3 p. 288 17 December, 1968
63　J. Barnett *Inside the Treasury* p. 42
64　*Castle Diaries 1965–70* p. 571 15 December, 1968
65　Ben Pimlott *Hugh Dalton* p. 181
66　*Castle Diaries 1965–70* pp. 74–5 12 December, 1965
67　*Castle Diaries 1965–70* p. 788 20 April, 1970
68　Ibid p. 724 8 April, 1976

Chapter Three: *Mandarins*

1　Civil Service Statistics 1984 HM Treasury HMSO 1984
2　*Guardian* 13 August, 1983
3　J. Morley *Life of William Ewart Gladstone* Vol. 1 p. 649 London 1903
4　H. Roseveare *The Treasury; The Evolution of a British Institution* London 1969
5　J. Pellew *The Home Office 1848–1914* London 1982
6　Royal Commission on the Civil Service Second Report 1888 Q 19975
7　Leathes Committee Report on the Scheme of Examination

8   Royal Commission on the Civil Service 1931 (Tomlin Commission) Q 22320
9   Ninth Report of the Select Committee on the Estimates. Session 1947–48 Evidence by Sir F. Waterfield Q 1885
10 Royal Commission on the Civil Service 1931
11 Minutes of Evidence of Royal Commission on the Civil Service 1929–31 Paper by the First Civil Service Commissioner para 3
12 See R A Chapman *Leadership in the British Civil Service* London 1984
13 Eleventh Report from the Expenditure Committee 1976–77 (The English Committee) "The Civil Service" HC 535 Vol. II–I p. 269–70
14 Cmnd 4156 Davis Committee Report on Method II.
15 PRO/CSC/5/281
16 Letter from Financial Secretary to the Treasury to Sir Arnold Wilson MP PRO/CSC/5/81
17 Ninth Report of the Estimates Committee Session 1947–48 HC 203, 205 Q 1987
18 "English Committee" Report HC 535 Vol. II–I p. 809
19 Lord Bridges *Portrait of a Profession* London 1950
20 C. H. Sisson *The Spirit of British Administration* London 1957
21 Royal Commission on the Civil Service 1929–31
22 H. E. Dale *The Higher Civil Service of Great Britain* London 1941
23 "English" Committee Report HC 535 Vol. III–I Q92 p. 74
24 Ibid Vol. II-11 p. 483
25 Ibid Vol. II–11 p. 626 Evidence by the Head of the Government Accountancy Service
26 Tribunal of Enquiry into the Crown Agents Affair HL 149/HC 364 1982
27 Royal Commission on the Civil Service 1955 Q3623
28 Sir Douglas Wass *Government and the Governed* p. 48 London 1984
29 Sir Patrick Nairne Managing the DHSS Elephant: Reflections on a Giant Department *Political Quarterly* Vol. 54 No. 3 1983
30 P. M. Williams (ed) *The Diaries of Hugh Gaitskell 1945–56* pp. 41–2 8th October, 1947
31 Quoted in G. C. Peden *British Rearmament and the Treasury* p. 56 Edinburgh 1979
32 *Castle Diaries 1965–70* p. 607 25 February, 1969
33 op cit pp. 118–9
34 Sir Patrick Nairne op cit.
35 op cit p. 52
36 *Crossman Diaries* Vol. 1 p. 24 22 October, 1964
37 H. Young & A. Sloman *No Minister* p. 70
38 Ibid
39 *Castle Diaries 1974–76* pp. 198–3 21 October, 1974
40 Equal Opportunities for Women in the Civil Service. Report by the Management and Personnel Office. HMSO 1982
41 'English Committee' Q768
42 1976 Royal Commission on Standards of Conduct in Public Life (Cmnd

6524) Select Committee on Expenditure 11th Report (1976–77) HC.535-I. Eighth Report from the Treasury and Civil Service Committee (1983–4) HC.302

Chapter Four: *Power in Whitehall*

1   L. Pliatzky *Getting and Spending: Public Expenditure, Employment and Inflation* p. 12 Oxford 1982
2   H. Young & A. Sloman *But Chancellor, An Inquiry into the Treasury* p. 71 London 1984
3   Quoted in P. Hennessy, S. Morrison & R. Townsend, *Routine Punctuated by Orgies: The Central Policy Review Staff 1970–83* Strathclyde Papers on Government and Politics No. 31
4   'English' Committee Vol. II–II p. 752 Q.1833
5   *Castle Diaries 1965–70* p. 277 12 July, 1967
6   Ibid p. 119 28 April, 1966
7   *Observer* 25 February, 1979
8   P. M. Williams (ed) *The Diary of Hugh Gaitskell 1945–56* p. 36
9   *Crossman Diaries* Vol. 1 p. 80 3 December, 1964
10 Ibid p. 84 4 December, 1964
11 *Castle Diaries 1965–70* p. 114 8–17 April, 1966
12 Ibid p. 168–9 14 September, 1966
13 Ibid p. 360 25 January, 1968
14 *Crossman Diaries* Vol. 1 p. 95 11 December 1965
15 *Castle Diaries 1974–76* p. 123 27 June, 1974
16 *Castle Diaries 1965–70* p. 485 12 July, 1968
17 Ibid p. 142 14 July, 1966
18 Joel Barnett *Inside the Treasury*
19 *Castle Diaries 1965–70* pp. 258–9 23 May, 1967
20 Ibid p. 160 10 August, 1966
21 *Castle Diaries* 1974–76 p. 227 20 November, 1974
22 Quoted in Lord Hankey *Diplomacy by Conference* London 1946
23 'English' Committee Vol. II–II p. 758 Evidence by Sir John Hunt Q.1860
24 For example the discussion in 1967 of the remarriage of Lord Harewood. *Castle Diaries* Vol. 1 p. 210 19 January, 1967
25 *Crossman Diaries* Vol. 1 p. 282 20 July, 1965
26 Ibid p. 103 15 December, 1965
27 Pliatzky op.cit. p. 27
28 PRO CAB 21/1626 21 April, 1950. I am grateful to Peter Hennessy for this reference.
29 Cmnd 1432
30 Sir Richard Clarke *Public Expenditure Management and Control* p. 3 London 1968
31 Samuel Goldman *The Developing System of Public Expenditure Management and Control* p. 53 HMSO 1973
32 See for example the discussions in Cabinet on 30 June, 1966 (*Castle Diaries 1965–70* pp. 140–1) 15 July, 1968 (Ibid p. 486) and the Strategic

Economic Policy Committee 21 June, 1967, paper SEP (67) 105. (*Crossman Diaries* Vol. 2 pp. 390–1)

33   S. Jenkins The Star Chamber, PESC and the Cabinet. *Political Quarterly* Vol. 56 No. 2 (April–June 1985) pp. 113–121
34   J. Barnett *Inside the Treasury* p. 59
35   *Castle Diaries 1974–76* p. 596 14 December, 1975
36   J. Barnett op.cit. pp. 81–2
37   *Castle Diaries 1974–76* p. 481 3 August, 1975
38   Ibid p. 600 11 December 1975
39   J. Barnett op.cit. p. 103
40   *Crossman Diaries* Vol. 2 p. 463 5 September, 1967
41   C. Pollitt *Manipulating the Machine: Changing the Pattern of Ministerial Departments 1960–83* p. 81 London 1984
42   *Castle Diaries 1965–70* p. 720 15 October, 1969
43   *Crossman Diaries* Vol. 1 p. 315 1 September, 1965
44   *Castle Diaries* 1974–76 pp. 415–6 11 June, 1975
45   *Guardian* 1 August, 1985
46   *Guardian* 31 August 1985
47   *Crossman Diaries* Vol. 2 p. 410 5 July, 1967
48   *Castle Diaries* 1974–76 p. 315 21 February, 1975
49   *Castle Diaries* 1965–70 p. 295 19 September, 1967
50   Ibid p. 305 4 October, 1967
51   Ibid p. 314–15 25–27 October, 1967
52   *Crossman Diaries* Vol. 3 p. 839 1 March, 1970
53   Ibid Vol. 2 pp. 238–9 14 February, 1967
54   *Castle Diaries 1965–70* p. 602 6 February, 1969

Chapter Five: *Secrecy, Propaganda and Accountability*

1   A. Palmer *The History of the D-Notice Committee* in C. Andrew and D. Dilks (ed) *The Missing Dimension: Governments and Intelligence Communities in the Twentieth Century* London 1984
2   *Guardian* 27 August, 1985
3   G. Kaufman *How to be a Minister* p. 43 London 1980
4   Sir J. Hoskyns Conservatism is not Enough *Political Quarterly* Vol. 55 No. 1 pp. 3–16
5   Quoted in P. Hennessy. M. Cockerell. D. Walker *Sources Close to the Prime Minister: Inside the hidden world of the news manipulators* p. 139 London 1984
6   Ibid p. 40
7   *Castle Diaries 1965–70* p. 740 15 December, 1969
8   Ibid p. 25 25 Mach, 1965
9   *Crossman Diaries* Vol. 1 p. 161 18 February, 1965
10   Ibid p. 214 10 May, 1965
11   Hennessy, Cockerell, Walker op cit p. 137
12   *Crossman Diaries* Vol. 1 p. 394 29 November, 1965
13   Ibid pp. 215–7 11–12 May, 1965
14   Hennessy, Cockerell, Walker op cit pp. 138–9
15   *Crossman Diaries* Vol. 2 pp. 607–9 18 December, 1967

16   Quoted in A. Palmer *The History of the D-Notice Committee* op cit p. 232
17   R. H. S. Crossman *Inside View* p. 34
18   House of Commons Debates Vol. 850 Col.222
19   Third Report from the Select Committee on Science and Technology Session 1972–3 "Tracked Hovercraft Ltd." HC420 para 39
20   *Crossman Diaries* Vol. 1 p. 628 24 August, 1966
21   Sir D. Wass *Government and the Governed* p. 69
22   *Crossman Diaries* Vol. 2 p. 308 11 April, 1967
23   First Report from the Select Committee on Procedure 1977–78 Vol. 1 p. 40–45
24   Sir P. Nairne Managing the DHSS Elephant: Reflections on a Giant Department. *Political Quarterly* Vol. 54 No. 3 1983
25   Cmnd 4641 Government Organisation for Defence Procurement and Civil Aerospace para 22

Chapter Six: *Behind the Scenes in Whitehall*

1   *Crossman Diaries* Vol. 3 pp. 696–7 24 October, 1969
2   Cmnd 8787 Falkland Islands Review: Report by a Committee of Privy Counsellors (Franks Committee)
3   Franks Committee Report para 93
4   House of Lords Hansard 30 June, 1981 Col. 185
5   Franks Committee Report para 95
6   Ibid para 96
7   Ibid paras 98–9
8   Ibid para 100
9   Ibid para 104
10   Ibid paras 124–5
11   Ibid para 133
12   Ibid para 147
13   Ibid paras 152–3
14   Report of the Crown Agents Tribunal 1982 HL 149/HC 364 para 4.87
15   Ibid para 3.15
16   Ibid para 14.55
17   Ibid para 15.38
18   Ibid para 15.70
19   Ibid para 18.37
20   Ibid para 18.54
21   Ibid para 20.134
22   Ibid para 31.12
23   H. Wilson *The Governance of Britain* p. 27 London 1976
24   *Castle Diaries 1974–76* pp. 220–224 17 November, 1974
25   See *Observer* 3 March, 1985. House of Commons Debates 29 March, 1985 Cols. 876–884

Chapter Seven: *Whitehall Defeats the Critics*

1   The Civil Service Report by the Fulton Committee Cmnd 3638

2 Ibid paras 1 and 14
3 Ibid para 15
4 Ibid paras 16 and 17
5 Ibid paras 18–20
6 *Castle Diaries 1965–70* p. 464 20 June, 1968
7 *Crossman Diaries* Vol. 3 p. 103 20 June, 1968
8 Ibid p. 107 25 June 1968
9 Sir L. Pliatzky *Getting and Spending* p. 91
10 HM Treasury: Management Training in the Civil Service, Report of a Working Party. HMSO 1967
11 Quoted in P. Kellner and Lord Crowther-Hunt *The Civil Servants* p. 63
12 Fulton op cit para 240
13 Kellner and Crowther-Hunt op cit p. 70
14 Ibid p. 71
15 Eleventh Report from the Expenditure Committee 1976–77 "The Civil Service" HC 535 3 Vols. HMSO 1977. Government Observations on the Eleventh Report from the Expenditure Committee. Cmnd 7117 (March 1978)
16 "English Committee" Vol.II–I p. 51
17 Ibid Vol.II–I pp. 191–5
18 Report on Civil Service Training. Civil Service Department 1974 Para 5.3 (Heaton/Williams Report)
19 Report of the Administration Trainee Review Committee. Civil Service Department 1978
20 Sir P. Nairne. Managing the DHSS Elephant: Reflections on a Giant Department. *Political Quarterly* Vol. 54 No. 3
21 See also my *The Right to Know*, Chapter 2. Sphere Books 1985
22 Hansard 24 November,1976
23 The full text is in *The Right to Know (op cit) pp. 53–7*
24 P. Hennessy, M. Cockerell and D. Walker *Sources Close to the Prime Minister* pp. 14–15
25 H. Young *The Crossman Affair* London 1976 p. 11
26 Cmnd 6386 Committee of Privy Councillors on Ministerial Memoirs
27 Ibid para 69
28 D. West "Taking the Axe out of Storage" *Times* 26 June, 1985
29 L. Chapman *Your Disobeident Servant*, Penguin ed. 1979
30 Ibid p. 75
31 N. Warner Raynerism in Practice: Anatomy of a Rayner Scrutiny *Public Administration* Spring 1984 pp. 7–22
32 *Observer* 24 February, 1985
33 *Guardian* 1 November, 1985
34 *Times* 21 June, 1982
35 Cmd 3909 Royal Commission on the Civil Service (Tomlin Commission 1929–31) Cmd 9613 Royal Commission on the Civil Service (Priestley Commission 1953–55)
36 Ibid para 96
37 W. A. Pridmore *The Statistical Validity of the Civil Service Pay Research*

Process. Cmnd 8590 "Inquiry into Civil Service Pay" (The Megaw Committee) Vol. 2 pp. 170–192

38   R. Layard, A. Marin, A. Zabalza, *Trends in Civil Service Pay Relative to the Private Sector*. Megaw Report (Cmnd 8590) Vol. 2 pp. 95–128

39   Cmnd 8590 para 5

40   Cmnd 8147 Inquiry into the Value of Pensions (Scott Report)

41   Civil Service Statistics 1978 Table 1

42   Civil Service Statistics 1984 Table 5

43   Cmnd 9430 Statement on the Defence Estimates 1985 Vol. 2 Table 5.6

44   *Guardian* 8 July 1985

45   Hansard 3 April 1985

46   *Guardian* 20 March 1985

47   Hansard 18 March 1985

48   25th Report from the Committee of Public Accounts "Profit Formula for non-competitive contracts" July 1985

Chapter Eight: *Transforming Whitehall*

1   Sir D. Wass *Government and the Governed* p. 86

2   Fulton Report Cmnd 3638 para 190

3   Ibid Appendix C

4   *Times* 21 March, 1985

5   *Guardian* 7 February, 1985

6   Sir L. Pliatzky *Getting and Spending* p. 31

7   Ibid

8   Sir D. Wass The Civil Service at the Crossroads *Political Quarterly* Summer 1985 Vol.56 No.3 pp. 227–241

ROBERT KEE

The World We Left Behind

A CHRONICLE OF THE YEAR

1939

In THE WORLD WE LEFT BEHIND
broadcaster Robert Kee vividly recaptures the
moods and sensations of 1939 – the news that
made the headlines in politics, fashion,
entertainment and sport – and the growing
anxiety of the British people as the Second
World War loomed.

This is a unique portrait of the year as it
unfolded, filled with the incident, drama and
excitement of one of the most historic twelve
months in living memory.

'Authentic . . . absorbing and worth any
number of conventional histories.' *The Times*
'All recounted with such brio as can be gobbled
up in one day.' *Daily Telegraph*
'Fascinating.' *The New York Times*
'Brilliant.' *Daily Mail*

HISTORY   0 7221 5204 3   £4.95

LOVE WAS AN EASY GAME UNTIL SHE BROKE ALL THE RULES . . .

MANDY RICE DAVIES

The sensational, unstoppable story of high class seduction and ruthless international intrigue

In 1963, Mandy Rice Davies created a storm for her part in the series of political and sexual scandals surrounding the Profumo affair. Now, drawing on a controversial and colourful life of bizarre adventure, she has written TODAY AND TOMORROW, a novel as riveting and readable as it is robust . . .

0 7221 2847 9   GENERAL FICTION   £2.95